THE EMERALD DAWN

Book 1 of the Demon Wielder Series
By Allison Trebacz

Ephemeral
publishing

First Edition 2024

Paperback: 979-8-9906214-3-5

EBook: 979-8-9906214-0-4

Book Cover by Fakel Barros at Stardust Designs

Map by Josh Hoskins at Stardust Designs

To everyone who could've been a badass princess, but now you're paid to sit at a desk and say things like "circle back" and "Hope this email finds you well."

—this one's for you.

Don't stop dreaming.

WARNINGS

This book contains depictions of sexually explicit scenes and violence. It contains mature language, themes, and content that may not be suitable for all readers. Reader discretion is advised. Find a detailed list & mild spoilers below:

allisonimagining.com/content-warning

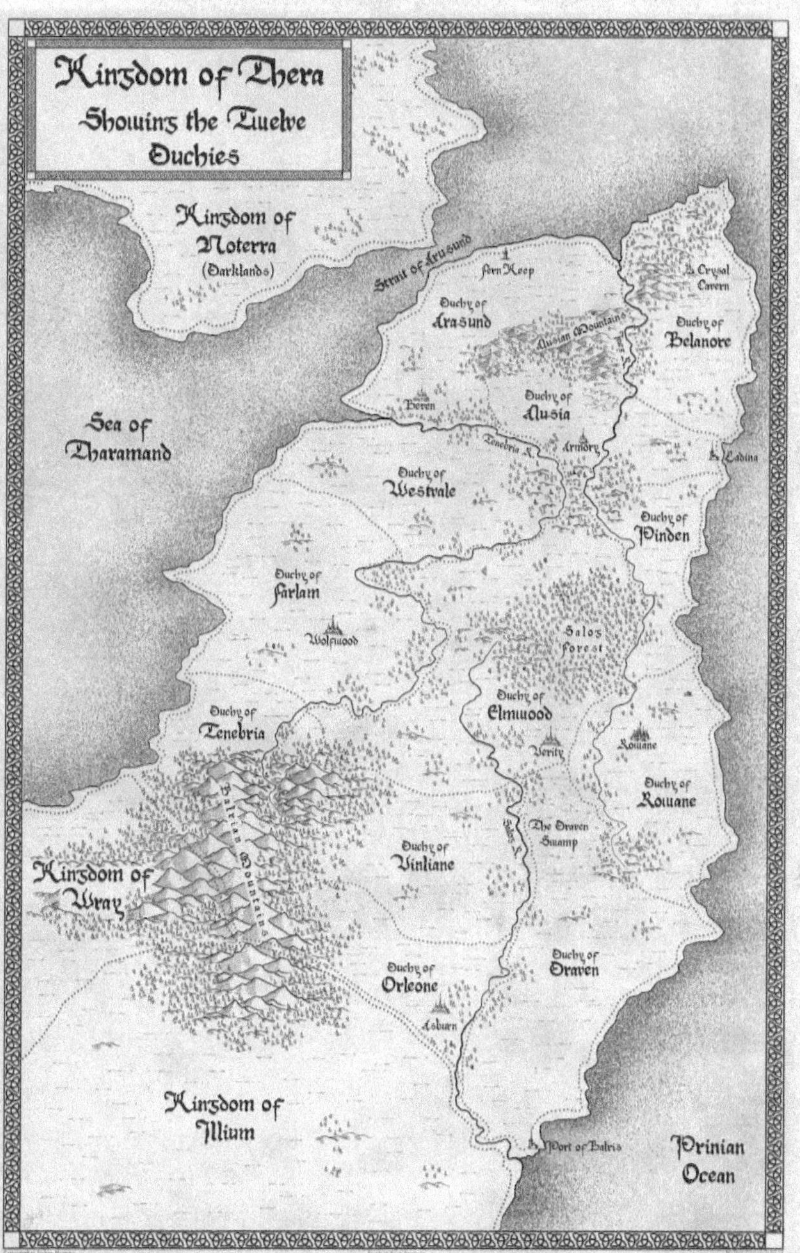

Kingdom of Thera
Showing the Twelve Duchies
Kingdom of Noterra
(Darklands)
Strait of Arusund
Fern Keep
Duchy of Arasund
Ausian Mountains
Crystal Cavern
Duchy of Belanore
Duchy of Ausia
Boren
Sea of Tharamand
Tenebria R.
Armory
Ladina
Duchy of Westvale
Duchy of Vinden
Duchy of Farlam
Salos Forest
Wolfwood
Duchy of Elmwood
Duchy of Tenebria
Verity
Rowane
Duchy of Rowane
Baltrian Mountains
Kingdom of Wray
Duchy of Vinliane
The Draven Swamp
Duchy of Draven
Duchy of Orleone
Auburn
Kingdom of Illium
Port of Balris
Prinian Ocean

Glossary

Names:

Aixen: Ayx - en

Avernought: AV - er - NAWT

Avi (Aviliana) Ah - Vee (Ah - vill - ee- Ahn - a)

Balris: BAL - riss (Goddess of Life)

Damien Arden: DAY – mee -EN ARE – den

Declan: DECK - lan

Dreonna: DRAY - on - Ah (Goddess of Death)

Farran: FEHR - ahN

Jaxon: JACK - son

Raion: RAY - on (King of Gods)

Reina: RAIN - ah

Leena: LEEN - ah

Olios: O - lee - OSE (God of Water)

Varyn: Ver - IN

Valois: val -Wah

Places:

Alusia: AH – loo – shuh

Arasund: ERR – uh – sund

Bal: Bahl (Heaven)

Balria: BAL - ree - AH

Beven: BEHV - in

Illium: ILL – ee – UHM

Noterra: NUH - tare - AH

Rowane: ROW - ayne
Tir: Terr (Underworld)
Tharamund: THER – uh – mund
Thera: THER – ah

Catharian Terms:
Aristone: AIR – ess – TONE (Silver Wielder)
Balen: BAY – len (Nature Bound)
Braan: Brahn (Burn)
Braagen: BRAH – ghen (Fire Wielder)
Dreos: DRAY - ose (Demon)
Dreosen: DRAY- ose - EN (Demon Wielder)
Lumen: Loo – MEN (Light Wielder)
Ontaros: ON - tar - OSE (Siphon / Magic wielder)
Sunderone: sun – DER – own(Shadow Wielder)
Vainnen: VAYN – en (Propulsionist)
Valdronna: VAHL – dro – SEN (Chosen by Dreonna)
Vistone: VIST – own (Illusionist)

PROLOGUE

THE CEILING OF THE stark white temple shrank as a thirteen-year-old girl and a priest walked below it. The white of her gown matched the bleached slate, giving way to iridescent slabs of marble as the sound of dripping water grew louder. Around a corner, the hallway opened up, revealing a wide, empty courtyard.

Part of it was enclosed. Small, leafy shrub trees grew along the walls, curling around pillars and stone overhangs in search of light. In the center was a large stone table stretched over a gurgling pond.

"This temple is older than all of the Seven combined," the priest remarked.

The girl traced a pillar with her fingertips as she walked around. She'd never stood in a room like this; it seemed to step into a different time when the gods still ruled and dragons were free. A warmth burgeoned in her chest, just behind her ribs as if something was waking up.

He continued, "Some practices aren't meant to change, though everything around them does."

"Was this a temple for the old gods?" the girl asked.

He nodded and took a step closer to the pond, arms crossed over his white linen robes. "And the gods before them."

Before? She shook the thought off. "Have you met the Seven?" she asked instead.

She asked because she wanted to believe. If she could find one, maybe they could help. She knew no one but a god could erase the blood oath that committed her to the knighthood, but she was already tired of training.

She didn't want to be a knight. She wanted to be on the islands of Sol and weeks away from Rowane because she didn't care about the Crown, the queen, or the people of Thera—she wanted to be nothing.

"I have." He nodded. "Every priest has. They want the best for us and the future of Thera. That's what the Rite is about. In moments, you'll see what the gods see in you."

"What if I don't want to know?" Her fingers twined around the branch of a small tree. Her brown eyes looked back at him.

The priest didn't move, and his eyes bore down. "Are you afraid?"

"No." Never. Fear wasn't something she'd allow herself to feel.

The girl walked toward the table and laid her hand on the stone. It was smooth and warm as if it had sat in the sun all morning, but that was impossible; it was far too early.

"Good." He swallowed. "Please, sit. It will be brief. And know that, on my life, I am sworn to secrecy. It is your Rite and your future to tell as you see fit."

She pursed her lips and climbed onto the table. It wasn't ladylike, as her hand caught her dress and the fabric tore. But she didn't care. There was no one to throw a fit.

Clouds flitted across the sky above her, and even a bird flew past. With the gurgle of the pond, it was almost peaceful until the priest's hand touched her shoulder.

"I've kept a great many secrets from the Crown, including those of princes, kings, and queens."

He held a cup towards her filled with something red and thick. She turned up her nose. Yet, he pushed it closer. "This is the blood from one of the Seven. The magic coursing through it was chosen just for you, Reina Sangrey. It will show you the future the gods need you to see."

She took the cup in her hands and swirled it around. Just one gulp. She could do it. "Can I change the future if I don't like it?" she asked.

The priest's expression was careful and measured as he replied, "Many try, but few are able to thwart the gods. Drink."

She brought the cup to her lips and closed her eyes, tilting it to her mouth. The blood was thick, warm, and sweet as honey—no hint of iron. It coated her mouth and warmed her skin. She laid back on the warm stone, watching the framed blue sky above as her head swam.

The dull thrum of what must have been magic pressed against her skin.

A sudden spark of energy skittered across her neck when the priest brushed her bare shoulder. She stiffened, nearly ready to run, but his voice soothed the instinct. "Close your eyes. You'll feel the magic tug at you as I say a prayer. Whatever you see, don't be alarmed. No harm will come to you."

She wasn't comforted, but nonetheless she closed her eyes. The pulse grew warmer, deeper, as the priest muttered his prayers.

The magic writhed and twisted in her chest as if it were a knot of fabric tying and untying itself as the god's power coated every muscle and fiber. Then something sharp twisted in her gut, and she fell.

Her eyes flew open, but she saw through another's.

Shadows receded. Her body wasn't hers—it was tired, heavier, different.

She clutched the handle of a dagger, and she wasn't alone.

Warm blood poured over her hands from the chest of a woman beneath her. Rage she couldn't remember surged through her. The woman's silver crown was askew as the Queen of Thera choked beneath her.

The girl tugged the knife back, eyes wide in fear. Blood rushed from the wound, seeping into the white tunic beneath the queen's navy jacket.

"The kingdom you rule will be devoid of life." The queen gasped as spittle struck her cheek. "You'll have nothing, Reina Sangrey."

No, no, no. Someone else was in this room watching her, but Reina didn't dare turn. She stared as the queen shook and the crown fell from her temple. Before Reina could move, a hand grabbed and dragged her back.

She blinked again. The blue sky and the temple ceiling stretched above once more, and magic leached from her skin as the priest withdrew.

Yet she didn't move. She couldn't. *The kingdom you rule will be devoid of life.* No. No, no, no. She would rule nothing, she would have nothing. *I will rise to the Queensguard, and I will—*

"You will kill the queen," the priest whispered. She bolted up. *Would he kill me here? Should he?*

"I can't," she stammered. "I won't. I..."

The priest's hand settled on her cheek. "I feared this the moment I saw you, Lady Reina. The gods give you a heavy burden to bear, but you must carry it."

She adamantly shook her head. "I don't want this."

"I pray for anyone who would." His hand fell from her face. "May I offer some advice? Protect yourself with everything you have, but above all, protect your humanity. Rite visions can destroy."

The gods could have shown her anything else, and she would have accepted it. This 'future' was a trap with nowhere to go but down.

The girl ran from the temple, head still abuzz from the god's blood; this was supposed to be a celebration, a step into adulthood, and all she could feel was the painful thump of her heart.

The two men she arrived with ran to keep up as she barreled down an empty alley, when something deep inside her snapped.

The wider man, a merchant, waved a hand around, and she winced as the crush of magicked wards slammed up and silenced everything but the rage in her head. The other man, tall and elegant, gripped her shoulders, but she refused to look in his eyes.

"Damien, that girl you have," the merchant said, voice dire, "that's the girl who kills the queen."

She turned to stone, her eyes locked on Damien's. There was no escape.

"Is that what you saw?" His voice was gentle but soothed nothing.

She straightened her shoulders. With all the things she couldn't choose to be, she could choose to be brave. "Yes."

"Congratulations on your Rite, Reina Sangrey," the merchant said with a sly smile she'd never forget.

Chapter I

I ALWAYS WONDERED WHETHER the old gods gave up because they hated their creation as much as I did. Surely, they never imagined a kingdom would have the gall to build an armory out of the humans who'd once inherited their gifts as a symbol of peace.

Surely the gods never imagined those humans would pit those gifted against each other to vie for the favor of a queen who had never deserved her throne.

I had to believe that if the gods knew how wrong it all was, they would fucking do something. Maybe they all abandoned us so we could destroy ourselves.

Thera was one of the five kingdoms—a kingdom of the new gods, the Seven, where the others hadn't caught up. The old gods shaped and formed our mountains, rivers, plains, and forests. They sculpted a world from nothing and filled it with creatures that needed them. It was a garden they tended until the joy of creation started to ebb and turn into resentment.

Then the gods forged one last creature, one made in their likeness, blessed with ripples of their magic, and assigned the humans to be the stewards of the land.

The gods and humans worked alongside one another for thousands of years. Houses turned to villages, then to towns, and eventually, cities. As time went on, the humans needed less and less from the old gods. The old gods retreated and turned bitter.

In their absence, new gods rose. Unlike the old gods embroidered into the fabric of the natural world, who begged for sacrifice by name, the seven new gods required tithes and honor. They were not known by individual names, only as the Seven.

I grew up firmly believing neither old nor new existed; they were merely stories my parents told my brother and me before they died.

Even now, I couldn't believe it. Sleeping or dead, it didn't matter. The gods had abandoned their creation. Priests could reassure us that the new gods roamed the lands, but I'd never seen them, and they'd done nothing for me.

As far as I knew, there were no gods in Thera. And if there were, they were especially absent from the Armory, which was a death sentence for most of us.

It was an academy for gifted soldiers chosen by the wealthy for the opportunity to prove worthy of the Queensguard Knighthood. The Armory was isolated in the duchy of Alusia by pine trees, rocky cliffs, and treacherous rivers.

The land wasn't well guarded; it was entirely remote and stood between two rivers and the jagged earth they'd formed. Woods stretched out in all directions in a mess of hills, cliffs, and canyons.

The river on the eastern flank flowed past the capital city of Rowane, where the queen sat on her throne in the duchy overlooking the Prinian Ocean. A western river coursed from the southern Balrian mountain range and filtered into the sea bordering the lonely and disconnected peninsula of the Goddess Dreonna, the Darklands.

Once, a thousand years ago, the Armory was a castle for one errant king and then another. Today, it was divided into three massive sections. The first one was large, old, and made of crumbling gray stone that towered over a bare yard and the southern forest.

The newer, northern section was built with the modern craftsmanship of the time in pewter slate. That section loomed over an overgrown garden with buttresses, towers, and gargoyles that spit when it rained.

The third section was the smallest and the grandest. It served as the courtyard between two castles until some war ended. Then it became the Atrium: a beacon of Thera's power.

The Crown let their architect cover the stone floor with marble and encased it in high glass walls supported with iron beams. All to show the new gods what the Crown could do to their finest gifted soldiers before the end of three years.

If the new gods were watching, instead of showing them what I was capable of, I stared at the ceiling. They wouldn't see anything anyway through the churning gray clouds and the sheets of rain.

The deafening sound of water crashing on the glass drowned the din of chatter and the subtle *thump* of pine striking pine. If they let us have real swords, perhaps we'd hear the metal tang over the dull drum of a downpour, but the Crown wanted control over our death and mandated all first-year weapons be carved from local trees.

I stood away from a building crowd as I surveyed the scene. Two men from my house lashed at each other with their wooden swords as if they were children playing knights in the shadow of a castle—their movements clunky and unsure because there was no elegance in pine.

It was meant to be humbling. All of our first year had been. We weren't trusted; we hadn't earned anything. But somehow we were all chosen because someone thought we might be worth something.

That was why they observed us within the glass walls of the Atrium.

Although, today's observation was counterintuitive. We weren't supposed to stand out until after our first trial, unless we wanted a target on our backs.

Our instructors told us as much, but not everyone in the Emerald House—my house—was keen on listening. This was the first time our makers would see us in the Armory. Makers were nobles who funded and filled their houses with soldiers. They found joy gambling on our lives and using us as proxies to duel each other.

We'd nearly made it through our first year, which was unimpressive. Over the next two years, we'd be tested, picked apart, and raked over coals by the makers as they watched, coached, and took notes on our trial performances—if we survived to receive them.

Maybe I was prepared for it, maybe I wasn't, but I wasn't showing my hand. Not yet.

I had too much to lose, which made the iron-weighted gaze on my back from one maker extremely unwelcome. If I died before I became a champion, Damien Arden wouldn't have to honor our agreement, and my brother would be responsible for the debt I shouldered with my life.

Declan, my brother, wasn't like me. He would be a scholar, turning pages in the archives and translating tomes. No blade or blood would touch his hands the way they marred mine.

But we all become what we need to be. I sucked in a breath, straightened my back, and pretended I could disappear. Everything about the Armory would be easier if I could slip through mostly unnoticed and mostly alive.

I didn't have to turn to know which maker was staring at me. He was a squat, middle-aged man with a weathered face and narrowed blue eyes. Today he wore a merchant's robe in deep emerald-green with silver threads embroidered into spring lilies: the flower of Thera.

I would recognize him anywhere, and he promised he'd follow my lead.

First-years weren't worth knowing when half of us would die in our first trial. The maker knew better than to call any attention to me.

My hand wrapped around the hilt of a stupid wooden sword with no intention of using it.

We had spent the last year honing our skills with fakes just for them to push us into our first trial with real steel, and I was counting down the hours. The Armory believed we'd either figure it out or die trying and end up with our name carved on the Atrium floor like the thousands before us.

That's why they kept first-years formally separate from the second and third years.

"They're such fucking show-offs," a familiar voice tsked beside me.

I glanced left, and there stood Leena, willowy with her silken chin pointed up. I didn't see her leave the sparring group, but I was relieved to have some distraction from the makers.

"You've certainly found the better spot, Reina. He's watching you." Leena re-tied her thigh-length, coiled blonde hair back in a green ribbon. She loved her hair, despite the impracticality. I rarely felt the same way about my auburn hair which was too stubborn to grow much past my shoulders.

We'd found the ribbon buried in a chapel cabinet while searching for wine last year, shortly after we arrived. She'd cut it in half with her teeth, and we promised each other that we'd both make it out of the Armory alive no matter what.

There had been a bit more to it, but that was all either of us remembered. *No matter what.*

"Makers don't make pledges to first-years," I grumbled as my hands swept against my hair, smoothing any imperfections before I tightened my own green ribbon.

Leena stared ahead and crossed her arms as she continued to watch our housemates make fools of themselves. She was sizing them up. I always knew, because her thin lips would curl into the slyest of smiles and her eyes would narrow out of sheer scrutiny.

I'd seen Leena take down every man in our house with her bare hands. In a prior life, she'd danced for the royal court with one of the largest dance companies in Rowane, the capital of Thera. She ended up here on a whim, something about becoming someone new.

While she enjoyed the discipline of performing, when an invitation from a patron found her, she left without a second thought because there was far more honor in the knighthood.

"You could take them all," she finally said to me. "Even with your stick."

I looked down at the piece of pine in my hand and frowned. It had to be a joke; my hands were made to hold steel. "I'm sure I could put Tomas down with a stalk of corn. Haven't we watched a wall take him down? Several times?" I retorted.

We both stifled a laugh at the sad truth, but reality was less funny. Three days from now, there was no assurance we would be alive, and perhaps we'd gotten too comfortable with one another.

Without warning, a sickening crack rang through the room, followed by a scream. Our attention pivoted, and so did the makers'.

A man with flaxen hair and soft brown eyes named Aixen lay sprawled on the marble floor, clutching his elbow, which was bent at an unnatural angle. Tomas hovered above him with a horrified look, wiping sweat from his brow.

No one moved until Varyn, our healer, pushed through the crowd. Varyn had a better heart than most of us, and he hid it with sarcasm. I never understood why he signed his soul to the Armory when he could've had a place in any city, any kingdom he wanted. Instead, he was here, crouched beside Aixen, trying to brace his arm so it would set with healing magic.

After nearly a year of living in close quarters, it was impossible not to learn what made each of us human. Worse, our cohort of twenty was one of the smaller houses, and the sheer size of the Atrium dwarfed us. I looked around, hoping for some reprieve.

I had no intention of showing the makers I could spar. No intention of showing them what I could truly do. Not yet.

I tapped my foot and glanced at the too-small clock on the far side of the room—there was still a half hour left. We'd never been dismissed early, and it certainly wouldn't start now.

It was just us and the four stoic makers who watched us like cattle at an auction.

The minutes of waiting ticked by. The rest of the house was too timid to do anything more than talk after what happened to Aixen.

Varyn kneeled beside him and tried to use his healing gift, but nerves got the best of him. Only a few white tendrils wrapped around Aixen's arm, but none set. They dissipated before they touched his skin.

"His magic has always sets," Leena whispered, her brows scrunched in confusion.

Aixen's breath hitched as Varyn tried again to no avail. Another housemate of ours, Eral, stepped between them to ease Aixen back to his feet.

"Maybe he's nervous?" I supplied.

"*You* could help," Leena insisted.

"We talked about this." I looked hard at Leena. She knew exactly what our survival strategy was.

"Right, we're not showing our hand," she shot me a caustic glare and lowered her voice, "even if we can help."

My cheeks burned at the accusation. Leena didn't have to remind me—I knew I could heal—but I wasn't ready for anyone else to figure it out. "If they want to show off before the trial, let them. We know better. I'm not doing anything to make myself a target."

She merely shrugged. "It's healing magic, nothing that works in a battle."

"The makers don't need to know. Not yet. I want to get through the first trial."

Leena crossed her arms then. She had a life before this, and it made her a better person. I didn't; the Armory was my purpose. If I failed, death was the only option waiting for me. It was a guarantee, carved into my spine—my life and freedom—traded for my brother's safety.

I knew who I was and exactly where I needed to be.

"Well," Leena huffed, cutting through my thoughts, "I'm gonna see if I can do anything."

Lightning flashed, and another sheet of rain pounded the glass above us. I frowned. The first trial would be miserable if it didn't stop raining soon.

Looking back at the makers, my stomach dropped. The man, the merchant in green, had stepped off the dais and was heading right for me. His choice didn't go unnoticed.

My mouth went dry as I straightened my shoulders and steeled my face.

I would give anything to disappear; the heat of every gaze in the room scorched like a sunburn on my back. I knew exactly who he was, and I'd remind him who I was.

Thunder shook the frame of the Atrium, and another ribbon of rain peeled through. Fear raked its claws across my bones.

The maker stopped a few feet from me with a smile on his face. *Fuck.* I forced my shoulders to stay straight.

I'd met him years ago in Damien Arden's den; he was the man who insisted I see a priest for my Rite at thirteen, and I'd seen him many times since. The Rite was important to the nobles and the Crown. It was a coming of age where a priest would grant a child a glimpse of their future.

For some it was harmless, for others it shook the foundation of who they were.

I was the latter, and without the merchant in front of me, I wouldn't know the lengths of violence I would be capable of.

"May we speak privately?" His deep voice reverberated in every crevice of my skull as he peered past me.

"Of course, my lord." The words left my lips quicker than expected. I fell into a practiced bow. *Gods fucking help me.* Fluidly, he led me into an alcove with a heavy locking door. We stood in silence, my eyes roving over the finery of his robe.

It had been nearly a year since I'd last seen him. I wanted to run.

"I reckon you haven't forgotten me, Reina Sangrey?" he drawled.

I forced a polite smile. "Never, Lord Avernought."

"Call me Lukas," he said, leaning against the wall. *I would never call him Lukas.* His robe was impeccable, full of intricate embroidered details in silver threads. My eyes flicked up to his, and he continued, "Emerald is my house, just as Damien Arden's guild of whores and assassins is mine. Neither would be anything—"

"A guild has a written code. Arden does not," I reminded him.

Avernought's glower implied my interruption was unappreciated, but I was always honest with clients of Arden's 'guild', which is exactly who Avernought was—his best client, in fact.

I added lowly, "My apologies. Damien is not an easy man to work with."

"But yet you do so, and loyally, might I add."

My eyebrow twitched. The way he looked at me was more exposing; he knew what I was to my core: assassin and traitor. Avernought had personally delivered my Armory invitation, and it seemed he would be a part of every pivotal moment of my life.

"Of course, my lord." I swallowed the rest of the sentence. What other options did I have?

Avernought breezed past my insinuation with a dismissive wave of his hand. "Reina, you are the finest he's ever trained. The nobles fear Arden's viper assassin. You know that?" I recoiled at the mention of the name, but Avernought didn't notice. "I know what you're capable of, and I pray the Crown sees the same. I've lost as much to them as you."

Something was coming together. I knew that, but then there was the way he said my name as his brows knit and that made me uneasy. A different fear crawled along my spine; certainly no one listened through the door, not while our other makers observed.

Avernought's words straddled the line of treason, and I picked my next words carefully. "I serve the Crown as we all do."

"The gods didn't give you those eyes, and I didn't give you the dragon-forged dagger to be complacent, *viper*." A slight smile turned the corners of his mouth as the word hung in the air like a curse.

My eyes narrowed slightly. "Calculated and complacent shouldn't be confused. I know why I'm here, and I have no intention of losing sight of that."

"You can count on the Emerald makers' support, so long as you prove me right." Avernought lowered his voice and leaned towards me. The man smelled like a burned cherry wood chest and bitter grapefruit perfume. "No one can know your relationship to Damien Arden or suspect you're his viper until you have the safety of a pledge, otherwise the nobles will turn quickly. I don't need to tell you why that will be a problem. I'll offer my pledge following the first trial."

Swallowing, my eyes flitted to the door. "I need to go back."

He'd said too much. I didn't need to hear any of it. None of it changed my goals, it only made my heart hammer.

The door opened with a groan, and I followed Avernought back into the Atrium where everyone watched us return. A wave of heat enveloped my body, burning in my cheeks as I walked towards Leena. She was the only person I dared to look at while everyone else gawked.

Makers never pulled a first year off the Atrium floor on the first day. I cursed Avernought as the bell rang and another roll of thunder rattled the Atrium.

We filed out in a single line of black leather with our green armbands, and none of us said a word as we passed the incoming Ruby soldiers and their silent line of black and red.

I hated being beholden to Lukas Avernought. He was a looming presence in my life as the only man who could get me into the Armory. And, again, as a man who had more money than the Crown itself. Though I still hadn't forgiven him for how long it took to get me here.

The day I turned nineteen, I was eligible, but Avernought spent four years deflecting until the time was right for himself.

Meanwhile, I served Arden as his beloved and feared viper, digging myself further down because the bottom was the only place I could go until I had the invitation.

I knew my purpose, but I was helpless to do anything until Lukas Avernought allowed it.

Chapter 2

Every eye in Emerald roasted my back as we filed through the narrow stone hallways of the Armory towards our floor. It was lit with torches every several paces. The flickering light exaggerated the scarred walls that held a hundred secrets from the thousand years this wing had seen.

Our house was on the fourth floor, and the moment my feet landed in our corridor, I bolted to the safety of my room before anyone could grab my arm and start asking questions.

Questions meant exposure, and I didn't appreciate being exposed.

I went straight for the washbasin and ignored the weight of Leena's own stare as it followed me. She even tapped her foot on the floorboards. This was her room too; she was the only person I couldn't escape from.

I toweled off my face and crossed my arms, mirroring her.

"What was that about?" Leena asked pointedly, pulling her own green ribbon out of her hair so her curls bounced freely in front of her shoulders. Her golden eyes narrowed. "A maker spoke to you."

"Yes, I was there." I frowned.

Leena only cocked her head to the side, even more impatient. "And?"

"And?" I repeated, feigning nonchalance. "It was nothing."

She scoffed. "No, it wasn't. By the Seven and the stars, Rein, they didn't talk to anyone else in Emerald." I attempted to shuffle past her towards my closet, but Leena caught my arm, forcing my eyes to hers. "Don't lie to me."

I let my face soften and sighed, sinking onto my bed. Leena was right.

"Fine. I knew him from before. He's a friend of Arden's. The maker is Lukas Avernought, and he's the silver merchant with more coin than the Crown and the one who invited me," I admitted.

"I thought I recognized him," she muttered, sinking onto the bed next to mine. Her tone grew quiet. "I danced for most of them."

Leena's hand squeezed my shoulder. The simple touch was overwhelming. It was easy to lose your humanity within the Armory walls when you're trapped for a year with no reprieve. It was even easier when you'd already lost most of it to begin with.

It was an honor to live in the Armory. We weren't allowed to contact our families; we weren't allowed to leave the grounds except for trials and Crown invitations. We were supposed to be nothing outside of these walls. However, there were no guards to enforce the bans on evening strolls or gallivanting to the nearer towns—though anything further was desertion.

The old wing had seven floors and each was dedicated to a house. Each house had their own kitchen, bedchambers, a training room, baths, a chapel for the old gods—and the new.

I spent no time at either but if I had to choose, I'd choose the old gods. It was their stories my mother would tell us at night, and the old gods my father would threaten us with.

The last room was a library with only enough material to get us through one year of daily classes, which were inconsistent at best.

Some days we'd pinch ourselves through a six-hour lecture on history, strategy, basic sigils, or realm geography. Other days, we'd learn a few phrases in Catharian, the language of the dragon age.

And occasionally we practiced bits of petty magic because our true gifts, our intrinsic gifts, were expected to remain secret until our first trial. Not all of us were gifted with intrinsic magic, but few made it through the first trial without.

I've read that fewer than a quarter of Theranians possessed intrinsic magic, but the ratio was higher in the Armory. Makers only granted Queensguard invitations to those they believed to be extraordinary.

If anyone survived the Armory without intrinsic magic, they sure as shit didn't have a maker, so I prayed my healing gift would be enough. Avernought wouldn't change his mind, but doubt made a home in the crook of my neck.

Halfway through our second year was when the makers considered pledging us to the Queensguard Knighthood. First, they waited to see who survived the first trials and who performed well enough before they invested any more time or influence. The makers wanted to show the queen the best champion they could find, as that's where makers made their money.

Formally, Armory champions were a bet paid out once a year. Informally, they paid out after every trial in Armory gambling dens.

It was a perfect system. The queen got more bodies for her elite Queensguard while the makers won money and another ear in the shadows of court or the borders of our kingdom. The Armory soldiers? Well, we got a job we'd be blessed to die in.

If we lived long enough to rise to the Queensguard, we'd be sworn to the life of a knight with no partners and no legacy.

Damien Arden wasn't a maker, but he ensured the Queensguard would be my only way out when I swore a blood oath to him at ten years old. There was no undoing it, and my debt would only be paid the moment I rose as a knight for the queen.

It was written on my skin in the shape of a snake and a sword, just where my spine joined my hips. I hated it for everything it made me, yet I owed the stupid promise my life and my brother's.

"We should get ready. We meet our house tonight."

I forgot Leena was sitting next to me. My mind had wandered off while I sat, staring at the stone wall. My left hand absently tugged at the buckles on my leathers; I wasn't in a hurry.

Tonight was the Maker's Ball or, less formally, the Black Banquet—named for the last meal given to prisoners before the gallows. It was the ball before our first trial and a celebration of our impending initiation into the real halls of the Armory after a year in the "shed."

The ball wasn't for us, though. It was for the champions who had just been presented to the queen before their solitary champion trial. In two days, they'd face their last and we'd face our first.

The Black Banquet was also the first time we would formally meet any second- or third-years in our house and the first time we were allowed to mingle with other houses.

The Armory was exceptional at keeping us separate. Every day was a reminder that proximity and relationships were weaknesses, but we forged them anyway, some of us more begrudging than others. Me? I was better off alone, but it was easier said than done.

The best trick for surviving the Armory was compartmentalization. In fact, the first test they gave us was to pack all our belongings into a single trunk. The trunk should hold everything a soldier believes important for the next three years of their life.

I brought my leathers, tunics, my mother's cardigan, a pad of paper, some ink, three books, and my dragon-forged dagger with an ornate gold hilt and onyx stone secured in the pommel. The dragon fire lightened all properties of steel, darkening the blade and creating a pattern of whorls across it, most visible in daylight.

Those were the only things important to me.

I had an entire bedroom in Arden's estate filled with other things that represented bits of me, but this was my only fresh start: my escape from being Arden's viper, Arden's anything. So I left behind the trinkets, the dresses, and anything that wouldn't be Dame Reina Sangrey.

This also meant I had nothing fit to wear to a ball. Luckily, the Armory provided. It always did.

Yesterday, they called us down to the first-level dungeons where they turned a hall of cells into a treasure trove, but it was merely a collection of the things the dead left behind. Who didn't love wearing the possessions of murdered ghosts? It wasn't a choice.

Leena stood up from the bed first, and I followed tentatively. We readied ourselves, trading our leathers and tunics for gossamer and tulle which felt foreign and uncomfortable after a year without.

I tugged at the bodice of the dress I picked out, frowning at how it cut into my shoulder.

Dresses, and the pretty pleasantries they came with them, reminded me of Arden—of a different time when I would plait my hair, wear his silk, and pretend I wasn't more than his bookkeeper and an object just out of his clients' reach. I'd sit on laps, and giggle, and talk in small words until Arden tapped my shoulder and slipped a note into the folds of my gown with a request for his viper and her fangs.

Leena stared at the mirror beside me, eyes downcast. We'd talked about our own pasts a thousand times because both of us were indebted in similar ways. She worked for a dance troupe under a noble named Moer; he had the money to be an Armory maker, but preferred to spend it in brothels that overcharged for discretion.

Leena chose a dress made of layers of rich emerald that clung to her frame. She pinned half of her hair on top of her head, letting the other half cascade down her back in spirals.

"It's strange, isn't it?" Leena's voice had a sad lilt as she glanced at her reflection before she stooped behind me to help pin and curl my hair. "To put on a dress after wearing leather for so long. Like there are steps I should remember for him."

"It does feel that way, doesn't it?" I mused, and memories of Arden's estate swelled back. There was always a catch when I wore a gown.

We were forced to pick clothes the color of our house, so I chose a dress in the darkest green I could find. It was an-line gown with a plunging neck. The interior was silk, and the exterior was a single layer of black-green tulle that shimmered in the light with tiny stars stitched along the seams.

A different version of me might have loved it, but I was a soldier now, on my way to becoming a knight.

Glancing in the mirror, I noticed every change in my face and my figure. My hair was lighter; I saw it even in the candlelight. My face looked tighter . . . more hollow, more tired. We had spent the last year training with our stupid pine weapons, hoping it was enough to stave off death when our time came. Of course, it was just part of the joke.

The bell chimed, and I squeezed Leena's hand before we departed our room. Dread gave way to tenuous excitement as our house walked together through the passageways of the Armory.

Our solemnity evaporated as we whispered and laughed as if this was our debut into nobility. It wasn't, but couldn't we try to have fun?

"Incredible. You picked the closest color to black you could find."

I spun to see Blaise smiling at me. Leena flashed me a knowing grin as she raised her brow and found a different conversation between Eral and Aixen.

"I promise you, it's green." I blushed as he laughed, but he had no room to talk.

He wore the deep shade of lichen: a coat with gold embroidery whorling around the chest. A year ago, Blaise was nothing but the thin, forgotten son of a noble who fell out of favor in a southern duchy. Now he was formidable, on track to be a captain, and notably well-fit.

"Either way," he said, "you're beautiful. Maybe you'll catch the eye of another maker."

I shoved him with my elbow. "I'm not talking about that tonight."

"Everyone else is." He shrugged.

"Do you want to dance with me later or not?" I glared. Blaise's saffron eyes looked taken aback, and I cursed myself. "Sorry."

"No, no," he stammered, his right hand running through his ruddy brown hair. "Don't be. I didn't realize a dance was on the table."

I gulped. I shouldn't have said anything. "Maybe."

"I'll take maybe." His lips quirked up.

We stopped at the closed Atrium doors, and I nearly collided with Leena. The Emerald instructor, Doris, had her hand on the handle. Doris was petite, unassuming, but her accuracy with a knife terrified us all.

She pressed two fingers to her throat; they sparked yellow, and her voice filled the hallway.

"Line up! I need two rows. They'll be announcing the Emerald House any second."

We scrambled. Leena stood in front of me, and Blaise was so close to my side our hands almost touched. I thanked the gods the hallway was dark, or someone would have seen the flush in my cheeks; I wasn't hiding anything well tonight.

Voices bounded off the stone walls as the next house approached. Before I could turn to look, the Atrium doors pulled open. A rush of cool air billowed through, and we walked in two steady lines toward the far side of the enormous glass Atrium where Ruby already stood below the lower glass ceiling of the gallery, between two pillars.

It was the wrong time to realize my strappy silver heels were too big, but I liked the way they sounded on the marbled floor. I stared straight ahead, focused on Leena's bouncing curls, and smiled as other people observed and dissected us for the second time today.

Doris gestured for us to stop below the gallery, in the section beside Ruby. We fanned out quickly as the next house was announced: Sapphire, and the few after—Diamond, Amethyst, Citrine, ending with Onyx.

There were no makers in the Atrium. I looked around again just in case I'd made a mistake. Music played from a few string instruments in the far corner, obscuring the intermittent ting of raindrops on the glass above.

The second- and third-years sat at tables in the center, beneath the tall, arching glass ceiling glittering like a million stars from the reflection of candlelight on the raindrops. Some soldiers had empty plates in front of them, and all wore their house colors just as we did. Colored banners hung from the rafters, distinctly different from the black ones strung up whenever an Armory soldier died.

"They're not going to feed us," I whispered to Leena as the music picked up. "Also, there aren't any makers at the Maker's Ball?"

"This could be bad." Her eyes widened as a server brought us glasses of deep red wine.

I nodded and took a glass. I needed it more than food. All the second- and third-years whispered and watched us. We stood, awkwardly clustered, in a pond of green because twenty of us were hardly a sea.

"Did Doris leave?" Blaise asked after a moment. That would be strange for something called the "Maker's Ball." They never left us unsupervised when makers were present.

"I don't know what's going on," Aixen whispered to Eral, loud enough for the other first-years standing around him.

The music stopped abruptly when a woman climbed onto a table in the center of the Atrium and whistled. The shrill noise bounded off the glass and metal above us. All the attention turned to her as she stood in a gown of crimson satin. Dual, silver champion cords draped over her bodice, and her black hair plaited perfectly as if she wore a crown.

She pressed her fingers to her neck, where wisps of pale yellow swirled and dissipated.

"Welcome, everyone. We've all been to this Atrium a thousand times, but tonight is different. Some of us have met the queen." She paused for a moment of raucous cheering. "And many of you are preparing for your first trial. I'm Freya, one of the champions of the Ruby House, which has yet to fail a single fucking trial this year."

Another pause, another round of cheering. Most came from our right, where the Ruby first-years gathered.

Leena leaned over and whispered, "I wonder what our champions look like."

I nodded in agreement and took a sip of wine. A flutter in my gut told me we'd find out tonight. My eyes swept the room, but all the second- and third-years were a bit too far away to make out.

Besides, it didn't matter; I'd survive regardless.

Freya continued, "Now that our makers and instructors have gone to bed, enjoy the night and let's see what you're all made of." She raised her glass of wine. "For Thera."

"*For Thera!*" Bounded off the walls and the glass, competing with the sudden pounding of rain on the glass as the weather picked up again. Everyone in the room toasted to the land we called home, even if it was the same land asking for our sacrifice.

Music resumed and so did my surveying of the faces around the Atrium. Something was amiss.

Made of.

The words stuck in my brain and prickled my skin as I watched the room. Second-and third-years all wore pins and signets we hadn't earned yet. Champions wore dual silver cords while single cords were worn by anyone pledged to a maker.

Then there were the silver epaulets on the shoulders of a few soldiers designating each house's captain and first officer in case their other visible honors weren't enough.

I needed more wine if I was dancing, and the fountain was all the way across the floor where several large glass doors had been propped open towards the overgrown garden, letting in the sticky summer air and the smell of rain.

I wasn't walking alone, so I flashed Leena a wicked grin. "Dare we get another?"

"Of course." She laughed, winding an arm through mine. "Much better than the stale stuff they keep under the altar."

That was saying something; tonight's wine was only a degree above vinegar, so the bar was low. At least there was plenty.

"Tomas said the third-years report everything to their makers," Leena remarked.

"Everything?" I winked at Leena as I filled my wine from the fountain that looked as if it were gurgling blood. Fitting.

"Well, hopefully not, but you know who Tomas knows. He is reliable."

I nodded, repeating like I'd studied for a test. "His dad is an advisor to the queen, and Tomas was invited here by the Duke of Westvale. His brother was a champion for Citrine last year."

She hummed, sipping from her glass. "Exactly."

Leena's eyes widened. I turned to see what she was looking at.

A large man from the Diamond House dressed in stark white rushed towards us, unknown blue magic dancing around his fingertips. Before I could react, a burst of heat erupted from him throwing me backwards, skidding across the marble toward a pillar, narrowly missing the wine fountain.

"*Traitor!*" he bellowed as he raised his other arm and gripped a sword.

I scrambled to stand as he charged and swung. I dodged the swing and ripped my dagger from the sheath on my thigh. Circling him, my eyes narrowed and lips turned up in an eager smile; all I needed was an opening. It'd been too long since I had a good fight.

Blindly, he charged, swinging the sword down, and I saw my chance.

Just as I was about to lunge, firm hands shoved me back to the floor to watch as another sword plunged into the attacker's chest, sending a spray of blood in my direction, across the white floor. Anger ticked across my temple because that was my fight.

The attacker was a second-year based on the pin I glimpsed as he swayed on his knees. He gave a bloody, spluttering cough before he fell to the floor, lifeless.

The Armory doesn't forgive.

I blinked, expecting to see Blaise standing above me. Instead, a beautiful man in a velvet green coat stood there and held out his hand. Curls of dark brown hair brushed his collar.

"The average response is 'thank you,'" he said curtly.

I glared at him, sheathing my dagger through the layers of my gown. "I could have done that myself. Next time you push me away from my fight, it will be your last." Brushing off his hand, I staggered onto my feet and straightened my shoulders.

The man stared and wiped the blood from his sword on the attacker's jacket.

Several realizations hit at once, and the blood left my face. Silver epaulets were pinned to his shoulders. He wore a single, silver cord—he'd been claimed by a maker, and he was—

"I'm not sure you should speak to your first officer that way, darling."

Fuck. Not a great start. Behind me, a single Armory guard crouched down and dragged the body from the floor. A stain of red followed him, streaking the white marble, seeping into the carved names of forgotten soldiers nearer to the north hallway. The blood would remain there the rest of the night as a warning.

The first officer placed a hand on his throat, and yellow tendrils wrapped around it. "This is your reminder: attacking a fellow soldier, willfully, and outside of a trial, is treason and punishable by death."

There was a sweep of murmuring through the Atrium, and I was suddenly aware I stood in a room full of people who were all certainly staring at me.

And maybe the blood.

"Did you know him?" the first officer asked. I think it was the second time. He looked at me impatiently, lips taut and jaw stiff.

I shook my head and mumbled, "No, I've never seen him before."

"Interesting. Do you have a lot of enemies you aren't aware of?"

I straightened and took a step closer to him. "Hard to quantify if I'm not aware of them, but I'm happy to add you to my list of known enemies if you keep prying."

Confusion furrowed his brow while blue eyes glared. "Are you alright?" he nearly scoffed.

"Where's Leena?" I bristled, averting my gaze to peer around him.

"Curly hair? Blonde?" he listed off.

"Yes."

"She's right there. Sangrey, isn't it?"

I nodded and stiffened; I wasn't enjoying this. He came a step closer, and I took one back. The man disarmed me with eyes of sapphire, a sharp chin, and an unsettling elegance. By how he stood, I figured he was a high-ranking noble. He didn't have to scramble for authority like some others around here who clung to any grasp of power.

"Why are you looking at me?" he asked, and then it became a smirk. "You really would kill me for that, wouldn't you?"

My arms crossed, and I doubled down, emboldened by the wine. "Without a second thought, First Officer."

"Fine, next time you're attacked, I'll stand back. Amazing the confidence a maker can grant." His blue eyes glimmered, and his lips turned up as he walked away.

Fuck. I didn't know why I stood my ground. The first officer was as important as the captain. In trial, they had nearly as much control over who would live or die. But that wasn't why my legs shook profusely.

I knew him. I knew those eyes. I had to. They were too familiar. Did he feel the same way? I wouldn't forget someone who looked like that, not if they'd spent any time at Arden's.

Leena appeared beside me, her hand steady on my elbow. "What was that about? And is he our first officer?" she whispered.

"Yes, and I don't feel good about it." Even now, bile rose in my throat.

"At least you can't see the blood on your dress." She frowned as I turned toward her, hand on my cheek.

"Is there any on my face?"

Leena gestured to her neck, and I took the hint. I grabbed a piece of my skirt and wiped at it until she nodded.

Within minutes, the Atrium became the grandest ballroom. The room of soldiers ignored the blood drying on the marble, and the space filled with talking and dancing as the Armory's nearly invisible staff cleared the tables.

Spilled blood wasn't a rare occurrence in the Armory, but it was a waste to kill a brother outside of our trials.

Leena stayed close as I crossed the room, walking towards Blaise as a wide grin spread across his face contrasting the pinch of concern in his eyes when he saw me.

Deciding it was best to give us privacy, Leena squeezed my shoulder and disappeared through the crowd with a knowing smile.

"Are you okay?" Blaise asked, closing the distance between us.

I nodded, and everything that happened felt secondary under his gaze. "Better now. Might even take you up on your offer," I joked.

"I was hoping you'd say that, Sangrey." His voice was low, gruff. And the heat of his body closed in; I'd been closer before, but this was different.

We were in something that almost felt like the real world. It wasn't a library or a training room, and I didn't have the protection of my leathers. It was a different heat between him and the fabric of my gown.

Tentatively, his arm grabbed my waist and pulled me into the rhythm of the music.

Dancing was never much of a choice for me. Arden always pushed me onto the floor and pointed out the people he needed leverage over.

I was Arden's viper because I could retract my fangs.

Blaise spun me, and the memory faded.

He was so close. The faint smell of cinnamon on his clothes somehow always lingered and permeated my senses. I always wanted more.

I wanted to taste it on his lips, his neck, and his shoulders. I was intoxicated too quickly. Perhaps it was the wine, because when his lips finally crashed into mine, my heart fluttered. He tasted like cinnamon. I knew this, but it was so much sweeter out here, in the Atrium, where it felt real.

Every other kiss was stolen in the shadows, but this . . . this was different. I pulled away first, and we stopped dancing as I tried to calm my racing heart.

"Better than I remember." His hands were still on my waist.

He'd changed completely in the year we'd been confined to these walls. He'd become more, somehow. More confident, more familiar, and more like someone who could fit into my life if we weren't doomed to be knights.

"I don't know. I almost prefer you sweaty and without the coat."

"Careful now." His thumb ran over my lip, the hunger in his eyes warming my belly. "We're still in the Atrium, Sangrey."

I looked around. Other pairs kissed around us on the floor, including Eral and Aixen, who practically clawed at one another. No one would pay any mind to what we did here. It was our Black Banquet, and all of us feared this could be our last night alive.

"We could leave?" I said with a demure smile.

Blaise's hands tightened on my waist. His desire pressed against my thigh, but he groaned and shook his head. "We haven't been dismissed."

"Later." Later sounded incredible, luxurious even. I grinned, kissing him again before I pulled away. I would have dragged the man into the shadows if I stood too close much longer. It was a habit.

He ran a hand through his hair as I stared at his lips.

"Right," he said. "I'm gonna get another drink. I'll find you later." Taking a deep breath, he nodded farewell.

Good, get away from me.

The regret crawled back as it did every time he walked away. I shouldn't feel empty, but I suppose that's what I'd become. Leena strode over, narrowly avoiding a collision with a dancing couple, preventing me from wallowing any further.

"Is it possible you feel something for him?" Leena whispered.

"No." I forced a frown. "No happy endings in the Armory, remember?"

She scoffed. "Depends on your definition of a happy ending because we've both had—"

I jabbed her with my elbow, and she giggled. Leena was never wrong. She just always said the quiet part aloud. It was one reason we could stand each other. She'd never play the game of politics with me, or anyone, if she didn't have to.

She differed from the noble-bred who held every emotion on their shoulders as if letting go of anything would open them to ruin.

In some ways, they certainly weren't wrong.

Emotions could always be exploited.

CHAPTER 3

THE MUSIC STOPPED AGAIN, and it wasn't Freya this time but a different champion wearing dual silver cords. This one was tall and lean, with black hair cascading down his waist. He looked infinitely more like a dreite, a dark priest of the Goddess Dreonna, than a warrior despite the deep scar across his cheek.

The man's voice reverberated through the room. "We welcome our first-year recruits and have been assured your training goes well. However, as tradition goes, we won't believe what we haven't seen."

A murmur rippled through the room among the first-years, while everyone else was stoic.

"Find your house captain and follow them to your test," the man ordered.

Sparks of color erupted in the Atrium. One for every house, each above a hallway door. I looked around for the Emerald, and a rock settled in my gut. *Of course, there'd be a test tonight.*

Who wouldn't want to get the first-years drunk and see what they can do?

Intrinsic magic, our gifts, took years to hone. In our twenties, most of us barely knew what we were capable of, or we were fairly good at concealing it. I was the latter, and dread filled me; I'd never tried to do anything outside of petty magic and healing.

I came to the Armory expecting my sword to keep me alive.

Beneath a flurry of green sparks, the first officer stood beside a red-haired woman who wore similar silver epaulets. Both were second-years, and she was the Emerald Captain. Behind them, Emerald's three champions stood, draped in their dual silver cords, observing.

We were supposed to have four champions I'd heard, but one must have died during the last trial. I swallowed over the lump in my throat. That could cost our house a portion of its funding in the coming year if we had empty-handed makers.

I didn't catch the first officer's name, but his blue eyes met mine and held the stare. Nerves bubbled up, along with something else.

The red-haired Emerald Captain wore a bright green gown, and her updo was coming undone in the humidity. She did a final count of first-years and whispered something to the champions before she turned on her heel.

The Atrium was near silent except for the patter of rain. Leena tensed beside me.

Emerald sparks sputtered out, and a door opened, leading to a staircase.

We followed the captain, descending well below the Atrium. A few of us conjured light in our hands to fill the cold, damp void of the cobbled stairway, but it didn't last long.

The further we went, the more the wine warmed and curdled in my chest as though we approached something foreboding. It took extra focus to keep the lights from flickering out as we followed our house down several flights of stairs.

At seventy-eight steps, our lights went out just as a horrific, ear-piercing screech echoed through the dark.

I tried to conjure the light again, snapping and twisting my wrist, but only managed a single spark between my fingers. I wasn't the only one struggling. Everything about my magic felt wrong and unsettled.

Another screech shot through the silence, and I instinctively covered my ears. It resounded off the walls and rattled my skull. *This is what death sounds like.* It dragged all the warmth out of my body as natural firelight, from a torch held by an undecorated second-year, filled the narrow hallway.

We were well below the dungeons, where the ground had turned from stone to well-packed dirt.

"Right, follow me," the captain shouted and darted down another hallway.

We followed, but I sure wish we hadn't.

Around the corner, a creature screeched again. Too loud, too close, and as the light from the torch spilled around the corner, it screamed even louder. Something behind my ribs warmed and twisted.

I pushed towards the front of the crowd of green to see what we were up against.

The hallway opened into a large cavern where giant stone pillars stretched toward the ceiling and held up the Armory far above. In the center was a large silver cage containing a grotesque creature.

I gasped.

Its scaled skin was as if made from obsidian—dark, reflecting the flames of the torch as it stood crouched on two skinny legs. Its long talons reached around the bars, searching. Smoke rose from its fingertips as it wailed again. Leather black wings spread out behind its body, flapping like a caught butterfly.

It snatched its taloned hands back and retreated, distorting itself to become as small as possible.

A demon.

Its presence dragged the breath from my lungs as it wailed again, baring stark white fangs that glowed against the shadowy depths of its void-black scales.

It was so human and nonhuman in equal parts . . .

My stomach pitted.

"From today on," the captain said, "you all serve Thera until the Seven call you home. Emerald is one of two houses specializing in demons and dreite priests from the Darklands. Her Majesty will rely on us and Amethyst to face and hold back the dark forces that come for us from the North, across the Sea of Tharamund."

The beast screamed again, and it sent something in me writhing loose. I'd heard a hundred stories about demons in my life. I knew it was possible we'd face them in Emerald, but I wasn't prepared for *this.*

"When the old kingdom collapsed, the gods unleashed a final curse to remind us evil is never far." The captain paused as the demon growled and hissed while she surveyed us. "Demons are the purest form of dark magic. They are botched creations of the Goddess Dreonna. Their teeth and claws are laced with the venom running in their blood."

Another scream of rage from the demon, another pause.

"They feed on humans and can only be contained by powerful sigils, silver, and iron. There is nothing else we can count on. During the Second War of Kings, it was only by Thera's dragons we defeated their demon wielder and forced the Darklands to retreat, resulting in Thera's independence."

A woman named Tessa collapsed beside Eral. My stomach coiled with dread.

His face darkened as he pressed two fingers to her neck and shook his head. Gently, he placed her back on the ground. She was stiff, pale, and her eyes unseeing. I wish I hadn't seen it.

A shiver ran down my spine: Tessa was dead, and she would only be the first of many. In the blink of an eye, we were nineteen.

The demon screamed again, and I swallowed the fear as it turned to sour desperation. *I needed to live.* I needed to serve on the Queensguard, or Arden would never let my brother go.

I could break a person in as many ways as I could fix them, but that was it. Where would I start with a demon? My gifts were of no use here. Healers were never granted another gift, so I was about to be disposable, which was the last thing I could be, or what good were fourteen years of training? At least I could fight better than Varyn, but that wasn't a comfort.

"Amethyst is the other demon house," the first officer said. "We will partner most closely with them and the griffon riders of

Onyx. The remaining houses serve the queen and their makers as needed."

I looked at Leena, and something in me twisted. Gods and stars above. She looked horrified. Every one of us was horrified. We were here to become champions for our makers and knights for the queen. We'd made peace with the blood, war, and violence that came with our future, but now we faced the first of many unimaginable monsters.

Aixen stepped forward first, his flaxen hair combed back handsomely and his arm still in a sling. I don't know what possessed him. The second- and third-years applauded while the rest of us held our breath.

"I believe most of you in this room wield something critical to Thera's defense, and tonight you'll show us. Remember, the gods grant us only what we need."

Everything else will die. The words our first officer didn't say were the ones hanging in the air.

The demon threw itself against the wall of its cage again, screeching as its flesh came in contact with the silver. Some part of me felt guilty, but every part of that creature would destroy me. I had no room to give a monster sympathy.

Aixen took a wobbling step forward. He'd chosen a mint-green vest which looked handsome in the Atrium, but now it paled him.

Leena nudged my arm and whispered, "You told me we wouldn't die tonight."

I shrugged, trying to appear calm. "I say a lot of things."

There was nothing worse than dying before the first trial started. Though, if you were dead, it was hard to worry about anything else. Tessa would be committed to the gods and burned with a soldier's honors having never faced an Armory trial. Maybe she was the lucky one.

Aixen looked at the captain and then back at the demon. He lifted his good arm, squinted, and focused as tendrils of silver extended from it. Eral gritted his teeth and watched.

At first, the demon batted away the dust with a hiss, but then it choked. Aixen twisted his hand. The tendrils turned into ropes, and the demon screamed as the silver drifted around it, becoming solid. Aixen heaved, sweat beaded on his brow. He wouldn't hold it any longer. The ropes shattered into pieces. He stumbled backward into Eral's arms as the captain applauded.

Next was Tomas. He showered the creature in a firestorm, warming the whole cavern. The demon roared, backing into the corner of its cage. Tomas smiled and took a step back.

Something in me felt restless and sharp as the frantic black eyes of the beast watched through the bars of its cage, wings tucked. Was it looking at me?

I never thought Tomas would have power like that; I'd think the gods would know better than to make someone so reckless a *Braagen.*

I'd seen everyone in Emerald wield petty magic in their palms like whispers of fire, wind, and water, but it was nothing next to the gifts my house showed off now. This was the magic that qualified us for knighthood.

One woman, Niela, her entire arm turned to liquid silver, and she fashioned it into a sword as silver wings unfolded behind her. Another wielded the wind and pushed the demon from one side of the cage to the other. It's called propulsion. There was a Catharian word for it, but it escaped me. Another man doused the demon with water, a trick which was coolly regarded as the water rolled off the scales.

I gulped. *All I could do was fix bones.*

Blaise stepped up, and my heart skipped a beat. He stood still, hands at his sides, eyes steadfast on the demon. A few seconds ticked by, and without raising a finger, the demon retreated and curled up on the ground, screaming.

"What did you do?" the captain asked, lips pursed as she tried to work it out.

Blaise smiled. "*Vistone.* I showed it an illusion: the same room but with a shrinking cage."

The demon slowly realized it wasn't real as Blaise stepped back into the crowd of first-years. It stood back up and spread its wings, roaring again; black venom dripped from pearlescent fangs.

"Sangrey."

I winced at the sound of my name. The first officer was suddenly beside me and nudged my arm. I hesitated, shaking my head, weighing the right words to say. "I'm a healer."

"Avernought doesn't invite healers to the Armory," he rebuffed.

"Perhaps he's wrong."

"Doubtful. Show us what you can do." His voice clipped as he gestured toward the cage.

Nothing. I gulped. There wasn't another gift in me, not an intrinsic one. I was even average at petty magic. Regardless, I walked forward, knowing there was nothing a healer could do for a demon.

Minutes before, we all watched Varyn twist his face in concentration as he tried to break the demon's arm and put it back from a safe distance. The demon only snarled and reared its wings at him.

I swallowed my nerves as I took a step.

Something else. I had to do something else. I crept closer, seeing burn marks on its obsidian scales as it folded its wings and lowered itself. It appeared to kneel and cast its eyes down. Perhaps it could sense I was a healer from the way I looked at the black blood oozing from its arm.

My magic reached forward, white tendrils nudging the wounds and turning iridescent as they sank into the charred skin of the creature.

The demon's beady eyes surveyed and mocked the magic in me that barely worked. Blood still trickled. I was more useless than I realized.

I closed my eyes again. *If I just had a knife, I could carve it like a ham, surely.* Sweat beaded on my forehead. I twisted my hands and fingers again in another motion I'd memorized for healing burns. Something warm bloomed in my chest and I gasped. My eyes flew open.

Nothing. I took a step closer to the cage, then another. I needed to see what it saw.

It didn't scream, move, or blink. It just stared at me. The wound had closed.

I reached out to touch it, sticking my hand through the bars, and the demon remained—kneeling and complacent as something wet and cold shifted between my ribs, contrasting the heat in the room.

"Sangrey!"

Blaise shouted my name and pulled me out of whatever trance the demon lured me into. I snatched my hand back just before it touched the scales. There was no applause as I returned.

A few people moved out of my way as if they were afraid. Even Leena had wide eyes.

The only one who didn't was the first officer. He looked pleased, his lips curling up as if he had found something he'd been waiting for.

I stopped and turned around to watch the rest of us go. I did not know what I did until the first officer leaned towards me and whispered, "I told you Avernought doesn't speak to healers, *dreosen.*" Something warm twisted in my chest and folded over. "The queen was hoping for a demon wielder."

"Oh." Me? Demon wielders were legends, myths from a by-gone time. It had been almost two hundred fucking years.

"My name is Farran."

I filed the name away, but my attention shifted as the cage rattled and the demon fell from the trance, throwing itself at the bars. It wailed as its skin came in contact with the silver.

Then, Leena stepped out from the crowd.

She was the last to go.

"Put it out of its misery," Farran commanded, loud enough for the room to hear. He walked back towards our red-haired captain whose sallow face pinched and concentrated.

I couldn't see Leena's, her back was turned to me. But I knew she'd never taken a life, not from anything. She was nothing like me in all the ways that mattered. She still had softness and feeling where Arden had numbed me.

"You'll never survive the Armory if you're still crying about your mother!" Arden shouted through the locked door as I tried to clean the bloody slice he'd taken out of my arm.

I cried out of rage. He had no fucking right to use her.

I was fourteen then, but maybe he was right. At twenty-four, I was still alive and hadn't cried in years. I could hardly remember her face or my father's; they were my past, and this was my future.

Leena's hand rose slowly. She strained and twisted her fingers as if turning on a faucet. A few perilous seconds ticked by before tendrils of black extended from her hand. The tendrils mingled, multiplied, and wrapped around the demon. So much so that they filled the cage and obscured the grotesque shape of the creature as it writhed and screamed.

Then she closed her fist. There was a crack, followed by silence. Pain lanced through my chest and stole my breath only to dissipate a second later.

The blackness vanished, and the room stood still. The demon's body was bent and broken across the cage floor as an unmoving heap of scales, wings, and gangly limbs.

We were in a state of shock, but Leena looked calm as she walked back.

"What the fuck was that?" I whispered in horror.

Leena merely smiled and said, "Shadows."

Chapter 4

We went back upstairs and mingled in the Atrium for a little longer. Half of the room had lost their appetite for wine, while the other half couldn't drink enough.

Emerald was the second house to make it back. Only Amethyst, our demon counterpart, looked as forlorn as we did. I'd bet they met a demon, too. Their house wasn't any different from us, aside from the color they wore.

As we stood around, someone in our house said the last demon wielder appeared in the Second War of Kings two-hundred and thirty years prior, while the one before served five hundred years ago in the first War of Kings which created the five kingdoms.

Any *dreosen* in between was killed the moment their gift was known.

The shock of it all made the rest of the night a blur.

I woke up sweating the next morning, every muscle heavy and joint tight as I pushed against the weight of yesterday. Sunlight streamed through the narrow window beside me, dust glittering in the beam of light.

Outside, fog had settled on the forest floor and rolled through the grounds.

Today was the last training day before our first trial: the day they'd swap our fake weapons for real ones. We were supposed to have enough skill to use them without being a danger to ourselves, but there was a vast difference between steel and pine.

I pulled on pants, strapped on my leathers, and shrugged into my mother's old cardigan. Luckily, Leena was asleep.

The soft tap of my footsteps against the stone echoed through the empty hallway as I left our floor and descended the stair tower to the grounds.

The door at the bottom groaned as it opened. A few first-years were already sparring on the lawn, leaving footprints on the grass in the silvery morning dew as their metal swords scraped one another in a draw.

I couldn't tell what house they were in, but it didn't matter; I'd missed the sound. The clack of wood we'd all gotten used to had nothing on the elegant clang of metal striking metal.

I ambled down a path leading into the forest where the trees seemed impossibly tall. Viridescent pines stretched up and choked most of the foliage and brush below. It was a far cry from the thick, haunted forests of Rowane where berries, vines, and brush raced to fill any space between.

Though the Armory woods were hollow and forlorn, I'd learned some of its secrets. There were hidden riverbanks, a few cliffs, and even some villages a quarter day's walk away if you followed the right trails.

I clambered down the rocks to my rendezvous point on the riverbank, expecting to see one of Arden's men half drunk, staggering across the river. Instead, there was a horse tied to one of the willow trees sagging over the water.

It wasn't the same speckled horse I was used to. This one was taller and a deep chocolate-brown. It sized me up as I approached, then it blinked and shook its head; we knew each other.

A rock skipped across the water, drawing my eyes toward the lanky figure of my brother. Anger flushed my cheeks. *Arden promised me.*

"You shouldn't be here, Declan," I said, my hands fisted in my pockets as he turned around on the bank.

We shared the same face and the same straight auburn hair. Both of us looked painfully like our mother, but Declan had her eyes: blue as light as a sunny day, where I had my father's brown and his storminess to match. Declan also took my mother's kindness but it was rare for me to see it. I only ever saw the part of him that resented me for dragging us to Arden's doorstep.

He was a few inches taller than me. Taller than I remembered. He crossed his arms and walked closer, lips pursed.

"Only doing what I'm told, Reina. Arden is paranoid again, convinced himself Tristan read the letters and wanted to send someone he trusted," he retorted.

"He trusts you?" I almost scoffed.

"No, but he trusts you, and that's enough."

"What does he want?"

"You're not even going to ask how I've been?" Declan snapped.

I lifted my chin. "I mean, you look well."

He kicked the ground with an embroidered boot and gave a short laugh. He was dressed as a noble and held himself like one.

When I left for the Armory, Declan was supposed to become an apprentice to a librarian in the lower city. Prior to this, messages came from Arden or whoever else he could spare from his *guild*—he had plenty of bodies eager to please him and rise through the ranks.

It was a three-day trip from his estate; until today, he'd never risked anyone of value.

"Arden wishes I was you, you know?" Declan took a step towards me and tilted his face up. The sun caught his light blue eyes, and memories dredged up at the sight.

I squared my shoulders. "I'm sorry you're still there."

"All because you haven't paid your debt." He glared. "I don't know what deal you struck with him, but I'm polishing his silver and mopping up the mistakes the others keep making now you're not there. Another girl came back half-dead the other night."

"I'm sorry." I meant it. "Arden promised me he would help you, not use you."

Declan ignored me and pulled a letter from his coat pocket, holding it out for me. I grabbed it and tore it open. The writing was so familiar; I'd notice Arden's penmanship anywhere. His letters twisted and curled around the sentences in the most haphazard, practiced way. It was chaotic and balanced all at once, a combination of two worlds—exactly the space he occupied.

The letter even smelled like his damned house. Old wood, dust, and cigar smoke. Unmistakable.

"Your trial is tomorrow," Declan said. I nodded but barely heard him. The words scrawled by Arden were louder than any rumble of thunder or the constant pang of guilt.

To my viper,

I've placed many bets on your success at trial. By now, Avernought has approached you in front of the other makers to make his intention clear. As you know, he's waited for this day as you have, and he intends to offer you as much of his protection as he can.

Avernought has not told me what your gift is, but he assures me it can only benefit you and it's complimentary to Prince Farran's. This endangers you, and I cannot protect you in the Armory, but there are plenty who can. Hold your loyalties close, and don't get distracted. I'm doing what I can from Rowane to influence your trials.

Remember your promise to me. Remember your destiny.

May the old gods rise again to be the wind at your back.

Prince Farran. Not a noble, but the son of a queen with the blood of thousands on her hands. Thousands, including our mother.

That's why his name was familiar. That's why I recognized his face. Rage simmered below my skin, a slow, frothing boil. *I should have known.* I'd heard the announcement once, I'm sure, but it wasn't important enough to remember. I was preoccupied.

"Did you know any of this?" I asked Declan, slowly raising my eyes to meet his.

"Arden tells me nothing," he said flatly. "Especially when it comes to *you*."

The words hurt more than they should have. "Tell him I protect myself."

"Fine." Declan paused. He kicked a rock on the riverbank and watched it splash into the shallow water before looking back at me. "Have you seen anyone I would know?"

A hurt I hadn't seen before swirled in his eyes. I said lowly, "First-years barely see the other houses."

Declan looked at the sand clinging to his boots. "Right until you have to kill each other."

"We don't kill each other," I mumbled.

"You think I believe that? The Armory builds weapons. That's all you are to the makers. They only need a few of you to survive." He wasn't wrong. We'd talked about it before.

I sat silent over dinner at Arden's estate many times as Declan pleaded with me to find another way. He knew nothing of the oath, and I felt guilty enough. If I told him I'd die if I didn't fulfill it, his resentment would turn to pity, and that would be worse. I preferred his anger.

The sun climbed higher into the sky, and the morning mist began to disappear as the day settled in. "This was my choice, and it's kept you safe," I said quietly.

"I can protect myself."

I nearly rolled my eyes. "I need to go."

This wasn't enough time, but it was all I could give. His chin dipped to look at the river lapping at the bank. Softly, I added, "I miss you, Declan."

"Arden will send me back in a month at the same time."

I took a breath and looked at him tightly. "He doesn't own you. He owns me."

"This isn't about me. He gave me every tutor I ever asked for; I've never felt confined the way you did." He lowered his voice. "There were other ways out for you, Reina."

I winced at the sharp edge in his tone and stepped back towards the trail. "There weren't. I've told you a hundred times."

"What's your gift?" he asked after a moment of silence.

"Not right now." I wasn't ready to answer—gods, I wasn't ready to admit it to myself. I was sure he'd find out soon. The Armory criers would be out in full force, collecting bets as soon as they had a report. "I need to go."

"It has to be good if he sent you out of Rowane." Declan smirked and stepped back. "Suppose I'll find out from the criers."

I began walking back. "Sure. Goodbye. Please, be careful," I called over my shoulder.

"Good luck, Rein."

I murmured a thanks and retreated into the woods, leaving Declan and his horse on the bank. Only getting out of this alive would repay my debt. Then I would carve the life out of Damien Arden.

Until then, killing him would kill me, too.

CHAPTER 5

EACH FIRST-YEAR HOUSE HAD their own dining room. Tonight, the Emerald dining room was the second quietest it had ever been following several hours of training. The first happened when a recruit was accused of treason and dragged from the dining hall by his hair.

The Crown could excuse fraud, murder, and other heinous things, but *never* treason.

We all pretended to eat as we heard the guards snap his neck in the hallway.

That was a year ago, and so much had changed since then.

Reality sunk in slowly . . . somehow, there would be less of us tomorrow.

I chased a potato around my plate with my fork. It was certainly cold by now, but I couldn't find my appetite. I kept thinking about the letter, my brother, and the power pulsing through my blood—a power far beyond anything I imagined.

I hoped to every god, new and old, it would be enough to keep me alive.

Leena cleared her throat, and we made eye contact across the table. "You should eat."

"You should, too." I lowered my gaze to her food.

Her plate was as untouched as mine: potatoes piled on one side, a cut of some meat on the other, and a dinner roll.

"Did you know you could do that yesterday? With the shadows?" I asked.

Leena nodded. "Some of it. I'd always thought I could move them, and I used it in the woods a few times before, but the demon made it come alive. What about you, *dreosen*? Blaise almost dragged you out of the room when you reached for it."

"I had no idea," I admitted. "I . . . I knew demons were real. Just never thought I'd be so close to one."

Leena stabbed a piece of meat. "Now you can command an army of them."

"That might be a stretch." I winced.

"I can see it now: General Reina Sangrey, *dreosen*. You're in black leathers. I can be your first in command and rain shadows down as the *sunderone* of Thera. We'll be legends."

"It does sound like a song, doesn't it?" I smiled slightly.

"It does." Leena smirked, taking a bite of food. "Almost wish I could hear what the criers will say. Or maybe not, the ones in Lower Rowane were awful."

Leena ate a cold potato and I did the same. Both of us let our minds wander and said nothing. I thought about Farran, the first officer and prince. I didn't need any protection, not from someone born loyal to the tyrant queen.

I already felt sick every time I looked at the stars, wolves, and lilies of the Theranian crest. How would it feel to stand beside the prince himself? If that was my fate, I didn't want it.

How much money did Arden stand to make from Avernought if I made it to the Queensguard? He was already wealthy, but it must be life-changing if my name was somehow intertwined with a Theranian Prince and the richest maker in the Armory.

I tried not to think about my Rite vision all those years ago: my dagger clutched in my hands, sticking out of the queen. It was a nightmare I couldn't shake.

I'd become a Queensguard Knight and pay my debt to Arden. Then I'd get close enough to the queen to take her life exactly as I'd seen it at thirteen.

"Are you sure you're alright?" Leena's voice cut through my thoughts. "That was a—"

"I'm fine." I pushed my plate forward as I stood. "I'm going for a walk."

Leena sighed; she knew better than to follow me. I'd find her later, either in the library sprawled across one of the overstuffed chairs or in her bed, scribbling out letters for her family. Armory letters weren't sent until after we died or came out as champions, but writing made her feel better.

I wasn't even sure Declan would read my letters if I died. I was ten and he was seven when we first came into Arden's care. Our parents died in a fire set by Crown soldiers, and Arden's was the best bargain I could make.

Torches warmed the stone walls of the Emerald floor as I wandered. The rap of my footsteps echoed, and I didn't stop until I pushed open the door to the training room. Only one torch was lit inside, so I flicked my wrist, bringing another to life with a soft *whoosh* of flames.

I smiled; that kind of magic never got old. Petty or not, power was power.

Another storm blew in outside. Lightning flashed and filled the room with light every few minutes, while rain pounded the few slender windows gracing the long, narrow space of the training room.

Targets were fastened onto the far walls on either side, and mats sat in the middle where we spent the last months practicing maneuvers and sparring with training weapons.

Today was the first and only day the Armory provided first-years with real steel. It was late but still gleamed. I ran my fingers admirably over the cold hilts and scarred blades. They would certainly be gone by morning, but it was a thrill to use something real, no matter how beaten and battered it was after so long without.

The soreness in my arms was settling in, but I didn't want to waste time, not when I had the whole room to myself. Besides, I'd hardly touched the knives, and they were always my favorite.

I grabbed one from the rack and held it, memorizing the weight, the pull, and the angle of the blade. With my feet planted firmly on a mat, I measured a clear shot and threw.

It hissed through the air and landed with a *thunk* on the target. It wasn't centered, but at least I hit something. When I started training with Arden, I spent months dodging blades as they ricocheted off the wall in his garden.

That was nearly twelve years ago. Now, I could hit my mark from yards away.

"Demon wielder," a voice echoed through the room, and I jumped.

The next knife missed the target and hit the wall with a metallic clang. I growled and spun around to see Prince Farran standing in the doorway.

"Your Highness," I greeted and gave a curt bow.

A voice in my head reminded me to be respectful. His trust would be invaluable, even if the thought of it made my skin crawl.

I cleared my throat. "Don't second-years have their own training room?"

"We do." Farran walked closer with a nod.

He was the opposite of royalty, dressed in a white tunic and riding pants. Heat rolled over in my chest, between my ribs, as he drew near. He wore no cords, pins, or epaulets to designate his rank, and his dark hair was loose around his shoulders as he watched.

"Were you looking for me?" I asked.

"I was looking to practice; this room is longer. Better for archery than what they give the second- and third-years. I didn't expect any first-years to be practicing tonight, so you being here is coincidental. You know it is the last night before your first trial?"

"If I wanted to drink and fuck, I would be," I said plainly, and his eyebrows rose. "I'm doing exactly what I want to be doing."

"Throwing knives?" he mused.

"Yes, and if I miss during trial, I'll just stand behind our *sunderone*."

He smirked. "You're not worried about her burning out?"

"Burning out?" My brow raised in question.

"The Armory gave everyone a tonic yesterday to wake their gift. It calls it forward, but it will still take years to master. The beasts in the first trial won't kill you. Reaching too far into your power and draining it will. Before a chemist found the tonic, gifts came about much slower."

That made too much sense. Everything felt heightened and strange since last night. Power was an incessant buzzing against my skin. "Is that what happened to Tessa?"

He paused. "Most likely. Not everyone's gift is meant to be woken so abruptly."

I grabbed another knife and threw it. This time, I hit the target. Farran's eyes widened as I turned back. "Since you think you know mine, what gift did the Seven give a Prince of Thera?"

His hands stopped on a bow leaning on the rack. A crack of thunder shook the floor. "Wouldn't you like to know?"

"In fact, I would," I retorted.

"Perhaps you'll find out tomorrow." He raised the bow and nocked an arrow on it. Casually, he pulled back, released. He hit the target dead center. "Avernought suspected the *dreosen* might be in Emerald. I am surprised it's you."

"What is that supposed to mean?" I grabbed another knife from the rack. I aimed and threw it hard, splitting his arrow down the center. I bit back a smile.

His sapphire eyes stared at the target as he answered, "Nothing. Just seems like a lot of power to give to someone so small. It's gonna take all the gods to keep you alive, isn't it?" Something deeper reverberated in his voice, and I couldn't quite place it.

"I don't remember saying I needed protection." I looked back at Farran, my jaw tensed. "In fact, I thought I made myself clear."

He lowered the arrow in his hand to look at me with a hard gaze. "Do you plan to test that?"

"I only plan to leave here alive, Prince."

"First Officer is the title that matters."

"That's incredibly hard to believe." I scoffed.

"Even after meeting a demon yesterday?"

"Especially after meeting a demon," I muttered. I grabbed one more knife, aimed, and threw.

It hit the target several inches from the center, and I exhaled, peering at Farran. His sapphire eyes watched me.

Black lines drifted and waded across the bit of his chest exposed by his shirt. Something about it was familiar, and I stared shamelessly as he tightened the laces to hide it. I cleared my throat, eyes snapping at the wall.

"What do I need to do tomorrow?"

"Fight." He shrugged. I rolled my eyes, but he continued as nearby thunder rumbled, "Fight and don't burn yourself out trying to show off. That's what's going to kill most of you in the first few trials. Some powers shouldn't exist."

"Like a demon wielder?" I looked at him as another flash of lightning illuminated the training room.

"Historically, it's the treason that kills them, but certainly you would never. Not as the first, true *dreosen* of Thera?"

His stare was disarming. My heart skipped a beat. Thank gods it steadied before panic completely seized me. I knew better than to let words shake me, and I answered with the calmest voice I could.

"Luckily, I'm here to dedicate my life to the queen." *Not a lie.*

"As am I." Farran walked around me and set his bow back on the rack. "Reina Sangrey, any relation to the noble house?"

I shook my head. My last name sounded strange when he said it, ass if he were savoring it. "There are many Sangreys in Thera. Mine descend from shopkeepers and tavern maids. My father did dream of serving the Crown, if dreams of nobility count?"

That *was* a lie. My mother was a Theranian noble, and my father was no one.

My life was tied to the Crown, and I hated it. I hated the nobles, the royals, and anyone who served them blindly, but I needed to be here. If the prince left me alone, I could grit my teeth and bear my fate.

"Interesting," he mused, a flicker of curiosity crossing his face.

My face scrunched. "Why?"

He shrugged, and a curl fell in front of his eye. He pushed it back. "I have a hard time believing someone with eyes like yours who throws knives better than any knight I've met, ever spent much time in shops or taverns."

"Brown eyes? Hardly anything special," I retorted, ignoring how the comment mirrored exactly what Avernought said. "And if a prince knew anything about taverns, the knives should come as no surprise."

"You'd be surprised what I know about taverns, darling."

I glared. "I wouldn't be terribly surprised to learn you've been drunk in a tavern once."

"It was twice." He grinned. "Well, I'll leave you to it then. Suppose you're right about my own training room."

With that, Farran backed away and left. I sighed, relieved, and walked across the room to grab the knives from the target. A few more throws, and I'd let myself go to bed.

But something about the way Farran looked at me was unsettling. I didn't pick up another knife. I felt like prey because perhaps, that's what I was to them. A prince wouldn't waste his time talking to me if he ever found out about Arden, let alone the destiny awaiting me.

In fact, he'd sink a thousand of those arrows into my chest before I spoke another word.

His footsteps faded, and I left shortly after with a gaping chasm in my gut I couldn't find a name for.

CHAPTER 6

My first day at the Armory, a year ago, felt like coming home. I had traveled alone from Rowane, hoping to every god my trunk arrived safely. The idea of anything happening to my mother's cardigan or any of my books enraged me. My trunk had the last slivers of my life before I belonged to anyone—perhaps the only.

I remembered arriving the same way I remembered fever dreams. It happened in flashes, blurred together as it was the prologue of a story.

Instructors ushered several of us past the Atrium, our mouths agape at the sight of the impossible glass Atrium as sunlight streamed through it. They pushed us into the stair tower, toward our assigned rooms where my chest sunk at the sight of fresh leathers laid out over a bed. A soldier's pin set gingerly atop an emerald armband: the house Avernought invited me to despite my indifference to the color.

Once we dressed, they gathered us in the Atrium where we lined up before a makeshift dais. On it stood General Linden of the Queensguard, with a gaggle of Crown knights and priests wearing the white robes of the Seven.

Seven priests, to be exact. It was the most important number in all of Thera: seven gods, seven temples, seven stars, seven houses, and seven dire wolves guarding the gates of Tir.

The priests fanned out and one by one, took our hands in theirs as they muttered a string of incoherent prayers before they moved on to the next. The language of the prayer was neither

Catharian nor the tongue of the realm, but something in the middle that only the Seven wanted to listen to.

House instructors stood along the outer walls, watching us. Perhaps a few Armory soldiers watched, too. My memory was hazy.

Blood pounded in my ears with every step closer they came. The soldier's uniform itched. I didn't deserve the honor or the trust and suddenly, a priest's hands gripped mine.

Cold tendrils of magic wrapped around my skin, binding me to the Crown I was more than delighted to betray.

That was my first day in the Armory. I'd survived one year, and I'll survive another.

Leena woke up before me. She paced the room, bare feet slapping against cold stone. By the time I sat up, she was already tying the strings on an armored bodice. She'd pull a tunic over it once she was done and layered her leathers over both.

It would be hot as the fires of Tir outside, but more protection was better than less when anyone could turn on us.

That was the standard issue uniform in the Armory. The only difference among first-years would be what color band we'd tie on our arms because we hadn't earned anything else.

I readied, twisting my hair into a braid with my fraying half of our green ribbon. We looked at each other. Since we arrived a year ago, outside of our first day, we never had to put on our complete uniform . . . until today. And gods be damned did we look like soldiers for the Crown; we were soldiers for the Crown. The leather was trimmed in silver with the queen's sigil embroidered over hearts.

"Are you taking anything else with you?" I asked Leena as I finished tying my boots.

She shook her head and walked over to the window, watching where the sun was just beginning to color the sky. "I'll take a sword from the field. You should take one too; dragon-forged or not, your dagger isn't enough."

I tied on my emerald armband and pulled open the drawer where I kept my dragon-forged dagger. I hardly needed it in the

Armory, but everything was about to change on the trial field, and I wouldn't be without it.

Inhaling a breath, I secured it in the sheath on my thigh.

"Reina?" my roommate prompted.

"Yeah?"

I turned, finding Leena by the window with her eyes cast down. "If anything happens to me—"

"No," I cut her off.

"No?" she said, spinning around. "You know what today is."

"Yeah, not the day we die."

Her eyes narrowed as she pursed her lips. "Well, if I do, you'll find my family and make sure they get the gold I have. It's theirs. I keep a letter on the nightstand beside it. It's everything Moer gave me the day I left."

"You know I will," I said solemnly, but I wouldn't entertain the possibility.

We would make it out of this. We had to.

A bell rang, reverberating through the halls. It was time; Leena went first, and I followed close behind. Doris lined us up in the hallway. Blaise stood behind me, and Leena stood in front.

I didn't dare look at him; today, any attachment was a weakness, and I already cared too much. None of us knew what we'd face in the trial, and after the demon, anything was possible. Only the gods saw what was in front of us now, and I doubted they were looking.

We marched down the stairs, maintaining our lines in the Atrium as the glass stretched above us. The skies had cleared. It'd be damp in the forest, but damp was better than trudging through pouring rain and mud.

Each house lined up beside the other. The second- and third-years joined us after a few minutes. Our captain took the lead, and the champions went to the back. The tension was thicker than the oppressive summer humidity as we waited for a signal.

There was a whistle, and someone from the Atrium loudly asked us to turn our attention toward the dais, which sat opposite the open doors.

Standing at the top of the balcony was the Queensguard General, Ephesus Linden. His most decorated lieutenants and knights of the Queensguard flanked him, all of them dressed in the queen's colors of navy and silver: blessed by the stars above.

The general pressed a hand to his stiff throat; nearly imperceptible wisps of yellow came from it, and his voice rattled the Atrium glass.

"The Queen of Thera extends her welcome. May the gods bless you all as you embark on your trials. Congratulations to the champions for whom this is the last, and to the new captains and first officers in our midst. You continue to do a great service for the queen and Thera. Because of you, the darkness and its legions are kept at bay and our borders secure.

"Finally, I welcome our newest soldiers. You've spent a year training and have made a great bargain for the future of Thera. I hope to see you all on the other side. As it's been said before, the gods don't make mistakes."

He's lying. My nails dug into my palm as I struggled not to clench my jaw. Linden knew many of us wouldn't see the end of today. That was by design.

Linden continued, voice unwavering, "Those who make it through this first trial can expect their bravery to be awarded. You are the first and last defense the Crown has. Without your sacrifice and your service, we wouldn't be as gods blessed with the peace we've had. Few warriors have the chance to test themselves within the Armory.

"To stand here today makes all of you an elite member of our forces from this moment forward. Lives will be lost, and they are the cost of the Crown and the price of peace. Know that any of you who die will be committed to the gods with the full honors of knighthood and the queen's mark.

"The trial is not a drill. Your champions and captains have earned the respect of the Crown, Armory, and their makers.

They have shown great skill and character. Many have trained alongside the finest in our military, faced battles, and made unimaginable decisions in the wake of tragedy. They will be your guiding compass as you face your trials.

"Darkness on the edge of our lands threatens the stability and peace of the Crown. It is our responsibility to protect Thera from these threats. The North is the land of the old gods, demons, and dark magic. My lieutenants and I have taken great care to organize this trial to the strength of each house. The captains have a map containing directions to one of the border keeps.

"Desertion and murder of brethren are considered treason and will be punished accordingly. I'm told weapons are set in the yard. You will gather them as you're dismissed. Please only take what you can carry. I will see you all here again in a week."

Linden's hand fell from his neck. Tense silence swept through the Atrium.

The houses were dismissed in order. Emerald was second to last, with Ruby behind us as always. There was no clear rhyme to the order, but that's how it had always been.

Leena glanced back as we waited. We'd all imagined what the first trial might be like. Last year, during the first trial, all houses were thrown into a series of brutal duels and physical challenges. The year before, Darkland rogues had landed on the shore of the Westvale duchy and the entire Armory greeted them in a haphazard battle. That trial lasted several agonizing hours. Today could be anything.

We walked in an orderly fashion out of the Atrium, into the yard where weapon racks and camping packs waited for us.

I grabbed a pack and a set of knives that I strapped to my leg. Leena opted for the elegance of a rapier. Blaise and some of the others briefly squabbled over a few broadswords and the single archer's bow.

Those of us in green gathered at the forest edge where four second-years contemplated the map they'd been given. The other second-years and our three champions stood near them, but their eyes roved over the first-years. All of them wore thick emerald capes which looked utterly miserable in the heat. We hadn't earned ours yet.

The Emerald Captain's long red hair was braided and tied into a knot. She wore a silver maker's cord and a captain's signet, with epaulets on her shoulders. She cleared her throat, and we straightened at attention.

"We're headed to Fern Keep, all thirty of us. It's on the northwest coast and three days on foot." Her eyes settled on Farran, and her voice lowered as she spoke directly to him. "Do you have any idea why they're doing this?"

He shrugged. "I know as much as you."

"Right, fine." The captain turned back toward the rest of the group. "We're on trial now. Expect danger in these woods. Don't trust a shadow, and we'll organize based on power. Landry, Phillip, and Jaxon are our Emerald champions. They'll watch our flank. Jaxon and Phillip are *lumen*, and they can see at night and strike lightning. Jaxon is also a dragon rider; ask her on your own time. Landry is an incredible *vainnen*, or propulsionist. They tracked a dragon as first-years in their second trial.

"I'm Avi, your Captain. Also, a *vainnen*." She gestured to Farran, who stood beside her. "Farran is your first officer, and he's an *ontaros*, also known as a siphon. He can wield almost any gift and absorb or share magic. Our other pledged are Devon, a *lumen*, and Vera, a *balen*—her gift is nature bound.

"This will be our third trial at this keep, so you'll follow our direction. Linden won't tolerate insubordination, and neither will we. We're soldiers, and we're here to serve Thera."

There was a murmur of agreement before we started the journey northwest. The air was hot and sticky, and several of us peeled off our leather jerkins, tying them to our packs. Even the sparse shade of the canopy wasn't helpful. I itched to take off the bodice I'd laced too tightly.

Hours out from the Armory, the forest was somehow more desolate than the Armory woods. There were no bushes, shrub trees, or any other sign of greenery beyond the pines stretching above us.

And for the next few hours of travel, no one spoke. All of us walked with our heads down and packs held tight, anticipating what threats might come our way.

Until Jaxon, one of the champions, stopped. Then Phillip stopped, too, and they looked at something in the distance, both with hands on their swords. The sun was setting, and a gloomy twilight had fallen in the last several minutes.

Avi exchanged glances with the other second-years. I couldn't see or hear what they did, but I wasn't very familiar with anything outside the walls of the Armory or the city walls of Rowane.

A howl ricocheted off the trees, followed by another from behind.

Jaxon spoke quietly, but we all heard. "Shadow hounds."

Proper fear seized me. I knew about shadow hounds. We were warned they roamed in packs outside the city walls. Twice the size of wolves and dark as night, they were heart-hunting creatures desperate for the pulse of magic thrumming through our veins.

Our new, enhanced magic rolled off of us like a beacon; I was sure of it.

Gods, we were a feast. The beasts would rip us to pieces. Shadow hounds relied on magic to stay alive, and our magic was a rare sight anywhere, especially this deep in the forest.

"Do we run?" Aixen asked aloud as all of us took steps closer to each other. His hand twitched for Eral's.

Another howl rang out.

Farran shook his head. "No, we won't outrun them. They can teleport short distances if they're willing to waste magic."

A chill went down my spine; with nearly thirty beating hearts, it was a safe bet they'd be willing.

Jaxon spoke up. "We have two minutes. Who's the shadow wielder? That's our best chance to buy time."

"Farrow," Farran said and looked at Leena, who was white as a sheet. "You'll stand next to me. Propulsionists, to the front. You'll try to push them off. Will that work?"

Jaxon looked into the woods as another howl came through. She shrugged. "It's been a while since we've faced one. With our numbers, they'll be bolder. We need to stand in a circle. Reina to the center. We'll need her for the trial. What else do we have?"

Fear lodged in my throat, and I didn't hear the rest of Jaxon's order. This is what it was. Aixen and Blaise stood in front of me. My back was to Avi and Farran. I could use petty magic to conjure some wind, but demon-wielding was probably useless without a demon to wield, and I had no idea where to begin, and no interest in touching the darkness coiled in my chest.

The howls came closer, and we waited. Precious seconds ticked by but it was an eternity as I tried to count the number of hounds rushing us.

I clutched my dagger in one hand, knife in another, bracing for whatever happened next.

They howled in unison now.

There could have been more than five. I looked at Blaise and realized I might regret it if either of us died, but it was too late to say anything.

A gust of wind rolled through from one of the *vainnen*. It disrupted the snarling beasts and sent at least one hound flying into a tree with a yelp of pain. The growls rumbled through my head. I wouldn't turn and look, not yet.

There was a scream, then the crunch of bone and flesh. I'd vomit later. I remained standing in the circle barely fucking armed, listening to everything fall apart at my back.

Yelling echoed through the trees. Several flashes of blinding white light and then screaming, followed by striking swords.

Blood splattered across my neck, and I shuddered.

"One down!" someone yelled.

Then one appeared in front of us, and every part of me froze. It was three times the size of a normal wolf, blacker than night, and bright red human blood dripped from its canines.

The hound growled at us and lunged. It caught the leg of the first-year in front of me, the one who struggled to conjure water in front of the demon. He screamed in agony as the beast tore into him.

I hurled a knife, striking the hound's shoulder, but it did nothing but anger the beast.

"GO, NOW!"

Two more first-years flew out with swords. They cut a gash through the hound's neck, but it hardly looked up. The first-year was dead, and the other gripped her leg where blood poured out.

I should have grabbed a sword from the field.

A rush of wind, the scream of a hound, a flash of light. I grabbed another knife because it was all I had.

"THREE LEFT."

Blaise ran towards the beast, his sword drawn and eyes alight. My heart pounded but the hound cried out as Blaise cut it down by the neck. Its head fell with a *thump* on top of the dead first-year.

He ran out of my line of sight as I attempted to keep my breathing steady.

Then, Jaxon's voice cut through.

"FARROW, *NOW*!"

I turned this time. True blackness extended from Leena's hands towards the two remaining beasts who feasted on the heart of a second- and first-year—no. It was Eral.

Leena shook beside me, and my attention snapped back. Her eyes watered.

She was trying to hold on and crush them like she'd done for the demon as more screaming tore through the woods.

"More!"

It was too much. The hounds collapsed, and so did Leena. She wasn't the only one on the ground, but she was the only one I cared about. I ran and dropped to my knees beside her. My hands grabbed her arm. Farran and Avi came quickly.

"Did she burn out?" I whispered, and my wild eyes met Farran's. "Did you let her burn out?"

Farran looked down at her, and his hand went to her neck. "She's fine. Just needs rest. She won't be able to do that again for a few days." His eyes moved to Avi, whose jaw was stern and face pinched as it calculated. "Can we set camp here? We can't go much further."

Avi nodded and rose to her feet. Her hand reached for Vera. "If you could count the dead and set the pyre, we'll hang the hounds to scare off any others. I'll write reports."

Farran walked away to join Jaxon and Phillip, who assessed the hounds and the wounded. But I remained on my knees, clutching Leena's arm until her eyes finally fluttered open.

"Thank gods," I breathed, clutching my chest.

"We did it, right?" She asked, her voice distant.

I nodded. "Yes, we did."

"Good. Did it look as awesome as it felt?"

"Of course." I laughed, and it felt wrong, but gods be damned was I happy.

We'd nearly survived the first day of the trial. There was more to worry about, but this was what I needed to focus on as the last wisps of sunlight fell behind the horizon and darkness consumed the forest. *We survived.*

While my house had killed all five hounds, they killed four of us and injured three. Three dead were first-years, and one was a second-year. Among them was Eral.

My heart broke for Aixen. We all loved Eral but Aixen was in love with him. They had a plan to run away the moment they rose but now Aixen would go alone.

The dead would remain here, committed to the gods in a pyre. Later, their names would be carved into the stone floor of the Atrium and listed off by General Linden in some ceremony—a knight's funeral.

Farran, Jaxon, and Avi strung the bodies of the shadow hounds from various trees.

They assured us it would keep everything away and the only monster that would dare cross the line would be a demon or a measly scavenger.

I've stared down worse odds, I'm sure, but watching the outline of the creatures sway, their sinew and blood dripping to the earth, turned my stomach.

I'd served death a hundred times and seen it a thousand. Life with Arden in the lower Rowane wasn't glamorous. It was visceral and godless more often than it wasn't. But here, in the silence of the forest, wearing the leathers of a Theranian soldier, death was jarring.

After Varyn and I did what we could to heal the wounded, I sat in front of the fire pit, throwing pine needles into it and watching them burn.

I hoped the guilt of surviving and the pang of loss would burn with it. There were three other first-years who were still awake and sat silently, staring into the flickering flames the same way.

We kept watch, but not even the squirrels would dare to come within a stone's throw of our camp.

Across the fire, Jaxon and Avi whispered back and forth. Someone sat next to me. Dry pine needles snapped underfoot, and I looked to my left, half expecting to see Blaise and half hoping.

Instead, my eyes met sapphire ones. "How are we holding up, Sangrey?" Farran was much less intimidating when he sat cross-legged in the light of a fire, hair barely restrained with a tie. He looked tired but still alert with his short swords strapped on his back.

"You said most of us will get killed by burnout," I muttered.

He shrugged and tossed a handful of needles into the fire. "I didn't factor in a three-day trek to a northern keep. Sorry for your losses."

"Are the other paths just as dangerous as this one?"

His jaw ticked, and his eyes reflected the orange of the fire as he spoke. "You're asking if other houses will see as many dead?"

"Sure." *I guess that's one way of putting it.*

"Well, usually we'd travel in small groups," Farran stated. "This was a beacon for the hounds, since the potion hasn't fully worn off. Tomorrow, we'll divide up. Or so Avi promised."

"Why didn't we start with that?"

Farran took a deep breath. Several of the other first-years were certainly listening. "Avi and the other captains were told to get rid of dead weight. It was Jaxon's idea to test Leena."

"Is that what people are to you?" I whispered.

"*No.*"

I didn't believe him. I knew what this was. Arden had prepared me better than most, but somehow, the callousness of it caught me off guard. The Crown and the Armory were one and the same, and both were equally responsible for who I'd become: cruel enough to nod along.

Farran continued, mistaking my frown for disgust. "It's what it takes to survive. We're soldiers, darling. You should grab one of the swords for tomorrow. Your dagger and knives won't be much help against beasts."

"Don't call me darling." I glared.

A log in the fire shifted and sent embers flying up. I looked over at Farran, who was also watching it intently.

Neither of us moved, so I asked, "Why are you here? At the Armory?"

A smile spread across his face. "No one in the family takes a title they haven't earned. My oldest brother died trying, and I will, too. It's tradition."

"Some tradition," I scoffed.

"Avernought invited you, didn't he?"

I nodded, glancing at the darkness surrounding the camp. "He found me in Lower Rowane. I was a barmaid who didn't handle rudeness well."

"That's where you learned to throw knives?"

"Yes." *No.*

"Right."

I thought for a moment. A thousand questions came rearing back. I'd spent all day trying to find them until the hounds wrung everything from me.

"What exactly is an *ontaros*?" I remembered the word Arden used in his letter: complimentary.

Farran ran a hand through his dark hair, and several curls fell back into his eyes. "I control raw magic, which means I can protect others from burning out by supplementing the magic they spend. That's how I kept Leena from burning out. I can also use anyone's intrinsic gift without taking a life."

"So, if someone has a rare gift, like say demon wielding, you can match it?"

Farran nodded. "Only if you allow me. It's not something I prefer to take, but the queen is eager to claim two *dreosen* on her guard. You make Thera the strongest kingdom in the realm." His eyes settled on mine, searching for something I couldn't provide.

I looked back at the licking flames.

"Oh. Right." I was a weapon. Of course. My life was a symphony of changing hands and serving death. A beat passed before I looked back at him. "You're still not scared of me?"

He shook his head and laughed a little. "For other reasons, perhaps, but you'll need to do a little more than calm a demon and throw a knife to scare me."

"Then I'll try harder," I said, perhaps a little too bitterly.

He was quiet for a moment. "Do you have a problem with me?"

"Just cautious around princes."

"Yet, you're here to join the Queensguard."

"For the queen," I corrected. "And the glory of knighthood."

"The queen won't live forever."

Like fuck she will.

"There's a first time for everything. Perhaps she's immortal," I quipped.

His expression tightened. "You should get some sleep."

"Can you take magic from someone who's asleep?"

Farran's eyes narrowed. "I do have petty magic. I don't need anyone's gift."

I was too tired to ask for a demonstration, but I planned on figuring it out because any Theranian could technically take magic, and the Crown was no stranger to it. I just wanted to know what to expect when it happened.

I'd seen it before, forcibly taken when a Crown knight dragged a man from a tavern and took what the knight thought he was owed at the cost of the man's life.

The act was punishable by death, but he was properly protected by the Crown.

Surely, a prince had even more protection than a knight.

Chapter 7

ANY SMALL AMOUNT OF hope was gone the moment we crawled out of our bedrolls that morning. It was still fucking humid, and the sun had hardly risen. The thought of adding back another layer of leather sounded less pleasant than making the trek naked.

Even worse, all I could smell were the rotting carcasses of the hounds, made worse by the suffocating damp and lack of wind. At least nothing else had found us. Yet.

We were down to twenty-six, and it hadn't taken long. A shiver crept up my spine as the thoughts settled with me. I knew our numbers would dwindle, but I'd hoped for more combat and less senseless death. I wondered what the queen had to gain by trimming her numbers so aggressively.

I stretched and joined the few first-years who were awake by the fire, where Jaxon passed out provisions. Aixen, Varyn, and Blaise were among them.

There were a few others, but I'll spare the names—they're all written somewhere on the Armory floor. And in a few days, they'd briefly live again when the formal Armory reports were handed off to Crown criers and shared in the Armory gambling dens, one house at a time.

Rowane had four licensed dens, and one was just a stone's throw from Arden's estate. I was certain Avernought owned it. He didn't have to say anything; I remembered the way green banners hung from the ceiling and the oddness of the room in the heart of Lower Rowane. It was over decorated and out of fashion for the pubs lining that street, but it was clear which merchant owned it.

In my nineteenth year, when the crier arrived, I spent every day at the den, learning the trials, the soldiers, and the strategies as if any of it would help me.

But my hope slipped with every week that passed without an invitation. Weeks turned into months before I stopped going and then stretched into years.

By the time Avernought handed me my invitation, I stopped thinking about the Armory. Instead, I'd made peace with my oncoming death.

Now, it seemed silly that this was all I'd waited for. The criers wound the stories into something glamorous, something worth betting on and dying for, but sitting here I felt nothing.

It was the same hollow, meaningless waste of life I'd experienced while working for Arden.

Jaxon handed me a chunk of bread and a piece of dried meat with a forced smile. I took it gratefully. This was the first time I'd interacted with her, and the reaction was unexpected, but I was too tired to figure out what she was thinking.

I sat beside Aixen and avoided looking at Blaise. Grief was easier to swallow this morning than the words I couldn't say.

"Morning," I muttered to Aixen. His arm was still in a sling, and his eyes glazed over as he stared into the dying embers of the fire.

A breeze pushed his flaxen hair into his eyes, his voice cracked as he conceded, "It should have been me."

"No," Blaise interrupted, trying to be comforting. "The gods don't make mistakes. Not for us."

"You'd think the gods would be able to choose without this nonsense," Aixen's voice seared.

I winced. That was the wrong thing to say, even if Blaise did believe it. Aixen always made the mistake of letting his emotions in; Eral was more than a friend to him, so much more. I couldn't blame him. I knew the pain more than I could admit.

I gave Blaise a hard look and put a hand on Aixen's knee. "Eral would want us to go on. We don't have a choice."

Aixen shook his head and rasped, "Eral didn't want to be here."

"But here we are," I reminded him, though it didn't seem as comforting as I intended.

Aixen said nothing else; he stood and returned to his bedroll. Half of us wanted to be here, and the other half had found ourselves dragged here after being discovered by a maker at the right time. Eral was openly disdainful.

Blaise eyed me from the other side of the log. I could feel it as I watched the embers in the fire, but I didn't move. I wanted the ground to open up and swallow me whole.

"You did great," I said quietly, trying to keep my voice steady.

Blaise looked at me, his head cocked to the side so his ruddy hair fell away from the scar on his forehead.

Heat rose in my cheeks as I cleared my throat. "You slayed one of them. I saw it."

"I got lucky." He huffed a bitter laugh. "And you had knives when you should've had a sword."

"I'm fine, aren't I? I had a dagger too, but you didn't see that."

"Please, take a sword, Reina. I'm not watching you die from something stupid." He smiled, but a part of him was serious. The razor-sharp edge of his tone rang in my ears as he held a water skin out towards me. "None of us are, but you're worth more than most of the houses."

I took the skin, but I didn't want to hear it. No part of me was ready to wrap my head around whatever that meant.

He said nothing else as I took a swig. It was just a few seconds of pleasant silence until I handed it back.

Avoidance was what I needed. "I should wake up Leena." I sighed and rose to my feet.

Blaise grabbed my hand. I instinctively yanked it out of his grasp. He had a playful grin on his face, but a sadness in his eyes.

"I do mean it. I'll dance with you again," he murmured.

My face didn't move, and I couldn't say it back—not truly. Instead, I sputtered out, "Good, I'll have something to look forward to that isn't just eye contact with the queen."

A glib remark wasn't what he wanted to hear, but it's what I had. I yawned and looked up at the sky. It wasn't so much sky as it was a thick canopy of looming, dark green leaves that hardly let any of dawn's light though.

Leena was mostly dressed when I found her, strapping a dagger and a rapier to her hip as I approached. "I think we're leaving soon. How are you feeling?" I asked.

"Like I got hit by a dragon." She frowned. "How many died?" She looked straight at me, sensing my apprehension, and repeated her question. "How many?"

"Four," I said quietly. "Eral was one. And Emery."

Her gaze lowered to the ground. "Oh."

Only two weeks ago, Aixen had grinned at us from Eral's lap as we drank stale mead. My chest ached, and I was sure Leena's did too, mourning the loss of lighter days as we packed away the bedrolls.

I never meant to care about my house, but it was inevitable when we were trapped together. Now I realized how much the Armory had softened me.

The fear I felt had nothing to do with me and everything to do with losing them.

Avi waited in the center of camp, dressed in her cape and leathers. Her face was deadly serious and the sharp lines of it, combined with the way her hand wrapped around the hilt of her sword, made her look every part of the Armory captain she was.

"We need to get moving." Her red hair was braided to the side, but pieces were already trying to escape in the humidity. "We lost time yesterday, and we'll make up for it today. We won't have rations for an extra day. Divide into small groups and concentrate on your intrinsic magic. Too many of us together is a beacon, and it's going to get more dangerous the closer we get to the border and the keep.

"Lastly, we lost four last night. I've sent the report, and we committed their souls to the gods in a soldier's pyre. Their sacrifice will not be in vain but for the continuation of Thera," Avi continued and listed off our groups.

We would be in groups of three or four, each with a champion or a second-year. Leena was with Farran, Blaise was with Avi, and I was with Aixen and Jaxon.

Finally, the captain said, "We'll leave incrementally. I'll stop when I think we can stop. We won't wait for the other groups to set camp."

My group left second to last. I walked close to Jaxon while Aixen trailed behind, playing with his silver and folding in on himself. All I could think about was how I couldn't lose Blaise, no matter how complicated it was, but I had no way to tell him.

We were soldiers, and we didn't deserve love, not the proper kind; it was one thing to die but another to tear a heart in half while being forced to live.

The forest descended into rolling meadows for a while and then transitioned back into woods with odd trees that had thick trunks and gnarled branches. We only stopped once to drink water from a stream.

Above all, the forest still seemed empty. I was bored and counted the chirping birds on one hand and the squirrels on the other.

"Shouldn't there be animals around?" I finally said, louder than intended.

Jaxon looked over at me. "Probably not. We're not far from Vera. Animals can sense a *balen's* gift and tend to stay away. Doesn't work for other creatures, but gives us less to worry about."

I kicked aside a rock and nodded. "Ah."

"It's that or Aerno."

"Aerno?"

She nodded, lips pursed as she held out her sleeves to show me a sigil tattooed on her wrist. It appeared to pulse in the light. "My dragon—he's following us. He loves the mountains."

I had more questions, but the way her jaw feathered as she shook her sleeve back told me the conversation was over.

We were quiet for a while, and the forest trail shifted again; rocks jutted out in places, and the hills became sharper and more jagged until we were certainly climbing. The temperature dropped too, which was a welcome relief.

Jaxon glanced behind us. Aixen remained there, a silver dagger clutched in his palm, and his face was listless. Time was the only power capable of fixing grief. Anything else just staved it off.

"We'll stop when we get to the mountain meadow. That will put us half a day from the keep."

I nodded. I had no idea where we were, but I had to trust Jaxon. She was a champion and the former Emerald Captain from what I'd overheard between the second-years. She also had the map.

On this side of the mountain, the trees thinned and gave way to more rocks and low, sharp brush as we stumbled through it.

"You worked for Damien Arden." The words halted me in my tracks. My feet were lead.

Jaxon couldn't know. That was impossible.

I gripped the sword now hanging from my belt, because I didn't know what else to do, and choked out, "No, not me."

"I picked my father up from his den a few times," she recalled with an even tone, continuing ahead. "I recognize you."

"You must have me confused," I said, forcing my tone to be just as sure.

"I know what I saw," Jaxon insisted. Frustration poked at the back of my neck like needles. She didn't look at me as she continued, "You don't hide as well as you think. Because of Arden, my father died a traitor at the hands of the Crown? And my father often mentioned Arden's *other* service. None of Arden's whores would last a minute here, *Viper*."

I froze, my blood turning to ice. The mountain moved beneath me, and every bit of me screamed for flight. There was nowhere to go. No cover, no towns, no nothing. Arden was one thing but that part—the viper—was buried away from every-one but Arden's innermost circle. Even Leena didn't know that title.

Out here, Jaxon could kill me and claim it was an accident if she suspected I was a traitor.

Gods, she'd kill Aixen too, and I'd have no defense if I killed a champion . . . even in trial.

The trail sloped as I crafted my answer and wrung my hand around the hilt of my blade. I was sure my knuckles were white. "You're mistaken."

Jaxon looked straight at me and stopped walking. I nearly ran into her.

"No, I'm not," she pressed, and her words cut through me.

I tilted my chin and forced my eyes to meet hers. Vitriol swirled in the brown depths of her irises.

"You don't know me."

"And you don't know me. I've given my life to defending the Crown," Jaxon accused, and for a second, I thought she would reach out and grab my shoulders. Instead, she lowered her voice. "I will kill you if any part of you intends to harm the princes or my queen. Do you understand that? I know exactly who the fuck Arden is, and I swear on every sleeping god and the stars above, he will not ruin another part of my life."

That explained the way she looked at me. I slowly nodded and tried to calm my trembling knees. "I'm here to serve the Crown." I gritted. "Arden never made my choices."

That was a lie. Everything I was today had been decided by Arden, but she had no right to know.

Damien Arden was no friend of the Crown, nor the gods that came with it. His loyalties were well known, but Arden had enough of the nobles' gold and Avernought's to keep his head on his shoulders and the Crown looking the other way.

I did not have the same leverage. Neither did Jaxon's father, apparently.

She whipped around and continued walking without an-other word.

Every part of me shook, and I was going to be sick. She could kill me for being the viper. Everyone in the fucking kingdom of Thera was allowed to kill me.

If I truly wanted to serve the queen, I'd only have to cut my throat. Arden's viper was a known threat to the Crown and the nobility surrounding it, even without the prophecy haunting me.

Avernought had seen it all those years ago even before he forced me in front of a priest for my Rite. I saw it when the sweet taste of a god's blood turned sour in my mouth, as a single minute of my fate played out.

I never stopped thinking about it. Years later, I sat down with a seer for the old gods, and she saw it too. Her mystic gaze pinned me to the bare stone walls of her residence as she stared, mouth opening and closing like a fish. *"It can't be you,"* she wheezed, but she was wrong. *It was me. It was always me.*

I struck her dead with a single knife, straight to the heart, to protect the secret.

As we wandered through the meadow, the sun began to set over the silence. I couldn't worry about my secret. Instead, I hoped the queen lived in fear of the day her eyes would open and mine would be the last she saw.

Jaxon was right. She shouldn't trust me.

Chapter 8

We walked another hour, making it safely to our destination in time to set up camp in the meadow with the others. I helped Varyn by treating a few infections and fixing some bones before we collapsed on our bedrolls.

Jaxon didn't look at me, and Arden wasn't mentioned again, but she was very clear she was going to keep me at a distance, and I could sympathize with her hatred.

Luckily, she was a champion and after this trial, she'd rise from the Armory and be inducted into the Queensguard. What Jaxon had given me was a warning, and I intended to heed it.

I woke up the next morning thankful I wasn't murdered. In fact, I was surprised to walk out to the fire as if nothing had happened. All of us looked better this morning. The bags under Leena's eyes were gone. Varyn looked less like he would fall over, and while Aixen still looked lost, he stood straighter and had combed his hair back.

We'd all made the trek except for Devon and two first-years: Max and Rodrick. Max was recovering from an injury to his leg, which held them back by a few hours, but no one seemed eager to consider them dead yet.

Avi, in particular, looked exhausted and somber as she stood in front of us and gave today's instructions. "We're a few hours from the keep, and we'll be descending the mountain. Watch your footing. We'll follow a canyon upriver, and we'll be traveling by daylight, which should keep everything at bay, but we are closer to the darkness General Linden mentioned.

"Should anything happen, we'll take the same formation we had for the hounds. I want the *vainnen* up front, *lumen* in the back, and everyone else in the middle. Vera, let me know if you start slipping. We'll be close to the darklands."

Oh, we weren't waiting for Devon's group. Uneasiness rose in my throat.

No one had truly explained to us what the darkness was, but the legends went the old gods retreated to an eternal sleep after the Second War of Kings, two centuries ago, when Thera and the Darklands divided. It was that war when the Goddess Dreonna abandoned her creations—her demons—because they were beyond repair.

The rage and loss corrupted them, twisting them into something entirely *other*.

That unfettered dark magic manipulated the natural world and corrupted the dreite priests who created shadow hounds, along with a thousand other desperate, beastly creatures. The dreites intended to claw back power and magic from the new gods in Thera, claiming it was stolen from them.

That's one legend, anyway.

There were a few nights at Arden's where I'd heard a very different legend about the new gods creating the darkness so they could overtake the old gods.

Only the gods could tell us which was true, of course, but even if Dreonna dragged me down to Tir and told me herself, I wasn't sure I'd believe her.

The terrain shifted as we walked until we scrambled down the rocky side of the mountain, slipping on loose rocks. The only relief was at the bottom of a canyon where an overgrown riverbank opened into a faint trail.

The woods here were darker and thicker than any I'd seen before. Gnarled trees threatened us with thorns the size of my forefinger. Nettles lingered on the edge of the trail with purple thistles, and even the occasional caw of a bird sounded haunted.

The next hour passed as if it were three. We crawled through, single file, until the forest gave way to a wide clearing and the faint salt of sea air.

An old, imposing keep stood at the center. It was a walled structure with two spires rising above the trees. It certainly wasn't at the scale of the Armory, but it was large enough to be formidable.

Second and third-years rushed ahead of us to the gate.

Avi pressed a hand to her throat, and yellow tendrils wrapped around it, extending her voice to those beyond.

"The Emerald House of the Armory has arrived with your reinforcements at the order of General Ephesus Linden and Her Majesty, Queen Claudia MacLaine of Thera."

Minutes ticked by before the gate rose with a creak. Behind it was an entire battalion with their weapons drawn, spears, swords, and axes all pointed directly at us as they hid behind beaten-up shields and eyed us with suspicion.

Avi and Farran stepped forward with their hands held up, while the rest of us didn't dare to move.

It was a bit ridiculous; in hindsight, we all wore the same sanctioned leathers with silver trim, and the same pin of Thera's crest—the head of a wolf below the stars of the Seven, dressed in vines and lilies. The only difference was the color of their capes and the armbands we wore.

A man with a mustache, lieutenant signet, and silver champion cords stepped in front of his men and bellowed, "How do we know you are who you say? We've had shifters."

Jaxon pushed to the front and took the lead. "It's me, Caro. We fended the keep last year and lost half our numbers in the woods on our way here. We lost Levan to a demon out there. You were supposed to get a letter with a list of our numbers, but I'll assume it hasn't arrived."

Caro's shoulders slackened with relief. "Oh, thank the gods and stars."

He gestured for his men to lower their weapons and dragged Jaxon into an embrace.

Thank the stars, indeed. The soldiers backed down and moved aside to let us into the keep. Straight ahead was the main residence. Built of dark gray stone as was everything else, it rose several stories above us. Stables and other smaller stone buildings surrounded a courtyard.

Guards ushered us first years to a stable behind the main building, while second- and third-years went elsewhere.

I expected worse, but the stable was clean, warm, and had a roof—far more than we had with our meager bedrolls in the woods. A thick layer of hay was spread on the ground and provided welcome padding. The best part, there wasn't a horse in sight. I was almost excited at the prospect of a decent sleep.

Leena rolled her bedroll out next to mine, and Blaise laid his bedroll on my other side.

It was how I always imagined sleeping with Blaise: in a stable full of our closest friends. I mean, Blaise and I had fucked before, but I had a rule about sleeping together. This nearly toed my line.

Dinner wasn't for a few hours so Leena pulled out a deck of cards to pass the time as we all took turns cleaning up and changing out of our leathers and soiled clothes.

We waited now for the last of our house to arrive, and for the entirety of Onyx. Their griffon riders would be our counterparts for the trial. Suppose that meant it wouldn't take place at the keep, rather somewhere far enough away we needed wings.

We were in the middle of a trial, but we'd earned a little laughter as we waited for the loss to catch up, and I knew it would. Every time I saw Aixen, a twinge of grief rolled off him like a crack in a dam.

"Trial isn't so bad. It started rough, but I think we'll be okay," Blaise said and laid back on his bedroll with his eyes closed as I failed to repair a tear in my breeches with magic.

"Don't get too comfortable," Leena warned, shuffling the cards. "They could kill us in our sleep. What if they're actually the shifters?"

"Can't you choke them with shadows?" I asked and frowned at my leg. The fabric shivered again, so it felt like I was getting closer. I used to be good at mending, but apparently I'd lost my touch.

Leena shrugged. "I mean, I'd certainly try. Was it weird they were so worried about shifters?"

"No," Blaise answered and sat back up, arms wrapped around his knees. "There are shifters all over these parts. They scavenge on magic when it's around. My father had been to this keep once before. They had a run-in."

"But could they shift into the whole lot of us?" I wondered, raising a brow.

"They must be able to if they're so worried." His eyes paused on mine, and my heart tilted in my chest. It shouldn't have. "Silver kills shifters, and so does cutting off their heads. Maybe demons kill them, too?"

I hoped we wouldn't find out.

"I'm starving," I finally said, clearing my throat. "Let's go to the hall. Aixen will meet us there when he's done washing up, I'm sure."

I pushed myself up from the floor. Leena groaned as she did the same. I reached a hand out towards Blaise and helped him to his feet.

His eyes lingered on mine for a second too long. I shouldn't have done that either. Everything between us needed to stop. No matter how good his hand felt in mine for those few seconds, Blaise didn't deserve any share in the blood on my hands.

The main hall of the Fern Keep was nothing special. It was a giant stone room with three long rows of wooden tables. Wooden candelabras hung above us, lit by wielded light—an easy tell; magicked light was far more blue than natural flame.

The second-years and our champions sat at the table towards the front. They were engaged in a hushed conversation with Caro and a few of his own.

A messenger raven flew out of an open window with a thick letter attached to its leg which I imagined was Avi's report that would be rewritten and distributed to the criers. I wondered what they'd say.

Three of us sunk down on the far end of the same worn wooden table. Soldiers at another kept looking at us. We pretended not to notice.

"We'll have them serve dinner soon," Jaxon said, sitting beside Aixen. Worry pressed between her brow in two lines. "We can't wait all night."

"Have you seen Devon or the others?" Farran questioned us, and we shook our heads.

It was almost dark. Onyx still hadn't arrived, and neither had Devon and the two first-years. My finger traced a scar on the table as I pursed my lips, mind racing. Rodrik was one of our best fighters.

"Gates haven't opened as far as I know," Blaise added, cocking his head towards Farran. "Would we send a search out if they're not here by morning?"

Farran shook his head and sent black hair into his eyes as he sat in the space beside Blaise. "We have a trial to complete."

"Has a whole house ever died in a trial?" I asked, and maybe I shouldn't have.

Farran looked straight at me. "Not for decades."

"Good, so it's unlikely?" Judging by the blank faces around me, my positivity went unappreciated. I dropped my chin and went back to tracing the scars on the table, wondering who carved them.

Jaxon cleared her throat. "Don't worry. They'll be here. They've got plenty of experience and griffons. And even if they're not, we're Emerald and we'll find a fucking way. We do have some wings between us. It just won't be as fast."

"What's the trial?" I asked. All three of us looked expectantly at Jaxon.

Jaxon shook off the stares. "That's for your Captain to tell you. This is my champion trial. But I'll do what I can to make sure the whole house doesn't die."

A bell chimed through the hall. Jaxon looked around and saw a few soldiers get up and rush out.

"That's the gate. It has to be them," she remarked.

Jaxon swept out of the hall while the rest of us stayed put. Aixen joined us, with a few of the other first-years, just in time for hot stew. I'm sure it was barely fine, but after a few days of jerky and bread, the stew was gods-blessed, and we devoured it.

No one spoke until Jaxon walked back into the hall ten minutes later with Devon and Rodrick; Max was nowhere to be seen. A bad sign. Several spoons clattered back into their bowls.

Varyn was close behind them. His mouth kept opening and closing with words he didn't have. White healing magic clung to his fingertips.

Avi and Landry ran across the hall. Avi took Devon by the shoulders and stared at him, trying to keep her expression neutral. He looked as if he'd been torn apart. Rodrick looked worse, limping with one un-glamoured, feathered wing bent behind him and a mangled arm cradled in the other. Their leathers were shredded.

A deep gash across Devon's cheek was crusted with old blood. It wasn't good; Rodrick was the best swordsman we had, and now he looked white as a sheet, his arm beyond what Varyn or I could ever hope to repair.

Jaxon and Avi rested the two injured soldiers on the table beside us as Caro stalked towards them.

"Where's your healer?" Jaxon demanded of Caro as she held him upright with one hand on his shoulder. He winced at every movement.

"Isn't that yours?" Caro said pointedly, eyes taking in Varyn.

"He's a first-year," she answered. "He's learning, and this is venom."

Avi unbuckled Devon's jerkin and gingerly pulled off the tunic underneath. I looked closer and stifled a gasp. Claw marks lacerated his chest, and his veins had blackened. I'd heard about poisons like that, but I'd never seen one.

"Are my healers allowed to help?" Caro softened and looked only at Jaxon now. "I know how the Armory can be, and I don't want to—"

Avi glared at him, tearing her focus away from Devon. "If we don't get a trained healer, they will die, and you'll be down a swordsman, wings, and a *lumen*. It doesn't look like you can afford it." Avi matched his tone with a warning. "Especially if the griffons don't show."

Farran stepped around Jaxon. I don't know when he left the table, but he straightened his posture and slipped into something more like a prince than a soldier. "That's an order, Caro. If there's a problem with the Armory, I'll handle it."

Caro frowned, his eyes glued on Farran with a measured amount of derision. "Yes, of course, First Officer. Otto, get the healer."

I didn't move. I couldn't help. Leena clutched my arm as we watched, unable to look away. Varyn and I could do some healing, but we couldn't patch together a mangled arm. Not one this bad.

Even Devon was fading to the dregs as black spread and blistered along the edges of his wounds.

Avi and Farran peppered them with questions to keep them conscious until the Fern Keep healer arrived. We learned Max was dead. They didn't see any griffons, and they were attacked by a demon in broad daylight.

My heart twisted. For a trial, this was feeling more and more like a trap. If I were there, could I have stopped the demon?

Hurried footsteps caused all heads to jerk towards the door as the healer rushed into the hall. She was the only one in the keep wearing leathers at the moment, as though she'd just come in from outside.

Piercing gray eyes fixed on Devon and wasted no time. She kneeled before him, resting her hand on his chest as she closed her eyes. White tendrils of magic suffused into the black and drew out the venom in gasps of black smoke until the wound was clean and Devon's color returned.

The healer stepped back and motioned at Varyn to do the rest. Then she turned her attention to Rodrick. She placed a gangly hand on his arm and another on the side of his face.

The white tendrils didn't penetrate the way they settled on Devon.

Her gray eyes narrowed, churned, and the color of the tendrils changed to red before he suddenly slumped over.

We all gasped. Jaxon and Avi jumped to their feet.

Avi's hand held Devon down by the shoulder.

"What the fuck? You killed him!" Devon screeched.

The healer stood up calmly and crossed her arms as several soldiers moved away from her. "I'm sorry. I had to make a choice," she said smoothly.

"It was a fucking arm!" Avi shouted, her hand still pinning down Devon, who looked ready to lunge. "You could have healed it. The venom wasn't any different!"

The healer shrugged and dismissively waved her hand. Her eyes were unapologetic as she explained, "I saved the light wielder. The other was only going to hold you back. A swordsman isn't needed by your house. His gift was dismal, and magic has a cost."

"That was not the cost of healing him, and you know it," Jaxon warned, her voice on the edge of a growl as she stared at Rodrick's stiff form. "This will be reported to the Crown."

Devon shook off Avi's hand and stormed out of the hall. Landry followed him, casting one final glare over his shoulder. The healer left a heartbeat later, and no one followed her.

Farran's glare pivoted to Caro, his face taut. "Is this how things work here? That decision should have been left to the Emerald Captain," he barked.

"With all due respect, Your Highness," Caro enunciated, drawing out every syllable, "I outrank you in this keep. The lives of my own come before the disposable lives of your half-soldiers. I won't extend my healer to save someone who won't be a champion. You need my healer at full strength tomorrow when you'll face worse."

Caro turned sharply and walked out of the dining hall as the chill of his words settled in. His footsteps echoed off the stone and reverberated in the foreboding silence.

His soldiers followed and left our house alone with Rodrick's body laid out on their table. We all stiffened as Avi came over with Farran. In a split second, we were soldiers awaiting orders. I hated it. A different version of me would wake up in the dead of night and carve out the revenge we were owed, but *that* was certainly treason.

Farran cleared his throat, his eyes downcast but measured. "Phillip, Blaise, take his body outside. The keep should have everything for a pyre on the west side."

There was uncomfortable shuffling before Jaxon stated, "This is part of trial. Death is inevitable and shouldn't shake us. There will be time to honor their sacrifices later."

Avi straightened beside her. "All of you can retire for the evening except Aixen, Reina, and Leena. I need to speak with you about tomorrow," she said. "I'll also need to know who has wings in case Onyx doesn't make it."

The three of us rose to our feet, but we didn't leave the anchor of the table as the others departed for the stables. Leena grabbed my hand and squeezed as Avi approached. Her face darkened, and her jaw clenched tightly. Her hair had fallen out of its tie and hung limply around her shoulders in tangled curls.

Before she spoke, she glanced at the entrance to the hall. "I have a feeling Onyx isn't coming. We'll be without griffons tomorrow, which adds some complexity. If we're getting out of here alive, we need to be precise, and I need you three to learn as much as you can in the next two hours, out of sight from Caro and his men. Leena, you're with me. Aixen, you're with Vera, and Reina—you're with Farran."

My stomach bottomed out. Alone with the prince?

Leena squeezed my hand again and let go as she took a step forward and uttered, "Right, let's survive this."

Survive indeed. That was our only option, wasn't it?

Chapter 9

There was a visceral difference between dread and fear. Fear sat in my stomach and turned over in a torrent. Fear could be calmed and quieted with the right train of thought, even if it was a constant in Thera. I'd learned to tune it out and channel into something useful.

Dread, however, was like a fist on my chest or a hand wrapped around my spine. It hung in the air with all the weight and oppression of humidity in the highest days of summer.

The only way out of dread was to barrel through it.

After everything that happened today, fear had fully morphed into dread but I felt it less poignantly than I should have. Maybe it was the new power sparking under my skin. The gift from the goddess of death I was too afraid to touch.

But I wanted even less to do with it after what the demon had done to Rodrick and Devon.

I met Farran in the center of the keep and followed him through a trapdoor on the west side, left propped open with a rock.

Farran didn't say anything, and neither did I. I just prayed to the gods Jaxon hadn't told him about Arden, otherwise I was willingly walking to my execution.

Was he too quiet? Would the first officer take me away from the keep and execute me as a traitor?

Yes, actually. That sounded reasonable, and my heart pounded.

Would I let him kill me? Maybe not. We were remote enough I could kill a prince and run. The tree cover was fairly thick.

We walked through twisted woods and down a hill where the dirt became sand. I heard it before I saw it, the great roar I had only read in books. We stood on the shore of the Tharamund Sea.

I'd never seen a body of water larger than the lake outside of Rowane. As we rounded the corner, my mouth dropped. The majesty of the white rolling waves as they collided with rocks and sand stole my breath. It was imposing and beautiful all at once. None of the stories or dreams compared to the way it looked tonight under the luminance of the half-moon.

"Have you never seen the sea, darling?" Farran asked starkly, snapping me out of my thoughts. Some of my anxiety eased.

Certainly, an executioner wouldn't make small talk, but then again, I'd never faced one.

"I've hardly left Rowane," I whispered.

"Oh." He chewed his lip. I admired the view, forgetting I needed to hate him for what the Crown had done. "Well, if we survive this, there are plenty more wonders to see. This beach is nothing; you should see Illium or Sol where they seem to stretch forever."

I had a hard time believing it. "Those are completely different kingdoms."

And this beach was one of the most beautiful things I'd ever seen. The push and pull of the waves crashing against the shore made the trial feel silly—and human. We were nothing next to that kind of power, no matter what we wielded.

"There is more to the realm than Thera," the prince said.

"Have you been to other kingdoms?"

He shrugged. "I spent a summer in Illium once."

"Sounds princely."

"It was. I stayed in the palace." His gaze held mine as he watched my reaction.

I didn't know how he wanted me to react, so I didn't. It was strange. Both of us were in civilian clothes. He wore a cotton shirt, and I wore my belted tunic when I should have worn leathers.

"Must've been awful," I finally quipped, and my mind drifted to my own summers in Lower Rowane, drowning in the smell of human perspiration and rotted vegetables as I vacillated between letting silk run over my hands or blood—depended what tensions I was paid to soothe.

"It wasn't," Farran said finally. "However, I still want to get some sleep, so we need to figure this out."

He looked away and took a step towards the waves. Seashells and sand crunched beneath his feet like he walked on crushed shards of glass.

"This keep is on the Strait of Arasund. Out there is the Sea of Tharamund, and across the water are the Darklands, where they say the Goddess Dreonna festers." I tried to hide my wince as he described the old gods. Farran kept talking, "If the Darkness isn't attacking, this keep is tasked with crossing the sea to capture and destroy any dreites or demons they can.

"We're supposed to bring a dreite priest to the Armory, alive. We haven't done that before, and we especially haven't done it without griffon riders," he explained.

Too many questions turned over in my head. "What do I need to do?"

Farran shrugged and kicked at the sand again. "A *dreosen* can control aspects of Dreonna's creation and override the dreite priests and priestesses who control the demons. Two demon wielders could turn their whole command in battle."

I nodded slowly. I didn't know if I could do either, or whether I wanted to. Certainly not a few hours from now.

He asked, "Can you feel the magic? Your power comes from the old gods. We're about as close to it as we can get without being at an altar; the sea carries the old magic of the God Olios. You should feel it strengthening."

"If you can tap into another's gift, can't you answer that yourself, *ontaros*?" I retorted.

Farran's blue eyes narrowed. "I try not to impose if I don't have to. You might be getting me confused with the rumors of my brother. I've learned it's best to ask for permission."

"I can't confuse you with someone I've never met."

"So you don't hear rumors?" he pressed.

My gaze trailed to the frothing sea. "I don't listen to them. Anyone in Lower Rowane who claims to know the Crown is lying."

"You haven't answered my question."

I rolled my eyes. "Yes, I can feel it."

Feel was an understatement. Now I was looking for it, my blood was humming; there was a warm knot in my chest between my heart and my ribs that was heating and expanding.

I'd never experienced magic this strong before. I couldn't believe I was just now noticing it. Had it been there this whole time?

"You'll get used to it," the prince said.

I looked at Farran. "That's the least helpful thing you've said so far."

His lips quirked in amusement. "No one knows much about demon wielders. It has been two centuries."

"We know they win wars," I said sharply. "In the Second War of Kings, a demon wielder almost single-handedly faced down our dragons. She would have defeated them if her own generals hadn't turned and choked her magic. Surely, your princely education covered that if I could find it after one night of poking around the Emerald library."

Farran contemplated the words, his brows pinched. "There are competing theories. She could have been cursed, or gods-blessed. They also had a full army of shadow wielders at the time." He slowly turned away to face the waves. "The magic was different. The new gods were still learning how to contain it, and the old gods weren't fully asleep."

"Shame they're not rested yet."

He took a breath and turned back to me after a brief wander through his own thoughts I didn't care about. "What do you know about sigils?"

I relaxed. I knew sigils; they were the first type of magic I'd ever learned, and I answered easily. "The strongest are drawn in blood or carved into something with magical properties. Some bind, some leave marks, and curses require extra magic or compound sigils."

He pulled a dated sheet of paper from his pocket and held it out in front of me. "Have you seen one like this?"

I stepped closer and examined it in the moonlight, squinting as my eyes adjusted. It wasn't any sigil I'd seen before. The ones I knew were simple lines stacked on one another and layered specifically to channel the magic, as if it were a sentence.

Arden taught me how to draw several that weakened magic in a room or extended the life of a poison. Those were child's play next to the symbol staring back at me.

I shook my head. "I've never seen one like this before."

It wasn't just a mess of straight lines. This one had curves, circles, and triangles stacked over it at odd angles.

"This is how we bind a dreite priest," the prince elaborated. "It's only meant to be used by one priest on another, but the same magic runs through demon wielders. Both derived from Dreonna. I've practiced it before, but it wouldn't work for me. Magic can be particular."

"And you're sure it works?" I raised a curious brow.

"Confident. Draw it here, in the sand. You'll draw it in blood tomorrow."

I looked down at the moonlit sand and back to Farran. He was being serious, and that was a ridiculous sentence.

"This isn't the only way out tomorrow, is it? Me drawing some old sigil?"

Farran set the paper in my hands, his blue eyes narrowed. "You mean a sigil guarded for centuries by the royal families of Thera?"

I kneeled down in the sand with it and tried to memorize its curves, its lines, and the way it spoke to me as I willed them together. It was like learning a new dance. My finger dragged hesitantly through the wet, clumpy sand, getting caught on stones and shells.

His brow furrowed, and his voice didn't sound as confident. "You should be able to use it. *Dreosen* magic is ancient."

I finished, but nothing happened. No pulse, no light, no sign of life. Even without blood, sigils would still give you an inkling they were drawn correctly. I'd drawn enough to know. For years, I thought it was the only magic I'd be able to use.

"And if I don't get it?" I asked, frowning at the sight before me in the sand as I leaned back on my knees.

He stood over me, his arms crossed as he squinted in concentration. "Try again."

I erased the sand drawing and tried again, and again, and again. I tried it so many times my fingers forgot I could write anything else. I don't know how much time passed until something in me snapped with the crash of another wave.

I screamed and blasted sand away with a rush of petty magic. He caught the paper before it blew away.

"I can't do it." I seethed, glaring as the paper flapped in his hand.

Invisible walls closed in on me, even as the wind and salt battered my face—I gasped on it. Fear and doubt had wrung out my lungs, and I couldn't catch my breath.

"I can't do it. I'll be the reason we fail. Eral, and Rodrick, Emery . . ." I wrapped my arms around myself; the magic in my veins was pure lead weight. I shouldn't care, but I did. It was easier alone. *This* is what caring did for me. All of this was easier done alone, and I was the assassin who knew better. "They're dead, because—"

Farran's hand gripped my arm. Heat curled from his fingers and brushed against the magic pounding through my veins. I looked up through bleary eyes to see him kneeling across from me.

His face had softened, and wind pushed unruly hair into his eyes, but I could see through it. "You will not be the reason we fail, Reina. I promise."

His hand was steady. I shook my head furiously. Saying it didn't make it true.

"I will if I can't get this. That's how it goes."

I shook off his grip and dragged my finger through the sand again—it didn't work. Angry tears burned against my eyes. I wiped them off with the back of my hand and grimaced at the way it scratched my skin. Then I tried again, and again.

The sigil didn't so much as spark, no matter how I willed it; perhaps it was mocking me. I gritted my teeth. Maybe Farran brought me out here to humiliate me? To prove I was never worthy of the Queensguard and everything to this point was luck?

Maybe this was where he killed me because it's what I deserved? I'd dared him to try. In fact, I wanted him to. Fighting would bring me back to life.

Farran stuffed the paper in his pocket. His hand tightened around my arm and dragged me to my feet. I hissed, but I wouldn't break. Not here, not like this. I stepped back and wrapped my arms around myself, as if I could forge them into armor that would keep away the feeling, as I looked at the churning sea, praying he'd pull his sword from its sheath.

"Let's go back," he coaxed, voice soft, and I frowned. I know he moved; I could hear the crunch of sand.

I didn't want to go back and see the absence of everyone I had already let down, because I was useless against the hounds. I couldn't draw an ounce of my gift. Yet I was supposed to be the *dreosen*—a once-in-century demon wielder, the first of Thera.

I didn't want it; I resented whatever pulsed through me. If anyone asked, I would carve out my heart if it would return me to who I was.

Farran did nothing, and somehow that was the worse punishment.

"How do you get used to this?" I balked at the crashing wave, as though the gods would hear me. These soldiers didn't deserve their death the way I deserved mine; that was the tragedy of it all.

"You don't," Farran answered instead.

My head whipped around to see him standing beside me. His jaw ticked. Moonlight glimmered in his eyes where I was sure mine swallowed it.

He murmured, "You just learn to cope. They say the Armory takes so the gods don't have to . . . It's not your fault."

"I might have saved one of them, but I didn't."

A truth, that's what I'd admitted, and it lodged itself in my throat like a bite of bread too large and dry to swallow. Farran's hand reached out suddenly, softly tilting my chin towards him, forcing my eyes to meet his and jolting every part of me.

Every nerve fired something between a warning and a want I didn't ask for. Magic pressed against my ribs in strokes of heat. All of it was new, and I didn't pull away.

"It's not your fault. No one gets to blame you. Not even yourself, Sangrey."

"Then whose fault is it?" I demanded of the prince as his hand fell.

"Everyone who sent us here and the gods who gift us while they sleep on their hands." Farran took a large step back before he paced to the edge of the woods. "We should go back," he announced.

We should. But I didn't want to. None of this was what I expected.

Did the Prince of Thera actually see the Armory for what it fucking was?

That was so close to treason I tasted the metallic tang of an executioner's ax, and it was all I thought about as we walked back to the keep in stark silence. We both admitted something to ourselves, and my anger frayed, but it wasn't soothed. I balled my fists as we parted ways.

There was nothing the prince could say to change my mind about his Crown. Alive is what my parents would be without the Queen.

I intended to take: a *hand for a hand, gold for gold, and one heart for another*—or whatever it was the new gods said when they stole everything from the old all those centuries ago. One day, I would take from Thera in the same way.

There was nothing the prince could say to change my mind.

Chapter 10

We roused from the stable well before dawn broke. Jaxon and the other champions took it upon themselves to make sure all of us were dressed, ready, and standing in the cold, empty center of the keep before any of Caro's men had the chance to see it happen.

As we stood in our group, waiting for orders, Leena leaned over and whispered, "I learned how to make a shadow hound." She beamed with excitement.

I nodded. My night was nothing but an infuriating drawing lesson and a breakdown. But Leena didn't need to know, and if we failed to get the dreite priest, everyone would know soon enough.

I swallowed the thought and watched Farran walk in behind Avi. Both of them wore their epaulets and cords. If they were concerned, neither showed a hint.

Avi stepped forward, hand pressed to her neck where meager wisps of yellow lifted her voice. "Our trial is to cross the strait into the Darklands and return a living dreite priest to the Armory for interrogation by the Crown."

Unsettled whispers rippled through our house. Dread settled in as a heady morning fog.

Avi kept going. "Onyx will not be supporting us with griffons. I need anyone who can fly to stand to my left. Anyone who cannot, to my right."

We divided ourselves. Avi cursed, seeing only six standing to her left. Wings were a separate gift among Theranians passed down through a handful of bloodlines. Though it wasn't obvious, most Theranians kept theirs hidden with a glamour.

I was not one of them, nor was Leena, or we would've escaped the Armory far more often.

"Fuck. Right, okay." Avi scanned through all of us, her brow furrowed as she raced through her thoughts. "Those who can fly, can you carry another? We need to get as many of us over as possible." There weren't any objections, and she bit her lip before adding, "Jaxon offered to retrieve her dragon. She can take two."

"You can use mine," Caro said, descending the steps alone. "I can take three, and he's familiar with the routes. My ranks will stay behind and defend the keep. I don't have enough to send and assist. Not for this trial; we've lost too many on their shores."

Dragons were rare in Thera, but this was their land, and occasionally, they'd present themselves to Armory soldiers in trials.

Anyone who bonded a dragon was quickly chosen by a maker; a dragon easily doubled the price offered by the Crown. Dragon riders were also the only soldiers allowed to rise to the Queensguard in fewer than three years, depending on Thera's needs.

Currently, a second-year in the Onyx house was the only soldier with a dragon outside of Jaxon.

Avi dropped her hand, and the doors of the keep opened into the field. The sky hadn't even matured into the orange light of morning and dew clung to everything.

Farran stood off with Devon, Vera, and three first-years claiming to have wings. Jaxon and Caro walked into the field and summoned their dragons by tracing a sigil tattooed on their forearms.

Jaxon's dragon, Aerno, arrived first. He rose over the trees and landed in a gust of wind and a flurry of black, iridescent feathers covered his wings; the scales on his front and back matched. The creature was well over five times the size of the griffons Onyx was supposed to bring, and much more fearsome. It seemed aware it had an audience and blasted the ground with a display of white fire that scorched the grass.

Occasionally, dragons flew over lower Rowane but it was rare. Most dragon riders were stationed at keeps along our borders and in smaller towns throughout the kingdom like Caro.

A thundering caw echoed from above, shaking the ground before another dragon flew in. Caro's was a deep shade of brown, with green-tinged feathers and scales mirroring its wings. Battle scars dragged across the beast's belly in a massive raised gash where scales had since healed over. I wondered what battle it came from; Many dragons fought the wars of gods and kings—few were younger than a century.

Caro's dragon was larger than Jaxon's and had a long, feathered tail, where hers was scaled. The dragon landed with a huff, shaking the ground. There was no fearsome display; the dragon simply surveyed the small crowd on the other side of the field.

Dragons were enslaved for centuries by the dreites and their priests in the Darklands throughout the god wars. Thera liberated them in the Second War of Kings and since then, their partnership with Thera has remained unbreakable. So much so we continued to be the only kingdom with their power.

Avi raised her voice. "Right. Six volunteers for the dragons?" she called out.

Leena went to raise her hand, but I snatched it before she could and whispered, "Dragons will kill anything with dark magic."

She looked straight at me with an open mouth and punched back. "A demon wielder is safe?"

"I didn't raise my hand."

Aixen, Blaise, and Varyn raised their hands—made sense. A dragon might shiver at Aixen's ability to build silver chains, but they wouldn't strike him down on sight the way they would for Leena and me.

If dragons saw even a flicker of the darkness in our eyes, they'd turn us to ash.

Our intrinsic magic was indistinguishable from that of the dreites and would be treated with the same mercy. Darkland powers always had a way of creeping into Thera it seemed . . . if anything, just to keep the gods entertained.

"Claude and Blaise, go with Jaxon. Remember to bow to her dragon before you approach. Varyn, Jasper, and Evie, you'll join Caro. You also need to bow, but do not rise until asked. His dragon will not tolerate disrespect."

The five broke off and left the rest of us behind.

Avi continued, "There are six of us with wings and twelve without. We'll migrate in shifts; it takes a half hour to fly the strait and land outside of the tower. The dragons can cross in half the time and will scout for trouble once they drop their riders."

We followed Avi and the second-years onto the field and through a trail leading into the forest. A storm blew in from the sea; the wind was picking up as clouds rolled in. We reached the end of the trail in minutes when we all scrambled onto another beach. The great sea crashed into rocks, and the smell of salt and kelp seasoned the air.

A *whoosh* came from behind us. We all looked up to see the two dragons take off, flying side by side, headlong to where the water met the sky. It would have been beautiful, but I knew better.

There was nothing noble about death—no matter how many times Arden tried to convince me otherwise.

Avi called six names. None were Leena and I. Meaning we had the curse of waiting. A sudden rush of wind caused my eyes to snap up.

I'd never thought about wings. I mean, I dreamed about having them but never thought about what unfurling them would be like. Wings weren't common in Lower Rowane, as most of the winged bloodlines were noble, but they were fascinating to watch.

One first-year's wings sprang to life, nearly translucent, with white joints giving them form. Another first-year groaned in pain as black leather wings spread out behind him. Vera had verdant wings echoing her nature-bound powers, and I missed the others because Farran conjured his own, and I couldn't look away.

Of fucking course, the prince had wings. They were feathered and midnight blue, so dark they could be confused for black. Silver laced the tips of his feathers and matched the dual blades strapped to his back; they were exactly the set of wings a Prince of Thera should have.

I imagined him standing at the foot of a dais with those wings outstretched, and for a moment, I saw the beauty and power of the Crown. It was a stunning sight until I thought about the way he grabbed my chin and how he looked at me last night.

Fuck. I needed to forget that.

"Stop showing off," Avi snapped at Farran. I wasn't the only one caught staring. She turned toward the rest of us. "Right, those I called, please step towards someone with wings. They'll carry you over the sea. I'll wait here for the next. Good luck."

Waiting was excruciating. Avi kept going over what the plan was again and again, map in hand. There was nothing else to talk about while we waited on the shore for an hour.

Leena twisted her hands and formed her shadows into objects. I watched her fold them into a sphere, a flower, and finally, a sword. My heart ached. Only Leena would bend her shadows into a flower before spinning them into a weapon.

Meanwhile, I traced the damned sigil on the sand. The paper, tucked away in one of the many compartments of my leathers, but I knew the lines: the shapes in it were carved into my memory as fiercely as my failure to use it.

As Avi paced on the beach, she told us getting into the Darklands would be easy. Getting out would be the hard part.

They'd never tried to bring anything back alive before, so it was unclear what it would look like.

When I was younger, I read about sigils the way most of my peers read stories. I found it fascinating that even a knight, steeped in valor and silver, could be disarmed with a single, well-placed sketch. There was so much power in those lines for anyone who channeled them.

Several wings came down on us, prompting me to look up. I noticed Farran first; his wings reflected the sunlight. Beside him, the first-years stumbled onto their landing and looked out of breath, even a little awed, but it was a relief everyone made it back.

Farran folded back his wings and walked straight towards Avi. His face was severe, with Vera only steps behind him. They whispered something, and every part of the captain went rigid.

Avi pulled away and looked to the forest behind the few of us still waiting. "We need to go now." That was an order.

Farran took Avi, and I thanked the gods. Vera took me, and Leena was with a first-year named Ren. No one knew any other part of his name, but his wings were a deep green with scales shining iridescent in the sun. He was easily the strongest flyer out of the first-years.

Flying was both terrifying and incredible. Vera carried me only a few feet over the swells of the sea laid between us and the Darklands. She spent some of her magic extending vines around my legs to make the half-hour journey more comfortable for the both of us.

She was strong for her size, but I was awkwardly a few inches taller. I closed my eyes tightly, and her wings beat hard as we rose higher into the sky.

I willed my stomach to settle. Perhaps there was a good reason I couldn't fly.

After a half hour, she finally shouted, "There it is!"

I forced my eyes open to see we weren't skimming the sea waves anymore. Instead, we were far above them and approaching a land mass hidden by low clouds. The tops of trees poked out as we got closer. Between them were the ruins of what must have been the keep we needed.

Dread came around again. It was an icy hand around my spine, and it squeezed like a vise.

Vera's wings paused, and we glided towards the forested area in a brief, elegant free fall. Then she dove and my stomach twisted, perching itself in my throat until we stumbled onto solid ground.

Vera landed elegantly with a smile on her face while I sputtered forward and wretched in a nearby bush.

The woods here differed from the mainland. The trees were squat and sinewy. Moss and lichen coated the trunks, and the leaves formed a thick and nearly impenetrable canopy above.

The morning mist had almost dissolved, revealing just how endless the forest truly was. Despite how close we were to shore, there was nothing but an expanse of woods, sparsely dotted with bright red berries and ferns.

"Where is everyone?" I asked and wiped the sick from my mouth with my sleeve. My knees wobbled, but I was steady enough.

"Not far behind," Vera answered, and her eyes trailed up to the canopy of leaves as it rustled above us. "We beat everyone, if you were wondering."

I glared. "Is that what the dive was about?"

She shrugged nonchalantly, but a smug smile betrayed her. "Gotta keep Farran humble. Trial or no."

She stopped smiling when the others landed in the same clearing. There wasn't time to waste.

Caro's dragon circled us overhead, screeching. We looked up. Luckily, the sky above was clear. I was sure we'd know a dragon fight if one came to pass. Avi whistled and gestured for us to gather around. She spoke in a low, hurried voice, stealing glances over our shoulders into the shadow of the woods beyond.

"The champions are on their trial. The first group has infiltrated the keep, clearing out traps and setting our own. We want to paralyze any defense they might have and make sure the priest is cornered. Caro said it's been mostly abandoned, but the remaining traps are treacherous.

"All we need to do is bring back the dreite priest. And we know there is only one from Caro's scouts. Reina is tasked with finding them. The rest of you will receive orders as needed. We all play a role. There are other artifacts scattered around the keep that might be useful."

My hands tightened around the pommel of my sword. I was the one with the sigil. I was the one with a power dark enough to match the dreite's own. I gulped and prayed we weren't walking into a death trap.

Despite how many times I said I wouldn't die, I wasn't entirely convinced.

The walk was hardly ten minutes before we stood in an overgrown field where a single crumbling tower rose above the tree canopy. The surrounding walls weren't even half the size of the Fern Keep and smoke came from a chimney. It was utterly silent. No shouting, no clash of swords, not even the sound of conversation.

I shuddered. Something was off. It wasn't just the new magic humming in my blood—I was getting used to that. There was something else. I exchanged a wary glance with Leena.

Avi cleared her throat but kept her voice low. "Right, so they've gotten in and opened the drawbridge. One of our protection sigils is drawn beside the gate. It will not save you from a fatal blow, but will slow the damage. Have your weapons ready. First-years—steel before magic unless you want to be a banner in the Atrium."

I looked at Farran; his blue eyes shifted, warily surveying the surrounding forest. We followed Avi into the bare stone keep. The only difference between this one and the one we'd come from across the sea was that moss and grass grew along the floor, and ivy pushed stones apart.

The rest of our party had gathered in the center, waiting for our arrival. I'm sure Devon briefed them just as Avi had briefed us.

The building was larger once we were inside. At a glance, it didn't seem like there was much to it. We were surrounded by stone buildings, all haphazardly built. Some jutted out at odd angles, others with slanted walls and rotted thatched roofs. It was unclear what buildings stood alone and which were connected.

At one point, the keep might have housed a noble, but they had fallen now. Perhaps, unceremoniously to the dreite priest who laid in wait, somewhere within.

Caro's dragon circled above, but made no sound when it flew over us. It was scouting. Watching.

Jaxon was also nowhere to be seen, nor was her dragon, but I locked eyes with Aixen and the others who flew before us. The first-years were all accounted for. Gods knew what the champions were tasked with today. This was their champion trial and their orders would only be known to them.

Champions weren't allowed to help their house, nor was their house allowed to help them. Jaxon, Phillip, and Landry had to earn their knighthood alone. Two years from now, we would too.

Avi, Farran, and Vera pushed into the center and spoke with Caro in a low whisper. I watched as Farran nodded and strode towards me. "We're going in," he announced.

"What?" I looked at Leena, avoiding the way Blaise's eyes followed me. He was watching. The heat of his gaze prickled the skin on my back as my gaze returned to Farran. "I can handle it alone. I'll be fine."

I'd retrieved men and placed sigils before, and I could do it again. Anyone else would weigh me down.

"I'm going with you so you don't burn out if you use your magic," he explained.

"It's a sigil. I'm more than capable if I'm not slowed down." From the hard look he gave me, I wasn't getting out of this.

"I've also been here before. I know my way around," he added.

I raised my eyebrows. I hadn't seen a lot of keeps, but this one hardly had a second wing. "It doesn't look like anything to get lost in."

He lowered his voice. "It's built with dreite magic. You're not going in alone."

"Yes, Your Highness," I said with a smirk, but it went unappreciated.

Farran turned on his heel past the front line of the party, and I followed into the depths of the deserted Darkland keep.

As we walked, I said a prayer to the old gods because I wasn't taking any chances—we were a sea away from the new gods, after all.

And even if we weren't, I'd always pray to the gods who built the mountains, not the ones who begged for tithes.

CHAPTER II

Rusted hinges creaked as Farran pushed open a massive wooden door. The cry of iron scraping stone sang through the space, and an earthy, heavy smell of musk and moss tickled my nose.

Light fell through the door and cast across the chipped stone floor for the first time in what might have only been weeks, but it could easily have been eons. It was eerie and still, as if the slightest breath could trigger a trap. Every shadow was an impending threat.

Between my heart and my ribs, something warm stirred.

It turned over itself as if it were waking up, and my fingers fiddled with the leather strap of my jerkin laid over my breast.

"You said it was fucking with us?" I whispered.

It was too quiet. This wasn't a guarded keep; it couldn't be.

Skeptically, I watched Farran twist and look behind us, then above. Nothing but shadows, cobwebs, and dust. We were in a long hallway that only grew darker the further we moved from the daylight trickling through the door.

As I stretched out my hand and rotated my wrist, Farran's warm fingers snaked around my forearm, and my magic withdrew. I gasped. The magic may have sunk back into my skin, but it simmered below the surface of his touch until I snatched it back.

"What are you doing?" he snapped.

I narrowed my eyes. "I can't see a damn thing."

"Not here. We're not drawing attention."

"Attention? Did you siphon off a *lumen*? There isn't a gods-forsaken soul in here."

He lowered his voice to a gruff mumble, "That's what concerns me. It should concern you too, *soldier*."

Something cracked behind us and we turned, but there was nothing except for shadows thrown by the sliver of light from the open door. However, a second later, a door slammed closed and darkness swallowed us.

The echoing blast of an explosion ripped through the hall, shaking particles of dust and silt from the stone walls before everything stilled. Nothing crumbled, but now my fear was palpable. It sat so much higher in my chest than dread, and my hand drifted to my sword.

They were out there. Leena, Aixen, Blaise.

"We keep going," Farran pressed, voice thick. "The priest knows we're here."

"Only one?" I swallowed.

"One dreite priest who's laid traps through this whole keep."

Farran couldn't see it in the pitch blackness of the hall, but I glared—intentionally. "So, everyone out there is bait?"

"No," he scoffed, like what I said was ridiculous. "Why would you think that? We need them to fight; the Crown doesn't actually want to waste everyone, if that's what you're alluding to. But every step closer to the dreite is going to trigger something. The worst will hit the courtyard. It was an old defense mechanism to waste an army before they reach—"

"The throne room?" I guessed.

"Yes. If they get through traps, Avi will send in defense for us."

"Incredible." *It wasn't.*

I pulled my borrowed sword from the sheath and frowned. The weight was off, but it would have to do. I had my dagger to fall back on if the sword stopped serving me; I hoped I wouldn't need it either.

Farran shuffled forward, and I followed, using the dull sword to reach into the darkness.

"Ouch!" he sputtered as my sword likely knocked his ankle.

"Sorry." Not really.

"You nicked me," he grumbled.

"I needed to make sure you weren't a wall."

"Anyone would know swinging a sword around isn't helpful in the dark. *Especially* an Armory soldier."

"I'm not just anyone."

He scoffed. "That's been made quite clear."

He kept moving and I followed. A light flickered in the distance, but behind us was darkness and the faintest sound of steel striking steel. At least the walls didn't shake again.

But this was a trial, and somehow everything about it was almost familiar: I was grasping around in the shadows, sword clasped in my hand, looking for a target.

"Do you feel anything?" Farran asked, his voice shaking me out of the reverie.

"Marginally afraid."

"No, magic. Remember what I said about like power?" We trudged through, and it was so dark my eyes couldn't adjust.

"Right," I stuttered and refocused. "I think it's . . . it's picking up. Like heat. What should I feel?"

"I don't know," the prince admitted.

"Why would you ask if you don't know?"

"I've heard plenty of stories, Reina."

My name caught me off guard; the Prince of Thera had no reason to say my name, but the way he said it gave it power. I'd never imagined my name on the tongue of a prince, yet here we were.

I shoved the thought down and kicked dirt over it so it wouldn't rise again.

"Are we sure I can't light a torch?" I asked.

His feet stopped, and so did mine. This wasn't going anywhere fast. A scream ricocheted through the hall, and we both heard it.

He muttered, "Certainly, it couldn't be worse."

There wasn't a soul around us, and I couldn't draw the damn sigil without a fucking light.

Farran took a deep breath. It was the only thing I heard. Everything went silent again, and I didn't dwell on it. "Stay true. The throne room is where The light is coming through. That's where the scream came from."

"You know for sure?"

"I've been here before, darling," he reminded me.

I ignored the bait. "I've heard princes can be overconfident."

Farran's footsteps stopped. I shouldn't have said it. "Do you think now is a great time to say that when I'll be the one dragging you out?"

"Dragging me out?" It was my turn to scoff.

"Yes," he muttered and continued walking forward.

"I don't remember hearing that part of the plan."

He paid me no mind, and when we reached the part of the hallway where the light crawled over the stones, we stopped, beset by another large set of doors. Farran pushed them open, and the light spilled in, temporarily blinding me as we stepped into the throne room.

The ceiling arched towards the sky; it must have been as high as the walls of the keep. Abstract stained-glass windows lined both walls and stretched from the floor to the ceiling. The colors were muted but must have been vibrant once.

Pieces of broken glass and missing panels gave me a glimpse of what remained of a garden: a decrepit fountain and broken stone benches as ivy crept through the windows and pooled on the floor in a stream of lush, green carpet.

We stopped in the doorway.

The throne in front of us was empty and in the process of being reclaimed by the creeping vines and several odd piles of dirt or dust.

"Why is no one here?" I asked, and my hand tightened on the hilt of my sword.

Farran's eyes assessed all there was to see: the empty throne, the stillness. "Something is wrong."

"Perhaps news of the *dreosen* travels fast, and they've all vanished out of fear?"

He shook his head slowly. "No, that'd be more reason to defend it. Caro said they'd taken care of most of it. This one was left behind after an Armory invasion six years ago."

"Would Caro lie?" My stomach curdled with dread.

"No, I know him," Farran warned. "He's a lot of things, but he's deeply loyal to the Crown. They wouldn't send the Armory to a traitor. Not as part of the trial. I suspect they're pushing us over the border, hoping at least one house comes out with useful information about the Darklands."

My brow furrowed. "So, we go back and report the priest is gone?"

"I still feel the magic, and I'm sure you do, too. They're not gone yet. We'll go into the tunnels. Whoever it is probably left the throne when they heard the dragons."

"Right, let's find the tunnels."

"Gladly." He smiled, excitement etched into his face.

I couldn't feign such enthusiasm, but I followed his lead, both hands wrapped around the hilt of my sword as we stepped back into the hall, now illuminated by the open door to the throne room.

We paused for a moment. He stretched out his hand and turned his palm, beckoning a torch to life. He grabbed it from the wall and handed it to me.

"Thank you, Your Highness."

His face fell. "Can you handle a sword with one hand?"

"Patronize me more, First Officer. I love being underestimated," I muttered.

I held the sword out toward him. He opened his mouth to speak, but another piercing scream interrupted us. I needed to focus. We were losing time and needed this to work.

Farran decisively stepped forward and pushed a door in the hallway open. It led down a stairwell that appeared vast and unending, reeking of mildew. This entrance hadn't been used in years, but we descended anyway, and once we were several steps away from the door, it became entirely too quiet yet again.

Farran came to a screeching halt, staring straight at me. His eyes twinkled in the firelight like sapphires. I admired the way the shadows danced across his features, and something in me fluttered I thought I'd buried.

"What do you feel?" he whispered tentatively.

I paused and closed my eyes to focus on the pressure and the warmth building in my chest and twisting unrelated to the way he'd just looked at me. "We're getting closer. It feels . . . warm."

"Warm?" He squinted.

There was no further explanation. I simply didn't have one. It was warm, like the heat from beside the hearth in the dead of winter, or a cat sleeping on your chest.

Whatever it was stretched and untangled in front of my heart, spreading past my chest and twining itself into the muscles of my shoulder. I'd experienced it before, but this was the most palpable.

Three more stairs and we were in the dirt tunnel underneath the keep. The soft dirt insulated any small noise. But I could still hear the way our boots crunched on the floor, the strain of leather, and my own damn heartbeat.

The heat intensified and spread, tying knots around my muscles as we continued to get closer and closer to something inevitable.

"Left or right?" the prince asked.

I hesitated and looked in both directions. I needed to be quick. We'd already probably taken too long. They could be dying up there. Leena, Blaise, and Aixen could all be dead.

No, no, that's ridiculous.

"Right."

"You're sure?"

No.

"Yes," I said with the confidence of a noble.

If I was wrong, I'd be too dead to live it down—probably.

This was a dreite priest, after all, a keeper of the Darklands and descendant of the Goddess Dreonna. Farran took my word and barreled right. I struggled to keep up with the quickened pace.

The heat in my chest rose and rose until it was fire knocking on my ribs. "Stop."

Farran listened and eyed me with concern. An invisible weight had collapsed on my shoulders and squeezed my lungs; I couldn't breathe. I looked around, my eyes swirled, and something came back.

No, that was impossible. I hadn't been here before.

"The dungeons," I rasped. The magic was painful and seizing.

The prince trusted me, but a line of worry creased his brow; we were in the same house, in the same trial. Why shouldn't he be able to trust me?

The searing pain in my chest spread to my arms and wrapped around my core as intuition dragged us down several halls to the dungeons—or at least I hoped. I turned a corner and froze . . . we stood face to face with three demons. On their haunches, they growled and snapped. Inky black venom dribbled from bright white fangs, but none moved.

I prayed they wouldn't, and to this day, I don't know why I took a step closer, but they moved too—bending at the knees while I stared straight past them.

Three days ago, the hulking sight of three demons would have been why I gasped, but not today. I was made *new*. Behind their shoulders, a dreite was strung up in iron chains. Large gashes stretched across his chest and abdomen.

Any deeper and his entrails would grace the floor. Ruby-red blood dripped off him where I expected black . . . perhaps we didn't need the sigil.

"We need the sigil," Farran said blankly. "And you should move them."

I didn't have the capacity to wonder if he'd read my mind. Neither of us dared to move underneath the weight of the demon's stare. Let alone three.

Stepping back, I set down the torch. "I can't do both. There's no way I can do both. I don't know how to move them."

"They're not attacking. Maybe you could—"

"Not attacking yet," I snapped. "I'm not trusting anything, especially a gift I know nothing about."

"You're not walking up and grabbing him," he protested.

"Maybe I can?"

"You have a death wish."

"I call it bravery."

Farran relented, pinching his nose with fingers. "We need to do something. We don't have—"

I wasn't waiting. I lunged forward with my sword drawn and slashed at the demons. The fire in my chest burned, raged, and bellowed as my sword cut through scales black as night.

All three demons lashed out, but I knew steel better than anything. They wailed, and their talons scratched at me, exasperated as they tried to grab the sword from my hands. None of my cuts were clean, but they did the job as I somehow severed one head and some arms with my dull blade.

Behind me, Farran followed my lead, surgically carving them up with his much sharper dual blades. For a few moments, there was nothing but the sound of flesh, scale, and bone meeting the stinging trill of steel as the beasts roared until silence fell and the demons laid out in unmoving heaps.

It was, of course, a temporary solution; neither of us had silver, and Leena was far above ground.

I relaxed the grip on my sword. Farran looked straight at me with wide eyes and thin lips, waiting to say something. A splattering of black blood decorated his cheek, and the heat of his stare collided with the swell of power in my chest. "You could have *wielded* them."

"Avi said steel before magic," I replied, shrugging my shoulders as I shook sinew off my blade. "I know how to swing a sword."

Farran eyed me derisively as he kicked one of the demon's lifeless forms to see if it reacted. "They'll stay down for an hour."

Good.

"We don't have much time then." I rushed towards the dreite, examining his wounds.

He was an older man with light brown skin and a well-kept graying beard now splattered with inky demon blood. His tunic was shredded, and deep scars penetrated his chest almost exactly like Devon and Rodrick but without the venom. The priest's wounds were certainly infected, and he was deeply unconscious.

I turned to Farran, asking, "Are you sure this is the priest?"

"Not sure why it wouldn't be," he mumbled and took a step towards me, nearly tripping on a demon leg, but he quickly caught himself. With every pulse of my heart, my magic reeled back as if an outgoing tide. Whatever drew us here was gone, but I wasn't about to dwell on it.

Unless the fading power meant the dreite himself was fading away. He didn't look good.

I buried the consideration. "Do we still need the sigil? Someone clearly got to him first."

"The sigil is still the most important part," Farran said. "Draw it on his chest. Then he can't conjure when he comes to. It's a full stop of his magic."

"He's dying," I argued. But I didn't know why I cared. I'd seen death before, I'd seen torture, and fuck, I'd delivered both in Arden's name. This was a dreite of the Darklands, of the old gods. The Crown would smile at his suffering, and I should too.

"Yes, he is." Farran said nothing else. His jaw was so tight, muscles in his neck stood out. He was barely holding back.

The severed arm of a demon wriggled by my foot. I kicked it back in a hurry. It certainly hadn't been an hour. I pulled my dagger out and turned the blade towards the dreite. The lacerations on his chest were too deep, too close together.

We needed him off the wall.

Farran stepped over and scraped several sigils into the irons with his own knife, loosening them until the dreite's limp body fell forward into his arms.

The dreite didn't wake. A horrible, guttural noise came from him, deep and desperate, far away from where the gods could intervene. I shuddered. Arden always tried to stop me before it came to that but sometimes it was unavoidable.

"Turn him over," I commanded.

The man's back was pristine, and I kneeled beside him. Watching his ribs rise and fall for a moment. I wouldn't think about the dirt and tainted blood on the floor that would get into those wounds.

Why was I doing this for the Crown?

It didn't matter. This was survival, and this was who I needed to be. I'd done worse for Arden, and I'd do worse again.

I leaned forward, dagger in hand, and traced the sigil on the dreite's back.

His body stiffened and shook, but his breath remained even.

Farran watched intently as I worked the fine point of my dagger and wrote in all the lines and curves that failed me on the beach. When I finished, I leaned back on my knees and watched as the sigil gave a faint glow and absorbed into the man's back like a brand.

Black, ugly, with rushed and jagged lines, but I did it.

"You want to carry him, or should I?" Farran asked.

I stared at him blankly. It was very clear I wouldn't be dragging an unconscious body any further than a few feet on my own.

While I stood up and sheathed my dagger, Farran folded his left hand and lifted a closed fist. Yellow ropes extended and wrapped around the dreite, lifting him slightly into the air. Farran pulled the dreite's body over his shoulder as if he were a sack of wheat.

It was impressive for petty magic. Any time I tried to summon something larger than a book, I ended up winded.

We walked over to the demons and back the way we came in silence. A very distinct sinking feeling curdled in my abdomen as we walked back through the dungeon. All the heat in my chest subsided and folded itself back.

I had no idea what, if anything, it meant for what waited above ground. The magic and power simmering underneath my skin was a beast I was only beginning to understand.

Chapter 12

We topped the stairs and I stumbled into the hallway, hands gripping my knees as I fought to catch my breath—again. Farran stared at me, and I hated it. The slaughtering of a demon, even three, had been effortless, but it was the stairs that would be the end of me.

"I have short legs," I wheezed, chest heaving.

He ignored me and tugged at the neck of his jerkin. "You can heal."

"We've already established that."

"He won't make it like this." Farran glanced down the hallway, to the left and then the right. The man's labored breathing filled the otherwise silent hall. His rattling chest was louder than my own heavy breaths.

I nodded, my eyes fixed on Farran. "Do we have time, First Officer?"

"Yes. Remove the infection but keep him asleep. We don't have time to heal the wounds completely," he ordered.

The body thudded as Farran's summoning hold released. I kneeled beside the dreite and placed my hands on his abdomen. I had removed infections a handful of times; the books said you needed to connect with the blood, identify it, and drag it out.

If it didn't work, a drop of the healer's blood would make the connection easier. Though, with such a method, side effects could occur, and I wasn't keen on discovering those.

My eyes closed.

His heart was steady, despite the slow beat, and I pressed gently upon him with my magic pushing through the minuscule layers that make a person what they are, until I found a vein strong enough to have a fighting chance.

The infection struck back at my senses; a sour tang flooded my mouth and burned like swallowing the embers of a fire. His dreite blood was purging the venom, but the infection still spread faster.

I couldn't get it in one drag, so I tugged on the edges of it and did my best.

It took a few tries but with a last heave, yellow-green essence seeped into the air and dissipated above the body as I fell backwards. The dreite looked the same, but the edges of the lacerations looked less angry, and his face relaxed.

"Impressive." Farran marveled as his arm extended forward.

Ropes came from his fingertips again and wrapped around the priest once more. He hoisted him over his shoulder, and we kept walking. Every step was more unsettling than the last. *Every fucking one.*

When we made it to the entrance, it took all of my might to push open the giant wooden door leading to the courtyard of the keep. I struggled to swallow back the unease settling in my throat, but bile replaced it moments later.

The courtyard was covered in blood, shredded leather, and abandoned swords. It was a massacre.

Before I moved a muscle, Farran's free hand was on my shoulder, holding me back.

"What do you see?" he rasped.

"Same as you," I said through my teeth. I was on the verge of collapse. My knees trembled, the world tilted, and I fumbled, trying to grab for my sword against his steady grip. "A fucking massacre. It's . . . it's my—"

"They're fucking with us." Farran's voice was tight.

"What?"

He took a step closer, his arm brushing mine, and the warmth prickled my skin as his voice lowered to a cautious whisper. "I see a dead dragon and nothing else."

"No blood?" My eyes widened.

He lowered the dreite to the ground, still holding the summoning ropes as he shook his head. "It's empty. There isn't anyone here."

Illusory magic was new to me and our house library hardly had any books about it outside of brief mentions and a few myths. "What do we do now?" I asked, eyeballing the entrance of the corridor we'd just left . . . guttural growls resonated from it. I looked at him frantically. "How quickly do demons recover?"

Fuck.

His face fell, and we drew our swords on instinct, ready to slaughter again if need be, but I straightened.

I was a demon wielder. I'd figure it out.

I slid my sword slowly back into its sheath as the clip of talons on stone echoed through the hall, steady as a ticking clock.

I cocked my head toward Farran. "You can fly, take the dreite, and get out of here. I can handle this."

"I'm not leaving you," he argued.

"We need the dreite to complete the trial. Get him back to Thera," I ground out and squared my shoulders toward the door. "I'll be fine."

"As the First Officer—"

My eyes narrowed, and I didn't look at him. "As the First Officer, you know I'm right. I'm the fucking demon wielder."

Power, magic, something pulsed to life in my chest. I was afraid of it, but my curiosity was stronger.

"Sangrey—"

"Go. This is one of the times I protect myself."

Farran relented. However, something glinted in his eyes: a flash of frustration.

I ignored it as he sheathed his swords, grabbed the dreite, and spread his wings. The footsteps were so close. Heartbeats after he lifted off the ground, three demons emerged from the hall, and I braced myself with a reminder: *you can make them kneel.*

The demons snarled at me as they approached and flexed their claws. Anger rippled from them, but I wouldn't budge. The power behind my ribs expanded and twisted in a nest of threads, all of them warm and stretching as the creatures came closer.

This was a dumb, terrible idea. But here I was.

I held my left hand forward, trembling as I nudged the heat from my chest towards it, hoping that's where the magic needed to go.

I waited for them to lunge.

Nothing happened, but a few damp, cold threads moved among the others, and I shivered.

Was that it? I waited as the demons fell to a bow a few paces in front of me, followed by the clip of human footsteps from the hall. No, that couldn't be right.

"I see you've met my guard," a woman's voice chimed.

She strode into the courtyard, dressed in brown gossamer, and stopped between the three demons who'd bent on their knees. The woman's eyes narrowed as she watched them and looked back at me, quickly erasing the surprise. Her long brown hair was unbound and trailed to the base of her spine, while a circlet settled just above her brow with an onyx in its center.

"Fascinating; they weren't thrilled about being torn apart, but here they kneel." Gray eyes swiveled to mine and remained. "Your eyes betray you. If you are who I believe you to be, they will rise on your command, *valdronna.*"

"You know nothing about me." I drew my sword but kept my left hand poised, on the off chance I needed to do something with it. *Valdronna.* "Who are you?"

"The dreite priest*ess* you seek." She smirked. "We had a warning, and you should be thankful."

"Who was the man in the dungeons?"

"An advisor—and traitor. You can have him. He'll give Thera's Crown plenty, but it will change nothing. Everything is already on course. We know what your queen seeks, but perhaps we'll take it instead."

"And that is?" The demons remained kneeling; I wouldn't play my hand unless she forced it. Besides, I doubted they'd listen to me.

The dreite ignored my question. "The rest of your party departed. They left hours ago after facing my mirrors and the keep's defenses."

This had me taken aback. "Hours? We've hardly been here one."

"It only feels that way to you." She paused, grinning as she took a step towards me. Her demons watched. One snarled, but none made an attempt to stand. "You certainly have a darkness in you—Reina, is it? Of course, it is. Your father would never have named you anything else, I'm sure of it."

My eyes narrowed. "You know nothing of my father."

"Neither do you, but I suppose you'll see the truth soon enough," she drawled.

I snapped my left arm down, fist still closed, eyes on the dreite. The heat pulsed in my fingertips like another heart, however there was nothing in it but a flicker of my gift . . . a faint rush of wind and a ripple of power.

The demons rose and took a step away from the priestess. My sword dropped from my hand.

I lunged, pulling a dagger from my leathers in a single motion. She held up her hand, and neither I nor the demons moved. I froze before her, against my will.

She tutted. "I don't want to harm you, but if you take one more step towards me, I *will*. You will have to work harder to get a sigil on my skin or any of my brothers and sisters. I will not set a living foot in Thera. Their Crown has destroyed and imprisoned everything capable of goodness."

"You're mistaken," I gritted out. I didn't care. Every kingdom was a hero in their own story but they could all burn as far as I was concerned. My loyalty was to my friends and a destiny that would kill me. No kingdom was worth my life.

The dreite glared. Her thin lips pursed and quivered with the words she wanted to say. "I've said too much. Your party will return shortly for you; do not bring them back here or all will be made worse."

The woman turned away and hesitated. She looked back over her shoulder and met my eyes.

"And never harm a *dreos* again. It is below you and insults the Goddess Dreonna; we are not your enemy," she snapped.

She walked away without another word and the demons followed, the massive door creaking to a close behind them. I was alone in the empty keep. I replayed every word, every movement of the priestess like I'd find an answer in it while I waited for someone to retrieve me.

The sky above was painted in shades of deep purple and orange. It had been hours, so much longer than I thought or felt, and now I was sore, empty, and filled with dread.

"We are not your enemy."

I shuddered. I supposed it was true. In a way, they had every reason to hate Thera as much as I did.

She knew my father. No. She was mistaken. My father was a man, harmless and unassuming who charmed my mother into marrying below her status. He read us stories at night and made dragons out of rose cuttings from our garden. He'd never met a dreite priestess in his life.

I waved the thought away. More pressing was that we didn't complete our trial, not truly, and that was a rock in my chest dragging me down until I heard the beating of wings and a rush of wind. Someone had landed nearby.

I whipped around to see Farran standing a few paces away. His wings were completely black in the waning daylight except for the silver tips that glinted, and more feelings twisted sharply in my gut at the severe look in his eyes.

I swallowed down the surprise: he'd been sent back for me, out of everyone else in Emerald.

"You're in one piece, thank gods," Farran observed and took in the empty space around us.

The courtyard was deserted except for a handful of fallen leaves that skittered to the corners in a light breeze.

I nodded and crossed my arms. The dagger was still in my hand, which I forgot until I nearly nicked myself. "The man we found wasn't the priest," I said, looking up to meet his confused stare.

"What do you mean?"

"After you left, the priestess came out. She knew our party had left. She also knew we battled mirrors and slaughtered her demons."

Farran's forehead crumpled and lines appeared between his brows. "Who did I bring back?"

"One of her advisors and a traitor."

"Could be worse." His face relaxed as the gears in his brain appeared to turn. "We tell no one about the mistake. The Crown can use him, and we need to get back. A storm is coming in, and I'm not a fan of flying through the wind over an open sea."

I picked my sword up from the ground and sheathed it. "Did the champions complete their trials?" I asked.

His face hardened. "Jaxon did. Phillip and Landry did not. Emerald will have only one champion to offer the Crown."

"Oh, Gods. I'm sorry." The words sat heavier on his shoulders than mine, no doubt. I saw the glimmer of sadness, loss. "And Leena?"

"Leena is fine," he breathed.

Those words were the only relief I needed. I walked towards him but stopped abruptly, unsure of what to do next. His wings looked exquisite, and something about the fading daylight softened his features as he examined me.

Was there a question I should ask? I wasn't thinking.

I was looking at his lips, and the clearing of his throat shook me out of the brief trance.

"Right," Farran muttered. His voice seemed caught, too. "Let's go and try not to vomit. These are new leathers."

My cheeks flushed. Of course, Vera said something.

Without a word, powerful arms wrapped around me, and I became very aware that my back was pressed against his chest. The ripple of his muscles twinged against me as every part of his body worked to get us off the ground.

With one steady beat of his massive wings, we were off the ground, soaring into the air, away from the Darklands and over the sea, back onto Theranian land.

Magic shifted around my chest. Unsettled and frantic, like it reached for something . . .

It wasn't eager to return to Thera.

Chapter 13

Farran's wings pounded against the incoming storm as the waves churning below us turned white and frothing. He hardly slowed to land, and I tumbled into the sand, landing on all fours while he remained on his feet with an unhelpful grin.

I scrambled to my feet, belly in tight knots. Involuntarily, a spasm slid up my throat, and I dry-heaved, muscles attempting to empty my stomach, which was useless, as I hadn't eaten since last night.

After a minute or two, I felt better, but then I felt everything *else*.

"You're gonna have to get used to that, darling," Farran said lightly.

"You couldn't have taken us straight to the keep?" I glared.

I wiped my mouth with the back of my arm as he folded his wings away with the magic of a glamour. I blinked and they were gone, not a feather left behind.

He shrugged. "Felt like seeing the sea one more time. Thought maybe you would, too."

"Don't act like you know me." Fire burned in the glare I shot him before I stalked to the woods and up the trail leading back to the keep.

Leena was alive, but I wouldn't do anything wistful until I saw, with my own eyes, that everyone else was; not all of us get to be as callous about life as the Crown. Clearly, the Armory still had more of me to break.

It was fully dark as I approached. The brief flash of anger had ebbed, and I could hardly make out the warm glow of the torches on the lower walls. I trudged the last few paces across the yard until I reached the gate and pounded on it.

Farran caught up easily. I would walk faster next time.

The gate lifted, and standing behind it were a weary Avi and Vera who still had dried blood on their leathers. They ushered us into the main hall without a word. Jaxon and Caro stood with solemn faces.

Half of them wore their leathers, while the others had changed into tunics and breeches. It was just the six of us and the three bodies laid on a table, covered with sheets.

Death was different and more complicated when you knew whose life was cut. I thought I'd feel more, but I felt numb.

"The priest is in a cell. We'll move him tomorrow. He hasn't woken," Avi said plainly, but her voice stumbled.

Farran nodded. The gesture told me everything I needed to know: we shared a secret now.

"I'm sorry about Landry and Phillip," I murmured, eyes trained on Jaxon who had dressed down into a tunic, but splattered blood crusted on her neck.

"So am I." Her voice was razor-sharp. I'd never noticed how full her lashes were until she cast her eyes down. "It's part of the trial. I'll see you all in the morning."

She paused for a moment to look back at me. I held her gaze.

"You did good, Sangrey," she said with tired sincerity. "The Crown will be pleased."

I nodded, letting my doubts rest in the back of my throat like molasses. *The Crown will be pleased.* Arden's laugh echoed in the emptiness of my head. I dug my fingernails into my palm, the sharp pain a reminder: *this* is who I was supposed to be.

I hated it.

Jaxon and Caro excused themselves, leaving Avi and Vera behind. The four of us sat down at one table, and Caro's men brought out cold bowls of stew. It didn't smell good, but it didn't smell bad enough to pass.

Avi pulled her hair out of a twist and it fell down in stiff, uneven waves over her unbuttoned jerkin. She stretched out. "I've been waiting all day to do that."

"What happened?" I couldn't play this anymore. I didn't see Aixen or Blaise. If they were under one of those sheets, I would—I don't know what I'd do . . . but I couldn't take another minute of uncertainty.

"Devon is severely injured . . . again," Avi said about the second-year. "Jaxon is flying him back to the Armory at first light with her dragon. He needs an Armory healer. Varyn stabilized him for the night, but the wound was close to his heart. The mirrors had dragon-tipped blades."

My head jerked up. Dragon-tipped blades only became so when they stabbed a dragon; their power was brutal but temporary—dragon blood was a slow-working poison. It adhered to the blade for a few days, and if untreated, minor scratches would kill in weeks while large wounds would fester and burn, killing within days.

"Did anyone get hurt?" Farran asked.

Vera spoke instead. "Not as severely. Aixen took a strike to the arm, and Varyn took one to the leg, but Varyn scraped together a poultice from Caro's reserves. We'll be able to leave tomorrow."

"Leena?" I pressed, glancing around the table. Farran said she was fine, but I needed to hear it again.

"Leena is fine," Avi assured. "She nearly burned out, trying to choke the mirrors and cut their magic. It was brilliant, truly. The mirrors couldn't hold their forms as well in her shadows, so we owe her our lives."

Vera perked up. "Blaise kept the mirrors back from going down the hallway and making your work more complicated. He got scratched, but it's nothing. It wasn't with dragon blood."

"We lost two. Ren, the first-year with the wings and River."

Farran lowered his eyes. River was one of three second-years who wasn't pledged to a maker. If we lost many more second-years, one of our four makers might go without a champion next year which would certainly put Emerald's funding in jeopardy, especially now Jaxon was our only champion this year.

If a house doesn't have champions, makers can pull funding. Remaining soldiers get scattered to the other houses where alliances were already formed, tightening the competition to get a maker.

That disruption usually leads to violence, but it hasn't happened in over a decade.

"Ren burned out." Avi sighed, smoothing her forehead with her fingertips as if the motion could draw out sadness. "So did River. They were overwhelmed by the mirrors and lost control." She took a deep breath and looked at the table. "I already sent our report. Last item is the pyre."

She lifted her eyes to Farran.

"Can you help?" she asked. "I want them committed before first light." Avi's eyes shifted to me. "Sangrey, you're dismissed. Get some sleep. It's a long journey back, and you'll need your strength if the priest wakes and calls on any demons."

I shook my head, blowing out a breath. "Let me help." Avi had eased my worries; I could do more than pretend to sleep.

"It's not necessary. We can—"

"Please." I wanted to help. "I'm not tired yet."

Avi and Farran shared a quick look before they finally shrugged.

"Sure," Farran said, and his eyes fell to me. "Let's get the pyre set."

"I'll check on Jaxon," Avi muttered and stood. "She'll want to be there."

Hot on Farran's heels, we walked out of the hall and down a winding alley within the walls of the keep. He pushed open a wooden door leading out of the north wall towards a small stone path.

The path ended abruptly, with a funeral pyre positioned at the end, still smoldering from Rodrick's commitment last night. Thunder rumbled in the distance, threatening, but still far enough away.

Firewood was piled high against the wall. We stacked the logs and twigs waist-high without speaking. The tedium of the movement was welcome after everything we'd endured.

When we finally stepped back, I stole a glance at him. His jaw tightened, and he looked every part the first officer he was.

"Let's get the bodies," he muttered.

The words fell on the stones with all the weight and turmoil of a broadsword dropped in battle. I followed him back to the hall, passing Avi and Jaxon who carried another. A swirl of unease ran through me like a ghost.

I'd seen death before; I knew what death was.

But something shifted as I grabbed the knees of one of our soldiers and helped Farran carry them to the foot of the pyre for the first time. The ritual of commitment required carrying the body unaided so nothing could corrupt their journey. The weight was also supposed to be a reminder to the living.

On the second trip, whatever the emotion was, it fell sideways, and tears stung behind my eyes as we laid the last body beside the other two while Jaxon gingerly removed the shrouds.

They weren't sleeping; they were gray, cold, and so bereft of life. Landry should have been among them, but his body didn't come back, and a piece of my heart cracked.

He was supposed to be a champion, and so was Phillip. They had made it too far. I thought about my house, about our friendships, and what it would be like to reach the end and stand alone. I couldn't, and I couldn't fathom Jaxon's pain.

Phillip was first. Jaxon stiffened, the knuckles on her sword white as she watched Farran and Avi settle his body in the center of the unlit pyre. Phillip's leathers were ripped open. Black ooze coated him, and if I squinted, it had tangled into his veins and speckled his white hair.

"Sir Phillip Gable of Draven," Jaxon murmured as she held her hand out. The breeze picked up, and a few drops of rain fell. "We send you from one journey to the next, where you will rest and wake anew. The soul continues, and by the grace of the new gods and old, yours will never walk alone. May the wind be at your back, the gods at your side, and the meadows be in bloom for this life, the next, and all hereafter."

Farran and Avi lifted their hands simultaneously. I followed suit.

"This smoke will carry you." Jaxon lowered her voice, fire dancing along the tips of her fingers as she commanded the last word in Catharian, "*Braan.*"

Sparks flew from the four of us and ignited the pyre in a brilliant display. The orange glow of it twirled and consumed until we committed Phillip to the gods in full.

Thunder built in the distance as the storm approached.

We did the same two more times for Ren and River. With each body and flare of fire at Jaxon's command, their soldier's façade faded. As River burned, the wind changed, and rain fell faster.

Smoke curled towards us with the scent of burning pine, the singe of hair, and the tang of blood set alight. A smell so poignant and familiar it fractured a part of me. I wasn't prepared for the heaviness of loss, and now I couldn't look away.

Jaxon wept, and Avi trembled as she propped Jaxon up, trying to hold herself together too.

"Landry died alone," Jaxon choked. "I promised he wouldn't."

Farran moved in silence and wrapped an arm around both Avi and Jaxon. It was intimate, and I was an intruder, even as the acute twist of grief multiplied in my chest. They didn't know Ren, but I did. Just like I knew Eral and Rodrick, but my tears wouldn't come.

I backed away, slipping into the keep, where most of the torches were snuffed by the rain now coming down steadily. My footsteps echoed off the walls and reverberated through my bones as I walked back to the stables and crawled into my bedroll, swallowing the wave of grief threatening to drown me.

"You smell like smoke," Leena whispered. I turned onto my side; hearing her voice chased away the knot in my throat.

"You should be asleep," I whispered back.

Her eyes looked heavy, but the gold in them still glittered in the low light.

"Farran was frantic because he'd left you with demons. Forgive me for wanting to know you made it," she retorted.

"I told you I wasn't going to die." Even in the shadows, I saw her roll her eyes.

"You say a lot of shit."

"I haven't been wrong," I reminded her.

"You've definitely been wrong."

"Nope, can't remember."

"Sure," Leena quipped. "You got the priest?"

"We did." I'd tell her the real truth later. I always did. "You took on mirrors?"

She grinned. Hay rustled as she nodded. "Can't wait for you to see. Next trial, we'll fight side by side. Shadows and demons."

I mused. "You really want that to stick, don't you?"

"I just want someone to sing songs about us. It'd be a great ballad. Something about the cloak of night and black claws—the *sunderone* and the *dreosen*."

"You could write it yourself."

"It's not the same," she yawned. "Though, I wonder what the criers will say."

"Probably nothing that actually happened." I stretched out on the roll and swallowed a yawn.

I loathed the criers; they were there for the gamblers and makers. They only recounted what the Crown was willing to share, and usually, it wasn't much more than the list of the dead and some dramatized version of events.

"They don't always lie. Maybe Avi's report makes us sound incredible. Some of us *did* arrive on dragon-back."

I sighed. "We need to sleep."

"Fine." Leena closed her eyes eagerly and whispered, "Glad you're alive."

I said nothing back, but relief swelled in my chest as I turned onto my other side where Blaise slept. Heavy rain clattered the roof now, interrupted only by thunder.

A splatter of blood dappled his cheek, and I fought the urge to reach over and wipe it off. I knew how cold my hands were, and I didn't want to wake him. The defined lines of his cheekbones and the scar on his forehead were all smoothed in sleep. I wanted to be closer to him, but it felt impossible.

Everything about him was impossible, but it didn't mean I couldn't close my eyes and dream about a different life where maybe it wasn't, or maybe he was Farran.

My eyes shot open. *No, no. Absolutely fucking not.*

I knew who I was, and traitors died alone.

Chapter 14

We left the keep in a few small groups at first light as the rain was letting up. Now we were hours away from the coast, and the uphill portion of our trek was largely over. With a skilled horse, it would be easy enough to cross from the Armory to any of the northern keeps, but by foot, I kept slipping on the fucking rocks.

The landscape of northern Thera was hardly majestic, and the overnight storm made the already craggy path more treacherous. At this altitude, anything that wasn't stone was sparse and armed with thorns. Even the meadow grass pricked through my pants as we waded through it.

"You seem worried," Leena observed, striding up beside me.

Her gold eyes reflected the sun coming from the clear sky, and her curls escaped their light containment in the rising humidity. Clouds churned on the horizon to the south, quickly getting darker when we still had an hour or two of true daylight.

Ahead of us, Blaise and Farran walked with the dreite who remained unconscious and suspended by magic.

It wasn't worth lying. "Of course I'm worried." I sighed. "We have to survive two nights in the woods again."

"We can do that; we know we can do that," Leena reminded me. "Vera said next time, we'll get horses. We just weren't fast enough, and they were all claimed."

"Of course they were." The Armory only had space for thirty or so, and they weren't keen to waste them on first-years.

She paused, taking a breath as we descended another steep run of rocks. "Have you talked to Blaise? He's worried about you, especially after last night when Farran came back without you. I thought he was going to strangle the prince."

"I'm fine." I frowned. Blaise had no right to worry about me, nor would I accept it. "He doesn't have to worry."

"He absolutely does. You can't ask someone to stop caring," she said pointedly.

Gods, there it was: caring.

I scoffed and trudged ahead, because I'd never asked him to care about me. I'd never expect that from anyone.

The further inland we trekked, the grass became more supple, and late summer flowers bloomed in pockets of yellow and white across the rolling hills. I looked ahead to see the clouds covering the sun had turned heavy and gray.

I welcomed the rain; my leathers still had shadow-hound blood, sweat, and gods know what else stuck to them. I could smell it when the breeze stilled.

My mind wandered. Again, I replayed the conversation with the priestess. The surprise on her face, the way her demons regarded me, everything seemed off. What did she mean by "everything was on course" and "you'll find the truth soon enough"?

What truth? I was already the *dreosen*. Then there was the other word she used: *valdronna*—

"Demon wielder." The sudden timbre of Farran's voice cut off my thoughts.

My head snapped up, and his sapphire eyes met mine, stirring something deep within my chest. Every time I was alone with him, the ghost of Arden's words wormed their way up my throat and reminded me how precarious my life was, especially this close to the prince.

"First Officer," I greeted, matching his tone. "Have you heard the word valdronna?"

His brow raised. "Yes, why? It's Catharian."

"Do you know what it means? I know *dronna* like Dreonna the goddess, but I've never heard *val*."

He pursed his lips and chewed on it before answering. "Chosen or blessed is the nearest definition I can think of. Might mean "chosen by Dreonna" or "blessed by Dreonna." It's an old term for *dreosen* if I remember my Cathan Studies. Why?"

I glanced at him, fisting my hands in my pockets. "The priestess called me that."

"Oh." He considered it for a long second, the muscle in his neck straining as he swallowed. "I suppose it makes sense."

"It does." I nodded, watching his expression as something I couldn't understand flitted across it. "How is the dreite still sleeping?"

"Sleeping draught. Why?"

My eyes narrowed. "Someone with wings could have taken him, or Jaxon."

Farran lowered his voice. "Until he's brought to the palace, as a dreite priest, you'd be the only one in our house with the right magic to subdue him like this. The makers need to believe we're bringing back a priest."

"Aixen has silver, Leena has shadows. Their magic can also hold a dreite—or an *ontaros*."

"Depends on power." Farran tensed. "An ancient dreite priest would be no match. Those sigils are the only way to contain their magic, and they can only be cast by another priest, someone with true enough magic—"

"Or me," I said drily. "If it requires the magic of a dreite priest, how will the queen subdue him in the palace?"

"I wouldn't worry about what happens at the palace."

I stared. "The man isn't a priest. They'll know we didn't complete our trial in seconds."

Farran mulled over this and ran his hand through his hair; he had the audacity to smirk at me. "Is that why you've been so quiet? It's fine. The queen will be thankful for anyone who serves the Darklands."

"Seems easier when she won't have your head," I spat.

"She wouldn't have yours, either."

My brow furrowed. "You seem so sure."

"I have my reasons. Why do you think *I* wouldn't get punished?"

"She's your mother, for one," I muttered.

Farran laughed, which was something I hadn't heard before, and the lightness of it surprised me. "She's my mother, but she's also a mother who requires all of her children to go through the Armory and prove themselves. My oldest brother died in his champion trial, and she'd let me die in mine."

My stomach coiled. "Shit, I'm sorry."

His leathers shifted in a shrug. "I still have two brothers who survived. If I make it through, I'll replace my uncle as Prince Commander."

"You're not hoping for the Crown?"

He stopped walking, and I cursed myself. *Way too personal.* I was talking to a prince, not another soldier. I needed to be more aware of myself.

There was something disarming about him . . . something familiar that wriggled past my usual defenses.

"No, I'm not hoping my brothers die," he stated. "Why are you asking? Regardless of who the Crown is, you'll be there. The *dreosen* is invaluable, with or without a siphon. You are what Thera's been waiting for." He glanced over, searching for something. "You have no idea the stir it caused when they found out the other day."

"What do you mean?" I stiffened. *"We know what your queen seeks,"* the priestess had said, and I felt sick.

"Priests have been suggesting for years a demon wielder would be revealed in Thera's Armory for the first time in our history. Once the Crown knows the extent of your gift, they'll prepare to mount attacks on the Darklands and finally claim them."

My breath stilled. "That would mean war."

"You'll do as you're ordered on the Queensguard. We all will." Farran's voice held no emotion as he looked straight ahead to where trees came into view; the sky continued to churn in shades of gray.

"The other kingdoms would never allow it," I whispered.

"The other kingdoms don't have the *dreosen* or dragons."

"I—" Any words died in my throat. War had a different tenor to it when all I ever thought I'd be was just a Queens-guard knight.

"You act surprised every time someone reminds you of your gift."

"I am." It had only been a few days, and I wanted none of it. Silence drifted, and I changed the subject. "Are you worried about Emerald only putting up one champion?"

"Our makers are fine if Jaxon is the only one." He sighed. "You and I are about to fetch the best price they've ever seen. Avernought would probably split it with the lot of them to keep everyone happy."

"You and me?" It was my turn to laugh. "So, you're as-suming you could siphon my power?"

"I suppose I am, aren't I?"

"I expected you to ask nicer than that," I said, playing along.

"Do you? Since it seems you prefer threats, I'm simply meeting you at your level."

"Take anything from me and I'll cut you in half, prince or not."

His brow quirked up with his lips. "Careful, I might take you up on it."

"Shame I'm only armed with a dull sword, Your High-ness," I said congenially as Farran's face tensed when foot-steps came up behind us.

"I think you mean First Officer," Blaise said, and that was the end of the conversation. Blaise practically threw the body of the dreite towards Farran as we walked up the next hill, staring at me as he did it.

He wanted to talk. The unsaid words clung to every edge of the pause, but I wasn't ready.

I didn't know how I felt about him when every word I said to him took effort. He noticed it, of course he noticed, but nothing was the same. It had been so easy when our gifts were intangible things we wondered about in those first few months when we sat against the Armory wall and watched the stars.

But the first year in the Armory was a fever dream where anything felt possible. Everything changed in the dungeon when we learned exactly what weapon we'd be for the Crown.

The sooner I accepted the weapon I was, the easier it would be to turn off every part of myself that wasn't.

We stopped for the night on a ridge at the edge of a forest, where the ground was bare except for the pine needles scattered from the towering trees. It was just us, as the rest of Emerald had taken a different route.

Vera said there was a village along the way, but we couldn't walk up to an inn with an unconscious man, even if we were Crown soldiers.

Thunder clapped in the distance, and Blaise cursed. "I'll take the first watch," he said, giving no one else a chance to bring it up. He walked past me and sat on a fallen log. None of us stopped him.

"Milliard," Farran called after Blaise, and he turned back. "If the dreite wakes, you know what you need to do." There was a nod of acknowledgment.

I'd been poisoned with a sleeping draught before and it was strong, but not strong enough to last any longer than a few hours. If you wanted to keep someone unconscious for much longer, there were more effective poisons, like fharax root or blight blossom, but neither was easy to find this far north.

Leena tossed and turned beside me as the trees above bent and cracked in the rage of wind. One downpour came pounding through in a sheet of water.

The rain only lasted a few minutes before it moved on, but the threat never left. Thunder shook the ground, and lightning illuminated every corner of the forest at near constant intervals.

I fell asleep soaking wet, listening to the distant rumble until Blaise's gentle hand on my shoulder dragged me awake.

"It's your turn," he whispered.

I scrambled to my feet quietly, taking his place on the same log, eyes on the forest and sword in hand, even though it wouldn't do much.

The woods were silent aside from the biting wind. I shivered, unbuckling my jerkin, hoping the extra air would dry the tunic underneath even if it was cold.

After a minute, the needles crunched behind me. I knew exactly who it was.

"You should be sleeping," I scolded.

Blaise sank beside me, and I didn't move. He still smelled like cinnamon, even though none of us had bathed in days. It was as intoxicating as I remember, and it beckoned me. I knew myself, but I wasn't the same person I was a week ago.

I needed him to stay away from me.

"I can't sleep," he admitted, followed by a beat of silence and a gust of wind before he spoke again. "I can't stop thinking about you, Reina."

"Why?" I whispered.

"The night after the ball, I was ready. If it hadn't been for the demon, I was ready to make 'later' the start of something, Rein. Then, there were the hounds and all I could think about was *you.*

"And when the first officer came back from the keep without you, I almost lost my fucking mind.

"And now? Now, you've been avoiding me when all I've wanted to tell you is *that.*" His voice lowered, and I knew exactly how taut the lines on his forehead were as he spoke. I didn't have to torture myself by looking. "Are you afraid?"

Afraid? I almost laughed. I didn't know what I was feeling, but it certainly wasn't fear.

I knew fear. Fear was staring down a demon, and fear was the sinking desperation that gnawed at my temple when I dragged my brother to Arden's doorstep and begged him to take us in.

Fear was what I endured when Arden put a sword in my hand the first time and told me to be quiet. This twisting in my chest and emptiness in my belly wasn't fear; it was self-preservation.

"I'm not afraid, Blaise." I held his gaze as my nails dug into the rough bark of the tree. If he reached out, I'd let him. "It's different now. It's real."

"It doesn't have to be," he argued.

I turned to him. "I-I don't want to hurt you."

"I know you."

I blinked. The sweet smell of cinnamon swirled around me, and I wanted to lean into it but all that would do was make everything worse. "I'm not who I thought I was, Blaise. It's all fucked—"

His eyes broke contact. "Of course you are. You're strong, ambitious, a swordsman who rivals—"

"And the demon wielder," I pleaded.

His eyes found mine again, and the warmth of his hand covered my own as I leaned in. I shouldn't have done it, but I was weak, I was cold, and there was too much death.

I wanted the fucking warmth of someone else to remind me I was still *alive*.

"I don't care what you are," he murmured, and another gust of wind ripped through the trees.

I leaned closer. His forehead fell against mine, and tears burned my eyes. I didn't deserve the tender way his hand raised to my jaw, or the way his thumb stroked my cheek. But I was powerless.

"Blaise . . ."

"What if we just enjoy this?" he whispered, and his lips brushed mine.

Gods. Cinnamon and morning dew, just as I remembered, and I kissed back. Gods be damned. I kissed his tired, soft, and—*no.* I pulled a hairsbreadth away, and his hands clutched mine as my forehead rested against his.

I didn't want to run, but staying would destroy us both.

"What happens next?" I murmured.

"What do you mean?"

"I lose you, or you lose me."

"We're not dying," he reminded me, and I believed he believed it, but he was wrong. Love felt like dying. Love was delayed, cleaving grief hidden behind warm memories and safe words until those were the only things that remained of it.

"That's not what I'm talking about." My whisper turned pleading. "Even if we live."

Another gust of wind raged, and his saffron eyes narrowed. He drew back, staring at me. "I don't know what you're saying."

"I won't just be a Queensguard knight, Blaise. I'm the first *dreosen* in two fucking centuries and the first of Thera." My gaze tightened, and my hands squeezed; I needed him to hear me. I needed to hear myself. "I won't have a life outside of that. My life starts and ends with the Crown."

"That isn't what you wanted. You said it while we danced. I *heard* you." A shadow crossed his face; it was the first crack as I chipped away at him.

"I did. I did want that, but this isn't . . . I can't and I never should—"

"We could try." It was his turn to plead with me.

"Blaise, I know how this ends."

His hands fell out of mine, but his eyes still pinned me in place. "Tell me you don't want me," he whispered, voice stern.

"I don't deserve you."

"Say it, Reina," he muttered.

"Blaise." I drew his name out desperately. My hands fell to my sides. "I can't have anyone. I can't—"

He glared at me, and it shook something loose. "Can't or won't?"

"I can't," I whispered, a part of me breaking too. Maybe it was good we had this conversation before we got back to the Armory, or maybe it was worse.

Blaise got up and walked away without another word.

I never should have said what I did at the ball but *fuck*, I wanted something almost real, and he was my one last, choking gasp at it. Arden kept me well away from anything real because I was his viper, his favorite weapon, and I wasn't made for love.

I was made for old gods, the Crown, and the demons that haunted both.

The sooner I accepted that, the stronger I would be.

Chapter 15

Two days later, our footsteps echoed off the Atrium marble, below a sea of black banners as we dropped the body of the dreite at the feet of General Linden and several other Crown advisors. They stood around their dais as attendants buzzed around, preparing it with flowers and silk.

Linden said nothing, but his thin lips curled up in a sadistic smile, evaluating the success of the trial before he ever looked at Avi.

"Impressive work, Captain," he praised. "Ceremonies will start within the hour. Ready your house."

Two decorated knights in navy cloaks swept in from behind Linden. They picked up the dreite without magic and disappeared down a hallway.

I wouldn't know what happened next; we were dismissed to our quarters, which were painfully silent as the weight of who was missing settled in. Aixen leaned against the wall, staring at the door that had been Eral's. Beside it was Rodrick and the room he shared with Ren. No one but the Armory staff would open their door today.

Leena was bathing at the basin with a washrag when I reached our room. I tugged at the straps of my jerkin and froze when a new set of leathers caught my eye. They were draped over our beds and carefully arranged. The embroidered crest on the jerkin was clearly visible atop a soldier's cape in a deep, emerald green, trimmed with silver fringe—the Theranian crest on either side.

A pin rested on top of them in a small, opened navy box. We'd survived our first year in the Armory, and now we were fully soldiers for the Crown—one year closer to calling ourselves Queensguard knights.

Leena came up behind me, wrapped in a towel. "Your turn." She paused. "Capes? Gods, I can't imagine what Moer would think if I turned up to Rowane wearing that."

"Arden would laugh." I reached for the cape, stifling a grin as the silver fringe slipped through my fingers. A knock from Doris sounded on the door, warning us we only had five minutes to finish.

So much for a bath. I cursed and did my best to scrub the dirt off my face and braid my hair, but I still smelled like sweat and outside. It didn't matter. I put the leathers on anyway and prayed to the gods no one would notice.

The last part of the uniform was the thick green cape. I tried to fasten it, but my fingers kept sliding off the silver clips. It was rejecting me exactly the way I thought it should. By force, it finally gave in and didn't fall off my shoulders. The cape was askew when I glanced in the mirror, but it didn't diminish the effect; I looked like a fucking Queensguard knight.

Every hair on my body prickled and twisted with wrongness, but I couldn't dwell on it. Leena tugged my arm, and we left the room to line up outside the Atrium with the rest of our house.

We walked through the narrow stone halls, and Leena pushed something into my hand. Of course. How could I forget our ribbon? I smiled and tied it around the base of my braid as she did the same.

Ahead of us, Doris wore emerald robes instead of her usual riding pants and tunic. It was a special day, and everyone seemed to go out of their way to remind us. She raised her palm to stop us in the Atrium corridor while we waited for our name.

Looking around, many of us had survived, and I was grateful for it. But it all still felt wrong. Eral should have been here, Ren and Terra should have been here, Rodrick and Max should have been here.

Instead, they were black banners and names on a list to be etched on the Atrium floor.

The Armory made us soldiers and forged us into survivors.

Footsteps came up behind us. We swiveled to look as Jaxon, our only champion, walked in first with a vacant expression and her dual silver cords.

Behind her were our six second-years. Devon's usual dark brown complexion was pale as his hand grasped Avi's shoulder, while Farran stood on his other side. Both of them looked regal in their epaulets and cords.

Farran's eyes met mine, and I immediately looked away.

This was our first presentation following a trial and the first time we'd be on display for the Crown and the makers who represented the kingdom of Thera.

A soft pull on my cape turned me around. Farran looked down, brow lifted in amusement, but his hand remained on my cape.

"You have it fastened wrong," he said, voice low enough to qualify as a whisper.

Gods be damned, he smelled like the faint vanilla of an egg tart and wafting cedar while I was certain I smelled more like the horses out back. I frowned but didn't protest as his hands unfastened the cape, rearranged it on my shoulder, and clicked it back in place.

"There," he said with a nod.

My cheeks burned; everyone in the house had seen it.

I lifted my chin. "I could have done that myself."

He smiled, but it quickly fell away.

"*Emerald.*"

The word rumbled through the hallway from a booming voice in the Atrium, one I didn't recognize. Doris pushed open the doors and we marched in: heads high, backs straight, and our faces betraying no emotion . . . even as we walked beneath the rafters of the Atrium where nearly fifty black banners hung.

Ten of them were our own. I hoped the Crown was fucking proud.

We were the last house to enter for once, and the Atrium was silent as we took our place beside Ruby. The echo of our footsteps resounded off the glass. It was strange how hollow the room could be even when it was filled with people.

The dais was adorned with lilies and other white flowers woven around navy silk for the occasion. Nobles, makers, and high-ranking members of the queen's court stood on it, all outfitted in the midnight blue and silver of the crown we served.

General Linden stood at the center with the same sordid grin. The medals and honors boasted across his chest clinked as he walked. Behind him, other Queensguard knights and military designates stood, and I recognized Caro among them, his sharp mustache setting him apart.

Beside them stood all thirty-eight makers. All of them wore the color of their houses. Avernought stood closest to the general, and he flashed me a knowing smile.

The ceremony began with general remarks about our strength and the pride we've brought to our kingdom. The boasting was followed by a commemoration for the soldiers we lost, but they couldn't be bothered to list the names.

"All houses faced their trials admirably," Linden said as he took the podium again; yellow tendrils swirled around his neck, his voice growing louder. "However, only two houses completed theirs, and they will be rewarded with first dismissal."

The sound of uncomfortable shifting filled the Atrium, accented with whispers.

"Emerald House, please step forward."

Doris led us to the front of the dais. The steady burn of every eye in the fucking Atrium was on us now. Every soldier sized us up as we took our place before Linden and our makers.

"Welcome back from your trial," General Linden greeted. "We were all very impressed. The reports were harrowing, and we are deeply sorry for the losses you suffered. Their sacrifice will not be in vain. The gods don't make mistakes."

Those words were enough to make me lightheaded, or perhaps it was the overwhelming odor of the thousand white lilies decorating the dais. I wondered whose idea it was to make the kingdom flower one that reeked.

"Champion Jaxon Alderan, please step forward."

Alderan. I knew her father. I shivered as Jaxon pushed her way through us, standing in the space between the dais and our house. He died a traitor nearly three years ago when a Crown knight double-crossed Arden.

Linden continued, "In all of your trials, you have brought great pride to your maker, Lady Verdura. The Crown has an offer for your continued service, and hers."

Lady Verdura stepped around Avernought to stand beside Linden. She wore an unseasonably heavy gown of green, embroidered with silver thread in the shape of vines. The general handed her a folded piece of paper, which she snatched and read as quickly as she could.

Her eyes glanced at Jaxon, but her hesitation was nonexistent as she folded the paper and smiled at the general. "We accept your generous offer."

The makers owned their chosen and could reject the Crown's offer if they didn't find it fair. Or if they wanted to keep a champion on their own payroll and forfeit the Crown's payout. It didn't happen often, but it happened occasionally.

Jaxon knew what it meant. She lowered herself to one knee and remained stoic and unmoving.

"Jaxon Alderan, Knight of the Queensguard and protector of Thera. Do you vow to dedicate every part of yourself to the Crown and the continuation of peace? Do you offer your life to wear the cape and the weight of Thera's future?"

Jaxon closed a fist over her chest and spoke with an even voice, "I dedicate my life to the Crown, to Thera, from this day forward until my last dying breath."

"Rise and come forward," he beckoned.

Jaxon stepped onto the dais and kneeled again before the general. Someone walked out from behind him with the queen's cape of deep blue draped over his arms.

The man had dark, slicked-back hair and sharp features. A thin crown rested over his temple, and I had no doubts this was the crown prince; he was practically a twin to Farran if it wasn't for his olive-green eyes and well-groomed hair.

An advisor removed the emerald cape from Jaxon's shoulders as the crown prince placed and arranged the new one. He fastened it quickly and stuck a new pin on the right side of her lapel.

"You may rise, Dame Jaxon Alderan, Knight and Dragon Rider of Thera, guard of the queen, and defender of the Crown. I look forward to our partnership." The crown prince gave Jaxon a wry smile.

Jaxon stood and bowed.

A slow trickle of applause echoed in the Atrium.

From this day forward, she was a member of the Queensguard Knighthood: a knight for the Crown until the dawn of her last day.

For almost no reason, I thought about Farran's hands as they refastened my cape. I buried the thought; no part of me should have been thinking about his hands or how close he'd been earlier. I served the Crown, and those hands would never serve me.

"Dame Alderan, you are dismissed. Please gather your belongings. Our company will leave for Rowane at first light."

Jaxon left the Atrium without a word. This would be the last time we saw her unless we joined her in Rowane at the palace—if we joined her in Rowane, I supposed. Or wherever they decide to assign her.

There were still twelve other duchies and a hundred other keeps they could send us to. We were soldiers of the Crown, and it was our duty to serve.

Linden cleared his throat and surveyed my house. "Fine work on a complicated trial. Captain Valois, you lead well for your first trial at the helm. Lady Verdura, your maker, was more than pleased you secured a dreite priest. This gives the Crown an invaluable advantage.

"I apologize for the shadow hound attack. They are unpredictable, but the experience was formative, I'm sure. We worried withholding Onyx would hinder your progress, but you found a way across the Tharamund Sea by calling on your champions' dragons. The queen was duly impressed and provided an award to Lady Verdura for Captain Valois's quick thinking.

"The queen has also presented an award to Lord Avernought for the impressive first trial of Reina Sangrey, the first *dreosen* of Thera. While it's atypical to award a soldier before they're formally pledged, this is to ensure there is no confusion. Valuable assets have caused . . . unfortunate accidents."

At his words, I shifted on my feet and balled my hands into fists.

"Thank you again, Emerald House. Congratulations on your successful trial, and best of luck in the year to come. You are dismissed. May the wind be at your back and the gods at your side."

I hated the phrase more and more every time I heard it.

If the wind were at my back, my hair would be a tangled mess.

CHAPTER 16

GUARDS USHERED US OUT immediately. I was thankful to leave, but I'm sure it would have been helpful to hear what the other trials were and what gifts the other houses had. We'd all face each other eventually.

"Our trunks are packed," Leena said when we returned to our room, and she was right.

The room looked exactly as it had the day we moved in. Our single trunks, made beds, and a room that echoed with everything else emptied out.

We were second-years now. All it took: one trial and a pat on the back below the black banners of our friends. We survived.

Moments later came a timid knock on the door.

"Come in," I said warily.

Four servants shuffled in with wide eyes, wearing plain clothes and navy sashes with the Crown crest embroidered into them. The tallest of them walked towards my trunk and nodded at the others. They grabbed Leena's trunk, then disappeared into the hallway.

I'd seen servants in the Armory before. They served us meals and cleaned up. Some fixed the doors and windows, and there was even a rumor we had a blacksmith somewhere in the castle. They weren't allowed to speak to us as far as I knew.

There were rules, customs, and cruelty in the Armory I didn't understand where, in Arden's estate, several of the servants were as sharp as he was. It took me a few weeks to get used to the change.

"Do you think they speak in the palace?" I asked Leena, frowning slightly.

She shrugged, her braid falling over her left shoulder as she shifted her cape. "They speak in noble houses. That's how I learned about the Armory; a noble speaking about it with a serving girl. Are we supposed to follow them?"

I shook my head. "Let's wait for Doris."

"Fine," Leena sighed and sat on the edge of her bed. "I just hope the rooms are bigger."

"I do, too. Maybe we'll have a real tub and not a dumb basin."

"Oh, can you imagine?" Leena's golden eyes looked caught in a daydream. "We *are* soldiers of the Crown now. I've heard members of the Queensguard get whole houses in Rowane; surely, they could spare a bathtub for their newest pawns."

I flashed Leena a grin. "Pawns? Some might say that's treason."

Someone pounded on our door with the broadside of their fist. I opened it to see Doris standing there, small in stature but great in presence. As long as whatever happened next resulted in a feast or going to bed, I wouldn't complain.

"Follow me."

We were the last door she'd knocked on, and the rest of our newly minted second-years waited in the hallway. Aixen and Varyn looked exhausted. Blaise stood behind them, and I watched the tension in his face ripple as the ceiling became incredibly interesting.

Good to know our conversation was sitting well.

From the time we arrived, every part of our day was scheduled by Doris. No one left a room or walked down a hallway between breakfast and dinner with the approval of house leadership.

Doris was our house instructor and former lieutenant for the Queensguard. Instructors were always former lieutenants because their job was to protect and train the makers' investment until we made it through our first trial.

Then the responsibility passed to our captain.

Outside of instructors, the Crown saw little reason to dedicate any other military resources to watching us. The Armory was the most fortified keep in all of Thera, not because of the location or architecture, but because of those who inhabited it.

If we died within these walls, we didn't have what it took to be a Knight of the Queensguard.

Doris led us down the familiar passages, towards the Atrium. But where we always turned left, we now turned right and down another hallway we'd never walked down before. It led us into the newer wing of the Armory and up a rounded stairwell we climbed for three flights until she pushed open a door and ushered us into a wide room.

It was a cozy common area, filled with bookshelves and haphazard overstuffed furniture. Flames crackled in a fireplace at the far end, and several plush rugs were laid over stone floors, which gave the room a sense of warmth of home. It was unexpected after the coldness of first-year wing.

"You all get your own room. Names are on the doors and will be removed tomorrow. Your captain will show you around once you're settled. This will be your home for the next two years. Please respect it. Congratulations, soldiers, and thank you on behalf of Thera."

Doris offered a gracious nod and went back the way she came.

The second the door closed, Tomas whistled as he peeked through a bedroom door. "Damn, I didn't realize the first-years were prisoners."

Aixen and Varyn looked for their own. I counted the doors. If all the first years survived our first trial, we wouldn't have enough rooms. There were only twenty-two doors. Without Jaxon, our house was down to nineteen.

"Not dying certainly has its perks," Varyn concurred as he found his door.

"Makes sense, if we're almost the Queensguard," Aixen muttered. He found his name and quickly disappeared behind it. As much as we had to celebrate, we had plenty to mourn.

Leena squeezed my hand and smiled. "I'll miss sharing a room, I think."

"Me too," I said and squeezed back. "But my door is always open."

"Even if someone else is in it?" Her eyes twinkled mischievously, and my face broke into a grin. But deep down, the answer was no. I wouldn't make that mistake again—I couldn't. Every time I looked at Blaise, I felt the pang of guilt and grief.

"You're wicked, Leena," I mumbled.

"I'm honest."

Unsure whether Blaise had heard us or not, I watched him stalk forward and slam the door to his own room. I was losing sleep too, but if I was fine with my decision, he ought to be as well.

My room was beside Leena's and farthest from the stairs. I had to agree with Tomas. I opened the door and froze—first-years were prisoners.

A large four-poster bed sat in the middle of the room on a green rug. White curtains hung around it, and a lit fireplace sat opposite, which seemed odd for the last week of summer, but the nights had cooled off. Two small, grated windows looked over the Armory yard.

Beside the windows were a wardrobe and a desk. I opened the wardrobe to see it was stocked with formal leathers and lesser ones for training. Underneath them, I spotted a new pair of boots. *The Armory always provided.*

Gods, I didn't even care that everything had the crest of Thera on it.

On the desk, below the window, something glinted in the light and caught my breath. Set against a drape of navy silk was a sword I'd never be worthy of wielding.

Whorls of obsidian and steel flickered in the light cast across it—dragon-forged. I brushed my fingers along the golden hilt. The pommel was black with a familiar, large onyx stone set in the center; a perfect echo of my dagger. The same blacksmith must have forged them.

My fingers wrapped around the hilt and swung towards the bed, careful not to catch the blade. It was weightless and fit in my hand as if it was never meant to be held by anyone else.

I'd held many beautiful swords, but none sang like this one; this sword would be a part of me the same way my dagger was. I gingerly set it down and saw the note sitting beside it.

> *I've heard a viper has two fangs. Consider this your second. Be wise. May the gods be the wind at your back. We'll speak shortly. - Avernought*

I tore the note apart and threw it into the fire. The reminder was unnecessary; if anyone had seen that, I'd be dead where I stood.

Yes, I was the viper, and I was playing my part just fine.

Across the room, another door caught my attention. I pushed it open and doubled over.

A *bathroom*. And not just any bathroom: a lord's bathroom with a tub that filled on its own, a pedestal sink, and a toilet with a handle. *Plumbing*. Gods and fucking stars, I hadn't lived in a space with true plumbing in over a year now.

I stopped the drain, twisted the faucet, and dumped an entire vial of soap into it. A scent I couldn't place filled the bathroom, some blend of the woods and a spring meadow after all the flowers opened up. It was a little overwhelming, but it was better than smelling however I smelled.

I didn't hesitate. I shed my clothes and left them on the floor in a disgraceful heap before I dunked into the water.

The silence of being alone soothed every corner of my soul. Velvet suds and warm water relieved all of my apprehension and dread as I scrubbed off a week of dirt, blood, and sweat.

Once my fingers pruned, I dragged myself out and wrapped my body in a lush towel, but I was in no rush to get dressed. Instead, I laid across the bed, draping my wet hair in front of the fire.

I didn't wake until there was a pounding knock on my door; my door—no one else's.

"Just a minute," I yelled. I rushed to my trunk and pulled out a pair of soft, close-cut pants and a cotton tunic.

My hair was dreadfully wet, but it wouldn't dry if I strangled it into a braid now, so I left it. They pounded on my door again, and it rattled the hinges.

I yanked it open, expecting to see Leena. Instead, Farran stood there with books in his arms. His sapphire-blue eyes were deeply amused as he raised a brow and took in my wet hair and the tunic which was now too thin.

"Couldn't even wait for the tour to wash off? Might be a record."

"Can this wait?" I huffed, crossing my arms in dismay.

"Mind if I come in? I have some books and a question for our *dreosen*."

I looked past him to see if anyone else was in the common room.

He cocked his head to the side, and a dark curl sprang out from behind his ear. "It won't take long. Avi's whistling is un-mistakable. You'll hear it in a minute, I swear."

"Fine." I pulled the door open wider and moved aside.

He came in and headed straight for the desk. He intended to put the books there, but noticed the sword and set them on the floor with a pause. I tried not to admire how taut the muscles on his back looked through his fine silk tunic.

"I brought the books at Avi's request; several are from the Crown's library. They're all about powers from the old gods and what's known about demon wielding. There's another on sigils that came from my mother's private collection," he explained.

"Certainly, this could've waited." My eyes followed him as he strode away from the desk and leaned against the wall by the fireplace with his arms crossed. His dark hair was unbound, and he was barefoot, dressed in plain clothes not dissimilar to mine. His untied tunic revealed black swirls of a tattoo on his chest, and I tried not to look.

"Yes, however, I wanted to see what Avernought bought you as a reward." His gaze shifted to the sword on my desk. "I'd say I'm jealous, but mine is bigger."

My eyes narrowed at the prince. It was so obvious. "At least I know what to do with it."

His eyebrows raised. "It's dragon-forged, but I'm sure you knew that."

"I did," I said, keeping my tone even. "It's also very sharp."

"Then you also know," he continued and took a step closer to me for no reason, "it's not often the Crown grants an award to anyone on their first trial."

"General Linden did say that out loud."

"Just a warning," Farran said lightly. "I'd keep a weapon around. You're worth more than me, and you've already been attacked once."

"He didn't even scratch me," I muttered as I looked at the ground a second before looking back at him. His lips quirked up; gods, he was smug. "You seem awfully sure I'm worth more than a prince?"

He nodded. "A *third* prince."

"So that your brother today, the crown prince?"

"Cormac," he said, and some of the smugness faded as his eyes looked past me with an expression I couldn't read, something between wistful and concerned.

"Was he made by Avernought?" I pressed.

"No, he was a griffon rider in Onyx. Cormac was granted to Lord Lazure as a favor for thwarting an attempt on his life," the prince supplied. "He must be itching to get out of the palace. Usually, my uncle, the prince commander, does the knighthood ceremony."

"Interesting." I shifted on my feet, unsure what to do with the information that felt too personal. "Why were you granted to Avernought? Another life debt?"

He cocked his head and met my eyes again. Something about the way he looked left me craving more answers.

"No." He shook his head. "Avernought outbid the other makers and made my mother some promises. As her third living son, I don't think she's particularly strategic about my life so long as I keep it."

"Who was Avernought's champion this year?"

"Landry." Farran looked past me again as a flash of grief shadowed his eyes. "He almost made it to knighthood. But, had Landry risen, Avernought would have turned down the Crown's offer and kept him as a personal guard."

"Did he tell you that?" I asked.

Farran nodded, and a heartbeat later, a very loud and continuous whistle echoed from the common area. Farran smiled quickly before he left the room with me close behind.

I ignored a wide-eyed look from Leena, who definitely saw the prince leave my quarters. It struck me that I was probably supposed to bow at some point during the whole exchange, but I'd worry about formality when someone told me to.

Besides, he came into my room, and I didn't want to think about that either.

CHAPTER 17

Avi led us on a tour of the new wing of the castle. She showed us the amenities available to second and third-years: a training room, a library, a few study rooms, even a large underground pool for training and perhaps other reasons.

None of the rooms were exclusive to a single house. It was completely unlike the first-year wing where they kept us divided.

I swallowed hard. We'd be dining with everyone we faced in trial and training beside them. Farran was right to warn me about walking around unarmed, especially when guards weren't something the Armory had many of, unless a maker provided one from their own private militia . . . Which was far more of an embarrassment than an honor.

The tour ended in the dining hall, where two rows of long tables spanned the length of the room. Servers brought out wine and colorful plates of butter pepper stuffed hens, served on a bed of foraged greens with berries and citrus which had certainly traveled a great distance.

We stuffed our faces as if we hadn't seen a hot meal in months. The Armory had outdone itself, and the air of celebration was undeniable with all the chatter and laughter in the room.

After dessert, the captain from Onyx started a chorus of drinking songs. I shared a wide-eyed glance with Leena. We'd had some wine, sure, but not nearly enough to want to join, so we excused ourselves and went back to Leena's room. It was identical to mine, except she had already scattered around the contents of her trunk: papers, scarves, a little figurine of a dancing bear, and plenty more.

Out of pure curiosity, I poked around her wardrobe to see if she had anything different. She didn't, but I tugged on the green gown she'd worn to the Maker's Ball a week ago.

"Aren't we supposed to return these?" I wondered.

Leena's eyes flicked up from the book propped open on her lap where she sat on the bed. "No one said anything to me, so I'm keeping it." She shrugged.

The satin fabric rippled across my fingertips as it slipped from my hand and fell back into the shadows. I turned my attention back to Leena, and she must have seen my mischievous smile because her lips curled to match.

"You have an idea, don't you?"

"I do." A daring idea, in fact. Was it the wine, or was it the sick thrill of victory trickling through my veins? Honestly, I didn't care. "Do you still have that bottle from the last time we went to Mossford?"

"Of course I do!" Leena's smile turned into a wicked grin, and she shot to her feet without warning and pushed me aside, nearly putting my ass on the floor—admittedly, a hard thing to do.

After some rummaging through the trunk, she pulled out a bottle of amber liquor, and I couldn't think of a more rewarding sight.

Leena held it out towards me. "I don't think anyone's toasted Thera's demon wielder yet?"

I pushed it back towards her. "It's bad luck to toast alone. There's a cup by my sink. Let me grab it!" As quickly as I could, I left her room and ducked into mine. The cup by my sink was a thick, clear piece of hand-blown glass; it sat lopsided and uneven, but it would do.

"What are you doing?"

My eyes darted across the common room as I shut my door. Aixen stood in front of the fireplace, his arms crossed over a blue tunic and his flaxen hair dried flat against his head as eyed the cup in my hand.

"Drinking," I said. "Care to join?"

"Gods alive, *yes*," he groaned.

"Good. Grab a cup, we're in Leena's room."

Leena had already moved the bedside table to a more central place on the stone floor and set the bottle on it. I closed the door and said, "Aixen is joining us."

She grinned as I sat next to her, and a few seconds later, Aixen slipped in.

"I invited Varyn and Evie, too, if they wanted. Blaise declined. Tomas might come, Claude is out fucking. Sparrow might be too. You're really drinking in here?"

"Yes?" Leena's brow furrowed, as did mine. Aixen remained standing, as if he was ready to go. "Where else would we go?"

"Oh." He smiled and ran a hand through his hair, mussing it as mischief glimmered in his eyes. We were all about to get roped into something. "First-years won't be here for a few weeks; Emerald is deserted. We could do one last run in the chapel? Like the first night, bring it all full circle."

"Okay, yeah, that's a better idea." We stood, the bottle sloshing as Leena grabbed it by the neck. Caution gave her a brief pause. "You don't think we'll get stopped?"

Aixen shrugged. "There's no one in the common room if we move fast."

So, we moved fast—irresponsibly fast . . . fast in the way I nearly missed a stair and fell on my knees, but we made it across the Atrium, to the silent and empty fourth floor without getting caught by either our captain or first officer despite the giggling.

It was strange to be back, only hours later, listening to our footsteps echo through the stone halls we'd lived in for a year.

"Old gods or new?" Leena asked. It wasn't much of a question when two of us were from Lower Rowane; the grip of the old gods was strongest in the shadows of the new . . . or something like that.

"Old gods," I said easily.

The house chapels weren't different from each other, aside from the art hung on the walls, which was stodgy at best or indistinguishable at worst.

Supposedly, the chapel art was all repurposed trash, collected during purges and skirmishes that defined the last hundred years of Thera. I didn't believe in much, but that I believed.

Maybe, somewhere in a chapel, was a piece of my parents. After all, our whole house didn't burn, only the wing with their room. Promptly, the Crown emptied the rest of everything important before they leveled the estate into a park a month later. It was a memory just like they were but maybe something survived.

The chapel was just another stone room like our old quarters. Instead of two beds, four rows of benches faced a wooden altar where a stone slab sat on top of a table.

Scorch marks and dust had turned the rough red granite a dull shade of pink. Gaudy, threadbare tapestries hung on the walls, depicting stories of the old gods.

My favorite tapestry was about the Goddess Balris when she slayed a basilisk and took her kingdom, Balria, back from a human king. Even faded, she was poised, standing on the head of the basilisk with her sword hung at her side.

Worshipping the old gods wasn't illegal, but it was frowned upon. There were a hundred stories about nobles being cast from their circles and forced to leave court because they refused to recognize the Seven.

In the same vein, traitors were never hanged because they believed in the old gods, but most had the belief in common.

I sat on the floor beside a bench with my back propped against the wall, while Aixen sat across. A gentle *pop* sounded as Leena opened the bottle and settled, pouring three glasses.

"A toast." Leena grinned and raised her glass as we took ours. "To surviving."

"*To surviving,*" we echoed, and the words fell on the floor as we drank. The liquor burned the back of my throat, Aixen spluttered, and Leena seemed completely unaffected.

"It's better than I thought it would be." Her gold eyes stared at the thin, amber liquid as she swirled it and took the last gulp. "Almost smooth."

"It's poison." Aixen coughed. "You can't tell me that is anything other than poison."

"Want more?" Leena asked.

Aixen rolled his eyes and held his cup out. "Yes, of course I want more."

She poured another round as the first settled in our bones and warmed our blood.

Aixen closed his eyes and leaned against the wall. He murmured, "Remember the first time we were here? We were so damn afraid Doris would come in that Ren and Claude *insisted* on keeping watch in the hallway."

"Was that the same night Varyn learned he had petty magic outside of healing?" I remembered bits and pieces of the evening, but it was one of those memories that felt more like a legend. My eyes narrowed as I tried to recall. "Tomas burned himself to prove he could set a piece of paper on fire from across the room, and Varyn set it on first, then had to heal them both."

"Ah!" Leena squealed. "It *was* that night. How did we even get liquor on the first day?"

"Varyn brought it in his trunk." Aixen grabbed the bottle from Leena to pour more for himself. "He was saving it for a special occasion, but it wasn't hard to convince him our first night in the Armory *was* an occasion."

Aixen took a sip. We remembered that first night in different ways; I was sure. I watched a shadow drift over his face. Grief was the byproduct of love, and it was impossible to talk about our first night without thinking of Eral.

They'd kissed on a dare for the first time, in the corner of this very room, and now Eral was everything none of us wanted to be: a memory.

Leena cleared her throat and raised her glass again.

Aixen and I were apprehensive, but she ignored it. "I have another toast. This one's to the songs they'll sing about us. A silver wielder, a girl with shadows, and Thera's fucking demon wielder," she chimed.

"Here, here," Aixen and I muttered. Our glasses clinked, and we took our swigs.

Footsteps echoed in the hallway, and we stiffened. Aixen got up and poked his head out the door. His voice carried down the hallway, but judging from the way he stood, we weren't in trouble yet.

He sat down again as Varyn and Evie walked in.

It was always interesting to see the two of them together. Varyn was reserved, of average height with unassuming hazel-blue eyes, while Evie was tall and slender, with coils of raven black hair she kept short.

She was outgoing and always ready for a fight. She chalked it up to being raised at Thera's border with Illium, though her father was a commander of the calvary at a southern keep, which likely had more to do with it.

They made themselves comfortable on the floor.

"Aixen said we're getting fucked up tonight." Evie's eyes darted to Leena's with a mischievous glimmer.

"One could say that." Leena poured another round.

I hoped we had more than this bottle; it was already halfway gone, but maybe it was enough. My head swirled pleasantly, and the grief below my lungs transformed into a wispy, achy reminder.

Varyn took his glass and glanced at all of us. "Can I make a toast?"

"The floor is yours." Aixen bowed awkwardly from where he sat, and we giggled. "If you planned to toast to our intrinsic magic or surviving, you'll need to find something different."

"How about this?" Varyn held his glass as high as he could. "A toast to Emerald. May we crush our enemies and avenge the gods who gifted us."

"*Here, here!*" The clink of glasses bounced off the stone walls as we laughed.

"That was a really good fucking toast," Leena muttered. "We have to play a game. We can't do another toast again. It's over."

Aixen dug around in his pocket and pulled out several coins with a devious smirk. "It's been a while since anyone's laid down the gauntlet." Several *oohs* reverberated through the chapel as he turned the coins over in his fingers. "I'm challenging Evie: from here, one coin, center of the altar stone. Three turns."

"I accept your challenge." Evie rose, drawing three coins from her pocket.

They took turns throwing them at the altar stone. Varyn was the appointed judge. Evie won the first round by a hair's breadth, which meant Aixen had to take a drag from the bottle.

Next, Evie challenged me. For this round, Leena moved a lit candle to a more prominent place atop the altar. "The coin has to touch the flame."

I missed the altar entirely on the first toss. My second was worse. The third touched the flame, but it went careening into the wall, so Evie won again. And after that gulp, I had plenty to drink for the night.

We continued to play the game and laughed as it escalated. At one point, Leena conjured shadow rings and other obstacles as Aixen and Varyn became increasingly desperate to beat Evie. Aixen screamed and fell to his knees in utter defeat when a throw bounced off the ceiling and missed by a sliver.

"Gods, that hurt to watch." I stood and stretched my arms. "I think Evie is the true gauntlet champion."

Aixen's face darkened with competitive spirit and a sly grin. "I will never accept defeat, Sangrey."

"Right," I smirked. "Well, I'm going to bed. I hope to hear the story of your great triumph over breakfast, Reid."

"Oh, you will," Aixen promised.

"Good night, all." I yawned, walking out of the chapel.

The shouting of my friends faded as I ambled down the hall. In the stairwell, even more laughter echoed; we weren't the only house drinking where it all began.

Tonight was a celebration, despite the black banners. I moved through the Atrium like a ghost—or the drunk illusion of one as liquor lightened every part of me.

I even twirled across the marble floor, looking through the glass at the stars shining above; there was something magical about being alone in the Atrium in the dead of night, when all the threats and propriety were gone. It was just a beautiful, giant room—

"There you are."

Oh, good fucking gods. I spun around, wobbling on my heels as they slipped on the smooth marble. Farran stalked towards me, followed closely by Avi and Vera.

"Is everyone else in the chapel?" Avi asked with a sigh, the shadows under her eyes betraying how exhausted she was.

"Yes, but *I* was on my way to the library."

Farran's eyes narrowed, but he couldn't hide the amusement dancing across his lips. "Oh, you were?"

"Yes," I sassed, crossing my arms defiantly. *Too much to drink, far too much.* I tried to blink the boldness away, but it bubbled forward, unabashedly admiring the way Farran's cheekbones looked in the moonlight as it fell through the Atrium ceiling, knowing I'd regret it tomorrow.

"We'll get the rest of them," Avi said, exasperation graveling her voice. "Can you make sure the *dreosen* gets back, First Officer?"

"I'm perfectly capable of getting myself back," I slurred.

Avi frowned. "I'd believe it if you weren't drunk and standing unarmed in a military fortress after you were rewarded in front of every house—bit risky."

I opened my mouth to say something brash, or perhaps witty, but thought better of it. Avi was right, and the look on her face was a challenge I needed to back down from. I gestured to it, but neither she nor Farran were impressed by the dagger tucked in my breeches.

Indignant as a caught child, I didn't move. Avi and Vera left for the staircase to gather everyone else, leaving me with Farran.

"Which is it?" Farran asked. "Library or back to Emerald?"

Gods be damned. His eyes glittered in the fucking moonlight like a fishpond. No, wait, that was a bad analogy. They were blue. I had better words somewhere. They just weren't in a hurry.

I'd been alone with him before, but the alcohol twisted everything in me and pinched my words.

"Back. Let's just go back," I said, stiffening.

"Your wish is my command, darling." Farran gave a false bow, and a part of me shivered. It was such a delicious thought, but I needed my blood to stop humming in my ears and overriding the little sense I still had as we walked back. "You looked quite at peace twirling around the Atrium."

Heat flushed my cheeks as we walked down the narrow stone passage. "You didn't see that."

"Oh, but I did." He grinned and turned as his steps slowed. "Who were you before the Armory, Reina Sangrey? I'm still not buying barmaid."

"Too bad, Your Highness. That's the truth."

"Is it?" he drawled.

"Yes," I said. Not here, not now. There would never be a place for the truth, not between the two of us.

In fact, I looked around. We certainly weren't going to the common room. He took a turn I didn't recognize, and the corridor we stood in now had windows facing west. In the brief silence, a flicker of doubt brushed against my spine.

Icy sobriety inched my hand towards my dagger. "This isn't the way to the common room, First Officer."

"No, I suppose it's not."

"Where are we going?" I ground out, my fingers fully gripping the hilt of my dagger now.

Farran pointedly smirked. "You'll see."

Wrong thing to say, prince or no. I whipped around, my hand palmed his chest, and pinned him to the wall with my blade dangerously close to breaking the skin on his throat. The surprise on his face was palpable.

His sapphire eyes widened, but he had the nerve to chuckle as his hand wrapped around my wrist.

"Where are we fucking going?" I glared, pushing more of my weight into him.

His muscles twitched under my hand. If he wanted, it would only take a second—two moves—to disarm me. He could kill me right here, and I was at peace with it. Death meant avoiding several long conversations.

"As much as I enjoy being at the end of your blade, Sangrey, please let me go."

"Where are we going?" I pressed.

"Have you never heard of a surprise?"

I readjusted my grip, and he grunted as the cool metal kissed his neck. I smiled, though it didn't last long as I realized how fucking close we were.

It was intoxicating in a different way, and between the woodsy smell and the faint waft of vanilla, he disarmed me. Delicate lines traced his eyes, the bits of black stubble that shadowed his jaw . . . then there were his lips.

"Drop the knife," he warned.

I didn't. "You said we were going back to the common room. We aren't, and if you're here to kill me, you'll have to earn it."

The glare in his eyes cut through me like glass.

"I will *not* fucking hurt you," he said with such conviction, I believed him. My muscles loosened, yet I didn't let him go. I didn't step away.

"Where are we going?" I whispered.

"Emerald now. My mistake."

Finally, I dropped my arms and sheathed my dagger, but my feet didn't move. We were caught in some stalemate, his body nearly pressed against mine and the proximity muddled by liquor. My thoughts of him were a thousand stinging nettles rifling around my ribs.

He didn't touch me, but the magic continued to swirl and burn just below my skin.

It recognized him, and there was something between us that felt ancient, familiar, and impossible—I knew he wouldn't hurt me. I wouldn't hurt him either. The realization was a shock, and I took a step back, remembering who I was.

Farran touched his neck where my blade had been; there was no malice in his gaze, though he looked at me warily and took a step closer. I didn't flinch. I straightened and stared back.

Of course, he couldn't hurt me. My life was worth more. He'd said so himself.

His eyes flicked to my lips for the briefest second, and a different heat turned over between my thighs as a wicked, impulsive part of me had a much worse idea.

"Let's go back," he said. "I'll pretend you didn't pull a knife on your First Officer."

I crossed my arms. "My First Officer led a woman into an unfamiliar hallway under false pretenses."

"A surprise is not a false pretense."

"Depends on the surprise," I mused.

"Now you'll never know," he muttered, but the corner of his lip turned up in a half smile just before he broke away. He strode down the corridor, and I followed, drawn to where the heat had been and whatever the fuck that was.

I couldn't say something bad would happen, but every feeling crawling along my nerves insisted on the possibility.

Chapter 18

THE FIRST TIME I killed someone, I couldn't breathe. It was an accident; Arden let me go too far, and I had no idea how to pull myself back.

I caught an artery where I should have found a vein. Before I could stop it, the man's body slumped. I blinked, my hands were covered in blood and the dagger stuck out from his chest as the smell of copper and shit overwhelmed my senses.

I stumbled back, tripping over my untied shoe. Arden caught me and held me there until my breath steadied. I was only fifteen and already sullied. There wasn't a way back.

His voice cut through the screaming in my head.

"You did so well," Arden said into my hair. *"He deserved it. They all deserved it."*

A year later, the rumors about Arden's viper began to spread. From there, I became everything I needed to be; I wore every mask I was handed and said yes to anything that would make me worse because I wouldn't hesitate when I killed the Queen of Thera.

That was why I didn't deserve to be here. I didn't deserve to wear the crest, the honors, or the trust of anyone because every breath I took betrayed it. I woke up feeling sick about it because I couldn't stop thinking about the way Farran looked at me.

I crawled out of my room and knocked on Leena's, an hour past first light. We trudged to the dining hall, and I knew Leena was waiting for me to say something. I didn't; I just stared at the ground.

This morning, her hair was completely unbound and kept getting caught on my sweater. She broke the silence as we rounded a corner. "What did Farran want with you yesterday? In your room?"

I ignored her, mostly, and continued staring straight ahead. Thank gods she didn't know he walked me back from the chapel; that wasn't something I was ready to explain.

"He dropped off some books about demon wielders," I said, as if the sentence encapsulated everything. "It wasn't anything important."

She lowered her voice to match mine, a grin playing at her lips. "He is your *ontaros*."

"He's not anything but my first officer, the same way he's yours." I swiveled away from her and picked up my pace towards the dining hall, trying not to think about what Blaise had seen.

Leena ran to catch up. "I'm sorry. I'll stop, but you do owe me your stories. Perhaps a throwing lesson later? Like old times."

"Sure, but I promise you'll be disappointed. Secrets for secrets?" I raised my eyebrow and glanced at her. "I want to know more about your shadow hounds."

"Deal," she said as we sat down. Food was already laid on the table for the taking, and most of our house was already eating.

The next table over, there was a woman from Sapphire I remembered from Arden's; Declan would be pleased to know she'd made it through her first trial. A part of me wanted to talk to her, but there wasn't much to say.

Soldiers left their past at the door. The instructors, lieutenants, and generals all drilled it into us on our first day in the Armory, where we promised to be born anew and give our blood to the Crown: that was the first condition.

The second, to control us further, was contraception; we drank a vial of a moon thistle tincture monthly because a child of the Armory was unthinkable unless sanctioned by the Crown.

We drank our tinctures as Avi spread a piece of paper across the table she'd drawn up to look like a calendar. "We have two hours with the makers over lunch today. We're keeping a strict regimen in Emerald, and all of us participate."

She looked straight at Farran, who just settled on the bench and caught my eye.

"One hour of drills in the morning. Breakfast, weapons training, wielding, and night drills before dinner for another hour. We don't know what the next trial will be, or when, but I want to make sure we're getting at least four true hours of training in a day."

"Is this what the other houses are doing?" Tomas asked.

Avi looked straight at him and straightened her shoulders, drawing attention to the captain's epaulets she'd already put on this morning. "It doesn't matter what the other houses are doing. This is what Emerald is doing. We'll be ready for anything."

"It's no use talking her out of it," Farran warned Tomas as he spread jam on a muffin. "Avi knows a thing or two. She has no intention of losing a trial."

After breakfast, we changed into training leathers and met in the Atrium. The black banners had been removed, though the next trial would no doubt bring more. Overhead, the sky was a brilliant blue without a cloud in sight.

This was almost the brightest the Atrium ever got, and I struggled to open my eyes with the way the sun reflected off the expanse of white marble.

The four Emerald makers watched us from their dais while Doris stood with them, sipping on a glass of wine servants kept topping off. There were nineteen of us in total on the Atrium floor. Thirteen of us were newly minted second-years, while two were unpledged third-years, who all vied for the four open spots and the silver cords that came with being pledged to a maker.

Linden had made it clear I belonged to Avernought. There was no point in holding back the way I had before. I couldn't hide, I couldn't change my gift, but I could show them all what I was *always* capable of.

I crossed the floor and stopped at the weapons rack, grateful not to see a single wooden sword.

Several knives and daggers of varied weights and styles laid out on a table and glinted in the sunlight. It'd been so long since I'd seen something so delightful in this room, and I couldn't stop myself. Knives freed me; they were the first weapon Arden taught me once the blood dried on our oath.

I grabbed three, all similar enough, then I stood a distance from the targets on the far end of the Atrium.

I waited for Tomas to wander out of my firing line before throwing the first knife. It whistled through the air and hit its mark with a decisive *snap*. It was slightly off from the center, but I could live with it.

The second was dead center. A few of my housemates whistled; someone clapped. When I threw the third, it stuck just above the second. I'd hit exactly what I wanted.

I grinned, turning my attention to the dais where Avernought stood, but I was caught off guard by his company. Farran stood beside him, and pride pulled at the corner of his mouth. My breath caught.

"Avernought would like to speak with you." Avi's voice cut through my thoughts, and I nodded. As much as I wanted my house to know what I was capable of, without demons, I didn't want Avernought to forget either.

I charged toward our familiar alcove, and the maker pulled the door closed.

"Reina Sangrey, I wanted to give you my congratulations in person," he said with a genteel nod bordering on a bow I didn't deserve. "The Crown is impressed you brought back a dreite priest, and I am as well."

"All to serve the Crown," I said in a practiced voice. His green eyes looked me up and down. Today, he wore a plain blue doublet over riding breeches. "Has the priest woken up?"

"I wouldn't know. Merchants don't get answers, even when it's our coin paying for it." His eyes glimmered as his fingers played with a thin gold chain hanging around his neck. "What did you think of your reward?"

"Very generous and unnecessary, but it's beautiful. Thank you."

Avernought smiled. "Damien designed it but, alas, nothing is unnecessary when it comes to you."

The words struck me with sudden, choking force, and I stiffened. I thought about Farran and the careful words of the priestess. "Why do you think that?"

"I think you mean to ask how?"

"I wasn't invited to the Armory for grammar."

"Sharp. Bodes well for the upcoming trials." He chuckled, ignoring my question as something in my chest went taut. He lowered his gaze and leaned forward, pinning me in place. "There is much talk about your wielding ability, but soon they'll talk about your other abilities . . . Especially for what you did a minute ago."

"Is it a problem?" I asked, narrowing my eyes.

"I would never ask an artist to hold back, Reina. I've tied my hands to yours for a reason. You will honor the gods, and there is a plan so long as the prince doesn't become a threat to you." His gaze sharpened. "The Crown needs you both, as does Thera, but only for now. The queen will settle for one if she deems you too much trouble, and I can think of certain secrets which might come to light." Avernought's small blue eyes sparked with warning.

I straightened my shoulders. "I have no intention of letting that happen."

"I saw the way the prince looked at you. Don't tell me there isn't trouble."

"No one throws a knife quite like I do. He admired me the same as the rest of the room, Lord Avernought."

"Lukas," he corrected and crossed his arms, amused. "Regardless, tomorrow I'll formally make my pledge to be your maker. Expect to serve Her Majesty's knighthood in two years' time. Perhaps less if I can talk her into a waiver. The sooner you have the formal protection of Thera's Crown, the safer you'll be."

"I have no objections." An itch prickled my back where the blood oath was drawn. I never considered a rise to the Queensguard before three years. I could be released from Arden's debt sooner.

"Good. I will be in touch. I've heard a rumor Arden will be, as well. He may speak more freely than I." I knew they talked, but the acknowledgement here, in the hallways of the Armory, felt like treason. "One more thing, Reina."

I looked at him and held steady. "Yes?"

"You will formally belong to me, and I maintain a certain image. Your first trial was a success by completion, but when I receive the crier's recount of your next, I expect to hear how you used your demons or I will speak to Doris and Linden about organizing an arena trial."

My throat tightened. "Let's hope it doesn't come to that."

"Indeed," he said, and I followed Lukas Avernought, *my* maker, back to the Atrium.

I preferred a trial with the audience removed. It was barbaric to stand us all against each other in an arena melee. Though it had been years since the last true arena trial, they were a tax boon for whatever city hosted, and the makers loved any opportunity to watch their chess pieces tear each other apart; it was the closest they came to ripping apart one another.

My feet barely came to a stop beside the rack when a dull sword was thrust into my hand. I took it and glanced up; Farran stood on the other end.

The endlessness of his sapphire eyes gleamed. It was distracting and unfair for any human to have eyes like that, and everything that happened last night in the hallway came tumbling back with a tinge of embarrassment.

"Spar? We haven't had the opportunity yet, darling," he drawled.

"Don't patronize me, First Officer," I warned, but he only grinned. "Can't it wait until the makers aren't watching?"

"It doesn't matter if you've pledged, does it? Isn't that what he spoke to you about? Even if you lose terribly, you're still the *dreosen*."

Oh, he'd heard. I squinted. "So, this is where you try to kill me?"

"Me?" he scoffed. "If anything, I'm giving you the opportunity. You seemed excited to try last night." Farran's voice lowered, and the red in my cheeks deepened. "Or did you forget I was there when you slaughtered those demons? I know what you're capable of."

I stiffened, swallowing hard. "I didn't forget."

He rolled his shoulders back, and smugness pulled up the corners of his mouth as he nudged the sword dangling from my hand with his own. I looked around to see if I had any excuses. Leena sparred with Tomas, Aixen bent silver, while Blaise and Vera watched.

Everyone was training, and there was nowhere else for me to hide in the middle of the glass hall.

Fuck.

Farran took a step back, but the faint woodsy, sweet scent of him lingered. His legs spread apart, his sword pointed at the ground. "You do know how to spar, don't you?"

"Of course I do." I took a step back and sized him up. We were doing this.

Farran was decidedly taller than I, with much broader shoulders. This practice sword was steel and had none of the elegance of the one on my desk. Though it was heavy and awkward, Arden had taught me how to fight through an imperfect weapon; even the wrong one could be efficient.

I struck first, aiming straight and true, evaluating his reaction to see which side he favored.

Steel hit mine from the left. I let the momentum carry the sword around and gripped it with two hands as I spun. His sword came from above, but I evaded and moved underneath so quickly he stumbled a bit. Not enough to give me an entry point, but any lapse in balance could tip a spar.

I smiled. Then I unleashed myself.

We were a flurry of motion and clanging as one hit the other and we met block for block, parry for parry. The scrape of metal was music to my ears, and I reveled watching sweat build on the prince's temple.

I was made for this. Where his slices were delicate and deadly, mine were vicious and hungry. I was trained to strike in the shadows, where he was trained to show off in front of an audience.

Lithely, I ducked down, spun behind him, and stopped my sword at his throat. He came through a gap on my left, knocked the sword from my hand, and threw it several paces. Then he held the sword to my chin. *Gods be fucking damned.*

"I think I won," Farran said, voice smooth as silk.

He wiped his brow with the back of his hand as he dropped the sword. The Atrium was sweltering in the afternoon sun, and I was sweating too as I pushed myself back to my feet.

"I do have some notes about footwork we can address tomorrow," he added as he set his sword back on the rack and picked up mine.

I glared after him as the bell chimed.

CHAPTER 19

I AVOIDED MY GIFT despite Avernought's veiled threat.

Days dragged on since we'd returned from trial. I read about demon wielding obsessively. But the more I learned, the more I feared who it could turn me into.

There were only eight documented *dreosen*, and all faded into legends about brutal wars and traitors choked by friends before their destruction became irreversible. Only the first *dreosen* in recorded history hadn't been killed in war, and she'd been trained by the Goddess Dreonna—a concept which seemed far-fetched.

All magic had its limits and consequences; *dreosen* were cursed to figure theirs out alone.

Every time I considered touching the warm magic and darkness coiled in my chest, I thought about how the priestess had looked at me and the reverence the demons had even after I'd torn them apart.

It was a ridiculous gift that should have gone to someone else. I never needed a demon to meet my destiny. I needed the title, a solid sword, and the tenuous trust of the queen. I never wanted to be the queen's weapon in a war of kingdoms with the power to lay battlefields to waste; there wasn't an assassin alive who wanted the power.

I couldn't avoid it much longer. Eventually, I'd be cornered into using it. I groaned and rolled over in bed. There was no point in continuing to stare at the ceiling and wish for sleep. I was restless, and the moon was bright. Tonight was as good a night as any other.

Taking a deep breath, I got up and tucked my sword, dagger, and knives safely beneath my cloak.

Then I slipped out of my room. Only the embers in the fireplace lit the common room, but I didn't dwell on it as I started for the door.

"Where are you going?" My head snapped around at the sound of a voice.

Aixen sat on a couch, a book on his lap and several pieces of silver suspended around him as he sipped tea, as if this was a vacation and not the Armory. I also had no idea how he could read when it was this dark.

"For a walk," I said carefully.

"Alone?" He raised a curious brow.

I squinted as a few of the silver pieces fell on the couch; one was clearly a spoon, and another was a small bird. "You want to come?"

"Maybe another night." He thumbed another page in the book.

"Is Blaise around?" I asked, only because I didn't want to get trapped; throughout the first year, Blaise had a habit of finding me at the edge of the woods when I went on a walk.

Aixen's eyes flashed back up. "Not the prince?"

Gods' fucking sakes. "I don't want to see him either." I fought the urge to toss a knife to emphasize my point. "I'm going alone."

"Right, well, be safe. Here if you need me."

I left, descended the stairs, and walked out of the dark and empty Atrium. If there were any guards in the Armory, they were elsewhere. The air outside was cool and crisp as summer drew to a close. I tasted the start of autumn on the breeze as I walked through the overgrown yard towards the tree line.

Pine trees whispered in the wind, and haphazard slivers of moonlight fell on the forest floor as I wandered, looking for the right spot to shrug off my cloak and practice. I'd start with knives and maybe work up the courage to touch the smallest bit of magic in my chest.

The forest around the Armory was difficult to breach by an outside force. Steep hills sloped towards the Ines River, which ran north and had wide, muddy banks.

On the northwest stretch, large cliffs separated the hills and formed maze-like crevices that withstood the test of time. Nestled in one of them was an altar for the old gods I'd found a few times. I was always surprised the Crown hadn't destroyed it.

This altar wasn't anything like the chapel in the Armory: a powerless symbol. The altar in the woods was ancient, real, and called to the darkness roiling in my chest, drawing me closer towards the short ravine where it was nestled between walls of earth.

It wasn't obvious, it was just a slab of plain, gray stone. But that's what made it the true kind of altar devotees gave blood and magic to, hoping for an answered prayer.

I found it last year and occasionally came to admire it and listen to the silence. However, I'd never felt the magnetism I did now, with my gift awakened. I couldn't think of a better place to use my gift for the first time, but near the gods who gifted it.

I shrugged off my cloak, ignoring the way my skin sprouted goosebumps even under the sleeves of my cotton tunic. Maybe I should have worn leathers instead.

Dry pine needles crunched behind me, and the hairs on the back of my neck bristled. I wasn't alone, and I definitely should have worn leathers. I pivoted with precision, eyeing a moving mass in the shadows at the entrance of the ravine.

The knife clutched in my hand flew forward, striking a tree at the entrance with a *thwack*.

"*What the fuck?*" someone sputtered.

I drew my sword and took several steps closer. A man was stuck to the pine tree by his cloak, and in a second, I knew exactly who it was. "Farran?" I narrowed my eyes. Of course. "Is this another surprise? I thought I made myself very clear."

He had the audacity to *smile*. "As much as I admire your accuracy, I'm not eager to have any blade of yours on my neck again. Impressive, though—stuck my cloak and tunic to the damn tree."

I walked forward and stopped in front of him. He was right; it was a good hit.

I leaned in and pulled the knife from the tree with a *hmph* and ignored the way the smell of him mixed with the breeze; gods be damned, vanilla and cedar lingered like he'd been brined in it.

"You shouldn't be out here, darling."

My blood simmered. "No one told me the rules." I waved the knife near his neck as he held up his hands. "I can handle my own." And I was getting tired of saying it.

"Well aware, but I do think you were warned."

"Is that why you followed me?" I retorted.

"Follow is certainly a choice word. Maybe I had an idea."

When he took a step closer, I took one back. The way the moonlight reflected in his blue eyes was mesmerizing and otherworldly.

He was entirely too close. The other day, I didn't think he could hurt me, but something about the shadows contouring his chiseled face had me doubting that anyone would hear me scream.

"I'd think a first officer has more important duties."

"More important than ensuring the safety of his soldiers? Particularly when the most valuable one decides to go traipsing through the woods in the middle of the night?"

I smirked and straightened my posture as a breeze rustled the overhead branches. "I wield demons. You should be more worried about your own safety."

"I don't believe you'd hurt me," he said confidently as he dusted off his cloak and pants.

"Why not?"

"Because I've seen how much you want to and yet—here I stand."

"You're assuming again."

"Am I?" He smirked and took another step closer.

We weren't touching, but I was close enough for my breath to catch from the sudden heat and curl of magic against my ribs as it recognized him. My thoughts spun, and the memory of his hand gripping my chin on the beach made me shiver.

It was only because he was an *ontaros*, a siphon. His magic spoke to everyone's—I was sure of it. I should have taken a step back.

"You haven't wielded a demon," Farran said. "Do that, and maybe I'll be more worried about you." His chest was inches from mine, and his warm breath grazed my face; I didn't shy away. "Maybe this is part of your training, since you've been pretending you don't have a gift."

"What?" I mumbled, snapping out of the trance; I backed away from him.

He shrugged. "I see you holding back. You haven't tried. Was it your choice to come to the altar or—"

I stared at him. "Aren't you supposed to pretend the old gods don't exist?"

Farran relaxed, his voice dropping to a softer register. "I'm not my mother. My father's faith fell at the old gods' feet where my gift is from."

"Can you feel them too?" Everyone in Lower Rowane knew the late prince consort was of the old gods, but it went unspoken in polite company. To acknowledge it bordered on treason; the Crown of Thera belonged to the queen and the Seven.

"Of course I feel them. The woods here are swarming with the old gods' magic. The new ones aren't brave enough to leave the cities."

Treason. That's what edged his words, like he was cornering my thoughts and baiting me to agree. Arden had warned me that many in the Crown's court were trained to bend and twist trust into chains they could control.

A shiver ran up my spine. I didn't break away from his gaze, nor would I take the bait.

He added, "We could be called to another trial at any point. I doubt we'll get so lucky as the last one."

"We didn't get lucky," I reminded him. "We didn't get a dreite priest."

"The Crown sees it as a victory." After a moment of reflection, Farran switched topics quickly, as though he had a checklist. "Where did you learn to fight? I know plenty of men from Lower Rowane who don't have half the skill you do."

"Perhaps they didn't need to learn." That was too honest.

He stiffened, and his jaw tightened with more questions in the silence that followed. A breeze picked up through the trees, and we both looked up. I cursed the smell of him as it eddied around me. This wasn't the time, nor the place, to feel anything.

"For the last time, First Officer, why did you follow me?" I gritted out.

"You should wield a demon tonight."

"No," I spluttered and took a step back. "I'm not. I need to do it alone."

Where no one would know. I wasn't ready for my gift to be real, to know what I was capable of, or for anyone else to witness it. I wanted to live in the softness of denial just a little longer. I should have hidden my avoidance better.

Farran's face took on the same tenderness it had on the beach when I was screaming into the sand. He reached out as if to grab my arm, but thought better of it. "Are you afraid?"

I wished he'd stabbed me; betrayal was better than picking at my open wound. It didn't matter he was right.

"Of course I'm fucking afraid," I snapped. "I have a gift from the Goddess of Death. If you think it's so easy and important, then maybe you should just take it."

"I'm not taking anything from you."

"Why not? I'm offering." I glared.

His eyes narrowed . . . something burned in the blue brilliance of them. Maybe it was the shadow of contempt I deserved, but I wasn't done.

I snapped, "Why not? Crown guards never had a problem taking magic from the drunks in Lower Rowane, so why would a prince be any different? I have what you want; the queen can take the kingdoms with one *dreosen*, and I'm dying a soldier either way, so you might as well kill me here and get it over with."

Farran grabbed my arm and forced me to look him in his eyes; the moonlight in them was more distracting than the sun. I hardly noticed the tendrils of warmth where his hand was. Sheer anger overshadowed it.

"Why do you think I could kill you, Reina?" *Fuck.* The way he said my name and the strength of his grip . . .

I stumbled through the words and bristled. "Because there's no other way out, and I never wanted this." I wanted simple and quiet. Being at the helm of a demon army and conquering kingdoms for a tyrant queen was neither simple nor quiet.

Then there was the way he looked at me.

"I will not be the reason you die," he growled. Silent, dangerous anger flashed through his eyes like a silver knife turning over in a shadow.

I lifted my chin, refusing to back down. "I find that hard to believe."

"*Hard to believe?*" He stilled, his grip tightened on my arm. "If that was true, then tell me, why the fuck did we swear a blood oath before anyone knew who the gods damned *dreosen* was?"

He released my arm, and my voice dropped to a desperate gasp. "No, that's a lie."

The budding heat of magic was nothing compared to the coiling constriction of truth slipping out, and I stepped back. His eyes widened—he didn't mean to say it. I never should have heard it.

My mouth was agape. And still he tugged his tunic, lifting it up to display the full stretch of the tattoo on his chest; over his heart, thin black tendrils like vines folded in and over the abstract memory of a crest I knew. It wasn't written in ink, but the sinews of dried blood, magicked by destiny.

His hands fell to his sides. The fabric obscured it again, and I stumbled back another step as the world bowed.

"Do you know how much fucking danger someone with your power is in? At *all* times? Avernought and the queen demanded it. Avi also swore. And Landry. We swore it for the protection of the realm and whoever the *dreosen* would be."

"We?" I choked, tears burning in my eyes. "Who else?"

Farran bit his tongue; regret shadowed his face.

I narrowed my eyes and repeated my question slower, "*Who? Else?*" My hand twitched towards the hilt of my sword. I knew. I'd seen the mark. I'd traced it with my fingertips.

I just needed to hear it. I needed to know the truth.

"Blaise and Aixen."

I closed my eyes and tried to take a steadying breath. "You all pledged your lives to the *dreosen*?"

"I've said too much." Farran's voice hardened, and his jaw ground. "It happened before you knew, before any of us did. All we knew was Avernought believed he'd bring a wielder to Emerald, and they would need the protection of the strongest house in the Armory, as well as an *ontaros*. The oath was insurance, a promise to keep you alive. Nothing more."

"Nothing more?" I said erratically, my hand on the wall of the ravine to steady myself. "*Nothing more?* It's a fucking blood oath." I knew the weight better than anyone else.

His eyes lifted. "Only until you rise to the Queensguard."

If I had less self-control, I would have set his cloak on fire. I would have set myself on fire. The rage swirled and colored every shred of who I was. I stared at him, mouth open. "If I die, all of you die."

"You weren't supposed to know." Every part of him looked deflated as the words left his lips. "I was quite tired of you begging me to break the oath. I cannot kill you, Sangrey. And worse, I cannot let you kill yourself, which is already quite difficult when you have no regard for your life."

He wasn't wrong, and I'd deal with my truth later. I cleared my throat, but my voice still came out weak and scratchy. "How do I wield a demon?"

Farran looked at me. Not just a glance, but something deeper, something exposing. He said nothing, though I didn't know if there was truly anything else to say; a blood oath had been struck about me, without my permission or my knowledge.

They'd all pledged to protect Arden's viper, and not a single one fucking knew. All of them would curse their position if they found out who they truly protected.

I hoped Avernought was ready to meet the tip of his own sword. Maker or not, he'd made his way to the top of my list tonight. He knew exactly who I was and said nothing. Worse, he tied lives to mine.

Farran's voice cut through my thoughts. It was small . . . soft, even. "Reina, we can go back. I'm sorry, I—"

"No," I said, forcing strength, bolstering every word. "You're right. I'm wielding a demon tonight."

I stalked away, past him and out of the ravine, and steadied myself beneath the trees. I was afraid of my magic, sure, but the anger surging through me was stronger. Anger was a tool the same way magic was; they were twin flames folded and wound around the other, each kindling to a raging inferno.

"Not tonight, Reina," Farran bit out. Frustration bent the words as he ran to catch up.

I didn't give a fuck. I gritted my teeth and planted my feet on the ground. I wasn't leaving. "Fine. I'll see you tomorrow, then."

Farran stopped and stared back, shifting on his feet as he debated with himself. A moment later, he pinched the bridge of his nose and groaned while I closed my eyes and searched for the swell of heat.

This was my intrinsic gift; I didn't need help. The magic had curled itself into my chest when it sensed my anger, so I imagined it unfurling and expanding. I opened my eyes, and the abyss of the forest before us stared back at me. A pulse of magic warmed the space between my heart and ribs, building as I focused.

"What does the magic here feel like to you?" The edge in his voice was a razor blade against my temple.

"Like the center of a fire—pressure and heat, too hot to take color."

He sighed. *Good*. This was torture for both of us. "You could think of it like pulling threads if it's too much. My father said his magic felt the same as working on a loom," he added.

With my eyes forced closed to focus, I pushed through the fire. A rush of heat overwhelmed me as Farran stepped closer, vanilla and cedar briefly distracting my senses, but my fingers curled around the threads knotted in my chest, golden and warm.

I sifted through them, and then I pulled back. I was furious, but none of it meant I couldn't do the thing that scared me most.

Relief tingled against my skin as I found a cold, damp thread; imperceptible power rolled off it in waves and it beckoned me. Instinctively, I focused all of my energy, all of my anger, and yanked it into existence.

The wind tore through the trees. I opened my eyes. Farran stood beside me, watching as a figure came into being and rose from the forest floor.

The tether between me and the beast pulled taut as a tightrope. It stared at us. Its eyes were beady, black, and perceptive. Obsidian scales reflected the moonlight in a million perfect mirrors, and black venom dripped from white fangs as it kneeled.

Watching me, watching us.

"I think you did it." Farran breathed, awe replacing his earlier frustration.

The demon screeched into the night, but didn't move. If I died here, Emerald would almost be quartered. I gulped and took a step forward anyway. Farran remained at my back, unsheathing his sword, poised to strike if necessary.

The memory of the priestess struck me with perfect clarity: *"If you are who I believe you to be, they will rise on your command."*

I motioned for it to rise. The demon's eyes stayed on mine as it obeyed. There was something so familiar in its gaze, something known and unknown.

I gawked. What else did the priestess see in me?

The beating magic in my chest roared to life in the single step I took towards the creature I summoned. The buzzing, weighted power flooded my senses and settled in my shoulders.

Even with the moon's light, it was terribly dark. When I squinted, I could tell the demon wasn't whole. The ones in the keep were solid beings with oily scales in the deepest black I could imagine; this one was black, the scales shined, but it had soft edges. They faded in and out as though it hadn't been fully conjured. Something was missing.

Farran touched my shoulder. I nearly jumped. The demon hissed at him but made no move to attack.

"May I?" he asked lowly.

"May you what?" My brow furrowed, and he only moved closer, stopping just behind me before he reached for my hand.

"My gift works better when there isn't fabric in the way."

The proximity was intoxicating as my back settled against his broad chest; close enough his breath prickled the hair on my neck... I wouldn't—I couldn't—say no even if I hesitated. The way the power and magic thrummed made me feel complete, and I wanted to hold on as long as I could, even if it was getting harder to breathe.

I nodded. He gingerly peeled back the sleeve of the hand I'd stretched out. I close my fist in an attempt to funnel more power down the tether.

As his fingers touched my wrist, his magic tangled with mine.

Thick threads of heat wove into the cold, damp thread I held, and I'd felt nothing like it. The demon cocked its head as it regarded us, and my magic hummed with renewed vigor. The thread became warmer and stronger. The demon I'd summoned became sharper along the edges of its scales and wings until it was no longer an apparition.

We waited there, suspended, holding it up with bated breath until I had to let go. I fell back into Farran from the sudden plunge of magic, struggling to catch my breath. The demon disappeared in the breeze the same as ashes on a pyre, and the forest went still and silent.

"Incredible," Farran said, panting himself. "You're incredible."

My chest heaved as I scrambled away from him to stand on my own. A burning sensation inched its way through my body, starting with my fingers, as if the bones in them had turned to hot coals. I'd spent every part of me, and it had been out of my control.

I stared at him and rasped, "What did you do?"

"That was my gift keeping yours from burning out," the prince explained. The burning had started to subside.

I shivered as Farran looked at me, but I didn't shy away, even if I still felt the tug of anger fidgeting between my ribs. "That was your siphon power?" I questioned.

"Part of it. It's the part that allows me to enhance intrinsic power to prevent burnout. I did not take an ounce of your magic. I swear it."

"I've never felt magic like that."

A smirk crossed his face, and his eyes looked up at the black sky. "I find most women haven't."

I ignored him. "Does it only work through touch?"

"No." His eyes fell to mine again, and I shifted under the weight of his gaze. "It works a thousand other ways I'm still figuring out, but touch is most effective for avoiding burnout. Something about doubling magic and grounding."

It was silent for a moment before I murmured, "Let's go back."

He nodded and unfurled his wings. I looked up at the sky, and my body screamed.

Farran added, "It's five minutes flying or a half hour walking. You're pretending, but I can see your legs shaking. You spent a deadly amount of magic without an *ontaros*."

"I'll vomit," I said with a wince.

"Well aware."

Begrudgingly, I strode forward and found myself wrapped in his arms. The smell of him was overwhelming. I cursed myself, and I cursed him because he was right; my legs were ready to collapse, and I was far too tired to be angry.

His wings beat and pulled us into the sky, skimming just above the treetops.

A few minutes later, he dove toward the ground, and we landed. I stumbled toward a bush along the wall and dry-heaved, trying my hardest to keep the contents of my stomach within while Farran's hand stayed on my back until I waved it away.

"I'm fine," I forced out.

"Are you sure?"

I nodded quickly and tore away from him, pushing my trembling legs toward the Emerald as fast as they would go. Much to my chagrin, Farran kept up with my pace and followed me to my door. I thanked the gods it was late.

I didn't need anyone to see the way he looked at me. How his blue fucking eyes disarmed and pierced through my defense like he saw me for something I'd never be—like he knew me. He had no right, not after what his family did to mine . . . but it was getting harder to hold on to my anger, and I resented him for it.

He leaned against the wall with an easy familiarity, but his lips were thin with concern and something else he wanted to say.

"Good night," I said.

"I'm sorry," Farran murmured, somewhat awkwardly. He combed his hand through his hair, and I tried not to look. "It shouldn't have come from me."

"It's fine," I insisted and pushed open my door.

He leaned closer, his sapphire eyes locked onto mine. The smell of him still enveloped me, strong enough to make me dizzy and impulsive if I let another part of me slip.

There was a pain in his eyes . . . something deep and complicated. "It's not fine—"

"Good night, *Your Highness.*"

I didn't wait to see what withering look he gave me. I slipped through my door and locked it behind me. The moment I laid down, exhaustion struck me with the force of a poison. Instead of brooding, I drifted into a dreamless sleep, punctuated by the smell of vanilla, cedar, and the cold, musky stone of the Armory.

Chapter 20

I spent the next three days avoiding Farran and threw myself into training with renewed vigor. There was nothing I could do to change what had already been written. I wanted to scream, to cry, and to claw off Avernought's skin for lying when I deserved to know the truth.

I wondered what else he was hiding. I wished I'd asked the priestess even one more question about who she thought I was. Perhaps that was the truth she alluded to.

It didn't matter. I had to accept the bitterness of reality. Nothing had changed, and life in the Armory continued regardless of what I'd learned.

Later that week, we faced a brief trial in the Armory yard. It wasn't an arena trial, but it was a similar set of duels, restricted only to second-years and with no weapons allowed—only our magic.

We dueled Amethyst and I faced their water wielder. He cowered the moment I conjured a demon. But I had no idea what to do next. The soldier blinked a few times and recovered enough to strike me with a ball of water and knock me off balance. I lost my hold and couldn't call the demon back.

Then he struck me a second time and the force put me on my knees.

Frustration and anger blinded me. I ran at him, screaming, pummeling him with my fists, until Avi and Vera dragged me out of the ring.

Wielding lessons resumed that night. First with Avi and Farran, but a few sessions passed, and the captain had other duties.

After a week and a half of training together, the oath didn't come up again. In fact, we only spoke about two things: demons and whatever the weather happened to be. It was boring, but I was getting better.

By the second week, if I focused on the threads of magic and not the way Farran's hand felt on my arm, or the few times I'd caught him staring at me, I could conjure a solid demon well before my power waned.

On a particularly dreary night, I pulled on my boots, dragged my cloak over my shoulders, and fastened my sword.

Better wasn't good enough. I needed to do more. Tonight, I intended to hold one long enough to see what its claws could do to the trunk of a tree or something. I couldn't handle another embarrassment. Maybe it would spar with me if I asked.

Another set of footsteps echoed through the deserted Atrium. I glanced over my shoulder, expecting to see Farran, but there was no one. Nerves bubbled into my chest unbidden.

Against my usual instinct, I walked faster, nearly running for the doors, when a force struck me. *Vainnen.* I skidded across the floor and scrambled to stand, grasping for my sword as a second, stronger blast flung me into the Atrium wall like a ragdoll. My sword clattered to the ground. I was pinned to the glass, gasping for breath as a blinding pain pierced my temple.

My eyes peeled open. A man stalked towards me, one hand outstretched with a dagger in the other. The grip of his magic tightened. I was choking.

My head rang. Magic thrashed against my ribs, threatening to break free and seek reprisal. He stopped an arm's length away. Fire bloomed in his eyes as the hold released. My feet hit the ground just as his dagger thrust into my gut.

He snarled as he twisted it, and I screamed.

"Demon whore," he spat. "You don't deserve to live."

His eyes went wide, the blade withdrew, and I watched a set of massive talons perforate his chest as white fangs ripped his head from his neck.

Obsidian eyes met mine, and the demon dropped the man's crumpled body at my feet. Shock briefly overcame pain as I clutched my stomach and sank to the cool marble, too weak to cry out. Pain swelled and crested again with every breath—hot and white.

There was no thread tethering us, but the demon remained, solid and towering as sticky, hot liquid poured over my hand. *My blood.*

I was losing too much of it, with no strength to mend. The dagger might have caught my lung because the mark of my oath writhed on my back. Breathing came more like gasping.

"Reina!" That was Avi's voice.

I couldn't feel my feet. The room began to spin.

"Stay with us," Blaise said from too far away. Arms wound through mine. Someone lifted me.

Blackness closed in, and I fought it with every pounding step. Searing pain ricocheted through my body in a million sparks as everything that wasn't pain became a dream.

Where'd the demon go?

Avi peppered me with questions, but I said nothing; everything felt out of reach and unbearable.

If I closed my eyes, I saw the soldier's body torn apart at my feet. If I opened them, I saw everyone else.

I jolted again—the tattooed snake crawled up my back—a hundred voices and a hundred faces surrounded me as the pain blistered. Someone held down my shoulders and tipped cool liquid into my mouth.

Then the world went silent, black, and still.

I woke in my room, blinded by the sunlight streaming in. My head spun, and I forced myself to sit up, expecting hot, radiating pain as the memory swelled back.

To my surprise, the only pain I felt was an ache where the dagger had been, now tightly wound in bandages. I knew Armory healers had a gift, but this was impressive. In trial, this wound would have been fatal.

If I could sit up, I could stand, so I eased toward the edge of the bed and pushed onto unsteady legs. Immediately, I took back what I said about the soreness: all of my organs were bruised.

I winced as I put on my pants and tunic, but had no interest in lying around.

I needed to eat, so I dragged my disheveled self down to the dining hall. Unfortunately for me, it was filled with soldiers who all turned to gawk.

Leena gasped and ran over—I thought she was going to hug me. Instead, she grabbed my arm and helped me sit at the table, which was harder than it sounded. Aixen slid a mug of hot tea toward me with the same frown shared by everyone else.

"Thank gods, you're okay," Blaise said first, and the relief made sense.

The oath. That's how they found me so quickly, and that's how close we all came to death.

Gods be fucking damned.

Every complicated feeling swelled back and knotted in my throat. I wasn't worth worrying about, but here we were.

"He got you good," Avi said as she swallowed a bite of toast. "It was a dragon-tipped knife, so you're lucky you conjured a demon fast enough. If he stabbed you a second time, the healers weren't sure they could have gotten all the poison out."

"I didn't conjure it," I croaked. "I mean, I don't remember conjuring it." *I didn't. I couldn't.* I wasn't focused and there was no heat, no threads—nothing to tether it I could remember.

I opened my eyes and there it stood.

"You're getting better, then." Avi smirked, but there was a shadow of concern. I'm sure she'd ask about it later. "The man who attacked you was from Diamond. Connor, a third-year without a maker."

I looked at the table, grimacing. "He called me a demon whore."

"Glad he's dead," Blaise muttered.

My eyes darkened. "I just wish it'd been my own sword."

When I killed someone, I wanted to see the surprise in their eyes and feel the thrill of metal kissing flesh. I didn't want them gutted and left at my feet like a cat gifting a dead bird.

Leena squeezed my knee. "We know, Rein. We're just glad you're here."

"Also, glad your demon showed up," Avi remarked. "The Crown was notified, and they'll be sending more guards to make sure things don't get worse."

Great, exactly what I wanted to hear. There were probably more soldiers in these walls who didn't think I deserved to live. This was also the second time in a few months.

"As for any training," Avi continued, pausing for a moment until she had my attention, "I expect you to be accompanied by one of us any time you leave Emerald. If I find out you've gone anywhere on your own, you'll wish you'd been banished to Tir."

I frowned, but I expected it. Now I knew my death would destroy the house, but knowing didn't make it feel any less degrading. I forced myself to drink the tea and swallowed a few bites of egg before excusing myself.

I wasn't running today; I wasn't training. Not in this condition.

After breakfast, I settled into bed with several books and kept reading, even though it made my stomach turn.

Stories of the *dreosen* were tales, twisted by the biases of traitors . . . especially in the books Farran brought me from the Crown's archive. Outside of one wielder, long before Thera, they all ended the same.

The *dreosen* served well for a while and fought their wars, but something always changed. Something broke them. They always lost themselves and were executed—usually by a shadow wielder, sometimes by a dreite priest, and once a wielder was choked of their magic by a siphon.

I was surrounded by the very people who could carry out my execution. Was my whole life one organized, extravagant prison sentence? I'll bet the Crown finds some variation of the three when I'm executed.

Maybe my father never died in the fire, and he was a dreite priest. That would fill one requirement. My father would stand over me and carve sigils while Farran drained my magic and Leena crushed me? That would be the ultimate death for a *dreosen*.

No. I shook the thought away. I wasn't like the legends—I couldn't be. I felt grounded and sane, maybe a little angry and bitter, but not lost.

Or I was delusional about myself. They say that about delusion . . .

I must have fallen asleep, because my eyes flew open when hushed arguing outside of my door shook me out of the nightmares. My room was dark, and the wound on my side throbbed as I turned over. I pressed my hand against the bandages and tried to soothe it with a small spend of magic, but it spluttered out with a hiss like a flame doused in icy water.

The door cracked open without a knock, and light spilled in briefly. I knew it was Leena from the silhouette of her hair. She peered in, looking for me without saying a word, before she jumped in and slammed the door.

My brow furrowed as she walked over. A flick of her wrist lit the fireplace as I sat up, wincing.

"How are you feeling?" she asked. "I figured you were sleeping so I kept everyone out. Everyone—meaning Farran—he was going to come in without knocking, but I got here first."

"What does he want?" I inquired with a heavy sigh. The thoughts in my head rattled as my brain caught up. He was supposed to meet me in the forest last night.

Leena surveyed me from the edge of the bed. I truly believed her gold eyes could read my expression if she stared hard enough. Maybe her shadows came with more than any of us knew.

"He wanted to see you and apologize. He's blaming himself," she finally said.

"Did you remind him I saved myself and I'm perfectly fine?"

She frowned. The fireplace behind her shadowed the finer features of her face, but I knew Leena. "A demon saved you, and you are not perfectly fine. You're still recovering from the dragon blood, and the first officer is going to come in here to verify Avi and I aren't lying for you."

"Tell him I'm asleep," I grumbled, tugging at the blanket.

"That won't work." Leena's lips twitched on one side like she was biting back a smile. "I can delay him if you want to clean up first and change the bandage, but that's all the time I can buy."

"I'm fine," I pressed, swinging my legs to the other side of the bed. "I can take care of it myself." The soreness came back when I stood in a wave so sharp it sucked away my breath.

Nimbly, I padded towards my wardrobe and let out a long, dramatized hiss as I pulled my arms through my mother's old cardigan.

Leena's arms remained crossed. "At least let me braid your hair if you're going to be this stubborn. It's a mess."

Scrunching my nose, I gave in. "Fine."

Leena came over and deftly twisted the tangled auburn strands into a braid before she walked to the door. There wasn't a part of me that wasn't grateful for her friendship. Women in Arden's den came and went. Some were nice, but every kindness was a transaction.

"Thank you," I said as Leena opened the door; it was a small relief to know if I died, she wouldn't.

The door didn't even close before Farran appeared in my room. He looked disheveled, with his tunic half tucked into his breeches and the tie across it nearly coming undone, exposing a fraction of the oath I never wanted to see again.

His jaw was tight, and his damn blue eyes raked over me as I pulled the cardigan tighter.

"Come in," I retorted. Leena wasn't exaggerating; remorse visibly sagged off his shoulders.

"I'm sorry." The storm in his eyes softened. "I should have been there. I know how dangerous it is, and I'm the reason you were out at all."

I held up my hand to stop him; I didn't need the concern. . . the sincerity grated against my skin. "It's not your fault. It's the same thing that happened at the Maker's Ball. I fight my own battles, which I remember making very clear, several times."

Farran crossed his arms and remained a step away from the door. "Telling you about the oath was an accident, but I shouldn't have to keep reminding you—"

"Then don't," I ground out, taking a step closer. I stood in front of the fireplace, and the heat crept up my leg as my anger flared . . . Gods, I didn't need more guilt. "Not a second passes where I haven't thought about it. I've always taken care of myself, and I don't need a guard. This changes nothing."

"We all felt it, Reina. It should change everything. You know how the blood oath works, don't you?" His eyes flicked up to mine. The burn of his gaze struck me and rivaled even the heat rolling from the fireplace.

"Of course I know how it works." *I have one of my fucking own.*

Farran raised his chin and took a step forward, nearly closing the space between us. The room shrank, and I became prey again. The lines on his face deepened in severity.

"If that oath comes anywhere close to being broken, it burns against our skin like a brand, and it spreads. The closer you, *darling*, come to death and the further the dragon blood seeps into your veins, the more it burns and the tighter the grip gets around our necks until we end up like you. That was the second time we've felt it."

"And the first?" I whispered. The words sank in my chest like a lead weight. My thoughts jumbled as he chose the words he thought I needed to hear.

"Last year, a few weeks before you came to the Armory. We had no idea what happened, but I imagine you do." I wished he would look away because I was too proud to do it. He could pull me apart without ever lifting a hand; the power rippling from his words reminded me.

"It was a bad night at the bar," I mumbled. "It doesn't matter. I was fine then, just as I am now."

Farran's lips pursed as he watched me. He knew I was lying, but I didn't care. The prince had no right to know one of Arden's clients carried me back to the estate that night because I'd been set up.

He didn't need to know I would have died from the infection without my healing magic, and he had no right to know the scar from it rested just below my breast, between my ribs, and sometimes the memory of pain would tear me awake in the middle of the night.

Farran's jaw twitched as he stared. "Avi was terrified the first time and livid this time. She meant it. You will not be walking around the grounds alone; that's an order."

There was no amount of pertinence that superseded a captain's order in the Armory, unless I wanted to be miserable.

Farran looked past my shoulder at the fireplace, clearing his throat and the bite it had. "Avi also told me you conjured a demon without meaning to."

My skin prickled as the thud of the attacker's body creeped into my thoughts. I crossed and recrossed my arms. "It didn't feel like I conjured it. I didn't touch a thread of magic. Actually, I couldn't—not with the dragon blood."

"Perhaps you're getting stronger." His voice graveled as it raced through possibilities. He ran a hand through his hair, drawing several clumps of dark curls out of the tie as I watched. Some of the anger and tension subsided.

"Perhaps I'm losing control."

"We won't let that happen." Farran glanced at the books spread around my bed and then back at me. He didn't have to stand this close, yet here he was, and amusement tinged the shadows on his face. "Maybe some lighter reading wouldn't be a terrible idea since you're excused from training."

"If you find any stories where the demon wielder doesn't die brutally, I'll happily read them," I snarked, unable to hide the bitterness from my tone.

"Unlikely." He shoved his hand in his pocket. There was something else he wanted to say, but it remained a thought as he looked at everything but me. "Rest. You might be excused from Avi's drills, but you need to practice wielding and keep Avernought happy. Another trial is imminent. We were told in today's captain's meeting, and Doris is getting the last details. We'll all need to be ready."

He pulled a vial from his pocket and held it out for me; it was an unlabeled, dark purple jar with a plain stopper. The liquid inside chimed as it sloshed around.

"It's for your pain," he murmured.

I lifted my chin defiantly for no reason and said, "I'm not in pain."

A ghost of a smile tugged at his lips, and he took a step closer. Our toes practically touched, and the heady rush of cedar and the faint undertone of vanilla stilted my senses.

"So taking off the cardigan wouldn't be a problem?" he asked, and my breath stalled.

A warning flared against the side of my cheek, but my better judgment didn't understand the way the warmth built between my legs with every second he didn't look away. *What was I doing?*

I shook my head. "I'm in perfect fighting condition."

"So you definitely don't need this? Even if it matches your eyes?" The vial clinked as Farran dropped it back in his pocket with a smirk. No part of me needed to play this game, but I wanted to win.

I shrugged the cardigan off onto the floor and held his gaze with a measured stare, doing everything in my power not to wince.

The muscles healing in my gut protested and screamed, but I'd faked my way through worse. "No," I said, tilting my chin. "I don't think I do. You're also mistaken; my eyes are brown."

"Once again, I don't believe you." Farran's voice was thick, strained the same as when I pulled my dagger on him in the hallway a few weeks ago. He was baiting me, and I fell for it because I was staring at his fucking lips. "A dragon blood dagger went clean through you, and you're not in pain?"

My eyes flicked up. His stare was penetrating. Firelight sharpened his cheekbones as it bloomed.

"I don't believe you, Reina Sangrey."

"You're repeating yourself."

"I am very aware." He breathed, and it was my turn to catch him staring. We were at a very dangerous precipice as my churning anger was swept away by whatever dormant magic flickered in the space between us. "And very close to demanding proof, because I think you're lying to me about several things."

"I'm not showing you anything," I whispered, and my lips curled into a sardonic grin. My breasts were a hair's breadth away from his chest, and suddenly, they felt heavy and aching.

But the trance broke, Farran remembered himself and took a step back before he rushed across the room and pulled open the door.

Just before it closed, he glanced back at where I still stood, cardigan at my feet.

"Glad you're alive, Sangrey. Not just because half of us would be dead if you weren't. Now, get some rest. You're wielding tomorrow night." It wasn't a calming thought, but something in my chest fluttered as the door closed.

Chapter 21

The dull, bruised ache in my side kept me turning over like a roast left to smoke over cherry wood logs. I lost count of how many times I woke up before first light poked through the trees and cast a strip of deep amber across the ceiling.

With an exaggerated groan, I reached over to grab the cup of water from my nightstand when my hand hit something and sent it rolling off, clattering to the ground.

It was definitely glass, but it didn't shatter. Instead, it chimed as it rolled along the coarse stone. I grunted and peered over the bed. It was the purple vial Farran had teased me with: the stupid vial I declined.

I retrieved it and downed the contents without a second thought.

Almost immediately, the soreness dwindled as the potion set to work, tenderly cushioning all of my organs in something which felt akin to magical linen.

The potion melted the pain down to a mere memory that only tugged when I turned too sharply. Banned from any physical training, I didn't do much of anything until dusk, when I remembered to change the bandage. My body protested as I padded to the bathroom and held my breath, unwinding the gauze in front of my dusty mirror.

As the last of the bandage peeled away, I gasped. The scar was a straight line, just below my last rib, a few inches underneath the other scar that also nearly killed me. Several of the surrounding veins were bright red from the last vestiges of the poison.

Of course, the oath reacted—I'd killed men with similar jabs.

Salve cooled my skin as I applied a dollop over the closed wound and rebandaged. The pressure soothed the pain.

I managed to pull on a thicker tunic and a pair of breeches, but there was no point in putting leathers on, not without someone's help. Though, I was determined not to let a little bruising and some poison stop me; I was ready to train.

An hour later, Farran knocked on my door, and we left to begin my lessons once again. I ignored everything about him and focused on the sturdy floor underfoot until we arrived in the center of the Atrium. Moonlight streamed in, and a few lanterns had been lit.

My eyes drifted upwards to the single black banner strung up on the far side for my attacker. I ignored it and kept walking, letting Farran catch up as I steeled myself.

We crossed the tree line into the woods, and noticeable contemplation creased Farran's features. He bit his lip, wanting to say something.

"How are you feeling?" he finally asked.

I let the question hang in the air as pine needles crunched underfoot; that was too simple of a question.

"Fine," I said. "The pain is almost gone."

His eyebrows lifted, and the corner of his lip tipped up. "Almost?"

"I said I was fine, didn't I?" I bit back.

"Yesterday, you said you *weren't* in pain, which is quite different from *some* pain."

I pursed my lips as we walked down a hill. "Why the Armory and not university?"

He cast me a sidelong glance. "What?"

"You enjoy arguing semantics much more than the average soldier," I chided. "Maybe you belong at university, First Officer."

For a moment, Farran seemed ensnared by the question. His silence was compensated for by the ambiance of the forest: an owl hooted in the distance, the wind rustled the needles of the dark canopy above, and crickets chirped from the shadows. All getting in their last days before the frost finally came.

We took a sharp turn away from the river, and finally, he said something. "Did you get the potion?"

"Yes," I muttered. "Thank you."

"It's from my mother's healer. He makes it specifically to treat dragon wounds on the Queensguard. It's some blend of herbs and magic that's saved me a few times." He glanced out into the distance, looking for something. "And the makers are getting restless."

"The last trial didn't have enough bloodshed for them?" I snapped. "Four soldiers died in those duels."

Though the warmth of magic swelled in my chest as we came closer to the ravine where the altar was, remnants of poison still ticked away with every heartbeat, but I could feel it building back, hot and fast.

Instead of going into the ravine, I followed Farran north, up a hill. He stopped at the top and we came to stand in a wide clearing. Stars twinkled above, no longer obstructed by the endless trees.

"You're recovering, and I have an idea. But I don't want to push you too far," he said.

His deep blue eyes stared, cutting and reactive, as we stood too close. The scent of him mingled with the sharp autumn pine and a dumb, human part of me swooned from it.

"It's my job to make sure you're ready for the next trial," he continued. "You tell me if you need to stop. I'll never force—"

"I'm fine," I hissed with more venom than intended. He recoiled, but I was tired of saying it to him and everyone else. I'd lie as long as I needed to, because *I* needed to believe it.

"The demons listen to you, and they will defend you, it seems." Farran watched my reaction as he spoke. My scar twitched at the recollection and so did I—the searing pain, the thud of a body and head rolling on marble. "Their protection will be more valuable than any of ours once you learn how to use them. Last night proved it."

"What are you saying?" I tried to hold back the rush of anxiety as my hand knotted around the hilt of my blade.

"Avi told me there was a shadow hound spotted a little north of here."

I froze and hoped he saw the flash of panic. The screams and howls of the hounds from our first trial were still fresh enough in my memory to wake me up in the middle of the night.

"You think that's a good idea?" I asked slowly, my voice holding a warning.

Farran's jaw tightened. "No, but do you think it's worth a try?"

The thoughts pieced themselves together: no matter how many demons I strung together, there were only two of us, and I wasn't sure if my magic would unfurl enough. Worse, I couldn't use my sword properly.

We needed Leena if this would be a good idea, but that didn't mean I wasn't considering it. It was far too late to go back now.

Farran's eyes narrowed on mine. Something resembling pride swirled through them as he took a step closer. I thought he might tilt my chin again, but his hands remained at his sides. "With everything I've read, I believe those demons won't let harm come to you. Do you believe that?" he whispered.

I bit my lip; part of me believed him. There was a reverence in their black eyes, and not just in the ones I conjured, but even in the ones belonging to the dreite at the keep and the one caged below the Armory. I *saw* it.

The priestess remarked about it, *"They will rise on your command."*

Fear tried to claw its way through my body, tightening and tensing, but I wouldn't let it make my choice. Not now.

"Let's see what happens," I decided.

There was no turning back; the First Officer of Emerald didn't waste any time. Swiftly, he held up both hands and a ripple of magic pulsed from them, causing the trees to shake and pine needles to rain down. The threads of magic in my chest flashed like hot oil as the magic brushed me. I blanched at the far-off howl in the distance.

The howling came closer and closer, and the forest seemed to tremble with me. Fear pulled on every nerve until Farran's voice cut through it all with a single command, "*Now.*"

I closed my eyes and yanked on the single dark, damp thread floating above the others.

The coiled threads of magic spun apart, and what was tepid before burned now. Another howl, then the drum of massive paws shook the ground. My eyes flew open; Farran stood at my back with his sword drawn as a form materialized from the shadows.

"Keep going," he urged.

A demon kneeled before me, its ears twitching and onyx eyes scanning the perimeter.

"Rise." The command was foreign, but the demon obeyed.

I prayed to the gods it wouldn't turn to ash and held my breath as it turned to the commotion. Three hounds howled and skittered across the forest floor, barreling towards Farran's magic, which tangled in and flared against my own.

One hound lunged at me. I swung my sword, but the demon blocked my cut as a cry rang out, followed by the wet, decisive sound of torn flesh and broken bone.

I gaped as the demon shook the hound's viscera from its talons. The putrid stench of the hound's blood stirred my stomach. I held the demon's thread as I looked around. My hold started to shake.

Another hound growled behind me, focused on Farran, who only had one short sword poised because his other hand gripped mine, feeding me his magic, which was also slipping.

This was a dumb fucking idea.

The demon leaped between them and brought its talons down on the hound with a roar, and the reek of hound blood sprayed us.

Too much. My vision wavered, my knees almost buckled, and I gasped. I couldn't hold it. The demon fell apart. The one remaining hound stalked us . . . our best defense had fallen.

Farran cursed, and his hand fell from my arm. He unsheathed his other sword, and I held mine out, ignoring the twinge in my side and wavering vision. The hound was straight ahead of me, licking its stark white teeth before it broke into a run.

Fuck. I didn't have time to feel anything, or to second-guess myself.

I plunged my sword straight through its chest just before its teeth could snap. Bone cracked as it yelped and collapsed, nearly on top of me. The forest went silent save for the frantic beating of my heart as I fell to my knees, trying to catch my breath.

Farran sprang, dropping both swords to catch me by the shoulders before I fell into the dead hound.

It was over. We did it. My head felt too big for my neck, and my new scar stung beneath the bandages, the pain getting more apparent with every heartbeat.

"We did it." I heaved, trying to catch my breath. Farran did the same as he held me there.

"*You* did it." He scanned the forest over my shoulder, but then he looked at me and every bit of adrenaline surged forward.

Something shifted, and my thoughts disintegrated. There was no smell of carrion, just the dizzying scent of vanilla and cedar as magic pressed and warmed my ribs.

His face was so close to mine. I should have moved.

"Can you stand?" he murmured.

I swallowed. "Of course I can stand."

His hands held my arms as I staggered onto weak legs. The world twisted on its axis, and I stumbled again, but into his steady arms as his gaze disarmed me. It wasn't pride that lingered there, in the swirling blue. It was desire, and it burned through me like an unruly flame.

"We should go," I breathed. My core tightened, betraying warmth pooled between my thighs and fuck, I should have taken a step back.

"Or we could stay." His arm wrapped around my back as his hand tilted my chin. His thumb grazed my lips, and my body shuddered. Heat closed every space between us. "You're wondering too, aren't you?"

My lips parted at the slightest invitation, and he kissed me as though he was at the edge of his self-control. My back arched into his touch, desperate to know exactly what I'd been denying myself.

He tasted like warm spices and the woods of Rowane. It was everything, but so much *more*. There was nothing like this. I bit his lip. He groaned, and it nearly undid me as my fingers tangled in his tunic, dragging his body closer, but something else dripped into my mind through the haze of lust.

I stopped and drew back. Magic turned over in my chest as his sapphire eyes stared at me, and I stared back—wide-eyed and awed. We were two feral animals caught in a trap.

He's the son of the queen who sanctioned my mother's murder—the same queen who was to blame for everything I've had to become. But his swollen lips were the most beautiful thing I ever tasted, even if he was everything I shouldn't have.

I was ready to be an idiot because the man in front of me was exactly as undone as I was.

Against rational thought, I closed the space—no hesitation, and no apology as though I'd waited my whole life for it.

Farran ripped off my cloak and devoured me.

I purred when cold air prickled the back of my neck as his teeth tugged my lower lip. His tongue grazed my jaw and lingered on the sensitive skin just below, almost hard enough to leave a mark I wouldn't be able to explain.

"Hold on to me," he rasped and I did as ordered: my arms wrapped around his broad frame. Then he hoisted me off the ground and pinned me to the tree, his hard chest on mine.

I whimpered as he kissed me, all pretense and composure gone as hands slid up my thighs and squeezed, edging closer to the waist of my breeches.

My hips ground into his, needing to feel more than just the strain in his pants against the apex of my thighs. I wanted more. My fists bunched the back of his shirt as I bit his lip again. He moaned with a shaky ferocity that almost unwound me.

On the fucking Seven.

The ache between my thighs was unbearable, and I knew what I wanted. I reached for the laces on his pants, not caring that I was sore and tired, or that he was a Prince of Thera until my feet hit the ground, and he stopped.

My eyes opened in a daze. Farran stared at me while reality whirred back. His arms still cupped my back as my fingers touched my lips, unsure of what was real or what I'd done.

He didn't look afraid; he looked amused. "I'd be lying if I said I never imagined that."

I found my feet enough to stand and wriggled free from his grasp. "We can't . . . it was . . ."

"You're incredible." He gawked. I ducked under his arm.

"A mistake," I said, feeling cornered. That was someone else—a different Reina.

"Call it what you want," he said, sharper than I expected. "But don't make me call it a mistake." The storm in his sapphire eyes raged. I felt every torrent of his tone as he watched me pull my cloak off the ground. "I'll take you back."

A rush of air moved around us before I could protest, and Farran's wings unfolded, black as night.

He wrapped his arms around me, and I let myself fall into the faint vanilla, cedar, and heat of his touch, knowing I couldn't indulge again.

Some things were far too complicated, and this was number one on my list. I cursed in my head the whole way back and ran to my room the moment my feet hit the ground.

CHAPTER 22

As long as I kept my eyes closed, the day couldn't start. That's what I told Declan the first morning we spent at Arden's. He'd cried all night, and the room was nothing like the home we'd lost, but it was better than the streets of Rowane.

Arden kept us on the second floor, with old, creaking floorboards, worn furniture, and several threadbare rugs layered on top of one another.

That first morning, we squeezed our eyes shut and clutched the crimson comforter as tightly as we could to keep out the morning light. It was a nice thought, but it never stopped the day from coming.

The same was true this morning as a booming crack of thunder peeled through the Armory and forced me awake.

Today was here, and it didn't give a fuck that I still tasted Farran. I couldn't even think about the demon I wielded or anything else.

A second later, the rain came down in deafening sheets and I swore.

This was the punishment I deserved. Now I had to trudge through torrential rain to meet Declan on a riverbank.

I dressed quickly, strapped my sword to my hip, and grabbed my cloak from the floor. Good *gods*, it was covered with pine needles. Only a handful fluttered to the ground when I shook it, wincing—as my wound was no less sore than yesterday.

Heat crawled up my cheeks and thunder clapped again, so the cloak covered in needles would have to do.

The walk across the yard was dreadful. My clothes were soaked through by the time I reached the treeline. Lightning struck, summoning a deep rumble of thunder that shook my bones as the wind picked up and knocked down my hood a second time.

There was no point in pulling it back over my head. I was wet, and I would stay wet until I was back inside. I just had to pray I returned before Avi realized I'd gone anywhere.

At the riverbank, Declan's brown horse was tied to the same willow. I clambered down the steep embankment, slipped, and cursed every single god I could name, including the Seven, if they could hear me.

My hands sunk into the cold and revolting mud. I tried to stand, and it took too many tries for someone who was supposed to be an elite soldier for the Crown.

"Going well for you, Reina?" my brother drawled.

I heard Declan's voice before I saw him sheltering under the sinewy canopy of the willow starting to turn yellow with the season. His plain riding boots were caked in mud, and he must have stood there for quite a while to look as dry as he did.

Meanwhile, I looked like a drowned rat with my hair plastered to my skull in a useless helmet and both hands covered in muck.

"Do you want a hug?" I said wryly and spread my arms as I walked towards him.

"Absolutely fucking not." He laughed as I joined him under the tree.

Our last meeting sat heavy. It was nice to see him laugh even at my expense. His light blue eyes and crooked smile were so incredibly like our mother's.

"Maven is on his way to the Armory," Declan said blankly. "Received his letter three weeks ago."

My heart sank, but I wasn't entirely surprised. Maven had been in Arden's care for years; he'd grown up alongside us.

As a soft-spoken kid similar to Declan, they became friends, but Maven was alone and Arden took advantage of him, running the kid into the ground until he finally ran off and took a job wiping tables at a tavern three streets over.

"Why?" I murmured, gazing out at the river as rain pummeled it.

Declan shrugged as his eyes fell to the ground. His too-long brown hair fell into his eyes. "Wanted to try something, I guess. Just like you."

"That's not why I did it," I bit out, but I didn't want to have this conversation. Why did I have to explain myself every time we spoke? I bent down and rinsed my hands in the rushing river water before my attention returned to him. "You have a letter for me?"

"I do," he muttered, watching my reaction as he reached under his cloak and into his *leathers*.

My stomach knotted; he never wore leathers, and now Arden's letter was tucked in them. And though he tried to keep it hidden under his cloak, I caught the glint of a sword hilt. Declan covered it swiftly, but it was too late—I'd seen it, and I knew Arden's steel well enough to know it was a blade from his personal collection.

Anger pressed against my temple. I knew the route . . . if he traveled by day and stopped at the inns, the woods weren't dangerous. I took a deep breath and tried to calm myself.

Declan held the letter out. Before I said anything else, I snatched it.

My viper, your success has not gone unnoticed. I wish you the best in the next trial. Several makers seem to think it will be in the north again.

I'm sure by now you know what Prince Farran's gift is, as I am also very aware of yours. The dreosen *is a true blessing from the old gods and Dreonna herself. This will help us immensely and it makes you one of the greatest assets of the Crown.*

*Other forces will also know who you are. Av-
ernought's protection is great, but it has its limits.
As does mine.*

*What awaits you is bigger than us all, but you
will weather it. I trust Avernought with my life
and encourage you to do the same. Stay your course,
as your future is with the Queensguard. My only
advice is to make yourself indispensable, or the
Queen will only take what she wants and discard
the rest.*

*The house misses you. Declan is safe, and you have
my word so long as you hold yours, viper.*

*May the old gods rise again to be the wind at your
back. Enjoy your new steel.*

Declan was only safe from being used by Arden as he had used me. There were plenty of things Damien Arden could do without crossing the lines I'd drawn.

Biting back a curse, I crumpled the paper and threw it at Declan.

"When did you start wearing leathers? Is Arden training you?" I snapped.

His eyes narrowed. "It's a three-day trek to get here, Rein. Do you not know what's going on?"

"Going on? The main roads are safe." My voice lowered, and a thousand possibilities raced through it. "Did something happen in Rowane?"

Declan shook his head as thunder made the ground quake. "The Darklands have been sending rogues into Thera, even dreites and their priests. Attacks are getting closer. In fact, they razed a village to the ground a few hours south of here. They're emboldened, and the Crown has been going door to door, looking for soldiers. Maven would have said yes if he hadn't gotten an Armory invitation from Avernought."

My eyes narrowed. "Don't you dare say yes to them."

"I won't," he said, brushing hair out of his eyes. "You've made it clear you'd kill me before anyone else could, and I was certain that included the Crown."

"Keep it that way."

Declan looked at me, and thunder rattled again. "Rich coming from Thera's first demon wielder."

"*Dreosen* is the formal term," I said, tucking hair behind my ears as he froze.

"Fucking gods. It is true." Declan gaped at me before his lips curled into a smile. "I mean, I heard what the criers said. I just . . . why you?"

I wished he wouldn't look at me. I didn't have an answer.

He went on. "You're the most valuable weapon in the realm, not just Thera. So you cannot be mad at me for asking Arden how to use a sword. You, of all people, know I could be used against you."

"Fine," I gritted—I knew it was true. There wasn't a part of me ready to consider it. "Only defense. Make sure Arden knows I'm paying attention. One word of employing you, and I'll set demons on him."

"Can you do that?" he wondered with a grin.

I shrugged. "Sure." If the gods trusted demons to a bitter twenty-four-year-old, then why not? Anything was possible.

"You should get back before your head gets cut as a deserter." He sighed, frowning at the rain sluicing over the river. "I'll be back in a month Arden said."

I walked out from beneath the willow and took one more glance at my little brother. He'd grown so much . . . He wasn't the same child I'd bargained my life for to protect. Not anymore. "Be safe. Don't forget I'm the only one allowed to kill you."

"Never," he chuffed.

The rain ebbed to a trickle as I walked back to the Armory, and I left Declan feeling lighter than I thought I would. Maybe

Avi would delay our drills. I'd give anything for a hot bath now that I was thoroughly drenched and freezing.

Only Leena saw me drag myself through the common room. She raised an eyebrow but said nothing as she turned another page in her book.

I thanked the gods that I had more time than I thought, turning on the faucet to run a bath. As I sunk my foot into the deliciously hot water, Leena knocked on the door and announced she was coming in. *So be it.* I submerged myself as the door opened and closed with a *click*.

When I surfaced, Leena stood in the doorway, her unbound hair floating around in wild curls.

She seemed conflicted, like there was something she wanted to say, and she wasn't sure how. "Are you okay? We've barely spoken since . . ."

I looked at the wall, because I didn't have an answer. "I'm fine, mostly healed. What if we make a date of it tonight? I'll catch you up, and you can tell me everything I've missed in training when I'm not naked."

I ducked under the water again, and she waited for me to come up before she sat herself at the edge of the tub. I loved Leena; she always knew I was lying to myself about something, which made her all the more determined to find out what it was.

"Now is fine for me. You're the one who thinks it's weird," she teased. "I've barely seen you since you almost died. I also know you were with Farran again last night."

My eyes met hers for only a moment before I glanced away, but it had been enough.

She looked so proud of herself for having put the pieces together. "I knew it!"

"It's nothing." I scowled and rubbed a bar of lavender-scented soap over my scalp; it was noxious, but it was better than smelling the prince every time I breathed. I glanced at Leena. "How about we go to Mossford tonight and I'll tell you everything? Including what Arden warned me about."

Leena froze. "Arden? Not Declan?" she clarified.

"Well, Declan was the messenger, but it was Arden's letter." I shrugged.

"Fine, it's a deal." Her eyes narrowed. "You're not getting out of this one. I have too much to tell you."

A whistle echoed through the hall, and Leena gave me a withering look before she left. I wasn't getting out of anything. I jumped out of the bath and forced my wet limbs into proper clothes with great difficulty, biting my lip when I moved the wrong way.

Avi stood in the center of the common room with her arms crossed, her wild red hair unbound. Devon, Farran, and Vera stood beside her, and the remaining fourteen of our house stood around.

I accidentally made eye contact with Farran, and he had the nerve to hold my gaze when I hoped he would look away. He was nothing like the boys in Lower Rowane.

Avi cleared her throat. "We've been assigned another trial. You have ten minutes to pack. Wear your Emerald capes and any designations; we're representing the Crown on official business."

Farran's blue eyes caught mine again, and he smirked. How dare he smirk.

I looked away and swore in my head. Nothing about this was good. My hair was dripping wet, and I was in the thinnest tunic I owned—I had no doubt everyone saw my damn nipples.

Before embarrassment reached my cheeks, I ducked back into my room, stuffed a bag, and forced myself into leathers, trying not to think about how constrictive they felt against my healing wound. In a few minutes, I was back in the common room.

Avi used the time to braid her hair, and she looked more like the captain we knew. Her face still appeared shaken, but she pushed it down as she passed a stack of paper to Vera and Devon.

"Right, so there was a dreite attack on the city of Beven, which is the seat of the Arasund Duchy in the Northwest," she explained. "On horseback, it's only a day away from the Armory, on the Tenebria River. We're to aid survivors and clear any immediate danger before the Crown arrives. We're scouting for them because we can reach the city faster. I'm not counting on help from other houses. Questions?"

Aixen raised his hand. "Why us?" he asked.

"I do not know," Avi said quickly, but something flashed in her eyes. "Anything else? No? Fine, follow Farran to the stables. Second-years will need to partner up. Doris didn't reserve enough horses on short notice, and several houses are on trial. No one flies unless it's on my command."

She added, looking straight at Farran who was securing his officer epaulets to his shoulders. "Rogues are known to shoot through wings with dragon blood arrows, and I'm not taking a risk."

"Point taken," Farran muttered. His hair was tied back in a knot making his sharp features look more severe as he brushed past her and toward the hall.

I constantly forgot the Armory had stables even as we trudged towards them through the muddy yard and reticent rain. Horses weren't something wasted on first-year recruits; there were hardly enough for two houses, let alone two houses and their first-years.

Personally, I'd never had any desire to be around a creature that could trample me if it saw a snake. Horses were useless in the streets of Lower Rowane, and they were useless for carrying out Arden's requests: my legs were faster, smarter, and more agile than a horse ever could be.

I also smelled better—most of the time.

"You coming?" Aixen asked me, his straight hair matted to his forehead by the drizzling rain. I didn't realize I'd stopped walking.

Instinctively, my arms crossed over my chest and I eyed the stable door. It wasn't anything special, just a thatch roof on some wooden walls. The temporary reprieve from the rain wouldn't be worth it. "I'm fine out here."

"Right." He looked at me with a gleam of amusement, lifting a single brow. "Are you afraid of horses?"

"That's ridiculous," I snapped, but the accusation held a bit of truth.

I disliked everything about them: riding, maintenance, temperament. I had to imagine thet for every natural-born rider, there was someone like me who had no interest in them at all; riding was an expectation of the cavalry, *not* the Armory.

"Enjoy the rain," he chuckled and walked into the stable. The earthy smell of wet hay wafted from within.

Leena lingered outside with me and gave me a weird look. "Can you ride?"

"Sort of," I mumbled. Another crack of thunder peeled through, and I grimaced.

"Then you'll be no help." Leena sighed as she eyed Tomas, who walked out with a horse on a lead.

Oh gods, if I wasn't riding with Leena, what if I had to sit for hours with my back against Farran with no space between us? My entire body felt warm and tingly at the thought . . .

Immediate heat bloomed between my thighs as something in my chest twisted into a knot—there was no way. Absolutely *not*. If he so much as whispered about the weather so close to me, I'd be a mess. In another time and place, I might be thrilled at the opportunity. But not here, not today, not like this.

I'd even take Blaise. No, actually, that was the only worse choice.

All six third-years walked out of the stables, each with a saddled horse. Farran brought his closest to me. When it snorted, I jumped back and cursed louder than I intended. Several people stifled laughter, including Aixen and Farran.

Sure, maybe I was afraid of horses . . . In Rowane, I tolerated being around Declan and Arden's horses, but they'd long given up asking me to ride.

Avi cleared her throat. "I'm assigning anyone else standing around. Leena, you're with Mianen, Vera take Claude. Tomas, you have Evie—and Reina, you're with Devon."

A swell of relief rippled through me as I walked towards Devon. He held the reins of a sleek black horse standing much taller than the others, and I wasn't thrilled. Devon watched me with an amused grin. It was easy to see what endeared him to Avi; he was excessively tall and held himself like a lord. His hair was nearly white in the sunlight and contrasted with his dark complexion in a striking way, but he had a deep, quiet kindness in his eyes when he wasn't injured.

I stood reasonably far away from the front of the horse and put both hands on its hind, unsure of how to mount it.

"Have you ever done this before?" Devon asked incredulously.

"Of course I have." Years ago, I nearly broke both my back trying to coax Declan's horse out of its stall when it saw a mouse and kicked me into the wall.

Compared to Declan's, this was a big fucking horse . . . certainly bigger than it needed to be. I looked over at Leena; she was teetering, but she was already on the back of Mianen's gray horse.

I put both hands on the saddle and did my best to mount it, trying to heft my weight over its side. I slid off again and again, and even the horse seemed to laugh as it snorted and shook its head. I'd scaled walls, broken into the palace, thrown myself out of a window, and spent a night standing on a narrow ledge in a snowstorm—I could do this. How difficult could a horse really be?

"Dreonna's fucking tits, I can't keep watching this," Aixen cursed. He motioned for Devon, who jumped onto the horse with effortless grace.

"What are you doing?" I demanded, trying to hold out my chin in a dignified way.

"Helping." Aixen laughed and got down on one knee beside the beast, his hands outstretched and clasped together. "Give me your right foot, give Devon your hand, and when I say up, we're all going to work together."

Secretly, I was grateful for Aixen, and grateful this was Devon and not Farran . . . even if he was watching. I grabbed Devon, looked down at Aixen, and set my foot in his cupped hands.

"Ready?" Aixen asked.

I nodded. On his command, I pushed off from his hands as Devon pulled, and it gave me just enough leverage to get my other leg over the damn horse and seated on the saddle.

Aixen looked at me smugly. "Good now, *Princess*?"

"I am." I smiled. "Thank you."

Avi whistled, signaling the start of our ride to Beven for the trial, and Aixen returned to his horse. With little effort, he placed his foot in the stirrup and swung his leg over as if it were child's play.

Devon's arms wrapped around me as he guided the horse. His arms were sturdy, but his bony body poked me through the back of my leathers. It wasn't the same toned muscle that rippled through Farran every time we flew. He was another thing entirely.

I heaved a sigh. This would be a long ride if I didn't pull it together.

The first part of the trek was a leisurely gallop; we wound around the forest trees, and the motion nearly lulled me to sleep. Surely, this wasn't the pace Avi wanted to keep, not with the look in her eyes and the urgency with which she had woken up.

"Reina." Devon's voice in my ear jolted me awake, and his grip on me tightened. "Whoa, still me. Just wanted to let you know that once we get onto the flatter trail in a few minutes, I'm going to see how fast this horse can go. Avi wants to be there as soon as possible."

It had stopped raining, and I nodded groggily. "Sorry, yeah, that's fine. I'm good." I desperately needed to stop lying.

Even at this pace, my thighs cramped and chafed. Every few feet, a pain like lightning shot through my back and pelvis. The only thing keeping me on the horse was knowing it would be worse if I fell off. I survived being stabbed a few days ago. I could survive a horse.

Night fell as we crossed a bridge at the edge of a forest. From there, the trail spilled into round river hills punctuated with brush trees. A flat trail wound through them and everyone set their horses to a sprint. I held on for dear life, begging Devon to let me walk while he laughed and told me it was almost over.

We didn't stop until we reached the gates of Beven, which were drawn closed. The city behind them was silent, which was strange for the tenth largest city in all of Thera.

Avi approached and pounded on the thick wood paneling; the gates didn't budge. Then she stepped back and announced her name: *Lady Aviliana Valois of Arasund, here at the order of the Theranian Crown and Queensguard General Ephesus Linden.*

She was home, and the gates opened.

CHAPTER 23

AVI LED US THROUGH the empty streets of the walled city to a stable near an inn. Every instinct of mine wanted to slink off into the shadows and poke around the way I'd always operated in Rowane.

Moving as a group through the streets, dressed in our leathers and capes, felt more like a spectacle than an order.

Perhaps there'd be time later to sneak off and do things my way.

We only passed a few townsmen with their swords drawn and no one else. But relief washed over their pale faces when they saw us marked all over with the Crown's crest. If there were any knights or soldiers in Beven, they were far away from the entrance to the city.

Avi led us to a small stone courtyard outside the stable and inn where I hung back with Leena, my hand firmly placed upon the hilt of my sword as the rest of our house stabled the horses. In a few minutes, we all stood around staring at each other.

It was much too quiet for a duchy city.

"We are welcome to the inn above this tavern," Avi said as she trudged over and gestured at the tall stone inn behind us. "We have the entire third floor. Room assignments are yours to figure out. Beven was struck by a dreite priest and two demons. They're holding hostages. I need three groups to survey and secure; Beven officers will yield to your command. There could be rogues, dreites, or traps anywhere in the city.

"We're to secure it before the Crown arrives tomorrow. Devon, you have one squad. Vera, you have the second, and Jasper, you have the third. Amethyst is due to join us but won't be here until morning. Destroy any demons unless the *dreosen* is near. Reina and Farran, you're with me. Devon has the city maps."

Avi left no room for questions. She strode towards the inn and up the stairs with Farran and I close behind; she didn't stop until we reached a room with a desk overlooking the city from the fifth floor.

Farran stopped short, and the magic between us sparked in recognition as I remembered exactly why we shouldn't be this close. Gods fucking damnit.

"Farran told me you were able to take on shadow hounds with a demon. I don't know what else is happening between you two, and I don't care—this is a trial. You are soldiers for the Crown, and lives are on the line. My parents are being held hostage by a dreite and his demons." Avi looked straight at me. "I won't know anything else until I find the damn general."

Several suspicions clicked into place, knotting behind my ribs.

"A demon loyal to even a dreite priest will listen to her," Farran said, and I gave him a look. *How did he know? He missed the whole exchange.*

Avi's brow scrunched. "Will a dreite listen? If demons kneel like Farran says, maybe—"

I nodded, and the memory of the priestess resurfaced like a dream. "If the first trial was—"

"That wasn't a real priest," Avi said blankly, and my face turned white. Hurried reassurance bolstered her voice. "Farran told me the truth. No one else. It helped the Crown, but all three of us know."

"If anything, I can pull the demons off," I said. "And give you enough time to get your family."

Avi's gaze swept to Farran, and he nodded. "It's true."

"And the dreite? If he's a true priest?" Avi asked, looking straight at me.

She wanted my answer, but the truth was, I didn't know. I thought about the priestess and the odd way she looked at me. She had no interest in being commanded. Her voice chimed from my memories, "*They will rise on your command.*"

Farran cleared his throat and spoke in my stead, "She can do it, Avi."

Avi pursed her lips, dropping her voice. "It's my family, Far. If you lie, I know where you sleep, and I don't give a fuck about the Crown because we both know your mother isn't waging wars over you."

I shivered at the sharpness in her accusation, but Farran didn't wince; he straightened and nodded. "You have my word, Valois. Always."

"Mine too," I said sheepishly. I needed to say something, even if it wasn't helpful.

She and I had only been through two trials together with some training. She and Farran had shared too many to count.

Avi ignored me, but it wasn't completely dismissive. "We're going to the Valois Estate. It's not far, and I know the entrances." Her gaze shifted to mine. "Reina, if there's anything you need, ask. Magic is fickle, especially a gift as strong as yours."

"I've got it handled." I didn't need to look; Farran's blue eyes bore into the back of my head along with the shit-eating smirk he was trying to hide.

"Right," Avi said. She stood up, sword in hand. "Let's go."

She guided us through the empty streets of the city with ease. I chose to ignore Farran and instead focused on the budding heat around my heart as we got closer to what I could only assume were demons.

Threads of magic turned over and knotted further in an uncomfortable heap of slimy, wet, hot tendrils. *Why was it so intense? What was different?*

Avi stopped in the middle of the street as the feeling became unbearable. She lifted a grate and ignored Farran's pointed glare. "Just jump. You'll be fine, *Your Highness.*"

We descended into a damp, narrow cellar where the stone crumbled and the stench was noxious enough I couldn't get distracted by Farran. The foulness kept my head clear as I slinked through the tunnel, following Avi until she pushed open a heavy iron door opened into a basement after several winding turns.

The weight in my chest doubled, and I stumbled forward. Farran gripped my arm and kept me on my feet.

"Are you okay?" Avi asked, her brow creased in concern.

"Always," I remarked and shook off Farran's grip. I just needed to breathe and focus. "It's more than two demons."

"How do you know?" Avi's face was as white as a sheet. She was running through worst-case scenarios. This wasn't just a trial. For Avi, this was a test made just for her, and I shuddered at the thought. I hoped it wasn't her maker's request.

"I don't," I muttered. "But I've felt three before. They don't feel like this."

Avi looked at Farran. "We've only ever seen three at once," he amended.

Defeat had already settled on her shoulders, but she stared ahead. "The staircase will put us in the dining room. Reina goes first." Farran opened his mouth to protest, but I was already moving. Avi held a hand on his chest. "That's an order, Farran. I don't give a shit."

The door at the top of the stairs opened to the center of an estate house, with parquet floors, chandeliers, matching drapes, and crown molding in colors varying from room to room. Avi was clearly a lady who declined the title in search of something else.

My chest twisted, and dread pooled in my gut at the mess made of it. Despite the once beautiful decor, everything was wrong: tables were overturned, wallpaper cut apart, and glassware shattered across the floor. The threads in my chest clenched, and overwhelming pain shot throughout my body.

It felt as though a dagger was being dragged across my arms and my legs, over and over again. *Fuck.* This task was mine, and mine alone. I couldn't explain why, but I didn't think the dreite would allow it any other way. Footsteps sounded on the steps below me.

"I need to go alone," I ground out, voice fighting over the building pain and heat. My eyes met Avi's. "They're upstairs. I'll go."

"*Reina.*" It was Farran who protested, but I didn't care. I knew myself, and I knew the burning power under my skin. At least I *thought* I did.

Avi would keep him here until I said so. I watched her hands tense on her sword, and Farran unsheathed both of his. I wasn't truly alone, and I wasn't afraid of a few demons. Swallowing the pain, I darted up the stairs, no weapon in hand save for the magic and power searing through me.

A scream rang from down the hall. I ran towards a room with double doors and threw them open. It was a library, and five demons lowered their eyes and dropped to their knees as I rushed in.

Their cold threads tangled with the heat of my own, forging a balance. I could have grabbed them if I wanted, but I didn't need them. I'd handle this on my own.

Behind them was an elder dreite priest dressed in robes with knowing silver eyes. He held a dragon-forged dagger to the throat of a man who was gagged and tied to a chair. A woman's body sagged beside him, one with the same red hair as Avi, though it was peppered with silver.

Behind them, several brutalized bodies were slumped over each other.

They'd been torn to ribbons by the talons of the surrounding demons. I took a short breath and swallowed several thoughts that made me human. The room reeked of blood and decay.

The dreite lowered the dagger from the man's throat, and his voice cracked as he spoke, "It *is* you." There was recognition and awe in the way he looked at me. "You'll see they all deserved it, *valdronna.*"

I opened my mouth to ask a question, but the dreite disappeared into dust, and the demons went with him. The magic in my chest calmed and cooled to a dull sensation, like all the heat had been sucked from the room. *Valdronna.* There it was again, but I didn't have time to think.

My gaze fell on the man gagged in the chair.

"Father!" Avi shouted, running in from behind me.

She fell to her knees beside him, eyes wet with tears as she pulled the gag from his mouth and untied the binds around his hands. Without an order, Farran had done the same for the woman, but she didn't rouse.

"Get her out of here," Avi's father blustered, and his eyes settled on me. Avi looked at us as Farran's fingers pressed to the woman's throat to check her pulse.

"She's still alive," Farran muttered. "I can carry her to a room, and we'll—"

"There's no need, Your Highness," Avi's father said with as much respect as he could manage in his condition. "I will carry her myself. And that demon whore—get *her* out of here."

A shadow flitted across Farran's face. "Do not speak of an Armory soldier like that, Valois."

"Stand down," Avi said to Farran as she turned. "Father, you're in no—"

Avi's father held up his hand and groaned as he drew himself up, massaging his wrist. "That is my wife, and I will take care of her, Aviliana. If you're here, it's because the Crown believes there will be more attacks like this. Focus on your charge. We will be fine."

"Forgive me, Your Grace," Farran interrupted, his eyes glued to the space in the corner where several bodies were torn apart and discarded. "What was this attack?"

"There were five demons and a dreite priest," I said, ignoring the glare Duke Valois leveled at me with all the hospitality of a snake.

"Beven was under dreite siege," the duke spat. "A few more hours, and they might have succeeded. We are all that remains of the Arasund Council. The rest is piled behind me." *Piled* was putting it nicely. The bodies were indistinguishable . . . eviscerated and maimed beyond recognition. Bile rose in my throat.

"What do they gain from Beven?" Avi asked incredulously. Her face looked green, but she held herself straight despite seeming sick to her stomach. "There are closer towns if the land is what they want. Arasund is hardly populated."

"You know why, Aviliana," Valois said sharply. "Beven is four days removed from the protection of Rowane and the nearest seat to the sea and strait. All of your military training from Rowane and the Armory should tell you it's the best target to send a message to our Crown that they are returning."

Valois's gaze swiveled away from his daughter and settled on the prince. Farran stared him down; Farran was a whole head taller and could fell the duke with a single punch.

"Darkness is coming for Thera once more. Our queen knows demon wielders aren't gifted in times of peace. If you'll excuse me, I will tend to my wife. Take your *dreosen* with you." He spat out the last sentence.

"She serves the Crown, Valois," Farran warned, voice deadly.

"Not *mine*," the duke muttered as he lifted his unconscious wife and brushed past us out of the library. A chill settled in the room, and I shuddered against it.

The words of the dreite screamed in my head—the duke had certainly heard them, too. The priest had been waiting for me. I wouldn't consider why.

"I'm going to find someone to clean this up," Avi whispered. "Farran, you have command while I speak with my father. Take Reina; there's a tower just south of our estate, and the general should be there. He'll know if anything else can be done to secure the city. I want his assurance. And if I'm not back in a few hours, can you send the report?"

"Of course." Farran nodded, but there was a flicker of hesitation. "I'm sorry."

She shook it off and moved for the door. Her eyes drooped from exhaustion, but it wasn't the kind sleep could fix. "If you see Devon, just tell him I'm here. He needs to stay with Emerald."

The two of us left the Valois estate and the smell of death filling it. Outside, Beven was silent and dark as we made our way to the guard tower. Only a few of the street lamps had been lit in this part of the city, near the west wall.

We passed an entire street of burned houses, empty and black, now mere skeletons of what they'd been. Then we passed two more and the surrounding air smelled like a stale fire pit put out by the rain.

If it were recent, the rubble would be smoldering. I'd seen plenty of fires in Lower Rowane; it never took much to start a fire and level a house, but entire streets? Something was off.

"Did you hear about any fires in Beven?" I asked aloud as we passed a fourth burned street. Neither of us had spoken a word to the other yet. This wasn't the conversation we should have had, but I didn't want to have the other one.

Farran's brow furrowed as he thought. "City fires are more a question for my brothers. They don't come up in our captains' briefing."

I shook my head. "These fires were weeks ago. They'd be smoldering otherwise. Could dragons do this?"

"No. The streets are paved in Balrian slate. It would turn black when touched by dragon fire. They're still gray. Besides, dragon attacks would incinerate the roofs. Most are intact so the fires were set from the ground."

My brow knitted as we passed yet another burned street. It was desolate, and no part of it felt like the thriving city Beven was supposed to be. "Did you see a lot of dragon attacks?" I wondered.

"Only one outside of the Armory. I rode out with my brothers and father to watch. It was an ordered attack on a village staging a coup against their duke and our Crown. We watched from the hill and aided survivors after. My mother felt it was important for us to see the Crown's power."

"How old were you?"

"Twelve."

I shuddered. More questions poised on my tongue, but we approached the wall before I could ask.

A squat man stood in front of the staircase leading up to the tower. He wore a cape with the silver crest of the Crown embroidered over rich navy fabric; he belonged to Thera's army, but his pin boasted the crest of Arasund. The man bowed slightly when his eyes caught those of Farran. A general's signet was pinned to his collar.

Farran ignored the bow and didn't bother to tell the general to rise. "We're here from the Armory. I'm the First Officer for the Emerald House. The Duke and Duchess Valois are safe, and we've removed the demons and dreites.

"What else needs to be done to secure Beven? The soldiers of my house are on the streets tending to any injured and searching for additional threats. The Crown will arrive tomorrow to assess the damage and offer assistance."

"I owe many thanks to our queen for her timely response." His beady eyes slid to mine. "My men are of little use against dreites, but I've heard the rumors of Thera's *dreosen*. I fear we might be on the precipice of another war for the land that's rightfully ours."

"You and everyone else," Farran muttered, and the general's attention snapped back to the prince. "If *you* feel Beven is secure, General, I'll order my soldiers to patrol and give your men a chance to rest."

"Your kindness honors me, Your Highness. Do you see the fires burning in the towers across the city?" We peered over the wall, and Farran nodded stiffly. "My officers signal all is secure, however, the gates will remain closed through the night."

Farran's face tightened. "The duke would also appreciate this update from his general, if you find the time. Are you aware that the entire Arasund Council was slaughtered in the duke's palace?"

"I was not, Your Highness. Thank you for the update; we'll handle it. May the wind be at your back."

"And the gods at your side." Farran turned from the general and swiftly strode away.

I nearly broke into a run to keep up with him. He didn't slow down until we rounded a corner and were well out of the general's earshot. Farran stopped suddenly and spun around.

There was a storm brewing in his eyes as he stared at me. "You were right about something, *dreosen*."

"And that is?" I raised a brow.

A breeze rippled through the street. Cedar plagued with vanilla wafted over me and lowered the defenses warring with my better judgment.

Farran spoke quietly, "Something is wrong. I don't know what it is, but I find it odd that the Beven General was at the furthest watchtower instead of anywhere else."

"I haven't seen many soldiers," I remarked.

He nodded, peering into the street. "Neither have I."

The icy hand of dread crawled up my spine, and I shivered. We were surrounded by a street of burned buildings. "Is this a trap?"

Pinched lines appeared between his brows. "Can't be. The Crown wouldn't put a duke in harm's way for a trial. I don't know what's happening," he admitted. "When Avi returns, I'll speak with her. She knows Beven."

Farran turned and started walking again, though his pensive expression had relaxed.

"There were five demons in the library?" he asked.

"Yes. The priest said one thing to me and vanished with them before I could do anything."

The prince paused. "What did he say?"

"I don't remember." I did remember, but lying was easier when I didn't know what to think of it and I was far too tired to have that conversation.

All I could hear, in my head, was the priest saying, "*It is you*."

Silence drifted between us as we passed another street, and the smell of wet ash finally receded. The stillness remained . . . unnerving. The houses and shops were fine, but there wasn't a whisper of life; not a light left on, a face in a window, nor the click of footsteps.

Farran took a deep breath. "About the other night, Reina . . ."

My cheeks flamed. "It's fine—never again. It was irresponsible."

"*Never* again?" he mused, giving me a lopsided grin.

This had to be the end of it. I wouldn't be able to hide my allegiance to Arden forever, and I needed every bit of distance from him. Once this oath dissolved, my days were numbered.

I didn't deserve any more of his time—it would be wasted.

Farran opened his mouth to say something, but a shriek from a nearby street cut through the air like a knife. I broke into a run, away from the conversation.

In an instant, we were soldiers again, with no room for anything else.

I gasped when we rounded a corner. Standing in the cobblestone plaza was something that looked like a demon, but it wasn't anything I'd seen before: it was four times the size and towered above everyone with inky black wings and matching fangs brimmed with tar.

It snarled and growled as it lunged on all fours towards several people barricaded behind a wall of overturned tables at a cafe.

In front of the tables, Devon held his axe towards the creature. Lightning crackled on the blade, waiting to strike. On the opposite side of the square, at the creature's back, Aixen attempted to wrap silver chains around one of its legs, but he struggled to dredge up the silver he needed.

The little he did find burned as it collided with the creature's obsidian scales. It bellowed, but the massive beast broke out of the too thin chains in seconds, sending silver shards in all directions.

Leena stood a few paces away from Aixen, her face creased in concentration as shadowy tendrils reached towards it like a lake of black ichor. She willed the shadows to form, but they wouldn't obey. Something was stopping them.

A man bolted from behind the tables and ran for a nearby alleyway, but he wasn't fast enough. A razor-sharp scale flew out from the creature, striking the man dead to the ground.

Then the creature turned and charged straight for Aixen.

Fuck.

Devon's blast of lightning pushed the creature backwards. Talons screeched across the cobblestones. The distraction gave Aixen just enough time to refashion his silver into a shield, but it wouldn't work for long.

The creature was enormous. Its gangly limbs alone were double the size of the lampposts, and it lumbered around.

Parts of it looked like a demon, and if it came from a dreite priest, I should have some power over it. Maybe that's how the magic worked? I didn't know. I closed my eyes, groping around for any kind of tethering thread. The knot of warm magic in my chest tightened as I tried to spread it open.

Aixen screamed—his magic wouldn't hold. My eyes flew open. I had one chance, and it needed to work. Even a distraction was better than nothing.

I yanked through the threads and forced the damp, cold demon thread to show itself. It twisted into the warmth of my own magic, and I pulled. Something cracked open, and the burn of power erupted through me.

Three demons holding axes stood in the plaza, and the creature's attention whipped around to me. My demons looked like children next to it, but they stood at the ready as I held their threads. Farran gripped my forearm, and supplemental magic wove into mine, thrumming below my skin, drawing from a new well of power.

This was the most I'd ever felt, and only one thought rattled through my head.

Charge.

It was only a thought, but without fear, the demons attacked. They became a flurry of talons, steel, and teeth as they ran circles through its legs and cut where they could.

The creature cried out as one of its legs severed. And again, as a demon's axe plunged into its belly and sent black blood spewing onto the cobbles, but it wasn't enough. My vision shook.

"You have to let go," Farran whispered in my ear. His words curled around me, and the heat from his own threads flared.

"I can do it," I rasped back.

I couldn't.

"Let. Go."

Just another minute. I watched as one of my demons bared its fangs and bit into the creature's foot, sending oil-black blood flying in all directions.

Stars poked my vision as the threads I desperately clawed at slipped away from me. A breeze swept through the plaza, but my demons remained whole and fighting. I watched in awe as one buried its axe into the ribs of the creature in the same moment a flash of silver lurched through it.

Instantaneously, the massive creature shuddered and collapsed as I did the same.

Chapter 24

Birds chirped, and sunlight filtered through the window. It was too fucking bright, and the noise was abrasive as it pounded against my head.

I forced my eyes open only to shut them immediately, attempting to steady my head through sheer force of will.

My leathers were gone. I wore a clean tunic and a borrowed pair of breeches. Every part of me was exhausted, far worse than when I took on the shadow hounds in the Armory woods. The scar in my abdomen pulsed in pain, but it was dull compared to the way my head throbbed.

Prying open my eyes surely wasn't worth the pain that lanced through my entire body. *Fuck this*, I inwardly groaned. I couldn't lie here all day but I wouldn't.

We were still at trial.

A knock sounded on the door. Before I said anything, it opened; the smell of food wafted in with the sound of footfalls. Gods, I was starving.

"Headache, darling?"

I stiffened at the sound of Farran's voice. He'd brought me food . . . not Leena.

Here he was, of all people. His voice was chipper and grated against the pain seated behind my brow. More than ever, I needed to find a way to open my eyes so I could give him an appropriate glare.

"I woke up with a headache, too," he remarked. "You spent a fuck ton of magic last night. While impressive, next time, one or two demons might be enough with other Armory soldiers around."

"I'll be sure to coordinate with everyone," I grumbled.

"At least Avernought will be satisfied." Farran crossed the room, and the floorboards creaked under his steps. The rattling of the tray struck every nerve in my brain. "You need to eat, First Officer's orders. The matron also added something to help with the headache."

A curtain squealed as he pulled it closed and some of the light receded. I sat up, testing the change by opening one eye and then the other.

"What did I miss?" I asked, squinting. Farran set a warm piece of toast in my hand as if I was a child.

"Well, your demons made quick work of whatever the creature was. Took it out at the knees, while Aixen finished it with a silver lance to the chest," Farran said. "It was something conjured by a dreite, but I've never heard of anything like it before. Tomas and Blaise also found a dreite trying to flee over the east wall. He vanished before they could do anything. Everyone is safe, but the city isn't as secure as the general thought."

"Oh." My voice was weak. I cleared my throat, and it helped marginally. "Is Avi's mother—" I forced both eyes to open. The pain was more of a dull ache with the curtain pulled. But I had to think about every damn movement.

The prince frowned slightly. "She'll recover. It was a small dose of poison. Avi will be back in command once she sorts things with her father."

"Good." Yet Valois's words still stung. They were hot iron against my neck. *Demon whore.*

Farran leaned against the wall near the window, his arms crossed as he watched me and his sleeves rolled back. He was dressed as plainly as I was, his hair tied back. He glanced at the toast in my hand. "You do need to eat."

Begrudgingly, I took a bite of the sourdough laden with warm butter and then another just to appease him.

"The Crown arrives this afternoon. We'll tell them what we saw," he added. "Did you try to control the beast at all?"

"No," I answered, trying to recall but coming up short. "And that all sounds more like a first officer or captain responsibility."

He looked straight at me, his calm eyes pinning me where I sat. "They'll want to meet their first demon wielder."

Oh. Dread seized my spine and threatened to pull me down, back into the bed.

The floor creaked, and Farran walked away from the window, towards the door. He saw the dread in my eyes; I was sure of it, but then he gave me the mercy of not saying anything about it.

Instead, he vied for, "The innkeeper washed your leathers and cape. They're drying by the fire. Your sword and dagger are under the bed."

"Thank you." I hesitated.

"Thank Leena. She was the one who got them off of you." He smirked. "Not sure how you're able to move in those." I thanked the gods for how dark it was in the room, so he couldn't see me blush.

Farran twisted the door handle. It opened a crack and light spilled in—I slammed my eyelids.

"Training starts when you're ready," he said.

I groaned as the door closed . . . Gods, I needed to get up. With the last bit of toast popped into my mouth, I dressed slowly and swallowed the vial of potion that was supposed to help. It wasn't one I recognized, but I'd try anything if it made the morning more bearable.

Tired, sore legs took me downstairs to the tavern, where most of my house sat around two wooden banquet tables pushed together. Chandeliers holding lit candles flickered above, while two fireplaces roared on either side of the stone room.

Varyn loudly told a story, and everyone laughed. Well, almost everyone; Avi and Devon were nowhere to be seen.

Another group of soldiers sat at a table closest to the door. Most of them had Armory swords, and one wore a purple cape: Amethyst. So, reinforcements had arrived this time.

Farran sat at the table behind our house with his arms crossed, deep in thought about something else, with several papers and maps spread in front of him. He was the first one to notice me, and his eyes looked so damn blue in the morning light that I gawked. The soft orange glow suited him in a way I would never say out loud.

Inwardly, I cursed. *A mistake, that's all it was.*

Varyn noticed me and stopped talking mid-sentence.

I flashed an awkward smile from the stairs. "Morning."

Tomas stood, raised a steaming mug, and bowed his head as he scooted across the bench to clear a space. "Everyone, make way for Thera's demon wielder! Our *dreosen*!"

"Please don't," I grumbled and walked past the space to sit on the end beside Leena.

She squeezed my knee and gave a soft smile. If I didn't know better, I would have called it apologetic. This was exactly the attention I had no interest in today, or ever.

"Aixen said you were incredible." A smile tipped Varyn's lips. His arm was around Evie's shoulders. Though I was sure everyone drank tea and coffee, the hum in the air and the excitement could have fooled me. "*Three* demons is what you wielded from thin air. Amazing. Amazing and terrifying."

"It was both of those things." Aixen smirked and held a steaming mug of tea towards me.

I accepted it gladly; my hands were freezing. Fall had arrived in full with yesterday's storm.

"Does anyone know what that thing was?" I asked. The ache in my head dulled as the tonic settled.

Aixen shook his head. "Devon thinks it was a wight. Tomas thinks it was some weird shit the dreites conjured to see if it could take on demons since you've evened the playing field. And our first officer has been notably silent on the matter."

"We have dragons," Blaise interjected with a bite in his tone. "It's not an even field."

My head swiveled. I wanted to hear his voice again, like we could still be friends, but the conversation shifted quickly to something else, and I never got the chance.

Suddenly, he couldn't bother to look at me. Blaise blustered out of the room when Varyn began his next story about a time he thought he'd encountered a wight, which was, in fact, a man with a shifting gift on the third day of a tavern bender.

I turned to Leena and lowered my voice. "Thanks for your help. I owe you one."

Leena smoothed my braid and smiled softly, fingertips lingering on the green ribbon tied at the end. "It was the least I could do, Rein. But you ought to thank Farran. He carried you the entire way back after he'd nearly spent his own magic."

"Is that why he's so smug?" I frowned.

She lowered her voice even further and leaned forward with a wicked smile. "He insisted, and Aixen was in too much shock." I blushed as she leaned back again. "You heard he killed the thing with a lance?"

"I wasn't in shock, Leena." Aixen leaned into our conversation. "Just a state of surprise. I wasn't ready to see a demon and whatever the fuck that was. I also thought I'd miss."

Evie looked at me through the steam of her cup. "Do you think you could a thing like that?"

"I have no idea." I thought about it for the second time. Maybe I should have tried harder. "I hope not, but I'll try harder next time."

A shrill whistle silenced us. We all turned to see Farran standing, patiently awaiting our attention. I rubbed my temples. My head was better, but if I turned too quickly, a sharp pain tore through it. The whistle certainly hadn't helped.

"Avi will be here later," he announced. "Until then, I'm standing in as Captain, and Vera is First Officer. The Crown arrives this afternoon. We're waiting on any information from the Beven General, and for now, the city is tentatively secure. Mira, the innkeeper, has been gracious enough to let us use her courtyard. We'll begin with warmups and then sparring. You have fifteen minutes. In the meantime, Amethyst is on watch."

Emerald scrambled to finish breakfast and grab their swords. Except for me. Somehow, I was the only one who came downstairs prepared, which meant I'd be the first in the courtyard with Farran.

It was a clear day, but it was cold in the shadows as I paced across the cobblestones in just a tunic and breeches.

"Did you eat?" Farran asked, breaking the silence.

I glanced up. I couldn't avoid his eyes, especially when it was just the two of us. We were surrounded by stone walls, shielded from the morning light, and his voice echoed.

"I had a few bites and whatever the potion was," I muttered.

A flicker of concern shadowed his face. He'd tied his hair back again today and looked every bit the captain, even without the leathers and designations. "If you faint in front of the Crown, I'm not catching you."

"I'm perfectly capable of standing." I wrapped my arms tighter around myself, cursing how completely unaffected he was by everything. "Will they ask me to wield a demon?"

Farran shrugged. "It's possible. They may just ask questions. I have no idea what they're after. Since we have a moment, I also wanted to make sure I heard you correctly last night."

My voice shrank, but I tilted my chin up despite it. "Which part? I recall several conversations."

His sapphire gaze held mine. I didn't realize he was only two steps away from me. If he came any closer, I wouldn't be cold. "The never again part."

"Oh, right. *That.*" I paused, my face heating. "Yes. Sorry it happened in the first place. I was out of line. It was a mistake, and it won't happen again."

Farran looked at me, and whatever expression crossed his face was unreadable. "If that's what you want. But, for the record, nothing about you is a mistake to me," he said carefully.

"Duly noted," I squeaked, taking a step back as I ignored the fluttering in my heart.

Voices came around the corner of the stables, and I turned to see Leena, Aixen, and Blaise—the first to arrive. They were followed closely by Vera and the other two third-years, Jasper and Mianen, while the rest trickled in.

Our conversation was over, but by the fucking gods, was it screaming through my head? Couldn't he see I was venomous?

Of course not; somehow, those words had done nothing to him.

When the rest of Emerald arrived, he clapped his hands together and training started. For the first hour, he tortured us with stretches and poses to "improve our balance", which was far more taxing than he let on. Blaise and Aixen wore their leathers, and both looked ready to die by the time we were done.

"Ready to spar?" Farran finally asked as the first ray of sun tipped over a shorter building and onto the stones. "Who's first? Tomas? Vera?"

Farran stood in the center of us with a short sword in each hand. They weren't his dragon-forged blades, rather a pair of worn, dull Armory swords. Though,, dangling from each of his deft hands, they looked intimidating as his gaze swept over the house.

Vera stepped forward. "Swords or magic?" she inquired.

"Whatever you want, Vera. I would never stop you."

Her green eyes lit up. Vera managed fine when it came to combat, but there was nothing natural about seeing her with a sword in hand. Her strikes and blocks were heavy and awkward, regardless of the weapon.

Vera readied herself and faced Farran with green magic blooming just below her skin. Nature-bound powers drew from the earth and didn't put the wielder at risk of burning out the way many of the other gods' gifts did. If she were calculated,

Vera could wield forever and only get winded, as nature was a bottomless resource.

Farran lunged first, but Vera blocked him with a shield of vines fashioned in seconds.

His right sword caught in the sinewy wood, and she disarmed him using sheer momentum, forcing him to yield as vines gripped his forearm.

Her eyes narrowed as she smirked. "Don't you know not to strike a nature-bound weapon?"

Some of his hair came free of its knot and fell in front of his eyes. "Of course I know. I just thought we should all see what happens." He swiveled around. "Next? I should mention, please don't use your gift if it will kill me. We'll find other ways to get practice in."

I may have imagined it, but Farran looked at Tomas first and then, pointedly, at me. *I couldn't conjure anything if I tried.*

Blaise cleared his throat and strode to the center of the ring. The softness in his saffron eyes had been replaced with intensity as he gripped his saber with two hands. But this wasn't the saber I remembered. It was new, with a gold hilt and a much sharper edge than a training sword.

Farran squared up, but before his feet set, Blaise had already started towards him. Farran's short swords crossed to stop Blaise's blade from coming straight down on Farran's chest.

Farran held him there for a moment, then used the strength in his back and shoulders to push him off. Blaise stumbled backward, but quickly regained his footing and lunged for Farran. I was in awe of how much Blaise had improved since last year. His swings were precise, his blocks were exactly where they needed to be, and he was *fast*.

A loose stone tripped Blaise and gave Farran the briefest opening. Blaise caught himself, but the quarter of a second was enough for Farran to stop his right sword before it struck Blaise's neck.

He needed to yield. Instead, Blaise moved aside and swung his saber hard, knocking a sword from Farran's grasp. His sapphire eyes widened as he retreated, and Blaise wasted no time. Another cut and the other sword skittered across the stones.

One more fluid motion and the saber kissed Farran's neck, so close it drew blood.

Both men were caught, heaving and sweating, in a deadly stalemate. Farran looked worried, and Blaise leveled a hard stare, like he'd given his warning.

"Oi! Enough!" Avi's voice bounded off the walls as she walked to the center, her face severe as she stared Blaise down. "MacLaine yields. Let him walk, Milliard." Blaise shook out of a trance and sheathed his saber as he stepped several paces back.

Blaise spat, "I'm sorry."

"Sorry, *who*?" Farran glared. Rage swirled through his eyes like a storm over a sea.

He held his tunic to the cut on his throat, revealing a delicious bit of skin at his hip I shouldn't have looked at as I held my breath.

"I'm sorry, *First Officer*," Blaise bit out, but there wasn't a line of regret on his face.

Farran nodded and straightened. "Don't let it happen again."

Blaise stalked off towards the inn. Everyone else remained.

"Anyone else inclined to ignore sparring rules?" Avi asked loudly, glaring at our house.

There was fire in her eyes. She looked exhausted, and her unbound red hair whipped against her face in the breeze. Devon stood beside her, equally spent and no one said anything.

Avi nodded. "Good, I have no tolerance for it, and I'm not afraid to sway a maker's decision. Don't forget that."

Farran lowered his tunic; the cut was almost dry, but it never should have happened. I glimpsed some of the black tendrils of his tattoo: his oath to the demon wielder and the same mark Blaise wore.

Avi cleared her throat. "Crown forces are arriving. Everyone needs to be cleaned up, in capes, and ready to receive them. Few houses get an opportunity like this. Please act like you have some sense. Amethyst will stand with us. They've only sent their third-years."

Training was decidedly over. We walked back to the inn and readied ourselves. My stomach dropped. I dreaded this meeting.

And I knew why: meeting the Crown like this was different, more official. This was outside the Atrium, a public affair, and I wore their crest and the uniform of their soldiers, with a gift they needed for their war.

I was *the* demon wielder—the *dreosen* the Crown was promised. Or was it the realm? The mounting pressure kept confusing me.

When the Crown's company arrived, we lined up outside the inn with the Duke and Duchess Valois. I stood between Vera and Leena towards the front of the line, eyes watering in the bright light of noon as Avi stood between the General of Beven and Farran.

I tugged a loose silver thread off the hem of my cape and watched it flutter to the ground.

General Ephesus Linden was the first to step forward. Behind him was Prince Cormac, several other advisors, and knights from the Queensguard in their silver cords.

Jaxon stood among them, dressed in the midnight-blue cape of the Crown, the silver hilt of her sword fastened to her hip. The cry of her dragon, Aerno, echoed in the distance—its presence should be a deterrent to any remaining dreites.

Linden spoke first. He addressed our house but only spoke to Avi. "The Crown appreciates your expediency, Captain Valois. The duke assured me your house handled the situation within hours of arrival. While it's a shame to have lost much of the Arasund council, at least your mother and father were spared, thanks to our *dreosen*."

I froze, and Linden's beady gaze drifted in my direction. My hand wrapped around the hilt of my sword, and I stared ahead. Part of me waited for Duke Valois to correct him or offer what he'd heard the dreite say.

"It's our purpose to serve the Crown," Avi said coolly.

"Wonderful." General Linden grinned, and I swallowed my relief. "I've been assured that a room is prepared for a more detailed briefing. Is this correct?"

"Of course, General Linden. Matron Mira will lead the way." Avi gave a curt bow, and the rest of us did the same as the Crown's party strode past us into the inn.

Jaxon lingered a little longer and lowered her voice as she passed Avi. "They were impressed. You're doing great. We'll speak later."

Avi lifted her eyes and smiled. "I learned from the best."

The door closed behind Jaxon, and Avi had one more order.

"If I don't say your name, you are dismissed to be on your best behavior and remain in the tavern to eat. If any requests come through from General Linden in my absence, you will oblige." There was a murmur of agreement among us, and Avi continued, "First Officer MacLaine, Odinea, and Sangrey. You'll join the briefing. Captain Vinn, First Officer Carter, you'll also join us."

I took a deep breath as the rest of Emerald followed Vera and Leena into the inn. Blaise glanced back at me, but I ignored the weight of his saffron stare as I followed the captains, first officers, and Devon up the stairs.

Chapter 25

Avi stopped before we walked into the inn, gesturing us closer.

My mind buzzed when Farran's arm brushed mine as we huddled with our captain; even through our leathers, it felt electric. If he felt the same, he was hiding it frustratingly well, or he was used to it.

"I know your brother is in there, Farran," Avi whispered. His jaw tightened. "Do not let him rile you." Her eyes roved over to me. "Nothing we hear today leaves the room."

Devon held Avi's hand as we ascended the stairwell, though the two parted the moment we reached the hallway. The room the matron prepared for the Crown was the same room on the fifth floor from yesterday. Today, several paintings had been added to the walls and fresh-pressed navy curtains were draped around the windows.

In the room, Jaxon stood against the wall with Vinn, the Captain of Amethyst. He wore a purple cape, epaulets befitting an Armory captain, and shared the same severe expression as Avi.

Prince Cormac sat behind the desk with his hands folded, General Linden to his right and the General of Beven to his left. I didn't know how the duchess made it all the way up the stairs, but she sat—tired, bruised, and worn—on a chair in the corner beside the duke; her eyes glued to Avi.

The four of us bowed towards the prince in tandem and remained standing in the center of the room.

"A bow?" The crown prince looked incredulously at Farran.

Cormac wore the same grin and sharp cheekbones. The only difference was the thin crown nestled around his neatly trimmed hair and olive eyes.

"I never thought I'd see the day—unless Mother's threats finally got you," he quipped.

Farran smirked. "I thought you could use it, brother. Mother said your ego was bruised after you lost to a woman in the last tournament."

"The women of Thera are worthy opponents," the crown prince grumbled as he surveyed the room. "Everyone is quiet today. Why is that? You were victorious, few lives were lost. The Crown is granting an award to all of you. I also happen to know Beven needs a piece of its wall rebuilt. Consider it done, Your Grace, Duke Valois."

Duke Valois looked up at Cormac with a grimace. "That's extremely kind of you, Your Highness."

"We have ten holds and two other duchy seats, like Beven, that remain more than a three-day ride from Rowane, all of which sit closer to the Darklands." Cormac continued with a dismissive wave and a charmed smile. "You were protected by your proximity to our honored Armory, but this attack exposed a vulnerability."

Cormac glanced at General Linden, who nodded.

The crown prince continued, "Our queen will provide each duchy an additional two knights from the Queensguard. They will be considered first- and second-in-command to your own general. They are familiar with dreite magic."

Cormac looked straight at the Beven General then, whose lips were tight as though he bit his tongue. The prince continued, tone tinted with warning.

"Our knights will respond to your order, General, but they've sworn loyalty to the Crown which comes before all else. Beven and the duchy of Arasund are granted Dame Jaxon, a dragon-rider and skilled *lumen*. As well as Sir Irvin, who is known for his efficacy in combat, years of service to the Crown, and gift as a *braagen*."

Cormac's olive gaze stopped cold on Duke Valois.

"This is, of course, in exchange for your continued loyalty. We have no reason to assume anything but unwavering support, Your Grace. But I do need to remind you the duchies Arasund and Westvale were the first to fall in the last small war."

"Neither Beven nor Arasund will fall, Your Highness," Duke Valois said, his head bowed towards the prince as though eye contact was undeserved.

"Good," Cormac said lightly, rising to his feet. "Your queen will be glad to hear it. Her Majesty looks forward to your presence at court when you and the Duchess Valois are rested enough for the journey."

Farran watched his brother like a hawk as Cormac came around the desk and stopped only a few steps away from me. He wore completely impractical leathers that had never seen a training field. They were deep blue and lined with delicate threads of silver, his own silver champion cords boasted across his chest.

"I've been looking forward to formally meeting our *dreosen*. Up close, she is a sight to behold in more ways than one." Cormac took another step towards me, gazing with the same intensity Farran had when we first met.

I straightened my shoulders as Farran tensed beside me.

Cormac grinned and looked at his brother. "You left out quite a bit when you spoke of her, brother. Incredible someone so small contains those multitudes. I should have paid more attention when I was last at the Armory; she has all the features that would be envied at court."

"She's good with a dagger, Cormac," Farran warned, but the prince's olive gaze didn't leave mine. "If you get too close, she won't care if you're wearing a crown."

Cormac frowned. "The demons listen to you over a dreite if you enter a room. Is this correct? They kneel?"

I nodded slowly, and his hand stroked his chin where dark stubble shadowed it. Regal was an understatement. I couldn't help but wonder what Farran would look like in the same crown.

The prince mused, "You conjured three demons from thin air in the plaza and overtook whatever fucked-up beast the dreites created? That's true as well?"

"Yes, Your Highness." I stood straight. "Well, our silver wielder delivered the final blow."

Cormac wasn't the only one watching me; Linden's gaze was also unwavering.

"How do you do it?" the crown prince asked.

I hesitated, but it was pointless to lie. Farran nudged my arm. "I can find their threads of magic and hold them almost like reins. Once I have them, I believe it's similar to any other wielding—"

"Farran told me you killed three when you brought the dreite priest back from the Darklands."

I took a sharp breath and prayed no one could read my mind, which corrected the statement. "I didn't know how to wield them at the time; instinct kicked in."

"Of course." Cormac paused. "You understand why this power is valuable to the Crown, yes?"

"It comes once every few generations and only one *dreosen* can exist at any time." I could say more about treason and war, but I knew when to bite my tongue.

The crown prince smiled. "A demon wielder means Thera will supersede the power of the dreites and any other kingdom wishing us ill. The gods gift us what we need, yes, but *you* are what we prayed for. I'm sure my brother and Lord Avernought have told you as much. Thera has never had their *own Dreosen*."

I nodded, but I didn't like his tone. It was some hybrid of fascination, pride, and entitlement.

"Where are you going with this?" Farran asked, and an edge tugged at his voice as Avi shifted beside him.

"Nowhere. She looks like someone who's used to a little more freedom. I'll apologize for how much will be asked of her in service to the Crown." He paused and looked at Avi. "We'll also be adjusting Emerald's trials to keep her closer to Rowane, just in case she's needed sooner rather than later."

Farran's face shadowed, and his brows pinched. "We're not at war."

"Correct—for now. That's why I expressed my apologies; it's better to get ahead of the unavoidable." The crown prince looked straight at the Duke and Duchess of Arasund as he took several steps back and leaned on the desk. "I have one more point of business, and then we can adjourn. Duke Valois, I'm sorry to hear about your son. I have several leads I'd like to discuss—"

"What about my brother?" Avi blurted and whipped around to level a glare at her parents. "What's happened?"

"It's nothing, Aviliana," Duke Valois said, lips a thin line while every feature on Avi's face was fierce and demanding. Even Devon tensed. "Nothing we can't handle," he added.

"What happened? Do I need to withdraw?" she pressed.

General Linden coughed forcefully into his arm. She was a valuable pledge to Lady Verdura, a maker of Emerald. Withdrawal was complicated and uncommon unless you were a dragon rider.

"That's completely unnecessary, Aviliana." Her mother's voice shook.

The Beven general cleared his throat. "She deserves to know, Your Grace."

Avi's head swiveled around the room, looking for anyone to tell her what was going on, until Prince Cormac finally crossed his arms and spoke up. "Allow me, Captain Valois. Your brother went missing last week. It's nothing to be concerned about, yet. The Crown sent out a search for him and Beven's forces have also been looking—"

"That's not nothing," Avi said calmly, but a storm raged behind her words. "You know what happens if Eoin is found dead." She held up her chin. "You have no other heir."

"Aviliana." Duke Valois's voice rose to a breaking point. "This is not the time nor the place for this conversation."

Avi took a deep breath and stepped in line beside Devon. "I suppose you're right. It's nothing."

A pin drop would have been too loud in the silence that came over the room. Farran looked stunned, and Prince Cormac wore a similar expression but straightened it with royal precision.

"I think we can dismiss for now and enjoy the evening in Beven. We'll leave at first light and get out of your hair, Duke Valois. Your daughter has permission from the Crown to extend her stay, given the circumstances," Cormac said.

"That's not necessary." Avi glared.

"Right," the crown prince replied matter-of-factly. "Thank you all."

Without another word, everyone filed out of the room. Those of the Armory went straight for the tavern downstairs, where Devon ordered two large tankards of ale.

I sank down on the bench beside Leena; she was in the middle of a card game with Aixen, Varyn, and Evie. Farran and Devon sat beside them, but paid more attention to the door of the tavern. Further down the table, Vera and Tomas chatted across from Blaise, who focused on his mug as though he might conjured something in it. The rest of our house had scattered around the room.

Leena shrieked when she won her third round in a row. Her arms flew back, and a woman's hand caught her fist the moment before it went into her face. "Shouldn't your shadow wielder have better coordination?" Jaxon asked, pointedly looking at Farran.

Leena whirled around and apologized profusely, but Jaxon laughed.

It had only been a few weeks since we saw her, but in the navy cape with her pins and designations from the queen, she looked regal, perhaps a little older too, as she sat between Farran and Devon. "Feels like years since I sat in a tavern."

"That's because it's been at least one since we've been here," Farran mused. Both took a swig of beer and winced.

"That's vile," Jaxon spluttered. The beer tasted like cold, stale bread. "It was fine the last time we were in Beven."

"Did demons attack then, too?" Varyn asked across the table. He slammed down a hand of cards and sent Aixen reeling.

Farran ran a hand over his chin. I noticed the shadows under his eyes; he was more exhausted than he led on. "There was one demon, and we had to bring its head back to the Armory, right?" he recalled.

"Yeah." Jaxon's jaw stiffened at the memory. "It was terrible. We'd get it cornered and it would escape. Happened almost ten times before we finally got it down. Makers awarded us, though—we had the faster time compared to Amethyst. Speaking of, has anyone seen Avi? I wanted to talk to her."

"She's in her room," I answered with a shrug. "Not sure when she'll join us."

Jaxon sighed. "I figured as much. This was cruel, even for the Armory. This was the Crown testing her, and all of you. Amazing work, Aixen and Reina." She turned to me with a proud smile and none of the warning I expected.

"Thanks, but Aixen killed it," I muttered. I wanted to trust Jaxon, but she knew who I was, and that was a tenuous place to be.

"Does the city feel empty?" Farran asked, looking pointedly at Jaxon. "We ran into four blocks of houses burned down by the west tower. Couldn't be dragons; the roofs were intact, and the fire was weeks ago, at least."

Jaxon's eyes narrowed as she thought through the question. "Odd. I haven't heard anything."

"How many people were in the streets when you rode for the first time?" Aixen asked. "Amethyst spent the morning going door to door to tell them the city was secure. Only a handful of people answered."

"It was busy," Jaxon said slowly, her eyes scrunched as she took another painful sip of beer. "It wasn't different from Rowane, but you're right, hardly anyone's been in the streets. If this happened in Rowane, people would have been trampled."

"Maybe they're scared," Varyn offered. "I nearly pissed myself when I saw the thing in the plaza." Indeed, it was a sore sight.

But the nagging dread was back and prickled my neck. Farran shared a look with me hovering somewhere between confusion and worry.

"We could do rounds tonight," he added. "Just to be sure."

"Not a bad idea," Jaxon said and turned to me. "You saw the dreite, right? Did he say anything? I wonder how far word has spread about your gift." She swiveled back to Farran. "Your house might need to focus more on keeping her alive."

"She's already been stabbed." Aixen shrugged, and I watched Jaxon's face pale.

"In the Armory?" she sputtered.

"I'm fine," I said, surprised at the concern Jaxon had when she knew I was Arden's viper. "Some asshole from Diamond. He's a name on the Atrium floor now."

"Good," she breathed out, "but don't get complacent. There will be more. You're all still armed, right?"

There were nods around the table.

The din of conversation around us paused as everyone turned to look at the staircase where Prince Cormac swept in. Everyone rose to their feet as he walked straight for our table and took the seat across from his brother beside Jaxon.

We all started to bow, but Cormac waved his arms. "None of that. If you don't bow for Farran, don't do it for me. Not when it's just us Armory soldiers."

Farran's eyes narrowed. "You came downstairs? Seems ill advised in a city that's only just been secured," he remarked.

"Lonely in my room." Cormac shrugged. He'd taken off the crown but hadn't changed his leathers. Two short swords hung from his belt. "It's not any city. It's one of our duchies. Guards aren't far, and I'm surrounded by soldiers and knights. You also forget, brother, I *am* a champion."

Cormac gestured to the two cords strung across his chest. They matched Jaxon's and every other Queensguard knight.

"Did it occur to you that perhaps I wanted to meet your house? I've heard so much about Sapphire from Lorcan, but nothing from you. I almost called on Avernought to make sure you hadn't deserted," the crown prince mused.

"Well," Farran said and leaned back. "Here I am. Alive and well. Certainly not a deserter."

"Nice to see." Cormac looked around the table. "Jaxon told me a little about Emerald. Let me see what I remember. I'd know Reina, the *dreosen*, anywhere. Beside her must be Leena, the *sunderone*, also formidable. Blaise? Aixen? Something with silver. One of you is a *braagen*, another is a *vistone*, and there's a healer. Of course, I remember Vera. I have a soft spot for *balens* and their natural wiles."

"Impressive memory," Jaxon said, sounding pointedly unimpressed.

"Does Emerald still have the nonsensical common room? With all the chairs skewed around and such?" Cormac wondered.

"You were in Emerald?" Leena asked as Farran and Jaxon laughed. Cormac shot them a glare.

"I'd agree he was in Emerald in some ways," Farran said. "However, he was supposed to sleep in the Onyx rooms and wear their cape."

"Love is a strange thing," Cormac replied wistfully.

"Now you call it love?" Something softened in Farran's face as he let himself smile. I'd never seen this side of him and a spark of heat came to life in my chest. I swigged the beer to cool it off.

Cormac leaned back, arms crossed tight. "And what do you know of love, Farran?" he drawled.

"Absolutely nothing, and I'm content."

"Whatever helps you sleep at night," Cormac muttered, keen to change the subject. His eyes turned to Aixen, who looked flustered. "What game are you playing?"

"Verity," Leena answered. "Aixen can deal you in, Your Highness."

Farran watched his brother as if he were waiting for something to change or shift. I knew the look; I looked at Declan the same way when he was being too polite. It was waiting for the inevitable storm—something unspoken he'd figure out when his brother finished performing.

"Does it seem quiet to you out there?" Cormac pondered. There was a murmur of agreement around the table, accented by a couple of shrugs.

"It's probably nothing." Jaxon waved it off, but shared a contemplative look with Farran. "We suspect they're scared."

We played a few hands, and by the end of the third round, we smiled and laughed like a group of old friends—not a crown prince and a house from the Armory who had sworn their lives to him.

Farran remained across from me, and I let myself admire the view as the beer warmed my nerves. Between the second and third round, he stiffened, and I craned my neck to see three Crown guards hurry outside.

Varyn dealt another hand, but we never played it. Someone burst through the door of the tavern, and everyone turned to look. The man was covered in something oily and black. His mouth hung open, but no words came out as he collapsed in the doorway.

Every Crown-sworn soldier in the room jumped to their feet and ran to get their weapons.

Both princes were already armed and rushed outside. I was close behind with Jaxon, Leena, and most of our house because we understood the importance of being prepared.

Chapter 26

The streets of the city were silent aside from a light drizzle of rain tittering off the roofs and shop awnings. Anyone walking would have thought it was peaceful if they could ignore the building swell of magic with the distant rumble of an approaching storm.

Power warmed my chest as we moved through the streets, swelling and tangling itself around my ribs like yarn threaded through a loom. The pressure squeezed my heart and pounded in my ears. There were dreites here, and every pulse reminded me.

If anyone died in the presence of the Crown, it would be another act of war amid several escalations.

Farran stopped abruptly and grabbed my wrist while the others kept walking, swords drawn. The heat from his touch buzzed against my skin, and his gaze flicked over my shoulder for a split second.

"You don't have enough magic to do what you did last night," he murmured. "If it comes to that, you need to run." The concern in his voice was palpable, almost desperate.

Everyone in our party stopped to look at us. Notably, Cormac raised his brow as he stared at his brother.

I snatched my wrist back. "I'll be fine." I had a dagger and a sword, neither of which I was afraid to use. The storm in Farran's eyes said otherwise, but I didn't care. I stalked forward and joined everyone else.

Jaxon said something to Cormac before she disappeared. I had no doubts she was getting her dragon and Sir Irvin, the other knight. There were no demons, no hounds, not even a clop of hooves on the cobbles. It was desolate despite how charged the air was.

Heat unfolded in my limbs the closer we got. We kept our weapons poised, but there was nothing to swing at until we turned down another street and something shifted in the air. The others felt it, too.

Another rush of thunder peeled through. We moved as one until the alley spit us out. Something was *wrong*. This is where we were yesterday—surrounded by the streets of burned buildings. The smell of damp ash overwhelmed me, and a new fire raged in the distance. I could see the orange flames and rising smoke against the sky.

I reached for the magic in my chest, but it felt unsettled. The threads thrashed and tied into knots. Dread clamped around my spine.

Is this when I'm supposed to run? I wasn't going anywhere.

Lightning struck, but no thunder followed, and Leena bumped into my shoulder. Cormac loudly said, "What the fuck?"

And then I saw *them*.

Five dreites stood in the rubble of the burned houses, all wearing symbols of the old gods on their cloaks: ancient runes and sigils stitched in gold thread I recognized but wasn't close enough to make out. On the very end was the same priestess from the keep, but she didn't look at me. She looked at the princes.

I stepped in front of Farran. He grabbed my shoulder, but instead of pulling me back, he squeezed it. A wind swept through along with a ripple of magic, and I thought I'd know what to do next, but my brain stopped, my chest burned, and the threads kept sliding out of my grasp as the knot of it wound tighter.

The dreites all stared straight at me. The one in the middle was the same from last night, and the silver in his eyes swirled like molten metal in a blacksmith's forge.

I took another step closer, and Farran's hand slid from my shoulder.

I wanted to do something impressive. They were here for me. I knew it; I sensed it.

"You've brought two Theranian princes, *valdronna*? Interesting." My head was heavy and thick as the dreite's voice poured into it as though it was warm honey. There was the word again, old, muddled Catharian.

"What do you want?" Cormac bellowed, and the dreites' attention moved.

My mind screamed: *wrong*, this was *wrong*. The crown prince sounded so far away, but he was right there. I could see him.

"This city is defended by the Crown, and we will stop at nothing to ensure it stays that way."

Swords rattled behind me, but no one made any move to attack—no silver, no shadows, no fire or wind.

"You're sure about that?" the dreite asked with a wry smile. His silver eyes shifted from Cormac to Farran, then back to me. "You can't feel your *dreos* anymore, can you, Reina Sangrey? I'm sorry, but now we know it's you, you—"

Farran stepped in front of me, both swords drawn. "Don't you dare. She's sworn to the Theranian Crown—you do not know who she is."

"We'll see about that," the dreite drew out with a scoff, but he eyed me with misplaced concern. "We do not want to hurt her, but we will if that's what it takes. Her magic is more than you can fathom; the same goes for your girl with the shadows. Both belong to us, and we will take them back."

I exchanged a horrified glance with Leena. *Fuck*, he was right. The warmth leached from my body. I backed up to run, but something slammed into me, and my legs buckled.

"NO!" Farran cried out.

I scrambled to my feet, but my head was so heavy. *Could no one else feel it?* Out of the corner of my eye, Cormac expended a burst of power, sending the dreites scrambling.

Silver daggers flew from Aixen's grip. There was more, but Farran's arm lifted me over his shoulder, and he carried me back. He set me against a wall beside Leena, whose eyes fluttered as her skin paled.

"Don't you dare leave me here," I rasped. I pushed off the wall to stand, but couldn't. None of my limbs would obey me.

Farran didn't look back. I was melting, drowning, and something else. I wanted to scream, but words wouldn't come. Leena was limp beside me. This was what the end felt like—succumbing to immobility . . . all I could do was listen and feel. Steel hit steel and shivered against my consciousness.

A dragon screeched overhead. Then there was yelling, a rush of wind, and silence that didn't last because it was punctuated by screaming and a rush of fire.

"CLEAR!" Aixen screamed. There was nothing I could do.

My eyes wouldn't open; my body wouldn't move. It wasn't mine anymore, and I couldn't fight. A blast of sweltering heat struck. Someone jumped over us to shield off the dragon fire.

It roared overhead, and ash coated every breath I took.

"We need to go. Now. Beven is lost." Farran's voice was the last thing I heard before darkness claimed me.

I thought I'd only been out a few minutes, but when my eyes opened, I laid on a bedroll while willow trees bowed above me in rhythm with the gusts of wind. We were along a river, where there was no hum of magic or the hint of dread that had filled the streets of Beven.

A heated, hushed conversation between Farran, Avi, and Cormac drifted on the edge of the breeze. I didn't stir as I listened.

"We're going back to the Armory. It's closer," Avi hissed. "If dreites took Beven, what do you think they'd do if they came across the crown prince in the middle of the night? We took enough of a risk to get my father out."

"Avi is right," Farran agreed. His voice was tight; he was hiding something. "We need to get to safety, Cormac. Then you can go back with a full company. You know the road back to Rowane is crawling with rogues, and they'll be emboldened by Beven. There have been four attacks on Armory soldiers in the Salos Forest this month. Certainly, you've heard."

That must have been why Declan wore leathers and a sword.

"Rogues could be out here." Cormac sighed. "The Armory isn't a secret, Far."

"It's the difference between one day of traveling and four," Avi snapped. "We also have more cover along the damn river than we would in the central meadows. Don't act like you don't know this, Cormac. You served too, or have you been in the palace too long?" Avi said his name with no mind of titles.

Twigs and leaves crunched as someone moved. The river rushed in the distance, and Farran's voice softened. "It's one night in the Armory. You'll be fine, and you'll be safe. Then you can return with the makers. They'd be—"

Cormac groaned, and his voice hardened. "You don't understand, Farran. I *need* to be back in Rowane."

There was a pause. Then Farran asked, "What did you do?"

"I didn't *do* anything . . . Can you give us a minute, Aviliana?"

Avi's footsteps moved away as she sighed. I squeezed my eyes shut to keep listening.

Cormac's voice dropped to a whisper, "I'm supposed to be married in three days, and our mother will destroy me if I'm not home."

Farran hissed back, "Are you fucking kidding me? Why did you come out at all, and when was I supposed to hear about this? There are a hundred advisors you could have sent. General Linden was plenty."

"Calm down, Far." I practically heard the crown prince roll his eyes at Farran. "It's arranged, all Mother's idea. She wants—"

"I know it hasn't been easy after Lennox, but you don't have to do this. You can tell her no. You're the Crown Prince of Thera, for gods' sakes, you don't have to hide from her."

"Easy for you to say when you haven't said no to her recently." Cormac chided. "Mother's council agreed I needed to marry and secure a future for Thera. I'm not like you. I don't get to fuck around. I had my chance. I fucked up. This is the consequence."

Gods, I wanted to know everything. *Had Farran been in love before?* Maybe it was someone in the Armory or Rowane. Something in my chest twisted. It didn't matter. I had no reason to care.

"It's been *years*. Stop punishing yourself." Farran took a breath before he asked, "Who's the bride?"

"Rose Verdura. We'll have beautiful heirs and all of that."

"Why Verdura?"

"Mother believes the countess is interested in restoring the old gods, and she sees it as a threat to Thera. Marriage will force Verdura to keep her loyalty and not do anything rash."

"Mother has thought of everything, hasn't she?" Farran said sarcastically. "Jaxon could take you back on the dragon. Or I could draw a sigil door."

"I hate both of those things, quite viscerally."

"Griffons? You won trials flying those. I don't know, Cormac. Miss your wedding, then." Farran's voice hardened. "We're going to the Armory either way."

Cormac groaned and stalked away, his footsteps fading. Farran stayed behind. The rest of the camp was further. Now that their conversation was over, the low din of laughter between the gusts of wind carried over. I turned to my side, expecting to see Leena, who had been worse than me, but she wasn't there.

"They belong to us."

I sat straight up, and Farran's eyes met mine calmly, like he'd been expecting it. "Nice of you to join us," he murmured.

"Where's Leena?" I glowered.

He shrugged. "Woke two hours ago. She's eating with everyone."

Cedar and vanilla carried forward with the precision of a memory as he stepped closer, crouching down to sit beside me.

"Why am I all the way out here?" I demanded.

"So you could sleep." He absently brushed a piece of hair behind my ear, which I'd never asked for, but every part of me curled into it. "I've never seen anything drain like that. They took more from you than Leena."

His hand fell, but nothing in his gaze relented.

"You were right. Those houses were burned intentionally. It was a binding sigil for magic like yours and Leena's. That's why you couldn't run. They'd carefully placed every line in the ash over the last few weeks—they burned the last section while we met the Crown. It only affected you once it was complete. Jaxon saw it from the air and broke through it with dragon's fire, but it was too late; a sigil that size has far-reaching power once completed. We should have seen it earlier."

My voice was scratchy, and fog permeated every thought and memory. "How did we get out?" I rasped.

"We tried to fight, but they got away. Blaise took a nasty cut to the leg. The kid everyone calls Sparrow tried to hold them back, but he was cut down trying to get away. He was our only loss."

Farran hung his head. Sparrow was a first-year and only nineteen; no one knew his name or his family. My heart panged. Now we never would.

"Injuries?" I asked.

"Aixen might have broken his arm again. We all got our backs singed and capes burned, but thankfully, Varyn is good at healing burns."

"And Avi?" I pressed.

Farran took a sharp breath. "Duke and Duchess Valois are with us. They'll go back to court with Cormac and petition the queen to keep their titles while they prepare one of their other houses in Arasund. There isn't a clear route to restore Beven unless the queen is ready for war . . . but that isn't my choice."

Unbound black hair brushed his shoulders, and his eyes looked bruised, but he had the nerve to turn and ask, "Do you want something to eat?"

I moved to stand—I was starving—but Farran pinned me back to the bedroll with a pointed look.

"I'll bring it over." He tsked. "You really need to rest in case we need your demons. We'll ride out at dawn." He walked towards the group, and my whole body shuddered.

I looked for any threads of magic, and I found a single, cold knot like a stone . . . it was recovering and needed time. My head swirled as I tried to touch it. I gave up quickly as a steaming bowl of soup found itself in my hands.

Farran sat beside me. "Mira gave Devon and Avi everything for soup as a thank you. Aixen and Mianen are the ones who made it."

The heat was indulgent, and it smelled heavenly: a fragrant mix of onions, chicken, rosemary, and whatever else they'd stuffed in it tickled my nose.

While I ate, he pulled a rock from his pocket and turned it in his fingers absently. I watched, mesmerized. It picked up the barest light from the fire and the stars above us.

"What is that?" I asked.

"This?" He held it towards me with a smirk. "A rock."

"I know that," I said indignantly. "I've never seen one that looks like that."

His lips turned up. "It's from the southernmost point of Balria. It formed the same way as common quartz but some volcanic explosion a thousand years ago in that very place forged the layers and clarity of it."

"You brought it to trial?"

He shrugged and closed his fingers over it. "Brings me good luck, just like your ribbon."

It was an odd thing to notice. We weren't far from everyone else, but it felt private enough I wasn't guarding my words. "I'm sorry Blaise cut you earlier," I blurted.

Farran's expression tightened. "It's fine; it was my fault," he said, much to my surprise. "He has feelings for you. I'm not blind."

My eyes widened. *Fuck.* Farran was there when I ended whatever Blaise and I had. He was also at the Maker's Ball, and that dance was the closest I'd felt to love in years.

He added, "Blaise and Tomas made it to the square just in time to see Aixen lance the beast. They also saw me use my gift while you wielded the demons—"

"Blaise knows what your power is." And he had no right to be selfish.

Farran looked at me in a way that went deeper than a simple gaze . . . He was searching for something, but I looked away. "He might have offered to carry you back, and I insisted—"

"Blaise doesn't deserve to be pissed," I said in a small voice, ignoring the twinge in my chest. "The Armory is for weapons, and that's what we are. That's all I am, and I told him I'm not worth anyone's feelings."

"You believe that?" the prince whispered in disbelief.

I nodded and took another sip of the soup.

Farran thought for a moment. "Perhaps you're right." I don't know why hearing him say that was a lance to my heart.

"I've never been wrong." I stretched and yawned, keenly aware he watched me.

His smile faded, and the conversation was over. "Whatever the dreites did, they took almost all of what you had and bound it. Could be hours or days before you recover. It isn't clear."

"Great," I muttered and stretched across the bedroll. Farran remained there, sitting. "Is it strange they call me *valdronna*?"

"Perhaps not." His brow furrowed and he glanced at me. "Do you think it is?"

"I don't know," I sighed. "I don't like the way they say it or the way the dreites think I belong to them. They're not going to stop."

"They will not take you."

"You seem awfully sure." I yawned. "Are you sleeping or leaving? You don't get to sit there."

Farran blew out a breath, and dry leaves rustled as he grumbled back, "Sleeping."

I was too tired to argue, too tired to think about what a terrible idea this was as I turned over and let the darkness have me. I didn't dream, and I didn't wake until a bird chirped overhead.

When I woke up, I was under the trees, near the riverbank, and still in leathers. The faint thrum of magic shivered below my chest. It was cold and distant, but tiny pricks of heat poked out from the tangled mess of it.

My breath caught as I rolled over to see Farran still sleeping, and I stared. His hair was tangled, but his face was smooth as his eyelids fluttered. I couldn't look away.

There was a faint scar on his cheek, just under his eye, only visible when his face softened. Not that I'd ever looked before, but I saw it now and wondered if it was a glimpse of who he'd been before the Armory. Did he wonder about my scars?

No—I needed to pull myself together; this gawking and these feelings were ridiculous. I turned away and stared at the rocks and leaves, arms wrapped tightly around my legs.

Feelings were off the table for me, for a thousand gods-be-damned reasons.

I was Reina Sangrey, a traitor to the Crown—Arden's viper. No amount of affection could shadow that. My past always caught up and exacted its revenge. It was the Crown that created me, after all.

A rock digging into my back forced me to sit up. It was black out, but deep blue clung to the edges of the horizon. First light would be here within the hour. I'd gotten enough sleep, so I walked quietly towards the fire, which smoldered in front of

Aixen, a dark-haired Amethyst soldier, and Varyn who kept watch while everyone slept.

I grabbed a log and added it to the fire, hoping to warm my hands. The fire leaped, and a few sparks scuttled towards the low-hanging canopy.

The men turned and looked at me as though I'd grown a fourth arm, which would have been to Aixen's benefit. His other arm drooped on his leg in a sling of ripped tunics.

I shrugged. "What? No one else was feeding the fire."

"Cold? After being that close to the prince?" Aixen winked, and I glared.

"You ought to stop breaking your arm," I snapped. "That's almost every trial. You could be the first armless champion if you keep it up."

"Or you could turn the bone to silver," Varyn suggested.

"Silver? One of the softest metals?" Aixen scoffed.

"You flatter yourself if you think your bones are stronger. At least if it was silver you could heal it." Varyn shrugged.

A flash of consideration crossed Aixen's face as he looked at me.

"Let me see your arm," I demanded.

Aixen's brown eyes looked at me suspiciously, but he held his arm out. I took it in my hands, allowing my healing magic to reach out in tendrils as I gasped. The sudden heat of Aixen's pain shocked me. Usually, I felt a little warmth, but today it was heightened and the sear of it caught my breath.

Aixen noticed and snatched his arm back, wincing. Varyn raised his brow but said nothing. I'd healed bones before, *gods*, I'd healed his bones before, but usually, a broken bone felt like a dull ache to me, if anything at all.

"We're not supposed to let you use magic yet." Aixen glared. There was no reason for me to ask who *we* meant. I had my first officer's order suspicions.

"I won't tell if you don't scream." I smiled sweetly.

"Fine." He clenched his teeth.

Varyn watched, lips thin but said nothing.

Aixen extended his arm. I took it gingerly and focused, pre-pared this time for the intensity. The heat of my magic wrapped around the swollen tissue to dull the pain.

To fix the bone, I pushed through and imagined every layer around the clean break mended. Aixen tensed as I tightened my grip. The pain and bruising radiated as I fused and pinched back the blood vessels.

It took all of five minutes to heal, and instead of draining me, I felt refreshed. That magic was comfortable, somehow different from the threads tied to the demons. I had no idea where it came from, or what the cost was, but I thanked the gods they'd given it to me.

Aixen turned over his arm and gaped.

"How did you do it so quickly?" Varyn asked in wonder. "I've read a hundred books and mine doesn't work like yours."

I shrugged. "Learned I could do it years ago while working at a tavern."

It was a half-lie. I learned it while I was working in a tavern, but I was working for Arden when one of his men came after me. I broke a man's hand and realized I could remake and break it again to get my point across.

When everyone was awake, some sent a few sidelong glances at Aixen, who didn't hide his working arm despite promising me he'd lie about it.

Leena came up and hugged me tightly. Her voice was sleepy but calm. "Thank gods you're awake. The bind could have killed us."

"How are you feeling?" I asked as she slunk off me.

She stared at the embers of the fire. "I'll be fine, just like you." Her hair wasn't bound by anything. It was curly and wild, with dry leaves and twigs poking out of it.

Avi's whistle echoed through the clearing, and Leena looped her arm through mine as we walked. She yawned widely and said, "Don't think you've escaped just yet. You owe me *several* conversations now."

"Fine. When we're back in the Armory." I rolled my eyes with a smile.

We gathered around Avi. If Farran looked exhausted last night, Avi looked devastated. Her wild red hair had fallen out of its braid and freed her curls. The young, gold light coming up from behind the trees her turned her hair into a halo of fire against the backdrop of willows and brush.

"Horses are almost packed," Avi said, and her eyes stopped on the crown prince. "If we ride fast, we'll be at the Armory by early afternoon. Vera and Jaxon have gone ahead with her dragon to make sure we have accommodations for the Duke and Duchess Valois, His Highness, and your company."

Avi gave Cormac a quick bow and immediately mounted her horse. I walked the same way and stopped when the familiar warmth of a hand wrapped around my arm and stirred my damn magic like a ladle in a soup pot.

I yanked it back and turned to see Farran staring at me with an amused grin, holding the lead of a brown horse. The only blessing was that this horse was smaller than Devon's.

"You think you're riding on your own?" he mused.

"I—no. Obviously not."

"You're riding with me this time. Your magic is weak, and if we run into anything, you'll need to borrow mine."

"I'm fine. I have plenty," I ground out. This was exactly the situation I wanted to avoid—*needed* to avoid.

Farran's eyes narrowed on me, and heat crawled up my neck. "No, you don't. You can lie to everyone else, but you can't lie to me. I *know* your magic," he said pointedly.

"Then stop and let me lie to myself."

He scoffed. "No. Get on the horse."

"Are you about to pull rank?"

"Does it help?" he asked with a smirk, and my defenses crumbled apart. *Fuck, was that all it took?* "As your First Officer, I'm commanding you to get on the horse."

That *was* all it took. He pulled the horse around so the saddle and I were eye level, and I cursed every god I could name . . . Everyone in my house and Amethyst watched. Worse, I looked like I was in pain as I gripped the saddle, and the beast knew it. Then the horse whinnied, and I jumped back.

Instead of letting me struggle, Farran lifted me onto it in one fluid motion and something different twisted in my chest that I refused to acknowledge.

Farran, of course, slid onto the horse like he was born riding. The gods-be-damned cedar and faint trace of vanilla overwhelmed as his back pressed into mine; his arms wrapped around my waist. He took the reins, and this was so much worse than flying.

"Is this okay?" Farran asked, his voice almost a whisper against the shell of my ear.

"Yes," I said sharply. "It's fine." It was more than fine.

His warmth and magic tangled with my own. The heat in my chest built up again, and the threads of magic untangled themselves, slowly coming back with every pulse. The rational part of me hated how easy my magic was around him.

I knew it was his gift, but the effect was intoxicating.

We rode straight through to the Armory. I was sore two hours in, and we had at least two more to go. Farran's horse was smaller than Devon's, with far less cushion. I had no idea if I'd be able to stand when the time came—my back already hurt.

"You healed Aixen's arm, didn't you?" Farran murmured in my ear. The menace of the accusation warmed a part of me I was actively not thinking about.

I kept my head straight and watched the landscape shift. "You have no proof."

"It wasn't Varyn," he retorted.

"Varyn can. He just needs more practice."

"Was that an admission?"

"No," I said swiftly. "It was evasion."

"Why did you do it?" His voice lowered another octave, and his chest rumbled against my back—distracting wasn't a big enough word. There was no way he didn't know what he was doing, but two could play that game.

I leaned farther into him and readjusted my seat. My hips shifted, and he tensed against me, his arm tightening around my waist.

I shrugged. "Aixen was in pain. We're better off if I spend a little magic than be down one man, even in broad daylight," I said, keeping my voice even.

Farran was quiet and ground out, "Fine." I shifted my hips again and felt his chest press into my back. "Are you quite comfortable, darling?" he growled in my ear.

"Yes." My lips quirked up. "Thank you for asking."

His arm pulled tighter around my waist; heat and magic thrummed against my skin and exacerbated the heat and desire building between my thighs against my better judgment. I drove my hips into him again and delighted in the small gasp that escaped his lips; I was never good at restraint.

"Reina, weren't you the one who said never again?" the prince said, voice low and husky. "You're doing a particularly bad job of letting me believe it."

"You were the one who ordered me to ride with you. I never agreed, nor did you say I *couldn't* make it torturous."

Farran tried to lean back, but there was no escaping me. I rolled my hips again despite the soreness and reveled in the way his breath clipped. "I'll be sure to add the stipulation next time," he said through gritted teeth.

Relief came a few minutes later when Cormac and Avi rode up beside us and talked about their plans for returning to Rowane. The interruption served as a bucket of cold water, and I quickly remembered myself: I was in the company of the Crown, and Blaise was definitely watching. I should have felt guilty, but guilt never came.

Chapter 27

We made it to the Armory before the sun reached the highest point in the sky. The new first-year recruits had arrived the day before and were scattered around the yard, waving their wooden swords.

A small crop of servants waited for us outside the open doors of the Atrium. A lanky one with wide eyes and wispy auburn hair took the reins of Farran's horse and guided him to the stable.

I strode into the Atrium with my house, followed by Amethyst. We were greeted by Jaxon, Lady Verdura, and the makers of several other houses, all of whom wanted to take the time to greet the crown prince—or lick his boots. I didn't judge.

Of all the faces, the one most familiar was nowhere to be found. I wasn't sure whether to be surprised or concerned by Avernought's absence.

A tug on my hand pulled my attention away to see Leena standing beside me. "We're invited to the Maker's Dinner tonight. They're setting the Atrium for it, so we ought to get changed." Her golden eyes glittered.

Walking up the stairs was a slog, and every muscle in my body strained with each step. I was so fucking sore, but I could sit through dinner. We had two hours to drag ourselves together and transform into something presentable.

It wasn't unheard of for makers to request a dinner with the second and third-years of their house; it was part of the process.

Makers placed their bets on second-years and invested in the soldier they'd hand over to the queen as a knight. There would be a formal pledge, and a few weeks later, the soldier would be awarded their silver cord.

They would wear it as a sign they were taken whenever in the presence of other makers, because it was a stupid little ritual that made some of us better than the others, even if we'd all die for the same crown.

I bathed in my quarters and tried to forget about the makers, the first-years, and the ugly purple bruises blooming on my arms, legs, and ribs from gods know what.

I slipped under the hot water, and my hair spread around me like a mermaid. For exactly one summer, I dreamed of being one of the mythical mermaids in the islands of Sol. That was when my mother brushed my hair and begged me to sit still while my father laughed. It was long before I knew there would be a last time.

No one bothered to tell me there would be a last time until it was too late to gather the memories back in my arms. No one told me how painful remembering was or how easy it would be to forget and no one told me that the memories I wanted to hold on to would be the first to slip away.

If I closed my eyes hard enough, I could still feel her fingers comb through my hair. I still smelled the lilac bushes in our garden. And sometimes, I could see her, but I'd long forgotten her voice. Did it sound like mine? Did Declan sound like our father now? I'd never know.

Water rushed to the side of the tub as I sat up and held my knees to my chest. I knew better than to let my mind wander there.

My mother always deserved a better daughter than the one I whittled myself into. I'd cut away all the softness she gave me until it was unrecognizable. I wasn't her daughter, and I hadn't been for a long time. I was Arden's viper and the Crown's demon wielder. The only part of her clinging to me now was her hair, and even that was dull.

The clock in the common room struck some hour. I didn't know what time it was exactly, but I knew I had one hour left, which I thanked the gods for. I rose and toweled off.

Fresh leathers hung in the wardrobe, waiting for me with pristine, black polished silver buttons and buckles fit for a knight of the queen. A pressed emerald cape hung beside my clean cloak, bearing no trace of pine needles and the kiss I kept trying to forget.

I dressed and tied my wet hair in place with the emerald ribbon; my shoulders sagged as I fastened my cape.

A knight. That's exactly what I looked like. It was the only thing I'd ever allowed myself to want, but I was an imposter. No matter how deeply emblazoned the crest was; it couldn't burn away my destiny.

Leena entered my room without knocking and held something small and pointed out. "Do you want any?" she asked.

"What is it?" I squinted.

"Coal—for your eyes. I put some on for dinner." Leena gestured to the corners of her eyes, now darkened by a streak of black. It made her golden gaze catch the light like a sword struck by the sun's rays. It certainly wouldn't do the same for mine.

Yet, I shrugged. "Why not?"

"Sit on the bed and close your eyes," Leena said. Her face was pensive, but she tried to keep her voice pleasant. "Have you never worn coal before?"

"I have . . . it's just been a while."

"Ah." Leena walked towards the edge of the bed and stopped in front of me. She'd tied her hair back with a ribbon, but instead of braiding her blonde curls, she let them cascade down her left side. "I said close your eyes."

I complied and felt the coal pencil sweep across the corners of my lids. Leena pulled away, and I opened them again. "How do I look?"

"Like a very sexy demon wielder," she mused with a smile.

I grumbled, "I don't think it matters."

"Of course it does," Leena said lightly and turned for the door, but not before sending a devilish glance back at me. "We all deserve to dress up a little, even if we're stuck in the uniform."

She slipped out of the room before I could defend myself.

In my year at the Armory, the Atrium's transformations still amazed me. The space had once served as the courtyard for the castle long before it was encased in glass. It was large enough to hold everyone enrolled in the Armory, our makers, and near a hundred spectators, but it could also be turned into something private and personal with the right touch.

Tonight, it was personal. A long table had been lined up with the overgrown hedgerows, just outside the Atrium doors.. Candles glowed beside centerpieces of fall wildflowers, plucked from the forest.

Similar floral sprays stood around the table, one trick to make it feel smaller. While chandeliers hung low, with silver ribbons twined into them extending towards the navy banners above us. The silk banners draped over the table and pooled a few paces away from the chair, furthering the illusion of intimacy.

Our house was near the end of the table, far from the doors leading to the yard, which were propped open to let the cool night air waft in while the three fireplaces on the interior walls roared.

Several makers from a variety of houses sat with Amethyst, along with the Duke and Duchess Valois. When the crown prince strode into the room, everyone stood. He wore a regal blue coat over the same extravagant leathers, flanked by several advisors and guards.

I didn't know the Armory could provide a meal fit for the Crown, but I was every bit impressed as plate after plate came out with its own matching glass of wine. Conversation flowed easily, and per Theranian tradition, every course also came with a change of seats. This was to make sure everyone was equal by the end of a meal, regardless of titles.

It dated back to the earliest days of Thera, and usually, I loathed it because it meant six or seven pointless conversations, but something about tonight made it pleasurable.

I learned about tracking wild boar through the Wray Kingdom from one of Cormac's guards; I listened to Jaxon tell the story about how she bonded with her dragon in trial, and I learned about Southern customs from one of the Crown advisors and their cousin who was a Ruby maker before he'd retired. Perhaps Arden's dinners were only tedious because of the company he kept.

Dessert came around at nearly midnight, and we were all impossibly full and perhaps too satiated with wine. I switched seats with Farran to sit beside Leena and across from Jaxon.

Beside me, another of the advisors sank into the seat. He was short and round, but he had the most beautiful hazel eyes. "Do I know you from somewhere?" he asked pointedly, with an accent I didn't recognize.

Certainly not from Thera, and his skin had a sheen to it, like scales which many from the Kingdom of Sol had—it was a gift from Olios, the God of Water.

The room closed in at the edges, but I pulled my lips in a smile and put on my most comfortable mask. "Depends. Did you frequent the taverns in Lower Rowane? I served at almost all of them." I gave him a knowing look, despite knowing nothing—an old trick.

Jaxon looked at me, a wine glass frozen at her mouth.

The advisor vigorously shook his head and looked around. "No, no, that can't be. Never been. But you—" He wagged a finger in front of me and pointed at Leena. "I do remember you. That beautiful hair. No one in Rowane has anything half as magnificent. You danced for the Crown with Moer's troupe."

Leena nodded politely and gave a curt smile. "I'm delighted you remember. It was an honor to serve such revered clientele," she said kindly.

"So, what is a lady like yourself doing in the Armory?" the advisor asked. "Not many dancers find themselves here. I would know."

"I wanted to serve the Crown in a more meaningful way," Leena said, lips pressed together as she took another sip of wine. "Dancing and fighting aren't so different."

"She's our *sunderone*, Lord Ignatius," Jaxon interrupted. "None of us would be here without her grace and skill with shadows. Moer will find another dancer, but we won't find another Leena Farrow."

Lord Ignatius seemed satisfied with the answer. He took a gulp of wine and turned towards the guard next to him, beginning another conversation as a sweet potato tart was set in front of us.

"I had no idea the Armory could make food like this," I said to Leena.

"Only when they have a reason to," Jaxon chimed in with a laugh, taking a bite of the tart. "It's a shame, really. I should bring the crown prince back more often. The knights eat worse at the palace, so I'd prepare yourselves now."

By the time the plates were cleared away, most of the advisors and makers had said their goodnights and dismissed themselves. Most of my house stayed back, along with Amethyst, several Crown guards, and their charge—Prince Cormac.

Someone brought out a deck of cards, and the wine kept flowing.

We laughed and cheered, playing a few rounds of Verity. With my second, deeply losing hand, I slammed the cards down and excused myself for the privacy of my room.

It was late, but once I'd gotten to my room and traded my leathers for a sleeved satin nightgown and loosened my hair, I wanted to be anywhere but the castle. I pulled my cloak over my shoulders and strapped my dagger, along with several stolen knives, to my thigh.

It was certainly too late, but I wanted to be outside, in the open air, doing anything that made me feel like myself when I was everything but.

I also couldn't resist the delightful rush of wind as I pushed the window open and slipped onto the roof.

Chapter 28

Unlike the seven-story, ancient, utilitarian side of the Armory that housed the first-years, the second and third-year wing was newer and built in the gloating style of the Catharian castles. It had terraces, buttresses, and stones jutting out, along with flat roofs in strategic places for archers in the event of an attack.

Emerald was on the third floor, and I'd escaped taller buildings on wetter nights, in longer gowns.

Cold air tickled my face as I eased onto the flat section of roof below. With one hand against the stone to keep steady, I stepped carefully over a thin barrier to the adjacent section.

The next step was more challenging; a sloped roof into the next story was slick with drizzle, and I needed to jump at the right angle to catch the ledge. Deep breath in . . . deep breath out. I leaped. A few pebbles skittered as I landed on the ground with a soft thud, and the impact pounded through my knees.

Two guards patrolled the yard, and I waited patiently in the shadows for them to pass. No one glimpsed me—perhaps I should have found it concerning—but I continued, the cool night breeze caressing my face in a whisper of freedom.

On the northern side of the Armory, there was an old derelict garden with wild, untrimmed hedges that hadn't been manicured in several years. Tall, coarse grass and prickly weeds sprung up around parallel stone paths and brushed against my bare calves as I walked. A centuries-old line of trees created a looming wall on one side of the garden.

The trees at the farthest end had scars and scorch marks from a fire that nearly destroyed the Armory two centuries ago. At the time, it had been a keep for Theranian soldiers until dreites descended on it in one of the shortest, and bloodiest, battles of the Second War of Kings.

The bloodbath forced the two halves of one kingdom into negotiations which would eventually divide them. Shortly after the war, the keep became Thera's Armory as it is today.

There was an empty fountain near the entrance of the garden and an old, crumbling wall where a groundskeeper used to live.

I laid my cloak and knives on a flat, tiled bench across the tiered fountain. Like many things, it had once been beautiful but now the tiles chipped and the topmost tier was almost unrecognizable.

Opposite the fountain, straight paths ran the length of the garden toward the ancient trees. It was perfect for practice. I gripped a knife and threw.

It fell a few feet short and clattered, skittering across the stone. I was sore and tired from everything, but it wouldn't stop me. War didn't wait for soldiers to be rested . . . danger didn't, either.

Arden told me some variation every time I complained, so I stretched my arms and tried again.

This time I threw with more force from my core and less from the taut muscles in my shoulder. Throwing might have been a single motion, but it took coordination from every part of the body to be effective. Arden kept a cane just for that.

When my shoulder slumped, or my back twisted wrong, he'd tap the muscle and pose me again—always careful never to touch me with his hands as long as I held a blade.

The knife whistled as it flew, and it stuck in the tree. *Almost* exactly where I wanted it.

I threw another, and another, until I ran through the five I brought. Then I started over again and again until the air became welcoming and invigorating. I threw until something in me snapped as the eyes of dreites came back to my memory, their haunting words jumbling with the premonition of my Rite.

"You'll have nothing, Reina Sangrey."
This wasn't nothing. My chest collapsed underneath the weight of delayed grief. I felt everything: all the uncertainty I'd buried; the pain, the loneliness, the confusion . . . the crushing weight of something I never wanted.

I felt the guilt and fresh grief for my mother and father that I'd buried so deep I accidentally preserved it.

It came for me at last, gasping for air and clawing at my skin.

I'd never been myself. I lost every opportunity to find out because I *needed* to survive. Who would I be when I did? Who could I be?

I'd taken every desperate opportunity to keep Declan from having to do the same, but what would he think once he knew what I'd done to get here? Or Leena when my destiny passed? By the end of this, I'll have destroyed every bit of goodness in myself . . . and for what?

Would it mean anything if I was the monster in their stories?

Before Arden, I wanted nothing. I became his when he wrote the promise on my back in blood and ink. I was so close to becoming everything he'd wanted me to be—*everything I needed to be*—but none of it was me.

I had no self. The deeper and deeper I dug, all of it was Arden. *All of it.* Every, "Yes, my lord," stole me away, piece by piece, until I became this: only a viper would survive the Armory and my waiting fate . . .

Not a girl, not a human, not the daughter of a noble, but a creature, void and averse to the things that make us human.

I gave up everything until there was nothing left.

I sunk down on the bench and drew my knees to my chest. Tears wouldn't come; I was too far gone. I reached for the warmth of my magic: *mine and mine alone.* My chest ached as the threads brushed against my skin and tied me back to the ground until something crackled and snapped.

My eyes sprung open—I thought I'd conjured something.

The garden was empty, but I looked to my right and saw Farran standing there, nearly bewildered as he looked at me. I didn't have the energy to fight, so I just stared back.

He cleared his throat and asked, "Are you okay?"

"Sure." My voice cracked on the single word, and I cursed myself.

This wasn't me; I needed to drag the mask back on. Vulnerability and weakness were synonyms for a reason. I needed to be distant. Away was the only place I was safe.

He stared at me, not believing what I said. Neither of us moved. "You shouldn't be out here alone," he murmured.

I gestured next to me. "You can sit."

Leave me alone, I thought, but the words didn't come. Every part of me was so broken I couldn't. I loathed the way grief caught up no matter how fast I ran. It always found me at the worst times.

Farran stopped, looking down at the bench where my dagger glinted in the moonlight.

"Oh, sorry," I muttered and strapped it back on my leg. He eyed me, but I didn't have the energy to consider what he wasn't saying.

The familiar smell of a cedar forest and a vanilla tart swirled around him. His magic seemed to reach for me. Warm tendrils of it brushed my skin. It was similar, but different, almost softer—cautious.

Why did he have to be the siphon? Maybe all of this would have been more bearable if I had a choice—if the *ontaros* I needed didn't stand for the Crown who'd stolen my life.

Pulling my cloak tighter, I stretched my legs to the ground.

"I've never seen you in this garden," Farran said after a moment.

"It's good for practice."

"I don't think you need the extra practice." He stared at the tree where three of my knives stuck out of the tree trunk, excessively close.

I ignored the compliment. "Why are you out here?"

"Needed some fresh air, and I was tired of listening to the guards' stories. Aixen's not, though. He's still there and utterly enthralled."

"He loves a good story." I nodded.

"Are you okay? After Beven, I mean. I'm sure Leena already asked, but I've never seen you merely *sitting* in a garden. Or in a nightgown."

"I just sat down." I huffed, smoothing the skirt. "I'm fine."

Silence drifted between us. The cool breeze lifted my hair, and it caught in my lashes.

I took a languishing breath. "I was just thinking about how fucked up all of this is." *Not a lie.*

"How so?" Farran turned with the gaze that *saw* me, and something shifted in my chest and it wasn't the tendrils and threads of magic. Something in me wanted to tell him everything, toiling through my head and heart, but that would be humiliating.

I looked at the sky. A cloud drifted past the moon and obscured a handful of stars.

"We're close to a war we'll risk our lives for, but it's not ours. We didn't make the choice to start it, but we'll be the ones who finish it," I said, my voice barely above a whisper.

"It is a little fucked up, isn't it?"

His agreement caught me off guard.

Biting my lip, I added, "I never asked for this damned gift. But now I'm here with no other choice. If I run, they'll find me. If I deny the magic, they'll find a way to get to it."

"You do have choices."

"No, I don't—not really. You know that," I said, gaze drifting down to the ground.

My slippers were soggy and covered in dirt. His boots were clean. I could have chosen more sensible footwear, but I liked the way I felt every pebble and blade of grass beneath my feet.

"I'm the *dreosen*, first in centuries and first of Thera. Apparently, I'll helm a fucking demon army." I sighed.

"Maybe it's not our war," he said. "And maybe you couldn't choose your gift, but you don't have to do everything for them. Gods know I don't. There are other ways." His face turned wistful. "You know . . . one day, Cormac will take the Crown, and things will be different. I know most of Thera thinks we're all the same, but I hope it's not true. I know what my mother did. We grew up in the aftermath and the uprisings."

"You grew up in the palace." I wanted to scream at him about my mother, but it would accomplish nothing. Instead, I looked at him and asked, "You really think it could be different under Cormac?"

There was a brightness in his eyes. I was painfully aware of how close we were.

"I have to believe it, don't I? My future is tied to Thera just as yours is. And he's my brother."

I looked at the ground. "How do you stand everything in your life being decided for you?"

"I adapted," Farran said with a shrug. "I snuck out of the palace. Did things I wasn't supposed to—I tried to be better because I didn't want to be a pawn, and I don't believe you do either."

He was absolutely wrong, of course. I was a professional pawn, but his words sounded so pleasant, so *hopeful*.

A feeling swelled in my chest like a tide coming in. I sucked it back.

"I want you to be right—that it's as easy as just being *better*." The lie felt nice on my tongue. It had a sweetness to it, an impossibility.

"Me too." Farran sighed, closing his eyes before reopening them. "I should probably leave you to your knives."

Something in my chest lurched as he rose to his feet, and I stood too. "I should get some sleep."

I looked at the knives still stuck in the tree, but didn't move. Farran didn't, either. I glanced at him, and that was a mistake.

His eyes swirled in the moonlight, and suddenly I needed to feel something

"I think you should kiss me," I murmured.

His eyebrow rose, and his lips parted to say something as leaves rustled around the desolate garden. He took a dangerous step closer, then came the rush of cedar and the memory of vanilla as time stopped.

"Do you? I don't know if I believe you." A smirk crossed his face, and the warmth of his breath tangled with my own, igniting a fire. I needed him to touch me but yet the breath of space remained. "Last time, you called it a mistake."

"Well, good thing this is *my* choice." My choice to regret later. My mistake to pay for, and my own grief to bury.

I couldn't have him, not really, but desire was a funny thing that could overpower reason.

Farran's strong fingers clasped my chin and lifted it, his hungry gaze locking onto mine. "Then I'm going to kiss you, Reina Sangrey. Exactly how I've imagined."

His lips claimed mine—soft, gentle, and deliberate. Everything our kiss in the woods wasn't. Then it went deeper. Hunger and need thrummed through me, compounded by our magic as I melted into his embrace.

His hands roamed across my body. One from my chin to tangle in my hair. The other grabbed my waist and pulled me into his chiseled chest; my nightgown was hardly a barrier. I gasped against his lips. We were both breathless, hearts beating against one another.

Magic and heat entwined, rippling across our skin. He broke away but didn't let go. Why had I denied myself this?

I wasn't thinking about tomorrow; I wasn't thinking about who might see us. In fact, I wasn't thinking at all.

Our lips met again, and the fire burned as his hands glided down my hips. There was nothing to stop us, and I wasn't done. My defenses were gone.

I'd said the words, and I wouldn't take them back.

He pushed me against the old Armory wall. Everything fell away. Everything but him as his hand tangled in my hair while the other held my back, closing out any gap of space between us.

I bit his lip with a dangerous smirk, drawing out a whimper. He ignited the parts of me I'd forgotten about—parts of me the boys of Rowane couldn't find as his hand skimmed up the fabric of my gown and squeezed my bare thigh.

My hips pushed into his, and I came alive. Every bit of his desire pressed against me as his hand cupped back as my breath came faster.

"Tell me to stop," he whispered, fingers running up the inside of my thigh, teasing me. I shuddered at the cool touch, and again as he drew burning circles with his thumb at the apex of my thighs, so close and yet so far from where I wanted him.

"Never," I breathed.

I'd regret it later when I was done being selfish. Not now, while his fingers were toying with the damp heat between my thighs. Not now, as I rolled my hips into his hand to show him exactly how I wanted him to wring me dry.

He pressed one finger and then another into me and wrung out a gasp as we moved. I wanted to keep kissing him, but the faster he moved, the more ragged my breath came until he added a third. That was when tension edged and burned into desperate pleasure.

"Come for me, *darling*," he breathed in my ear. It was a command.

His teeth tugged my lip. Desire rushed through me as his hand surged forward and back until all the warmth and fire consumed and remade me. Until I lost control and cried into his shoulder as pleasure collapsed the world around me.

"Fucking beautiful," he praised against my lips, his forehead against mine as we both caught our breath.

I tried to compose any thoughts, but nothing came. His hands fisted in my gown as my legs shook. He brushed a kiss across my lips once, twice, and then he drew away.

"More," I whispered and tugged him back, delighting in the intoxicating vanilla of his kiss like the faintest reminder of a memory. The hardness of him pressed the inside of my thigh, and I was wicked. "I want to feel all of you."

Instead of giving me more, he didn't move. His gaze fixed on mine as the heat of him pulsed through me like wildfire: dangerous, hungry, and beautiful all the same.

He brushed the hair from my eyes and lingered. "I should go back."

"I don't believe you, Farran."

His hand gripped my waist again. He looked at me so fiercely that the breath in my throat hitched, and my legs shook.

"What?" I whispered, praying to Dreonna he changed his mind. There was plenty we could do before regret caught up.

Farran shook his head and drew closer, a smirk on his swollen lips. "I don't know that I've ever heard you say my name."

"Would you prefer Your Highness or First Officer?"

He kissed me slowly then rested his forehead on mine again. "Next time, call me anything you want."

"Anything?" I whispered. "Farran."

He groaned and pried himself off me. The cold came back, but the heat of his magic remained warm on my skin. Reminding me exactly where he'd touched me and where I wished he would again.

Stop. Reality crawled back. What had I fucking done?

"Training starts again tomorrow, *dreosen*—and bring the dagger."

A mistake. It didn't matter what I said to him; I didn't deserve a next time even if nothing about him felt like a mistake as I watched him walk back to the Armory.

I knew it was wrong, and I knew it on every god in the realm, sleeping and Seven.

I was a monster, drenched in blood, and everything I said to Blaise was true. The moment I cared was the moment it would all start to fray and wither. I wasn't worth it.

And it was worse with Farran. We were two colliding storms, circling and waiting. Once he learned the truth, he'd never look at me the same. In fact, he'd probably never look at me again, and that would be another kind of death.

The Crown needed me alive, but they never needed me whole.

Chapter 29

A few days passed, and I'd spent more hours than I was willing to admit thinking about Farran, wishing he would say my name against my skin once more.

I shouldn't want any part of him, but I warmed and tensed at the thought. I needed to get some fucking control. I couldn't have these feelings because I was broken and irreparable. A spark of happiness or a single release of pleasure was more than I deserved.

I needed to cut out the parts that felt anything before they became something worse.

Only the shuffle of my boots on the marble floor echoed through the Atrium as I walked. It was early in the morning as usual; the sun hadn't risen, and only a faint light came through the glass panels, adding to the chill. The long, warm days of summer were gone, and I pulled my cardigan tighter around my tunic . . . I should have grabbed my cloak.

With weather, I always assumed I'd be able to endure more than I actually could. And that was probably true of more things than one.

Above me, ten black banners were strung across the ceiling, rippling in a phantom breeze. They counted our single loss in Beven, the first-year we called Sparrow, and whatever trial the other houses had faced.

In the forest, mist hung heavily between the pines, waiting to evaporate under the warmth of the sun, which bled through the evergreen canopy in shades of orange and yellow.

I clambered down the riverbank and froze. All the blood left my face as Damien Arden's palomino horse stared at me. I hated his horse more than all the others because only one man could ride it, and a knot tightened in my back.

The icy grip of dread tightened on my spine as Damien Arden walked around the corner of the riverbank.

His brown hair was longer than before and imperceptibly thinning; his features sharper but as handsome as I remembered. Bright eyes, like creamed toffee, raked over me, assessing for any noticeable changes. I had no doubts he was trying to see what he'd missed, and how he could've overlooked that I was the demon wielder.

"Good to see you still keep time well, my viper," Arden said, and a sardonic smile stretched across his face, revealing inhumanly straight white teeth.

I never wanted to know what he'd traded for them.

He drawled, "Apologies for not sending your brother this time. He's busy."

My hand tightened around the hilt of my sword. "We had a deal, Damien."

Arden held up his hands. His violet doublet, embroidered with rose-gold filigree, shifted with the motion. "Be reasonable, *Reina*," he crooned. "I will never forget a promise I made to you. How can I? You mean everything to me. Declan is safe. I'm not interested in sparring with a Crown soldier."

The last words were tinged with venom and loathing as he took a step closer, stopping only an arm's length from me.

"Can't I want to see you, Reina?" he crooned. "The acclaimed demon wielder, the *dreosen,* raised as my own? I'm hurt that your hand is still on your sword. A sword I helped your maker pick out. Lovely, isn't it?"

My eyes narrowed and I watched him, but my fingers remained taut around the hilt. This was his game. "It's beautiful," I ground out. "Why are you here?"

"Declan was fine for passing messages, but I'm afraid what happens next requires a more precise touch." He came another breath closer. A breeze ruffled the branches around us and overwhelmed me with Arden's perfume of tobacco and a woman's jasmine.

"What do you mean next?" I spat.

He tilted his head, regarding me. "Can you wield one for me? A demon? Lukas says they kneel for you and see you as more than a wielder."

"No." I shook off what he said. They did kneel, but I knew Arden had a different fascination. "What do you know, Damien?"

"So glad you asked." Arden clapped his hands together and stared at me.

The toffee depths of his eyes eddied and shifted to an even lighter shade of brown. I never knew what Arden's gift was, but I knew it lived in his eyes, a secret from the world. There were a thousand rumors about the man I shut out over the years, but I wondered if he could compel others.

Arden smirked. "I know the Crown accepted Avernought's pledge for you. They also provided him with a handsome reward, although I don't believe it's necessary when Prince Farran is also pledged to him. Were you there when Beven fell? The criers outdid themselves recounting the story."

"Yes." I nodded. "Rumor has it their general betrayed them."

"Rumors hold truth." Arden looked out into the river. "Perhaps it was a betrayal. There are many forces at play." His eyes slid back to mine. "Many would love to pry you from Avernought's hand and stuff you away for a better war. Like the King of Illium, perhaps."

My eyes narrowed, and I stared through him with an accusation. "Avernought promised you his winnings on my rise to the Queensguard. Has the King of Illium made a better offer?"

"The King of Illium is of no concern to you, but Armory soldiers are weapons to trade." He frowned, and my back stiffened. "I cannot be blamed for playing their game when I saw your potential."

"I was *ten*." I seethed through clenched teeth.

"And I was right, wasn't I?" Arden took a scant breath and kicked the ground before he looked at me again with an expression I hardly ever saw.

It was filled with exhaustion and worry—a face I'd only seen him make when Crown soldiers came to his doors in the middle of the night demanding to see his accounts.

Finally, he straightened and continued, "I'll speak plainly: I'm not your villain, and it pains me you can't see the same. Everything I have done for you has been out of love."

"Love?" I laughed bitterly; that was rich. A thousand memories of love compounded at once. "I did everything you asked. I killed for you. I'm your weapon."

"Or a hero? It's all in the framing, you see." His voice piqued, and I looked at him again as a shadow darkened his face. That was the man I knew. "You and you alone will kill the queen, Reina. You know this—it's what fate has written for you. The oath was assurance, and the Queensguard is just the beginning."

My magic twisted and thrashed against my chest like a fish spilled from a bucket. Before my Rite, my oath was Arden's selfish choice until the priest provided an altruistic reason, and then Arden forgot the real order of events.

My oath was a secret, never to escape the two of us.

Surviving the Armory was always a question and a fantasy, but with every trial, *my* future became a pulsing inevitability.

Since thirteen, when my Rite revealed it, the death of the queen became the point of my existence. I grew up dreaming about how my dagger would feel between her ribs. I wondered if she'd still bleed red as the rest of us do, or if it ran black . . . and I wondered what I'd say as I withdrew the blade from her heart.

"There is a plan," Arden continued, and sickening hope flickered, creasing his brow. "It's fluid, of course. Details are being worked out, but you are not in this alone. Once you fulfill our oath, we'll have a different conversation."

"I don't enjoy being in the dark when it's my life and my future, Damien," I said tightly, nails digging into my palm to hold myself steady. "What happens next? Who takes the throne if she has three sons? Executing a full royal line is political suicide. I know my part, but I'm not destabilizing a kingdom."

Arden took another step forward. His face was only a breath away from mine. My magic retreated to the back of my ribcage as his presence swelled. If I were any other woman, I would have swooned, but instead, I felt sick.

"You aren't planning to kill her so soon, are you?" he drawled. "Let the adults worry. You keep staying pretty and alive, Reina. A premature attempt on the queen's life might keep you from the Queensguard."

"I'm well aware." Arden scared me once, but I've since learned he's just a man. "Tell me what the plan is, or you'll taste my blade."

"I forget the way you bite." Arden licked his lips as he mulled over his words carefully, his sweet breath curling around my face. "Fine. There are options. The old gods have protected and kept King Ara of Cathan alive in the Darklands—or so I've heard."

He watched for every brief twitch in my expression, and I knew this conversation was a test, a dance of wills. Gods, how I hated him.

"That's a legend," I bit out. "Even if it were true, it's been centuries. Ara is long dead, and anyone who tells you otherwise is lying. The Catharian King will not return to the Thera, nor will its people want to be ruled by a corpse."

A smile crawled across Arden's face. "Correct. The Catharian King would not return to Thera—he would restore the Darklands and unite with Thera by the power of the old gods. Haven't you heard the rumors about the God Raion returning to Illium? Or that Olios might live again? And haven't you seen when the last *dreosen* lived?

"You know how important your gift is, my dear. It scares the queen; as a demon wielder, *always* heralds change and destruction. Two things that look so beautiful on you."

My hand twisted on my sword. I knew exactly when the last demon wielder fell two hundred years ago. Their death cleaved

Thera and the Darklands to bring about the new gods. What Arden spoke of was impossible. King Ara was a story, told and retold to explain what came to be, and never fully true.

"Your mother wasn't a noble in the queen's court, you know."

My eyebrow lifted, and I almost scoffed. "You lied about that, too?"

Arden shook his head. "Your mother was a noble of the Darkland court, the kingdom called Noterra—the last Catharian hold which collapsed only decades ago."

I froze. Several pieces of my past made more sense. My parents never belonged in Thera. Is that what the dreite meant when they said I belonged to them? I wasn't Theranian by blood. Did that change the Queen's claim on me?

Arden continued, "She fled when the last Noterran King died in the last Theranian attack. Thera's dragons obliterated several Noterran cities, forcing most survivors to flee. The priests and their demons kept Thera from the throne, but everything else was destroyed."

"The king died in the streets of his city that day," I added as I pieced together what he was saying.

"King Garek. You've been to the Darklands; it's now a wasteland of keeps and unruled magic. King Ara will restore the seat of Cathan to Noterra, as it was always meant to be. Lukas assures me there's a part you'll play. You just need to trust him."

"I'm already committed to regicide. What's another count of treason?" I remarked drily.

"You say it as if your morals are any different from mine." Arden glared, and he was right. His morals and mine were inextricable from the other. I was made in his image. It was only by fate I wasn't strung from the gallows like the others Arden created, the boys I'd trained beside.

"I will honor my fate," I mumbled, and my eyes raised to his, even though I wanted to drag every truth from him at sword point. "I'll await your word."

Arden held his hand out towards me to reveal a small glass bottle with condensation and a mess of tangled roots inside. Fharax roots from the southern region of Thera, I knew from the mottled red and black gathering near the stem. "*Dreosen* or no," Arden said. "Courage is still an effective weapon when needed."

"Is that what they call *fharendought* now?" I countered, grabbing the vial anyway. Fharax root, boiled correctly with coriander and wraith venom, created a shield from most binding sigils.

"What's waiting is bigger than all of us, Reina," Arden whispered and took a step back, his hand reaching for the reins of his horse as he untied it from the tree. After he swung his legs over the mount, he delivered a parting remark that would have made a better conversation. "The next trial is soon. Your house and one other will be brought to Rowane, just in time to watch the war begin."

Arden snapped the reins, and I opened my mouth to say something, but he was already halfway across the shallow river before the words came to mind.

Just in time to watch the war begin.

I ran through the entire conversation six times as I trudged back to the Armory. The vial of roots weighed down my pocket.

I thought of Farran, and the betrayal compounded with the truth about Arden. It curled in my chest and turned to ash. His mother was responsible for the death of mine, and there was nothing that would overpower the fire of revenge burning within me: hate always burned strongest.

My fate belonged to the old gods who slept and the new gods who sealed them away.

It was all the same truth when I woke up, no matter what kingdom I was born in. Arden was powerless to change the course of anything.

Everyone was in the common room when I returned. Farran gave me a warning look from where he stood with Vera, Jasper, and Devon. Books were spread in front of them, and Avi was nowhere to be seen.

I sat on a couch between Leena and Aixen. No one asked where I'd been, but I could feel the tension of the rising question, and Farran's eyes lingered on mine until I looked away. I didn't know what he was thinking, but I was sure his thoughts didn't mirror my own.

Instead, I thought about two things in equal measure: killing the queen and how striking he looked in fresh leathers, with the Emerald cape draped over his shoulders and the first officer's epaulets.

It was a second favorite next to him in a silk tunic and thin breeches. None of these were things I should have been thinking as the first officer's hands clapped together.

"Our house and Ruby have been invited to Rowane at the pleasure of the Crown as a reward for our successes in trial." Farran's face and voice were severe as he spoke. Beven wasn't a success. My stomach dropped; Arden was right. "We leave at first light tomorrow with Ruby. The invitation includes celebrating Autane and the consequent masquerade.

"I expect we'll face some type of trial, so training will continue as usual while we're there. Avi and I expect you all to remember you represent your house and the Armory."

Farran didn't wait for questions before retreating to his quarters as everyone in the common room dispersed. Or that's what I thought until he stopped in front of the door and spun to look at me.

"Sangrey, a moment?" he murmured.

Did everyone in the room stop to look? I straightened and walked towards him.

Every part of me strained to pretend I didn't wake up tasting his lips, that everything between us was perfectly normal. Of course, the Emerald First Officer and Prince of Thera hadn't made me come in the garden last night.

Swallowing, I stopped in front of him with my arms crossed and forced indifference onto my face.

"Avi told me I'm supposed to give you this," Farran said with a small smile as he held a narrow box towards me.

I took it from him and opened it. Inside was a silver cord, and I immediately forgot about the hands holding it.

He added, "Congratulations, Sangrey. Your pledge with Avernought was accepted, and you'll wear the maker cord for the rest of your service."

The cord stared back at me. It was everything I'd worked for, everything I was supposed to be and now it stared back at me, a braided silver cord, nestled in a navy box. It was just an object, a collection of threads, held out to me with no other ceremony, but I couldn't breathe.

There was no going back—I had a maker, and I'd be a champion. I closed the box and went to my room as the swell of emotion became a torrential downpour in my head.

I belonged to the Crown, to Avernought, and to Arden all in equal measure as a soldier and traitor with a destiny that could destroy us all. What happened when the queen suspected? Or maybe she already knew. Maybe she played with her traitors before her gallows ate them.

I stuffed the cord in the drawer of my desk because I wasn't ready to think about it. Not until I had to.

CHAPTER 30

Some days, I hated the training room. It smelled like a pungent combination of blood, sweat, and the damp hay stuffed in the mats. Today, I had no desire to leave, and stayed an extra hour or two parrying with a few soldiers from Amethyst and Onyx and then Citrine while Aixen watched.

I didn't depart the room until my hands were raw. No part of me wanted to be in Emerald tonight. I needed the pain and practice to clear my head when everything else slipped between my fingers like sand.

It was dark when I finally dragged myself back upstairs to find Leena sitting on my bed, waiting in the soft moonlight. I flicked my hand and the fireplace lit, coating the room in amber.

"Something wrong?" I asked. The door clicked closed behind me, and I locked it.

Leena shook her head. Her hair was braided with our emerald ribbon wound into it. She wore a purple tunic and breeches, but something was wrong. Her shoulders slumped, and she wouldn't look at me.

"My sister joined the Armory while we were in Beven," she murmured.

A twinge of pain pierced my chest as I sank onto the bed beside her and squeezed her hand. "Oh, Leena." An embrace may have been more comforting, but I stank of sweat and she smelled like fresh fucking peonies. "Which house?"

"Sapphire," Leena croaked. "She was supposed to marry, not do this." Tears welled in her eyes as she turned to me, pleading.

"She's not like us, Rein. Bea won't make it through the first trial."

"We'll talk to her." There were options, and Leena didn't have to do this alone. I knew which floor was Sapphire's, and I knew the woods around the Armory well enough. I'd trained Leena and plenty of Arden's men. "We could help. We can train her so she's ready for next year."

"You'll help?" she asked. Hope filled her eyes.

"Of course I'll help." I tugged on Leena's hand and forced her to look at me. I *needed* her to know the sincerity of my promise. "You'd do the same if it was Declan. I know you would. Whatever you need, I'm yours," I assured her.

Leena gave a small smile as she wiped the tears with her sleeve. A promise didn't fix anything, but it came with hope, and sometimes that was enough.

"Anything, Rein. You know that." Leena wrangled me into a tight hug and whispered, "Thank you. For everything. I never thought I'd find a friend like you." I hugged her back as she breathed in sharply, her face twisted in disgust. "You need a bath."

"Well aware," I muttered and crossed the room. After I'd peeled off my sweat-laden tunic, I threw it at her and she squealed as it wrapped around her face. "I'll be back in a minute; I owe you some stories."

I bathed quickly, and the two of us sat on the floor in front of the fireplace, trading stories about the last few weeks and passing books between us.

Leena browsed the histories of shadow wielders while I flipped through the few books we had on sigils. I was missing something. I had to be. Sigils predated all magic in the realm, and if I just focused, I'd find some that would help during trials. In theory, I should be able to do anything a dreite priest could.

"Do you think a portal to Tir would be useful?" I asked aloud as I turned another page.

Her brow furrowed. "Maybe? For a quick escape?" She bit her lip as she mulled over another question. She glanced down at the book, then back to me. "With the blood oath. They truly had no idea it was you?"

"That's what Farran told me." I sighed. "I haven't asked anyone else; I'm not sure I want to know."

Nor had I told anyone else. She was the only one I trusted.

My gaze flicked up to hers. "I'm trapped, Leen. I never worried about it before, but four people die if I do? Fuck. Farran probably feels the same way about me Blaise does. I'm just an obligation."

Leena shook her head. "No, he looks—"

"*Don't*," I warned. "It happened once." It was a lie, but I wouldn't admit it. I hardened my gaze, and the next words needed to be true. "It won't happen again."

"Whatever you say," she said lightly and looked down at the book as she flipped over another page. "They must have felt it when you were stabbed. That would explain why everyone lost their minds."

I looked down at the floor and pulled at a frayed thread on my tunic. "Yeah, they all felt it, and it's probably what saved me."

"By the Seven and stars, Reina," Leena breathed out and gave me a warning look. "It's no wonder why everyone is so willing to put themselves in front of you. Are you okay?"

I nodded, with nothing else to say. She was right, but she didn't know the worst of it. She didn't need to know, not of my destiny, nor the blood oath on my back. She only loosely knew about my work for Arden as an assassin—but never as his Viper.

The night we found our ribbons, I decided she would never be an accomplice.

I'd rather have Leena's friendship and safety now. I could deal with the betrayal and hurt later. When the time finally came, I'd lose everything anyway.

A few minutes later, there was a quiet knock on the door.

I got up and opened it to see Farran standing there in his cloak, staring at me.

Leena yawned and quickly excused herself. "Oh, good evening, First Officer. I was just going to bed. Nice to see you—goodnight." She hurriedly stepped through the door past both of us, and we made no move until we heard her door close.

I cracked the door further and Farran eased inside, his eyes roving over me for a quarter second. I forgot I was only wearing a tunic. Shit.

"You might want to put on pants," he muttered and blushed.

I glared, crossing my arms instead, waiting for an explanation. The motion tugged the tunic up and exposed a significant amount of my thigh. I knew better, but there was a thrill in watching him retreat.

He cleared his throat. "I thought—you should get some training in before we leave. Sorry, I've been—"

"Yeah, no, it's fine. I'll get dressed." I sighed.

Farran turned around as I grabbed my breeches from the floor and pulled them on.

"You can turn around now. I'm decent."

"Good, I was worried about your honor." A small smile turned a corner of his mouth as he grabbed my cloak from its hook by the wall and held it out for me. Amusingly, Farran tried to look everywhere but at me as I put it on. "I was being respectful. Happy to be less so, if you'd prefer."

Thank gods I was underneath the cloak so he couldn't see the way my face flushed or how my hands froze. I hated this. I hated whatever it was.

There was a soft knock on the door, and Leena peered in. "I actually had a second thought," she said with a grimace. "Can I join? I can throw some shadow hounds at Reina and raise the stakes a bit . . . unless it's more of a—"

"No," I blurted. "Sounds like a great idea."

"Great," Leena smirked. "I'll grab my cloak then."

The door closed once more, and the heat of Farran's stare was palpable as I walked past him and into the common room with Leena, leaving him to catch up.

I wouldn't say it, but I was grateful for her company. After yesterday, I didn't trust myself alone with him. Not with the way he looked at me, nor the way his touch took down every defense I had, which was certainly a feat.

Outside the Armory, a cold, drizzling rain dragged me back to my senses while we walked towards the tree line.

"How do you feel about going back to Rowane?" Farran asked casually on our way through trees towards the altar. I'd memorized the path now, and Leena followed close and kept bumping into my arm.

"Looking forward to it." Leena's gold eyes glittered when I glanced over as the memories flitted back. I wished I had an ounce of the fondness she had. "I'd performed in the palace hall a few times."

"I've never been inside the palace," I lied.

I'd actually been in the palace twice. The last time, I was cleaning something up on Arden's account. It was my first time out with Avernought's first gift: my dagger. I christened it with the blood of a Crown page and the guard who saw me.

I casually added, "Suppose it will be nice to get out of the Armory and be somewhere better guarded than Beven. Hopefully, demons won't be necessary."

"Are you excited to go home?" Leena asked Farran, and I watched my feet.

The moon was a slivered crescent tonight, and we could hardly see what was in front of us.

"It's just a place," he muttered, hands stuffed in his pockets. "I'm looking forward to seeing my brothers." His gaze shifted to Leena and me as his voice lightened. "I've always wondered how doesLower Rowane celebrate Autane?"

His curiosity was genuine, and I smiled despite myself. "We don't have masquerades for one, but the streets are filled with vendors and performers. Lights get strung up. Someone conjures leaves, and it's like walking through a forest just at the end of fall, before the first snow."

"There's also the Lord of Gourd and bottle tossing," Leena chimed in. I laughed at the expression crossing Farran's face, some mix of confusion and recognition.

"The Lord of Gourd?" he repeated.

"Yes," Leena said with a light voice, as if we weren't about to practice some of the darkest magic in the realm. "He's a man who wears a pumpkin over his head. Fates decide who gets to be the lord, but there's only ever one, and his throne is in Lower Rowane, always in one of the squares. Children bring him sweets and jokes for good luck. If the lord gets drunk enough to fall and crack the pumpkin head, it means a winter of good fortune."

"Really? That's a tradition?" Farran's eyes were wide in awe.

"It is." I chuckled and glanced at him. "Does proper Rowane not have a Lord of Gourd?"

"It absolutely does not. I suppose I'll need to see it for myself."

An unrelated thought came to mind. I changed the subject and looked at Farran. "I overheard something the night we came back from Beven. I shouldn't have been listening. It was between you and—"

Farran's face softened into a sad smile. "I won't know if Cormac is married or not until we get there. If it's arranged, our mother won't make an affair of it unless public pressure is needed."

"Will you be forced into marriage?" Leena asked.

I nearly jabbed her with my elbow on instinct. There was a part of me that didn't want to know. It didn't matter at all.

"Gods no," Farran said, and his complexion sobered. "I'm the third son. I'll be my brother's Prince Commander following my rise—unless several bad things happen in very quick succession."

We stopped in front of the ravine leading to an altar, and my magic woke up abruptly; the threads warmed and shifted as Farran stopped and turned on his heel to face both of us.

He clapped his hands together with a wild grin. "I've been reading about the last demon wielder and wanted to see if we could try something. Avernought is going to ask for a show.

Doubt we'll have to go to the arena, but Linden will come up with something to keep the makers happy."

"What were you reading?" My eyes narrowed. I'd also read several things, but none of the accounts described any more than conjuring and controlling demons.

Farran walked between the narrow walls of the ravine, towards the altar, as we followed a few steps behind. "The power you used to conjure a demon can be reshaped. It's the essence of their blood a demon wielder controls. There was a story about the first *dreosen* who created a wall of darkness and claws that stopped an army."

I gaped after him. "I'll burn out long before I even conjure a cloud."

A shadow darkened his face. "I won't let that happen."

Leena shared a glance with me and I was sure I'd heard about later. We stopped in front of the altar at the end of the ravine. A sharp breeze sent leaves skittering across the smooth, stained stone.

"I'll try it, but you have to answer a question," I finally amended.

"I'm an open book, darling." He bowed toward me, bending at an awkward angle. Out here, in plain clothes, that was the only action that reminded me he was a prince. Both Leena and I snickered.

"You can wield other powers, but I've never seen you try. You only ever give your own magic," I said. Leena nodded beside me, and I had to admit it was nice having backup.

Farran sighed and crossed his arms as his gaze shifted to the stone altar in front of us. "I don't enjoy doing it. It takes absolute trust from the other wielder—or absolute force. There aren't many people in my life I would ask for that kind of trust."

"You don't trust me?" I challenged, raising a brow.

"No, *you* don't trust me." His eyes caught mine, and my heart stumbled. "And you'd never trust me if I forced you."

The drizzling rain stopped, leaving a dampness in the woods. He was right, and I didn't know what to say, so I opted to say nothing at all. He shifted on his feet.

Finally, he said, "Have you ever conjured a cloud or wind?"

"She can conjure mist," Leena answered for me. "I've seen her do it a few times. She's quite good."

I shuddered. Once Arden found out I could conjure mist with petty magic, he asked me to do it every night. *It adds to the aesthetic*, he would say every time.

"You okay?" Farran asked. I still hadn't said anything.

"Yes," I snapped and turned around to look down the ravine as I rooted around my threads of magic. There was no reason for this to take all night.

Farran extended his arm. Tendrils of blue light crept from his fingertips and formed a weightless globe. He tossed it in front of us, and the blue light filled the ravine, reflecting off the walls in waves like moonlight on ocean water. It was surreal and beautiful.

"So we can see if anything happens," he explained.

"It's quite pretty," I commented.

"It really is," Leena added with some admiration. "I wish they taught us more pretty magic, but when you're ready for terrifying shadow hounds, I'm here."

I'd gotten faster at untangling the threads, but the proximity to the altar helped. Warmth pulsed and filled my chest; the heat needled my skin as I formed the magic into a fine mist—just a little heavier than an autumn fog. It was like folding a paper swan, and every turn of hand mattered. Too much of one, and the mist became rain. Too much of the other, and it would vanish in seconds.

Slowly, the mist swelled into existence, and I smiled as the cool, wet air kissed my skin. It glowed by the light of the orb but didn't obscure it, not yet.

That was the familiar magic; next were the demons. I stretched both hands in front of me and pulled through the threads until I found the cold, damp one tethering us together.

I wove it into the magic holding the fog. When I opened both eyes, the glow of the orb had dimmed.

"Can you move it?" the prince asked.

I lifted my right hand, and the mist obeyed. It crashed against the ravine's wall in a shattering wave and reformed on the floor.

Leena watched with wide eyes. "If this is your style of petty magic, you hold back too much in the Atrium, Rein."

Of course I did. I focused again, imagining more of the cold and damp weaving into the mist to become something more ominous.

I imagined lightning, thunder, and the crush of pressure. Thunder rang as I held the mist and the demon in place until it practically consumed the orb. A strike of lightning seared through. Farran threw a rock into the center, but nothing happened.

"Maybe it won't work without a real threat." I measured my breathing. I sounded more winded than I was as I moved my hand again and watched the storm crash against the wall.

Farran turned to Leena. "Hounds, now."

There was a tinge of emotion—anxiousness, excitement, and worry—on the edge of his voice coming closer when he laid his hand on my arm.

Farran's magic wound into mine, strengthening it as I doubled the size of the storm. Leena reached forward, and the motion was followed by barking and howling. I caught the movement of a shadow inside of it and gasped, but I didn't let go.

I knew I was pushing my limit, but it felt incredible and enticing.

Hounds charged into the mist, only to be swallowed by silence. I held steady, despite the way my vision shivered. I concentrated on the mist until the hounds were suspended within it. With bated breath, I tugged a demon's thread and then imagined crushing it in my fist.

The ravine filled with the screams of the hounds, tearing flesh, and breaking bone until there was nothing else.

"Let go, Reina," Farran whispered in my ear. It was far off.

The wind picked up as his magic nudged mine, but I didn't relent.

He pressed his cheek to mine, and I swooned. "Let. *Go.*"

I looked to my left. Leena's hands were at her sides. I could hold this longer. I could do it again.

"Reina, let go," Farran pleaded. His hand had snaked around my waist to hold me against his chest. *Fine.* I could stay here.

I dropped the threads, and the silence returned as the wind calmed. All that remained in front of us were the mangled bodies of two shadow hounds and the undulating blue light of the orb.

It drizzled again as the world came back into focus. I pulled myself out of his grip, but my eyes didn't leave the massacre.

"I think it worked," I spluttered, glancing at Farran. He was also panting—I must have pulled more than I thought. My chest heaved, and my legs were definitely not steady, but I'd felt worse.

"That was fucking brilliant." Leena gawked from behind, and I'd almost forgotten she was here.

"More than I expected." Farran's hand squeezed his neck. He took a few steps towards the orb and squinted into the mist. "I can see how it would take down an army."

He motioned for us to come closer. We did, and I gasped.

The ground around the orb wasn't just covered in shadow hound entrails. It was covered in fatal, black demon blood. A storm like that would be a painful end to any unsuspecting army, the kind of end someone would write songs about—Leena might have her wish after all.

"It's not just claws," I muttered, my eyes taking in the scene.

Farran shook his head. "No, it's worse."

The world turned over. My vision narrowed, and I stumbled back. Farran and Leena yelled my name. *Gods fucking damnit.* I pushed too hard, and I wasn't strong enough.

I was thirteen again, lying on the warm slab of temple stone, a priest dragging me through my Rite. In a flash, I stood in a cave, warm and sticky blood pouring over my hand.

The queen stared at me, her lips and rasping voice not matching as the words choked out, "*The kingdom you rule will be devoid of life.*"

She said it again and again until a final breath rattled and extinguished.

It was impossible at thirteen; it was impossible now. I'd rule nothing, but the queen got one thing right: whatever I did would be devoid of life. That kind of destruction I was capable of.

Black blood clung to my feet as the body of the queen decomposed into mangled pieces of demon gore.

Another flash and I woke up, drenched in sweat.

I was in my room, no blood in sight and no temple priest. I forced myself to sit up with a grimace. Everything ached, and my head pounded. The sun hadn't come up yet, and a soft, orange glow emanated from the fireplace.

I looked at the door and swore out loud. Farran slumped in a common room chair he'd set in the corner near my bathroom. His eyes flew open when he heard me curse.

"Oh, thank gods." He sprang to his feet, but I shrank back. "I thought you burned out."

My eyes narrowed. "What do you mean?" I had more pressing questions, but this was a good starting point.

He rubbed his temple as he stopped a few steps away from the edge of my bed. "You didn't feel weak. Something in you just stopped," he explained.

I shook my head and held my chin higher. "I was fine, and then I wasn't. Just like every other time."

His blue eyes looked at me, studied me, and they swirled like the fucking ocean. "I thought you died, Reina. Your heart was barely beating. Leena ran back here—"

I shrugged. "I just passed out. You didn't feel the oath—"

"Yes, I fucking did."

The color drained from my face. "Did anyone—"

"No. It was a flutter. I lied to Avi, but don't tell me you just passed out."

There was silence for a long, tense moment as I gathered my thoughts. "How long have you been there?" I finally asked.

"An hour. Leena was here for the two hours before that. Someone needed to keep an eye on you . . . just in case."

"In case what?" I demanded.

"In case it was something more serious." His voice clipped. "You're surprised people care about you?"

I turned away from him and looked into the fire. Anger slithered into my words with all the venom I could muster. "Do they care about me, or is this all about what I can do for them? For you?"

"*You,*" Farran said without hesitation.

Something fluttered in my chest, but I let it fall, and I didn't look at him.

He sighed and left the room. The door closed with a gentle click. I took a shaky breath as anger and bitterness poisoned my thoughts and clenched my fists.

I never should have let anyone close enough to care. I wasn't worth it; I was inextricable from the demons and blood I controlled. I was slow dripping venom that would kill everything it touched, just as I had before.

Memories swelled back against my will.

I was sixteen and alone after I'd been used by the first love of my life. She kissed my fingertips and told me I mattered, that I was worth more than the blood I'd spilled only to rescind all of it when she got what she wanted. She vanished with Arden's prized map, and I never saw her again.

That was the last time I begged the gods to tear my oath from my flesh. I wanted to run after her and face her the way she wouldn't face me.

Arden wiped the tear from my cheek and said people like us needed to look in different places for meaning. Love was a gap in our armor we couldn't afford.

But I didn't listen to him. At nineteen, I let myself fall because I thought I could be different. I trusted, I cared, I let someone else make me feel whole in a way I couldn't alone.

It worked until my venom caught up to him. That's how I knew love felt like dying, and I never wanted to feel it again. I watched him, eyes closed, as he begged for his life in the court-yard with Arden's knife to his throat because there was no other way.

I closed my eyes as he screamed, and Arden drew the blade. It was a mistake, and I knew better this time. I'd learned my lesson.

No one was immune to me. Maybe that's why the Goddess of Death chose my body; Death is all a viper was good for, so perhaps I was the perfect fit.

Chapter 31

I DIDN'T FALL BACK asleep, and the morning light came too fast. I was awake to watch the ceiling change from black to a royal shade of blue, and then orange.

Every word I said last night and every memory clawed back and sat heavy on my chest. It wasn't until Leena pounded on my door and threatened to barge in that I mustered the strength to crawl out of bed and get dressed.

Once I clasped the last buckle on my leathers, I pulled open my desk drawer and took out the navy box. It opened with a pop, and inside was my cord—silver and pristine.

It was soft, spun silk braided carefully and painted silver. I removed it with only my fingertips, as if it was the most delicate fabric I'd ever touched. It wasn't, but it was lighter than I thought. Before my dingy mirror, I strapped it across my leathers. Clipping it on one side, then the other, just as I'd seen our chosen do.

It was strange that something so small could be so significant. Then, I clipped on the emerald cape and tears poked my eyes because no one would ever question what queen I served.

I buried all thoughts about what I deserved and who I was. It didn't matter. I was here now. Destiny crept closer with every passing day, and dwelling on it helped no one.

Just in time to watch the war begin.

We stood around the common room. Arden's words stilted every other thought. Farran was nowhere to be seen, but Avi swept in, epaulets on display and her own cord hung across her chest.

She motioned for the door after she'd counted heads and took a tally of sixteen of us as we lined up. After a several-day absence, it was a relief to see her.

We left the Armory and headed to the stables where Ruby was well ahead of us. Most of their house had already mounted on their horses.

"You can ride with me," Aixen said from behind, and I hardly turned. There may as well be iron chains around my wrists for the heaviness I felt. "Farran left half an hour ago with Ruby's first officer. Something about getting ahead. Apparently, the Ruby First Officer is also from the upper echelons of Rowane. His father is on the Queen's council."

I nodded, struggling to follow along. "Makes sense."

Relief swept over me in a warm breeze. Riding a horse with Farran was one thing I was grateful to avoid today, especially when his entire presence loomed in my memory like a ghost of a future I couldn't have.

I cursed and strapped my pack on one side of Aixen's light-colored horse, then I caught Aixen grinning from ear to ear as I scowled. Griffons were fine, and if a dragon wouldn't kill me on sight, I'd be fine with them too, but horses?

I was still sore from Beven, and that was a quick ride.

"I'll just walk. I'm not doing it," I growled.

"Oh, come on, Rein. You're not gonna try? He's docile."

"No. No, I am not." I'd already embarrassed myself once before, and I wasn't doing it again. I was a soldier for the Crown, and it was embarrassing enough I couldn't ride.

Aixen rolled his eyes, grabbed me by the hips, and hoisted me onto the horse. I seethed atop the saddle; another choice taken from me.

He jumped on and we left for Rowane, not far behind Ruby and the rest of our house. In the woods, we were a mess of red and green capes, all decorated with the silver crest of the Crown—a sure target if I'd ever seen one.

"Are there knives on your leg?" Aixen asked after an hour.

Sharp twinges ran through my thighs, and my pelvis was already bruising with every damn trot. None of this boded well for the sixteen hours of riding I still had to endure.

What if I walked? It would have been easy enough, being it was all inland even if our route wound through the haunted Salos Forest.

"Maybe." I turned and glanced at him. His eyebrows rose. "You do know I always carry knives."

"I've just never been so painfully reminded." He glowered and readjusted his leg again, nearly bucking me off as he stretched. The horse briefly craned its neck. *Are you quite done?* Its eyes seemed to ask.

"I'm not comfortable either, but I suppose I can adjust them." I twisted the strap so they'd dig in less, but I wasn't taking a single blade off. "Better now?"

"Yes, much. Thank you, Reina." This was exactly how I imagined riding a horse with Declan would be. "Anyway, do you remember when we went to Mossford last winter? I think we should go back. I know a knight who'll be returning," he remarked.

Maybe worse; instead of chatting about dragons like Declan, Aixen avoided anything too close to Eral by ranking the soldiers and knights he was currently "talking to". Then he began a list of suitors for me because, *"No one can pine after a prince forever."*

For the record, I wasn't pining; pining implied my heart was broken, which was impossible because mine was never whole.

A few hours later, shortly before I lost most awareness of my lower body, Avi whistled, and our party of two houses gathered around her and the other captain: a lanky man with blond hair and wide-set eyes.

We'd finally left the endless swathes of pine and were now at a break in the woods. This is where meadows sloped into the oak forests surrounding Rowane. Once we crossed the Ines River, we'd only be a day from Rowane, where I wouldn't have to smell horse shit for a few glorious days.

"For the rest of the day," Avi said loudly, "we're going to break into a single file line and try to move as fast as possible through the meadow. Farran and Keaton aren't far ahead, and we'll stop for the night when we catch up. We're outside this evening, but tomorrow we'll stay at an inn in the town of Feisch."

The Ruby Captain beside her cleared his throat. "Everyone can remove their capes; rogues will know we're soldiers by our leathers. Capes will get in the way if we're attacked."

Aixen shrugged off his cape and jumped off the horse. I handed him mine. He rolled them both so the crest didn't show and then we took off, riding the rest of the day and even beyond sunset.

We didn't stop until we saw a fire from our first officers in the space where two hills met, close to the tree line of the Salos forest that eagerly awaited our arrival.

Farran and Ruby's first officer, Keaton, stood around it with their arms crossed, talking about something as we approached.

My hips felt like I'd held an open flame against them, and I eagerly dismounted. The smell on the edge of the air was familiar, and every breath, unwillingly, brought a rush of memories.

I sat in front of the crackling fire pit with our company as a few soldiers passed around provisions. Renewed fatigue settled in my bones and aching muscles like an old friend I couldn't figure out how to lose.

As we shared stories over the fire, I placed my hands on the swell of my hips and conjured small white tendrils to soothe them. The relief was instantaneous, and I realized the pain had staved off my exhaustion. Without it, I could hardly keep my eyes open and after a few minutes of trying to, I promptly gave up.

I spread my bedroll on the other side of the hill without a single regret except how near to the horses I was. Otherwise, the meadow was peaceful between the rustling grass and the stories wafting on the breeze.

One Ruby soldier found a griffon in a snowstorm last winter, while two others were kidnapped by Dreites and tortured for a few days before their house could organize a rescue. While Jasper, the second-year from our house, nearly burned out at a siege trial last year trying to hold back a Citrine champion who nearly set the whole field on fire.

There was more, but it lulled me to sleep, and I didn't wake until Farran tugged my arm and dragged me from the black abyss with a start.

My eyes flew open; one hand reached for my dagger and the other for my sword. "What's—"

His finger pressed to his lips and hadn't let go of my arm. Something was wrong. Immediately I rose to my feet, following him around the base of the hill where Avi, Devon, Aixen, and two men from Ruby crouched, watching our camp from several yards away.

It was silent except for the crunch of grass and a wafting conversation from where our fire barely smoldered.

"*Rogues,*" Devon mouthed at me.

He didn't need to say anything else. That's why our fire was put out; that's why we were waiting behind this hill. I squinted, trying to hear better.

I counted four rogues speaking to our own soldiers, but I was certain there were more hiding just as we were. A tense minute of conversation quickly gave way to the unmistakable sound of a sword leaving its sheath and then the song of steel colliding.

That wasn't the signal. Farran didn't move; instead, we waited in excruciating silence, listening to screams, the clang of swords, and grunting.

My hand gripped my pommel, knuckles white, as Farran held both short swords out, ready to strike. Another scream, then another.

"*Now!*" a voice bellowed through the shadows.

We ran into the fold, swinging our weapons. We outnumbered the rogues by well over half. Their swords were strong, and magic wasn't an option this close to the Salos Forest; the beacon would draw out a lot more trouble than a few humans wielding blades.

Three rogues were already on the ground. Avi plunged her sword into the fourth, and Aixen cut the back of his knees for good measure. Shouting erupted behind as three more rogues ran for us.

A sword nicked my arm, and I spun back, my steel to a man's throat. His eyes widened as I plunged, and his body fell to the ground, gargling. Farran took one hit to his arm and responded to the assailant with a short sword in the ribs before sending a frantic look around the field.

There was only one more, and Avi's sword rested on his collarbone as several other soldiers closed in. The rogue begged for his life, tears streaming down his face.

Farran gave a nod, and Avi severed the head from his shoulders. It was a merciful death, and relief swelled as we all sheathed our weapons and scanned the perimeter.

We hadn't lost a single soldier, and none of our party was injured, save for a few deep cuts Varyn could heal.

The sky had already turned the darkest shade of blue. Dawn wasn't far off. We needed to carry on so we packed quickly and left the bodies to burn on a makeshift pyre. Then our houses set off for Rowane with only one full day of travel left.

I rode with Aixen again. He spent the first hour of the jaunt trying to figure out how the rogues appeared by recounting every detail several times over. By the time we moved on, I doubted whether I had slept last night because he more than caught me up on what I'd missed.

Eventually, we crossed the shallow Ines River on foot with the rest of the party, gently leading the horses. They were reluctant, but the water of Ines never went higher than their knobbed knees.

Once we clambered up the bank, we were at the edge of Salos forest and fully in the Duchy of Rowane. Soon, oak forests would stretch between the sparse wheat fields and guide us into the valleys of Rowane.

We rode hard, despite my loud complaining. Every step the horse took felt like a burst of lightning up my back, and my pelvis was certainly bruised. Humans weren't made to sit on top of a fucking animal for hours.

I could have kissed Avi when she finally called us to a stop outside the village of Feisch. I was done riding. I could walk the rest of the way without batting an eye. Rowane was only hours away.

Everything about Feisch was an echo of home: every rattle in the trees above as the leaves turned, the wafting smell of an oak fire in the hearths, and the musk of late season goldenrod that grew along the side of the road where the morning sun fell.

All of it was home.

Our captains arranged us between three inns. We all got a bed, and every screaming bone in my body rejoiced. All I wanted was to lie horizontal and unmoving, away from the horses.

It didn't matter that four of us were squeezed into one room, or that I had to listen to Varyn snore. We had four walls, a bed, and a meal of rich beef stew with potatoes. The next day, we all awoke refreshed and ready to face whatever awaited us in Rowane.

We arrived by the northern route in the midafternoon. Our company spilled into the valley as the sun reached its highest point in the sky.

Straight in front of us loomed the walled city of Rowane, the Palace of Thera at the very top. Behind it was the faint outline of Lower Rowane, which looked like it had been spilled out of a bucket into the expanse of the valley.

Two hundred years after the Second War of Kings, Lower Rowane stretched well beyond its city walls, through the valley, and up to the edge of the forest. The lower city became a refuge for thousands and surpassed the size of the walled city in only a few years. The only part of the valley Lower Rowane hadn't overtaken was the wide swath of land around the main gate.

Supposedly, the soil was too rocky and sparse to build a structure, but the legends claim it's haunted by centuries of unburied bodies who died trying to seize Rowane. I'd never been interested in finding out which was true.

Avi and the lanky Ruby Captain had stopped us all at the forest edge so we could clip on our Armory capes and signets for approach; we already wore our best leathers.

I pulled the cord from my pocket, silver and light, despite what it meant to everyone around me. I had a maker, and I belonged to Lukas Avernought. The proof was clipped to my left shoulder and draped across for everyone to see; for once, the honor felt earned.

From the edge of the forest to the gates of Rowane, it was a half hour by horse with the sun beating down. It remained un-seasonably warm despite the changing colors of leaves around the valley.

Rowane's gates opened easily, but the hard part came next: navigating our way through the busy, winding uphill streets until we reached the palace.

I should have expected the welcome, but it caught me off guard. Conjured leaves of Autane fell around us and swirled through the air alongside the cheers and shouts.

Farran and Keaton, the Ruby First Officer, took the lead while Avi and the Ruby Captain fell behind them. Keaton was the son of the second highest-ranking family in Thera and prac-tically a prince himself; the request came from the Crown.

I nodded and smiled at the people in the street who waved at us. We all represented the Crown, whether or not we deserved it. Some residents held out banners for our houses while others shouted out names to see if our faces matched the images they'd built in their heads from the crier reports. Within five minutes, I settled for staring straight ahead; I'd tuned out the shouts of *dreosen* and demon wielder.

We passed merchant tents, homes, and taverns in full celebration as they tapped their cider barrels. Above us, strung lights were twined with streamers made from leaves while two dragons flew past, to the street's delight. It was beautiful and strange to be riding through it, but I'd love to get off the damn horse. Walking to the palace was infinitely faster.

"How much further do you think?" I asked Aixen, suppressing a groan.

"A half hour at this pace," he replied with a shrug.

"On the fucking seven and stars. Can't we go faster?"

He chuckled. "Reina, we'd run over people."

Aixen was right. That's why he held the reins of the horse, and I didn't.

Frowning, I listened to the misplaced cheers and excitement of the gathered crowds.

These were the kinds of events I avoided when I lived here, and now I was in the middle. I was also bored and fighting off several intrusive thoughts, so I picked the most exciting one.

"Why did you swear an oath to the *dreosen*?" I grinned deviously as Aixen choked on air. "It's just a question."

He cleared his throat and craned his neck to look at me. Even the horse seemed to stiffen at my words. "Where the fuck did you hear that?" he sputtered.

"Does it change your answer?"

Aixen looked at the sky and swore. "Several of us did, *not* realizing it was you. We knew it would be someone in the house—and the Crown gave us protection."

"What kind of protection?" I genuinely wanted to know.

It had to be something convincing if it meant tying their own life to someone they never met. I made my oath when I was too young to understand, but I'd never do it again.

Aixen squinted at me and lowered his voice. "You do know we were sworn to secrecy, right?"

"Well, it's no longer a secret to me." I shrugged.

"Blaise or Farran?"

"Doesn't matter," I said with indignance. I didn't love the assumption.

Aixen looked at the strings of lights above us and sighed. He knew I wouldn't relent.

"Fine, it was different for each of us. For me, the Crown would support my family in the South. You've heard there isn't much down there, and the land is cursed, I swear. The oath means my sister can be a healer. It also means my parents can keep their butchery. I couldn't turn it down."

"You shouldn't have to make the choice. You were coerced," I said with creeping guilt.

A shadow crossed his features, and my shoulders sagged. I shouldn't have asked.

He said stiffly, "Choice looks different for all of us, Reina. I don't regret what I did. Besides, knowing now that it's you, I'd have taken the oath without the incentive." My eyes widened.

"You don't have to be kind," I mumbled. I hated it. I hated knowing anyone would tie their life to mine.

"I'm not. All of first year, I thought I sold my soul. I really didn't think any of us first-years could be the wielder. I thought they'd have to be some terrible, court-born magistrate, but I'm glad you proved me wrong. You're terrible in a different way."

"Thank you," I said, and I meant it deeper than he realized. "I'd do the same for you."

He smirked. "I appreciate it, but your death would kill nearly half of us. I'd wait to make any promises."

"Point taken. I'll stay alive a little longer."

"Much appreciated, Sangrey."

The clop of hooves against the cobbled streets was all I could hear. We were higher than I thought and close to the palace gates. I peered over the gleaming slate roofs of Merchant Street and well beyond the city where the valley spread below. It was a sight I could see a thousand times and never tire of.

If I squinted, I could almost see exactly where Arden's estate was. It was a gap of green property towards the outer edges of Lower Rowane. Once, it was the only estate. Several more had cropped up over the years as nobles sought land the walled city had run out of.

We stopped at the large iron gates of the Palace. Crown officials stood opposite the plaza on the palace steps to greet us with Prince Cormac. Queensguard knights, in their cords and cloaks, surrounded them—soon we'd be equals.

Royal stable hands swarmed us and took the reins as we came to a stop. They led the horses to our right, where the plaza descended around the palace.

The gaggle of officials approached our houses, and I knew immediately it was a blend of our makers and Ruby's. Four were dressed in shades of green, while the other five wore a variation of red. The crown prince walked out, and we all bowed.

"Rise. Welcome, honored houses of the Armory," Cormac said with a charming smile. "Your makers will take you to your quarters, and if I could borrow your captains for only a moment. Enjoy your time in Rowane and at the Autane festivities. There is no reason to pretend you are humorless unless you find yourself in the presence of my mother."

One guard glared at Cormac, the tall one I recognized from Beven—Sir Irvin.

Cormac ignored him. "Right, I won't keep you any longer. May the wind be at your back."

"And the gods at your side," we replied in unison, looking like the perfect soldiers to the perfect Crown.

The makers guided us towards the gardens, the same direction the horses went, and they hardly looked at us: Emerald and Ruby alike. Even Avernought's eyes stuck to the ground.

Fear nibbled at my neck. Something had shifted. It was more tense than I expected for a festival.

A large stone wing jutted out from below the palace. We walked towards it and stopped when a particularly tall Ruby maker, with her hair tied tightly atop her head, spoke in a light voice. "This is where we house participants for the queen's tournaments during the summer games and guests for the

Queen's Spectacle. Her Majesty believes you'll find it sufficient."

The maker pushed the doors open, and we filed in. It was a single hallway that must have had seventy rooms. Portraits of legendary tournament champions hung between every door. The walls were stone, trimmed in black wood, and lit by three large wooden chandeliers hanging a little too close to my head.

On either side of the hallway were staircases leading to the level below, and beside them were the only windows in the space. They stretched almost the entirety of either wall.

"You'll find more rooms downstairs," the maker said. "That's also where you'll find the doors to the stable, baths, and a pantry. It should go without saying that being unaccompanied within the palace is off-limits. You are all aware that the knights of the Queensguard are the best in Thera; do not test them. They also trained the guards."

She left the wing with the makers close behind. Avernought paused for a moment to meet my gaze, but his expression remained unreadable.

"I suppose we should find our room." Leena's arm snaked through mine.

CHAPTER 32

WE PICKED A ROOM near a staircase. The simple space held two made beds, a rack for clothes, and several empty shelves. Across from the door was a large window looking out over a garden.

Stable hands unloaded our bags in the hallway. We grabbed our own, and I tossed mine on the bed and laid out everything in it. I found a clean but severely wrinkled tunic. The Crown had sent in help for our laundry, but we still had nothing to wear to a Crown ball.

"Are they bringing us dress clothes?" Leena asked aloud as she poked around the cabinets.

She pulled on a creaking wardrobe door. Inside was a handful of gowns and doublets.

"Answered my own question," she mumbled.

Fingers picked at the lace of an offensively bright green gown that was modest and exposing all at once. The other two dresses weren't much better despite being more pleasant shades of green.

"We still have two days. I'll think of something. I don't think either of us should wear a borrowed dress tomorrow." By something, I meant Arden. He held my accounts, and I was too aware of how thrilled he'd be to help.

"Now what?" Leena asked, sinking into the bed with a huff.

I shrugged and said, "Wait for Avi to come back? I'm sure they've put a trial in this. The queen wouldn't bring us here if she didn't want to see something."

Leena and I played cards on the floor for about an hour before Avi's whistle cut through the thin door just as I'd almost won a hand.

Devon and Jasper shepherded all of us into a too-small room where Avi stood on a bed and counted us.

She wasted no time. "This isn't a formal trial, but the Queensguard wanted us to warn you. There have been a few isolated threats, and the Crown wanted additional protection. *We* are the protection if anything happens. If you receive a reasonable order from the Queensguard or court, you will honor it as if you're a true knight. Understood?"

There was a murmur of agreement in the room with a flicker of dread.

"Good. Please enjoy Autane. The Crown will not bail you out of jail. In fact, your capes will be taken away just as they would be for a real Queensguard knight," she warned.

We filed out of the room, but Avi said my name and Farran's. I spun around as Farran closed the door and looked straight at Avi. She sighed heavily, her gaze steady on his as if I wasn't in the room, then she lowered her voice.

"Your mother has concerns she's expressed to the Queensguard and certain members of the court," she said, voice cautious, testing Farran's reaction.

"Of course she does." He lifted an eyebrow. "And those concerns are?"

Avi looked at the ceiling and back at him. Whatever it was, she didn't want to have this conversation, but she forced the words out. "The concern is you're being too much like the late prince consort and have been influenced by Lord Avernought." She paused to shift her weight. "Your brother shared the same worry."

"*Too* much like my father?" he sputtered, pinching the bridge of his nose.

"You know how they feel about the old gods, Far."

Farran looked up from the floor at Avi, his arms crossed and shoulders stiff. "And what does she want to do about it?" he demanded.

Avi broke his gaze and looked at the floor. I felt strongly that I needed to leave the room.

"Cormac said the queen wants a reaffirmation of loyalty to the new gods so the court holds its tongue." She looked at her feet.

"Fine," he ground out, his eyes a raging tempest. "How does Reina fit into this? She's done everything that's been asked. She can't pretend her gift isn't old magic any more than I can."

Avi's eyes softened, and the shadow on her face receded as they continued to talk about me as if I weren't standing next to them. "You know why. She's formally pledged to Avernought, who is now under the queen's suspicion. Her gift is even more cause for concern. He owns the two most powerful soldiers in the kingdom."

Something in me twisted at hearing it so blankly. Avernought would never be killed for treason . . . Like Arden, he had too much money and too much power but he could be brought to heel.

"I'm sorry, I am," Avi said. "But I can't deny orders when they come from Linden. Nor can you unless you plan to talk to the queen about it."

Farran grunted. "What is our *reaffirmation quest*?"

I moved closer and focused on controlling my features. A thousand possibilities ran through my mind; we could be forced to duel in an arena melee or brought in front of the court to perform an execution.

What if the queen found my brother? What if she charged him with Arden's crimes and I had to—

"She wants the old palace altar destroyed before the nobles as an event for the Autane masquerade." A small relief that no one would die, but the thought pricked my skin. It was wrong to destroy an altar; it was the same as desecrating a grave. Worse, in fact, as each altar held centuries of sacrifices, all made in earnest to the old gods who couldn't hear.

Farran looked at Avi incredulously. "On the fucking Seven, what a—"

"You're allowed to be upset." Avi hardened. "But she's still your queen and your mother, Far. I don't need to remind you. Don't do anything stupid."

Silence drifted into the room like a frigid breeze. Farran's face darkened again, and he asked Avi one more nagging question that stilted my breath. "And Cormac said nothing about it?"

Avi looked at the ceiling. "I'm sure he did, but the queen made a decision. You know how it is."

"Right. Fine, we'll do it." Farran's head swiveled, and his eyes locked on mine. If I didn't know better, it looked like tears brimmed his eyes. "I'm sorry you're getting pulled into this, Reina."

"It's fine," I said evenly. "I couldn't choose my gift."

And I needed to stop expecting I'd have any say in how I used it. My skin bristled at the sheer thought of using my power to destroy something belonging to the old gods. I didn't want to. How could I?

The only consolation was that Farran was even more pissed than I was. He stormed out of the room in a flurry. For a second, I thought Avi would chase after him and talk him down. Instead, she sighed and went to her own room.

In our room, Leena had put on plain clothes and braided a silver ribbon into her hair with her emerald one. Outside, shadows were getting longer as night descended on Rowane. Once the sun fell, the festivities would begin.

Leena's golden eyes were calm. It was always a relief to see her. Even in the face of death, she would find the sliver of hope I needed tonight.

The idea of standing beside Farran, before the court, and using my gift to destroy an ancient altar felt so final and damning. Could the demons abandon me for that? Or would they be forced to listen to someone who desecrated their gods?

"Where are you going?"

"We're all going into the city. We promised Aixen a perfect Rowanian Autane. Join us? Don't stay locked up in here," she murmured, clearly calling out the pensiveness I hadn't bothered to hide.

"Sure." I pushed the corners of my mouth into a smile. I would not ruin Leena's day. It had been years since she was allowed to enjoy Autane. Perhaps I could too.

Every Autane, Leena was contracted to dance for most of the festival. She had scars on her feet to prove how grueling the seven-day stretch was. After the first time she told me, I'd promised myself I'd kill that bastard Moer if I ever ran into him again.

I peeled off the Crown-crested leathers and shrugged into the cleanest tunic and breeches I could find; they were wrinkled to Tir, but at least they weren't stained.

"Ready," I said to Leena, and we followed most of our house out of the palace grounds and into the streets of Rowane.

Varyn led us down an alley to a plaza lined with squat trees and filled to the brim with long tables. Within minutes of sitting, giant tankards of cider appeared in front of us, along with plates of bread, cheese, and Theranian sausage made with pork and apples. There were thirteen of us—almost our whole house. Even Blaise came along and sat next to Aixen with Avi and Devon.

"So," Blaise started after wiping cider from his mouth with his sleeve, saffron eyes looking at everyone but me, apparently. He didn't seem angry. "Has anyone seen this Lord of Gourd yet? We're taking bets on which tavern we'll find him at."

"Who's we?" Devon frowned, raising a brow. "Unfair, considering most of us aren't even from Rowane. How should we know what taverns are around?"

Aixen smirked and leaned forward. "I'd bet if we just strung random words together, we might come up with a tavern name despite not knowing a single one. I'll start: The Royal Flagon, The Brass Pub, Blue Dragon Inn, Stone Tav—"

Leena and I burst out laughing. "No, he's right," I said over giggles. "Stone Tavern is one street over. And it's not The Royal Flagon but The Royal Cup. Stars below. Aixen has a point."

"See!" Aixen exclaimed. "Tavern names are the only constant. Poisoned Apple? Is that anything?"

"Yeah," Leena snorted. "It's next door to an Armory den with a crier if you want trial reports too, but I wouldn't recommend it. It's a nickname for a very seedy cidery near the gate. Ten people were poisoned there years ago."

"What?" Varyn deadpanned as Evie sidled up beside him. "Poisoned at the Poisoned Apple? You don't say."

"I do say," Leena continued, trying not to giggle. "And they're still open to this day. We can go if anyone's feeling lucky? I'm sure their Autane festivities are life-changing."

Aixen raised his hand. "I love gambling, but I think I speak for everyone that I'd prefer to live through the night." He looked back at Varyn. "Tell me more about this Gourd Lord."

"Lord of Gourd," Varyn corrected with a grin. "The Rowanians have only been going on about it since we left."

"Honestly." Aixen waved a hand and leaned back. "Rowane isn't even the most interesting city in Thera. It's probably middle at best, maybe a little higher just because of the palace. Has anyone been south? The Duchy of Orleone is another world. I spent a summer in Ashburn helping my father—"

"*Orleone?*" Varyn exclaimed. "May as well ask us Northerners if we've been to fucking Tir or Bal. The answer is fuck *no.*"

Tomas interjected, "Certainly Westvale is better than Orleone. It has the shifting—"

"No, fuck Westvale. Worst duchy." Devon laughed, and there were several murmurs of agreement.

"Westvale is just misunderstood," Tomas defended and took a swig of cider.

"You don't have to defend Westvale because your father owns it; we're brothers in blood. You can be honest that Westvale is the fucking worst," Varyn said, cupping his hand over Tomas's, who frowned and snatched it back.

Avi laughed at her soldiers as Devon gulped cider and pulled her closer like she'd jump across the table if he hadn't anchored her with his hand on her thigh.

"Actually, I have been to Orleone and Westvale," Avi said, brushing hair out of her eyes while her brow wiggled. "Perks of being the daughter of a duke. It's beautiful. Aixen is right. The duchess's estate is twice the size of Rowane's palace. Legends say it was built for Olios himself. Westvale is so incredibly flat."

Leena's face lit up as she turned to Avi, wide-eyed. "The god? Where else have you been? I want to hear everything."

We drank, laughed, and feasted between shared stories, pretending we were just friends at Autane like everyone else. It was a wonderful release, and I smiled despite myself.

Even two of Cormac's guards who'd been in Beven joined us after a while. Aixen seemed thrilled at the company; he kept flashing a demure smile towards the taller one, and his flirting only became more obvious with every sip of cider.

They were number three and seven on his list, if I remembered correctly.

At nine sharp, massive bonfires roared to life in the center of every plaza in Rowane: Autane Fires. The fires accepted sacrifices to the new gods and mild prayers all for an easy winter.

The Seven because they loved a little bribery. In reality, the sacrifice meant shop owners put out their scrap buckets with apple peels and shreds of meat because the farmers who provided the harvest lived well outside the city.

We didn't do the same thing in Lower Rowane, but it wasn't dissimilar. We burned leaves and threw empty bottles against the walls of the temples. It was a show of thanks that sounds quite the opposite, but it was *fun*.

"Another round?" Varyn blustered as he stood and gathered up several empty flagons.

"Mead for us," Aixen said with a feral wink. He sat between the two guards now, and I was both happy for him and worried.

Leena shared my concern with a raised eyebrow.

"Mead it is," Aixen said. "And ciders for everyone else?"

"No, thank you," Avi said lightly.

She looked content, appearing like someone else entirely in just her tunic and leather pants with her unbound hair. She leaned into Devon without abandon as his arm propped around her shoulders.

I smiled at whatever they were tonight; genuine happiness was so fucking rare and brief, if it ever came at all.

"We're going back to the palace," she announced.

Whistling and hollering met the statement. Avi's cheeks flushed, and she pulled Devon away. His hand slipped into hers as they faded into the street crowd.

As the fire in our plaza waned, Leena gave me a knowing look.

"I think I'm going back too," I said, and it wasn't met with the same fervor.

I thought Aixen might say something about Farran, but he only nodded solemnly. Maybe Avi told everyone what I was supposed to do tomorrow. Maybe my emotions were obvious, but it didn't matter; they'd all find out eventually, and I had no desire to talk about it.

I walked back through the winding cobblestone streets and bumped shoulders with drunk revelers. Feelings crept into my thoughts, and I didn't know how much longer I could hold them down.

A hundred memories swelled back and threatened to overwhelm me: the vision of a dead queen, the priestess, the way my mother looked at me through the flames of our house. It all happened at once. Then, as suddenly as it came on, it stilled, and I thought only of Arden.

His words became crushing, *just in time to watch the war begin*.

I wanted no part in a war, but it felt inevitable as I walked through the gates and wandered down to our room.

Farran's voice rang in my head: *You do have choices.*

Maybe he was right, or maybe he overestimated how brave I was willing to be.

Chapter 33

A crisp chill prickled my skin as I returned to our room. The hall was deliciously quiet after being out in the taverns of Rowane.

I kicked off my boots and sank into the bed with a sigh, not bothering to close the door or blow out the light. I simply stared at the stone ceiling and wished I'd brought a book that wasn't about sigils. Everything was too heavy, and I needed something to quiet my mind.

Eventually, I settled for watching the shadows from the firelight dance across the ceiling until a knock on the damn doorframe interrupted me.

I sat up and met Farran's gaze. His sapphire eyes looked forlorn, but his face managed a tired smile as I noticed the cloak hung over his arm.

"I thought you'd be out with everyone else, but I saw the light on," he admitted.

"I was," I said, swinging my feet over the side of the bed. He stepped into the room, and my magic thrust itself against my ribs, but I ignored it. "I came back before things got too wild."

He nodded. "I intended to join, but found my brother instead."

"Cormac?"

"Lorcan," he corrected. "He works in the library and keeps threatening to renounce his titles, much to our mother's chagrin." Farran's eyes lifted to mine. "I'm sorry you're getting pulled into this performance. The queen believes the threats to Thera are growing."

"And the old gods are to blame?" My lips quirked up in amusement, even as my heart soured.

"My father never let go of the old gods, and it bothered her. They had a thousand arguments about it. She sees it as disloyalty."

My eyebrows lifted, and I didn't understand why he'd told me. "Is that why we're destroying the altar?" I replied.

Farran nodded. "A message of strength to please the new gods, the Crown priests, and to shake the other kingdoms."

My chest ached, the threads of magic in me coiling and turning as my voice lowered. "How do we do it?" I whispered.

Farran looked at me. "You'll need to trust me. It's guarded by a millennium of magic keen on protecting itself. Every sacrifice of blood and magic lives in the stone, as I'm sure you know."

I took a deep breath and held his gaze. Arden's words haunted me, the dreites' words haunted me, but nothing Farran said haunted me—not even the idea of a millennium's worth of magic. I opened my mouth to say something, but he stopped me.

"Are you tired, or does your offer to show me Lower Rowane still stand? I need a distraction."

I straightened at the change of subject. "It's a bit more depraved than Upper Rowane, Your Highness. Are you sure your royal sensibilities can handle it?"

Farran gave a tired smile. "I did say I wanted to see it, didn't I, darling? I'm also wounded you think my sensibilities would be so fragile," he retorted.

"Fine." I rose to my feet and grabbed my cloak from a hook on the wall. My mind raced as I strapped on my sword and a few knives, mapping the lower city in my head.

I'd have to avoid Arden, his dens, and anyone who might call me his.

"Is it *that* dangerous?" The prince lifted his eyebrow as I armed myself.

"Not usually, but I'll keep you safe if anything happens."

He chuckled darkly. "Consider yourself my guard for the evening."

Farran led us past the stables, through the garden, and down to a cellar door. He opened it and went first. It was terribly dark and wet, but he conjured a flame to light a torch. It reminded me of the first trial . . . Hopefully, we wouldn't come across anyone strung up and guarded by demons.

"If you've spent plenty of time in the taverns, why do you want to see it now?" I wondered and pulled up my hood as Farran did the same.

"I haven't seen it the way you have. I only ever went to the same taverns and dens recommended by Avernought, which means I've never seen your Lord of Gourd. Perhaps you can show me something new."

Lower Rowane came to be when a dreite blew a wall apart at the southeast edge of Rowane over a hundred years ago. It took twenty-five years to get the funds to repair it. However, Lower Rowane had sprawled so much in that time it couldn't be closed without impacting trade, so the gap remains.

We stumbled through it onto streets of Lower Rowane which were far more alive than the upper sections of the walled city. People spilled out of taverns and restaurants into the streets; even the dens were stuffed to the rafters. There was shouting and loud, off-key singing on every corner, punctuated by the chime of shattering glass from the Autane tradition.

Several topless women walked around with charmed smiles in gossamer skirts. Their smiles were genuine. They knew they'd make full coin tonight, and I wondered how many belonged to Arden.

Farran stayed close as we wove through the crowd, un-noticed, with our hoods drawn like most men. We passed a few plazas where Autane fires burned and briefly stopped to watch several revelers fling empty bottles at a tavern wall—drunk thunderous applause met every shatter.

Someone was also losing control of their petty magic, as small yellow leaves rained down in a thick flurry. I couldn't hide my smile as we trudged through them on our way to a quiet street where a large tavern sat nearly empty. The inside glowed orange, and its windows looked out over one of the many bridges.

This place was safe because the owner never knew I worked for Arden. In fact, it was always empty because of an ongoing feud with Arden and his clientele.

George stood behind the bar with his usual smile as he took a patron's order. I pulled my hood down, grabbed a knife off my belt, and strode in. Farran followed, tensing next to me. I couldn't blame him, but he wanted to know how *I* saw Lower Rowane, and this was it.

I threw the knife towards the dartboard behind the bar. It landed dead center.

George whistled, and a smile lit up his face. "By the gods and stars," he said and turned to us. "I thought you were too good for all of us down here now, my dear Reina." He came around the bar and dragged me into a tight hug.

"It's good to see you, George," I replied with a wide smile.

George ruffled my hair as he let go. "Sit anywhere. I'll bring out your favorites. And who's this?" He eyed Farran.

"Devon," I said quickly before Farran answered. "Friend from the Armory, if you pay any mind to the criers."

"Good, good. Not the *ontaros* prince, a shame. But it's a delight to see you again, Reina. Not tonight, but someday soon, you'll have to tell me some of your stories. I can only imagine what you've done. When it comes to you, I don't believe the criers exaggerate enough."

I smirked. "You have no idea, George."

George disappeared behind the bar while I led Farran to a small table in a cove near the back. He sank into a chair, looking at me with confusion, though I caught a flash of admiration.

"Do you announce yourself at every tavern by throwing a knife?" he wondered.

"Just this one." I shrugged. "George saved me a few years back after I accidentally stuck one in his bar trying to scare some man in the street. He thought he could take me; he couldn't, and he was lucky my knife missed."

"Is that how you learned to throw?" Farran stared at me.

I shrugged. "More or less." *Not a lie.*

George slammed down a tray of sausage, bread, and cheese. Briefly, we were normal people: eating tavern food, drinking beer from a place I occasionally called home as we carefully traded stories about who we thought we were before the Armory.

"You seem to get into a lot of bar fights," Farran said with a laugh.

"Perhaps you don't get into enough," I retorted, popping the last piece of cheese into my mouth. I leaned back in my chair and looked at him. "Can I show you something else?" I asked.

"Is it the Lord of Gourd?" His blue eyes looked relaxed and content, a stark contrast to earlier.

I shrugged. "Unlikely, but it might be better."

"Lead the way, demon wielder."

"*Great.*" I smiled, setting a few errant coins on the table. I waved to George before pulling my hood over my head. Farran did the same and followed me out.

The spread of the lower city was completely haphazard outside of the single main street. Some roads came to dead ends, while others looped around and turned into streets with different names. Other roads crossed over themselves like a bow.

It was a mess, and I cherished it as I followed the curve of the road running along a stream. Stone bridges crossed every few blocks until the fountain in the center of a small plaza peeked out.

This fountain was grand for Lower Rowane. It was three tiers carved from marble and donated over fifty years ago by some noble for his concubine. Moss grew over it, and the detail had chipped away with time but it was still beautiful in its decay.

I gestured for Farran to sit and ducked inside the only storefront with lights on. It was just a bakery. The rest of the square was long abandoned. I brought back two flaky pastries, filled with a decadent cream, and held one out for Farran.

He stared at it and turned it over as a smile crossed my face. "It's a pastry. It doesn't bite," I prodded.

"I know pastries don't bite," he said as I sat beside him, avoiding the warring emotions in my chest as he took a bite that ended with a decadent moan. *Way too close.* "Outstanding, but certainly not the Lord of Gourd."

I laughed. It was ridiculous. I was sitting with the prince, sharing a pastry.

"We'd have to poke around a few more taverns for any leads." I sighed and looked at him. "But hopefully the best pastry in all of Rowane makes up for it."

He contemplated as he chewed. "Nearly. Is that why you're quiet?" he asked.

"My mother always went out of her way to come here. She'd bring my brother and I down from the city proper." I took a deep breath. I don't know why I shared that. *Maybe it was too honest.* But the way he looked at me encouraged the words. "We stopped here, at this fountain, and had these same pastries three days before she died. This is my first time back in years."

Farran's hand touched my lower back, his thumb moving in soothing circles. I didn't stop him, but I *should* have. Next time it happened, I'd be stronger, but tonight I was too tired.

"I'm sorry you lost her, but she'd be proud of you," he murmured as I smiled sadly—she wouldn't be proud. Hopefully, he wouldn't ask what happened. "And where's your brother now?" he asked instead.

"Studying at a library so he might be invited to the archives," I answered. "He's incredibly smart and could tell you anything about the Dragon Age."

"You joined the Armory so he could study?"

I looked at the pastry and muttered, "Something like that."

Then I took a bite and *fuck*—it was just how I remembered: warm, impossibly light, and the cream had a hint of vanilla that was difficult to come by in Rowane, but here it was, preserved and perfect.

"So Lower Rowane to you is one tavern, a fountain, and a pastry?" Farran said with a raised brow.

"Don't forget the bottle throwing," I added. "There's more, but you don't want to see all of it."

"Maybe another day," he agreed, stretching his arms over his head. "Thank you for showing me." Farran was quiet for a moment, then he lowered his voice, "Could I show you something? I'm afraid it's only fair."

"You don't want to keep looking for the Lord of Gourd?" I mused.

Farran laughed, and the magic in my chest fluttered. "No, you were honest with me, so let me be honest with you. There is something back at the palace you should see."

"Of course. Lead the way, Your Highness."

Farran stood first and offered his hand. I let him pull me to my feet, and for a moment, he pulled me too close. I meant to step back, but then he brushed his lips across mine and I kissed him back, ignoring the shock of tenderness lumping in my throat and the tears it brought to my eyes.

I shouldn't kiss him. I should have run and left him here . . . but I couldn't.

He pulled away, and I smiled at him unwittingly like some shy fucking maiden.

"I've been wanting to do that since the garden," he admitted. If he saw my watering eyes, he granted me the mercy of saying nothing.

Me too, I thought, but only rational words left my lips as I pulled away. "We should go back." There was a gravity to him—to us—and I hated it.

I wanted to kiss him again. I wanted him to pin me up against the wall again and make me say his name, but I knew better . . . even if my thighs burned at the very thought of it. Instead, I took the lead and led us back to the palace when I was sure I should have run.

The streets were uproarious as we snaked through them back to the palace grounds. Neither of us cared as the clocks of Rowane struck one—time felt suspended. I followed Farran along the perimeter of the palace, moving from shadow to shadow to avoid the guards; which explained why he didn't bother with his wings.

We wound through several parts of a manicured garden sloping steeply downhill. The palace was behind us, and all I could see were the tallest towers.

Magic in my chest ebbed and flared as we descended, but the power of it roared to life the closer we came to the edge of the forest. Farran grabbed my hand and pulled me down a path through bushes with broad leaves. The touch left heat behind even after he'd let go. Everything felt heightened, and it wasn't the cider.

We turned down a narrow alcove filled with rose bushes all pruned back in anticipation of winter, but bare vines snaked into the surrounding hedges and filled the space; I was sure it was breathtaking in the spring, but that wasn't why my breath caught.

In front of us was the altar we were supposed to destroy. I knew inherently before Farran said anything.

It was just like the one outside of the Armory: a large slab of unkempt, flat stone. But unlike the Armory, a statue stood behind it of the Goddess Dreonna with her bow across her back beside two demons, wings outstretched on either side.

She served the King of Gods, Raion, as his warrioress. I reached out to touch the statue, expecting it to be cool. Instead, it was warm and thrummed with power. Centuries of sacrifices. I couldn't ask this of the demons. Even making them watch would feel akin to torture—Dreonna was their creator.

"My father would bring me here when I was upset," Farran said. His voice was low and soft. "He told me if I felt alone, Dreonna always listened. That she was in the wind, the shadows, and the magic she gifted. He planted roses here so he could more discreetly offer blood for her protection . . . Until my mother caught on. You've heard the prince consort was murdered, I'm sure?"

I nodded solemnly. I was sixteen, Arden was furious, and the sentiment echoed through Lower Rowane for weeks. No part of me could imagine what Farran endured. My throat tightened. Whatever truth came next, I couldn't match it. I was out of truths to share.

My hand reached for his, and the warmth of his magic threaded into mine as he continued, "I was here when it happened. I was with him. He was attacked by a knight. It happened so fast; I reacted and killed a Queensguard knight. I wasn't thinking."

"You defended your father." I would have done the same.

Farran's voice was hollow. "It's treason to kill one of the Queensguard knights. My mother has made it very clear."

"How old were you?" I whispered into the darkness.

"Newly sixteen. She made me sit in the dungeon for a week. Cormac begged her to let me out. That was my lesson for taking revenge. It's a part of why I swore the oath—I thought it might please her and make my life easier."

"There's nothing fair about that." I breathed and squeezed his hand, holding it as the breeze fluttered the leaves of the forest and a silence drifted between us.

Farran took a sharp breath and said, "I wanted you to see the altar the way it was meant to be seen. The way I've always seen it."

I didn't know what to say. My chest ached, and I didn't know if it was the pulse of magic in the air or the way our fingers intertwined—I didn't want to leave.

Tomorrow had no reason to come. I didn't want to destroy this. Not for the queen, not for anyone.

Wind rippled through the air, and there was something I needed to say despite the comfortable silence.

"Why do I need to trust you tomorrow?" I murmured.

Farran's hand dropped from mine to rake through his hair as he took a deep breath. He was flustered. "I—it's—"

"Complicated," I finished.

Slowly, hesitantly, he nodded. "Yes."

"If I'm going to trust you, I need to know."

Farran looked at the sky with a reverence as though he meant to pray. Then he turned back to me. "Let's go somewhere more private."

"Lead the way, Your Highness."

I followed Farran back up the hill. It was much worse going up than going down. I thought he would turn towards the wing where our house slept. Instead, he turned the opposite way, towards the large stone terrace at the center of the palace.

"We're going to the palace?" My body stiffened. I shouldn't have been surprised, but gods.

Farran shrugged. "Yes. Because I know exactly who's posted around my room, and I trust them with my life."

It made sense, but didn't change my apprehension. I followed the prince through a smaller door leading to the side of a hall. He nodded at the guards, who barely regarded him in return. The palace was desolate at this hour.

Our footsteps echoed off the stone after the navy carpet runners ended. We walked down a hallway and then turned sharply into a narrow staircase.

"I can give you a formal tour next time," he mused.

Next time—as a Queensguard knight when he was the Prince Commander.

He led us to a round stairwell. I counted six flights and was panting by the time we made it to the door of the seventh. There, I followed him through a doorway into another stone hall which was instantly more welcoming as I tried to catch my breath.

Portraits and landscapes hung from the walls. A few sconces were lit, and navy rugs lined the center, muffling our footfalls. A palace guard acknowledged us with a bow of his head, and another door opened.

Chapter 34

For a second, we were alone in a dark room that had to be Farran's by the embracing smell of cedar wisps and the memory of vanilla creme.

Tendrils of light left his fingertips, lighting several sconces around the room and igniting a fireplace. We stood in a common room where several uneven bookshelves lined one wall and a tapestry hung from another. An overstuffed couch sat with a few wingback chairs before a fireplace near a table with too much stacked on it.

"Is there a reason your room is all the way up here?" I asked.

Windows stretched the height of the room opposite the door, each framed with thick navy curtains trimmed with silver fringe. On either side of the room were archways. One led to a tiled bathroom, and through the other I saw posts of a bed draped in navy fabric similar to the curtains.

Farran explained, "Lorcan's is too. The views are better and away from court. Cormac almost moved up here, but when Duncan died and he became the crown prince, mother kept him closer to the heart of the palace."

I barely remembered that. It was well before the prince consort died, and possibly before I lived with Arden.

Intricate hilts and decorative blades drew my attention; several swords and a bow hung on a wall near the window, all beautiful in their own ways. I chided the part of me that wanted to reach out and touch them.

"Would you like tea?" Farran asked, breaking the silence.

"Sure, yes," I said with an edge of surprise.

He went back to the door and whispered something to his guard while I walked to the fireplace. Hundreds of letters were piled on the table and across from them was a pile of odd rocks and several open books. All covered in fine dust.

My brows creased. "Why do you have a pile of rocks?"

Farran turned around from the door with a sour face. "It's a *collection*; one of those is a rare silver-blue agate from a lost mountain in Vinliane."

"Seems irresponsible to lose an entire mountain." I smiled despite myself as I laid my cloak across a chair and took a seat on the couch; deeply aware, he watched me.

My thoughts churned as the heat of his gaze brushed my neck, and I shivered at the uneasiness belying it.

It was the shaky feeling of a betrayal yet to come. I knew it well; it was the same I felt every time he *looked* at me. It was guilt, inevitability, and hope all folded into the same expression.

I doubted there was anything he could say that would shake my trust, but if Farran knew a sliver about my service to Arden, or my destiny, there would be no rebuilding, no forgiveness. There was nothing worse he could admit to me.

I didn't hear the door open, and Farran rattled me when he set a tea tray on the table. He poured two cups and handed one to me as he sat in the closest chair, elbow propped on the arm.

"Were you close to your oldest brother?" I asked.

Farran shook his head. "I was eleven when he died."

"And your mother still made all of you go through the Armory?"

"She insisted," he muttered. "Cormac went easily, but Lorcan got into a fight. Mother said he'd be no son of hers if he didn't. That's when we moved our rooms up here. We could pretend we weren't part of the palace. Even appointed our own guards."

My brow furrowed. "Your own? Aren't they all yours, Prince?" I chuckled.

"The palace guard is supposed to be of noble blood. Only the Queensguard Knighthood and their magic get a pass, so we might have lied about *our* guards' parentage and appointed them, anyway."

My mind reeled. "Where did you find them?"

Farran leaned back and grinned. "One in a tavern near the north wall. Peter absolutely destroyed it to teach the asshole owner a lesson. The other was a shepherd. Kind and quiet, but can cut down a wolf with a single swing. That's the one who let us in—Creighton."

"They're truly loyal to you?" I watched the flames flicker in the fireplace.

He shrugged. "They never took an oath to the Crown. I mean, they'll defend the Crown, I'm sure. But if I told them to leave and never come back, they would listen to me before the queen. They swore an oath Lorcan and I halfway made up."

I kicked off my boots and pulled my knees to my chest, deep in thought. My attention slid to his gaze, intense and mesmerizing all at once. "Why do I need to trust you?"

"Touch is only one part of being an *ontaros*." Farran's eyes pinned me there, and my heart hammered. "I want you to know I would never jeopardize your trust, not for anything."

A pang of guilt prickled my throat as it went dry.

"Answer me one thing first," he murmured. "A secret for a secret."

"Anything." Except not *everything*. I couldn't be an open book, not tonight, and no matter how deep the pools of his eyes shone—no matter he trusted me in a way that ached.

"Why does a barmaid need glamour to hide her eyes?"

I stopped breathing. "There is no glamour."

He'd only joked about it before, but he wasn't the only one as I pieced several odd comments together and my breathing shallowed.

Farran leaned closer. There wasn't anger on his face, only curiosity, as though he was trying to peer into me. "My mother raised all of us to see glamour magic. We use it on our wings, and your eyes aren't brown, Reina. In fact, there are legends about eyes like yours. Did you know that?"

"You're lying." My voice shook; that was impossible, but I remembered several other impossible things.

Farran extended his hand. There wasn't a line of malice on his face. "Let me show you," he said as dread clamped around my spine.

I hesitated, but it was a half measure. I took his hand and he guided us across the room to a silver-plated mirror mounted on the wall. He stood behind me, and for the first time, I saw how we looked together: a pang of longing tangled with fear and guilt as I stared.

We were dressed in similar tunics and black pants, but the sharp lines of his jaw contrasted the softness of my own while his dark, unruly hair complimented my light shade of auburn. I also realized my forehead only reached his shoulders. I'd never thought about it until now.

He tucked a few loose strands of hair behind my ears as I watched my eyes; brown, like my father's as they'd always been. Until Farran turned his hand over below my chin.

Cold magic kissed my skin, and I shivered as it pulled away a mask I never knew I wore. The brown turned to a vibrant purple, freckles dotted my nose and cheeks, and even my hair took on a darker shade of brown. I looked like my mother . . . all traces of my father erased as though he never existed.

My hands reached up to a face that wasn't mine. *She couldn't be me.* I dodged away from the mirror and went to the window, gasping for air as my lungs constricted. *What else did I not know?*

"I was no one before this," I said softly, straining against the threat of tears. "I had no idea. I never lied, I swear it." His hand grazed my shoulder, and I spun with a rush of anger. "You brought me here just to do that. To humiliate me."

Sapphire eyes blinked at me.

"I'm sorry you didn't know," the prince said gently, but it didn't stop the tears brimming my eyes. "I'd never do anything to humiliate you. I didn't know."

The anger ebbed as quickly as it came on. I shook my head, but I didn't have words; if I said anything, I'd break, but that woman in the mirror wasn't me. Who was she?

Farran lifted my chin and wiped a tear away so tenderly my chest caved. "I'll put it back. I just—"

"*Please,*" I begged.

The icy shiver of the glamour magic ensconced me. I didn't need to look in the mirror. I knew the familiar mask had slipped into place, and I could pretend a little longer.

"A secret for a secret," I whispered. Farran blinked. If he'd laid me bare in this room, I would do the same. "Why haven't I seen you wield anyone's gift?"

"It's old magic, unwritten from most of our histories for a reason." His hand let me go, and he turned towards the fireplace, arms crossed tightly. "My father had the same curse, and it's part of why my mother married him."

My heart twisted. I needed to stop reminding myself that his family was the reason my mother was dead. We'd both been hurt in similar ways . . . I observed every small and nameless expression flitted across his face.

"There was a culling after the Third War of Gods and by the Second War of Kings, *ontaros* were believed to be extinct; any found alive were killed the moment the priests saw their power. And not just in Thera, but across the realm. Nearly all records were destroyed."

I stilled. The chime of his words punctuated by the crackle of the fire.

He continued, "My father's family kept their gift secret and remained close enough to the Darkland crown they were overlooked. It was even forgotten about . . . until my father made a mistake, and my mother caught it. The real power of it, my ability to duplicate gifts, comes from blood."

Farran took a breath and looked at the ceiling; I wrapped my arms tighter around myself as the weight of the words settled. "My mother would give him vials of different blood to shift his abilities into something she needed. If she didn't have vials ready, he was expected to find a different way, and do so privately, because the power was illegal in the realm for everyone but the Crown."

"How did she know you had it?" I asked, my voice trembling.

He turned and looked at me; the pain in his eyes rooted me in place. "On my thirteenth birthday, after my Rite, she held a dinner. She drugged my wine with the blood of a mind reader. It worked. Just as it worked on Duncan, when he was thirteen and he died in the Armory because he refused his gift."

Fear seized my body. I was going to be sick. I knew where this was going, but I took a step toward him. Theranian blood held more than magic; it held memories. He didn't have to tell me—I already knew. The Crown guards killed several of Arden's men the same gruesome way, but they rarely got magic out of it, only proof.

"I would never cross that line with you," Farran said fiercely. "I want you to trust me, but I'll also warn you my mother will stop at nothing."

"She'd force me, wouldn't she?"

Farran nodded. He stared at me, into me, trying to read the thoughts racing through my mind, which were all screaming to leave.

Theranian blood contained the very essence of who we were. While he took my blood, Farran could walk into my memories and drag out every truth I'd held back, and then he could *ruin* me. I couldn't die, but he could make me wish I had.

I looked at him again—*fuck*. I trusted him. For whatever gods damned reason, I trusted him. I loosened my arms because my mind was decided . . . at least in the moment.

"What do I need to do?" I asked tentatively.

Caution shadowed his face. "You mean that?"

"I'm not interested in seeing the queen's methods."

"I'm not keen either." Farran shuddered, looking back towards the fire as I reached into my breeches and pulled out my dagger. His eyes went wide. I took a step closer to him and leaned against the back of the sofa, waving it.

"What are you doing?" he asked.

"You trust these guards with your life." I shrugged. "It's already tomorrow, and you ought to know what my power feels like if we're going to put on a performance. Figured this would be fastest."

The pop of a burning log and the unexpected light pattering of rain on the windows was deafening against the utter silence.

"This is my choice," I assured him. *And on the Seven and all sleeping gods, did I pray this was the right one.*

His eyes were fierce on mine, but I didn't back down. "You don't have to do this if you don't—"

"I've never been more sure of anything."

I turned to the archway leading to a bed. I'd be damned if I passed out on a couch or chair in a prince's quarters.

The arch gave way to a massive, plush four-poster bed covered in Theranian navy and silver. I should have left, I should have resisted, but there was another quieter, ancient pull in the back of my head keeping me there, and I cursed it.

This was the most dangerous place Arden's viper could ever be, and yet, here I was, laying on my enemy's fucking bed ready to pull back my last defense—I deserved to die.

Farran sat beside me. "I promise I won't pry, Reina. I need you to know I mean that," he repeated for a third time.

I believed him.

The threads in my chest shifted and unfurled without apprehension; somehow, it wasn't afraid of what came next; not the way every other part of me was. I held up my left arm and placed the cool edge of my blade against it. As I dragged it across, I watched the crimson beads greet the dragon forged steel like an old friend.

Farran stopped my hand and whispered, "That's enough."

Tenderly, he took the dagger and set it on the bedside table. My head swirled as one of his hands cupped my back, while the other brought my arm to his lips.

I closed my eyes and thought only about the magic, the power, and the way it pounded behind my heart and filled my chest. I experienced no pain, only the ache and thrum as it gathered where his lips and tongue traced my skin, drawing it from me in heady drags.

Threads unfolded and reformed, weaving into his own to become something else, something more than warmth, more than the power I recognized . . . more than anything I imagined and nothing like the drain I'd expected.

He stopped abruptly and leaned me back. Stars clung to the edge of my vision, and his hand held my arm, but there was the way he looked at me. I held his gaze and said nothing. What was there to say?

The depths of his blue eyes swirled and glittered like the sea under a clear night sky. My pulse quickened, and warmth spread where the cut was.

I glanced as tendrils of white mended the wound. "You can heal?"

"No," he said, and his voice was light but far away, like a dream. "*You* can."

Right.

Farran broke my gaze and lay next to me. The scorch of his lips on my arm subsided, and the power waned ever so slightly, but everything still felt visceral, more alive like I had gained something where I'd lost.

His hand found mine. Magic danced between us, tangling and warming where our skin touched, tying us together. He'd kept his word, and my heart clenched. I didn't deserve his trust.

"Your magic is beautiful," he rasped, voice barely above a whisper. "You didn't tell me it was all of these warm, gold threads. I thought . . . I thought it was—"

"Darker? It can be; the threads holding the demons are cold, but the rest of it is usually like that. Gold, warm."

He marveled, "Truly the only one I've felt like this."

"How many have you . . . tried?"

"Twenty? Most are like smoke or mist. Some are light, some slippery. Others aren't anything but a weight in my head. I don't remember any that had a temperature, and now I can feel the threads tangling with you. Is it like this all the time?" he breathed.

"When I'm close to like magic," I said and looked at him again.

He smiled, his eyes still closed. I hoped he couldn't hear my thoughts: memories were dangerous, but thoughts were embarrassing because all of mine were soft and unbecoming of a soldier.

"How long will it last?" I whispered.

"Depends how much I spend."

We laid on the bed in comfortable silence. I didn't let go of his hand, and indulged in the warm hum of power between us that was weaving, multiplying, and reaching for what he'd taken—what I'd trusted him with.

The severe lines on his face melted away, and he smiled wider. I'd felt the flutter before, and I buried it just fine, but in this moment, I was fucked.

This was the precipice; this was the point of no return, and I hoped to every god, Seven and sleeping, that Farran couldn't hear the screaming in my head because I wanted whatever this was.

I wanted the strength and power of his body on mine. I wanted the fire, the warmth, and the tangled threads. And, more than anything, I wanted him. I hadn't felt this pull in years, and I'd deal with the consequences.

Arden couldn't take everything and *gods-be-fucking-damned*. This was my choice. I looked at the ceiling. His thumb roved in circles on my hand, and I waited for the onset of dread, the warning clamp on my spine, even a prickle on my neck but there was nothing. No part of me wanted to run.

He was dangerously close, and his body only a breath away from mine as he squeezed my hand. Then he rolled onto his side, and I said nothing as his palm slid up my arm and towards my neck. Warmth pooled below my waist as his other hand trailed down my ribs to the inside of my thigh. My breath caught, and I finally looked at him.

"Tell me what you want, Reina Sangrey."

He stared at my lips, and I'd let regret wash over me later.

"*You.*"

The warmth in my chest gave way to an ache as the tip of his tongue traced my mouth. His body closed in on me, and he kissed me patiently. I relished the power of his well-honed back and the strength with which he held me there, hands softly cupping the back of my neck as he took his time.

Too soon, he pulled away, standing at the edge of the bed. Both our chests rose and fell with hunger and uninhibited desire. I meant to say something, but he stared at me with the full weight of his azure eyes. I thought I'd done something wrong until he pulled off his tunic and I had my answer.

His wide, muscled chest gleamed in the moonlight spilling in from the window. Scars streaked across it in places I would ask about later, and my heart lurched as I truly saw the oath on display over his heart.

I ignored those feelings and grabbed the edge of my tunic, but his hands stopped me. Instead, he swept me to my feet in a single motion.

"Allow me." His breath was hot on my neck, and the words vibrated against my skin. I was going to come undone before he even laid a finger inside me. There was *nothing* like this.

I shuddered as his thumb brushed over my peaked nipple as his other hand trailed down the fabric and tugged at it, tantalizing and slow. His hands knotted into the hem of my tunic and exposed me.

The rush of cool air was brief as he kissed me desperately, closing all space with his hard chest and sturdy hands. If he felt the outline of the oath on my spine, it didn't matter. I'll lie to him if that's what it took. I was greedy, and I drug him deeper.

When we broke from the kiss, he didn't stop. His lips trailed down my neck, leaving my skin hot then cold in the absence as he traveled to kiss the swell of my breasts. Lowering to his knees, his lips traced the scars on my ribs while his hands held me in place, in ache, until his tongue flicked the edge of my pants with a promise.

Cold air pebbled my nipples as he untied the stays. His expression held mine calm and reverent, then he pushed his thumb against my clit.

I gasped; my legs jerked, he tugged off my fence in a swift motion, and I was bare before him. The sapphire pools of his eyes dazed as they locked on mine.

"Gods, you're incredible," he breathed.

Hands gripped my thighs, and his eager tongue teased just below my navel, sending shivers of anticipation racing through me like a quaking storm. While fingers pressed the space between my legs to find I was already slick and waiting.

"Fuck, you're so ready for me," Farran moaned.

His lips trailed along the scars on my belly. Then my thighs, and finally I shuddered as he finally found my center. The stroke of his tongue burned through me, and I arched into the pleasure while my grip on his hair tightened.

Farran was a tease who left me teetering on the edge as he ate his fill but I was impatient.

I dragged his lips to mine, tasting myself as I kissed him like I would never be satisfied. My tongue lashed as the fire of his fingers trailed up my thighs as I drew him to the bed. His hands didn't stop until they were between my legs.

Then he pressed two fingers into me, and I forgot I had ever been with anyone else. Every surge of his hand was the best kind of torture as he whispered again my cheek, "Come for me."

I angled myself so his gaze stuck to mine as I held him in place by the nape of his neck. "Watch me."

Slowly, his fingers slipped in, and my grip on him didn't relent as he withdrew and pressed in again—over, and over, and over until my breath came faster, until my thoughts were only of him, until—

"That's it, darling."

Another pulse of his hand, and I seized as every sliver of pleasure rushed forward and I cried out.

Farran withdrew his hand, but I needed more even as his forehead pressed to mine and he thumbed my swollen lips.

"Fucking perfect."

The strain of him pressed the space between my thighs. He still wore trousers. I tugged the laces, and he drew back. I shivered at the rush of air, but even the cold couldn't quell my desire as I watched him undress.

I don't know if I gasped, but in that moment, I'd never seen anything more beautiful than the way his scars faded into the dip of his hips and the way the length of him looked in the moonlight as he stroked it with his hand.

I propped myself up, legs spread open to show him how ready I was after how long I'd waited. His lips crashed into mine.

"Are you sure?" he mumbled as his hips moved and teased; the hardness of his cock against my thigh was all I could think about. He bit my earlobe and whispered, "I want to know if you feel as good as you taste."

The fullness I wanted to wring from him stole my thoughts. My answer should have been obvious. All of the hunger, all of the pleasure, and all of the throbbing heat coalesced between us as my legs wrapped around his waist.

"What do you need?" he crooned.

"I need you to fuck me," I breathed, well past lying.

Farran held my stare, his voice a feral growl. "Say that again."

"Fuck me, *Your Highness.*"

The teasing thrusts slowed as one hand gripped my back and the other guided his cock exactly where I needed him. Farran watched my face as he pressed, inch by inch, stretching me slowly, almost excruciating, as every stroke remade me and boiled the tension into hot coils of pleasure.

"*Gods and stars*, Reina," he groaned. Tenderness turned to frenzy as he moved in me, driving deeper and deeper until I knew nothing but *us*.

Farran threw back his head as I matched his pace.

"Fucking . . . made for me," he moaned, breath coming faster as every pulse between us overwhelmed in undulating waves of ecstasy until I shuddered against him. My body left its confines, and he came with it.

It was a release like no other. He stopped, satiated and awed, placing a gentle kiss on my lips. His movements slowed as my heart raced beside his. For a moment, I'd forgotten there was a world outside his room.

"Farran," I breathed, opening my eyes. Reality came back in degrees, but it was different now.

His hand caressed my cheek, and a new emotion settled in my chest. Something warm, ancient, and terrifying. From the glazed look on his face, I wondered if he felt it, too.

I didn't say anything else. I just kissed him again and tightened my thighs around his cock, which hardened on command. He moved inside me again, and I was free again. I rocked my hips into his, tangled my hands in his dark curls, forehead pressed to his and I kept pace until he moaned into my lips.

Then there was nothing left to say. We leaned back on the bed, and I stared at the ceiling as I caught my breath. The smartest thing I could do now was get up and leave. That's what I always did, but as I turned over, Farran pulled me back and kissed me too softly.

"Ever since that first kiss," he whispered and my chest caved under his touch and the reverence in his tone, "I've been desperate for you. You've broken something in me, Reina."

His lips curled around the shape of my name, and there was nothing else I wanted to hear him say. Not now, not tonight . . . or whatever was left of it. I wasn't leaving.

My voice cracked. "You've broken something in me, too."

He pulled me into his chest, and I closed my eyes, drowning in every part of him. I wanted to suspend the world, just like this: the two of us without destiny, without duty.

We could run away and have a life that was entirely our choice. But I killed the thought, and tears I wouldn't let him see glazed my eyes and lumped in the back of my throat.

I'd been here before.

Some people could outrun fate, but we never would—it closed in on us with every tick of the clock. And if time didn't, the slow-acting poison of who I was would sour everything. However, it broke my heart. This time, it would be my fault and mine alone.

I listened to his heartbeat as his thumb traced circles on my breast, silencing the part of me that wanted to flee. The warmth trailing his touch lulled me into a deep sleep; so deep I didn't know I'd fallen into it until Farran woke me with a gruff whisper. "I want to show you something."

I thought about kissing him again, but when I opened my eyes, he was gone. Perhaps I dreamed it. But then I opened my eyes.

Fuck no. Real. Real. Real. I was still in his room, buried under the covers of a prince's bed, overwhelmed and frozen in place.

Farran stood at his wardrobe.

I peered past the bed at the beautiful dips and curves of his well-honed back. His black trousers did nothing to stop my sly smile as he turned around with a robe in his hands.

The sun hadn't risen yet; it still waited below the horizon as the sky made its turn from black to blue.

Nothing felt quite real except for the way Farran watched me: eyes alight and deep as the sea . . . like he'd never seen another woman. Maybe he hadn't. I didn't ask.

There wasn't a power on earth that could drag me back to reality—not until the sun came up.

Farran held out the robe. "You'll want to put it on. There's frost outside."

I took it, but he caught my trepidation and leaned in to kiss my forehead. Adding, "I promise you'll like it. If not, perhaps I can make up for it."

Farran pulled me out of the bed roughly so I fell into him. Strong hands tangled in my hair as he kissed me. The desperation in his tongue matched mine, and there was nothing controlled about it.

"Good morning, darling." His hand groped my bare ass, teasing the wetness already gathering as my composure scattered. Then he stopped, draped the robe over my shoulders and helped my arms through the sleeves.

I realized it was a trick as he grabbed my hand and pulled me out of the bedroom into the common room where he shoved the desk aside and pushed open a window.

Outside was a narrow balcony, and I was too dazed to argue.

I climbed out and stood beside him: below us was the entire valley of Rowane. I'd seen a lot, but I had never seen this; not from a palace tower.

I shivered at the heat of Farran's arm as it snaked around my waist. He pulled me against his chest, and we stayed there as the world woke up.

"It's beautiful," I whispered.

To the east, the orange of the sun poked its way through the trees in fragile streams of light, melting frost across the roofs as it climbed. There wasn't a cloud in the sky, and even the chill of morning didn't bother me.

His chest rose and fell against my back, and it felt like a home I'd never known—this felt like peace.

"I thought you might like it," he mumbled into my hair. "It's officially my second favorite place in the palace."

"What's the first?" I wondered.

"My bed, with you in it." Warm, velvety breath brushed my ear with the lilt of a smile in his voice. "Or, perhaps, the desk. Wherever you want, darling."

The warm threads of our magic remained entwined, and pressure built in my throat, a painful lump between happy and sad. I blinked away the wetness in my eyes. A breeze drifted through, and silence came with it as we stood, watching the morning sun blossom and spread across Rowane.

"Farran?" I'd need to leave soon, and my voice cracked. The itch of reality clawed its way back. I pulled the robe tighter.

Today was here, and nothing changed. I was still the *dreosen*. "I need to go back, don't I? Before anyone notices."

"Only if you can promise me something." His free hand tilted my chin up to meet his eyes, and the threads of mine tumbled over themselves. "I've trusted you with my secrets. When we go back, please don't ask me to pretend this never happened. I'll lie to anyone, but I won't lie to you."

Farran kissed me softly, lips dancing on mine. When he pulled away, I held his gaze, promising all I could.

"No pretending," I said. The lies would come later, but I couldn't pretend he was just another man, not after last night. Not after this morning.

Whatever pull there was between us had been sealed between our magic and blood. And the worst part is, I'd make the same choice a thousand times over, no matter how doomed it was to fall apart because I wasn't strong enough to walk away.

CHAPTER 35

I INTENDED TO LET Leena sleep a little longer, but when I slipped into the room, she was already awake, pinning her hair for the day ahead. She watched me closely, and I tried to ignore her curious glances as I brushed through the mess of my hair.

There was no way I could ignore her, nor did I want to, but I didn't know where to start. Whatever happened last night barely felt real.

"I'm fairly certain there are, at least, two things you haven't told me," Leena finally said.

"Good morning to you, too," I retorted with a grimace. "How was the rest of your night in Rowane? Find the Lord of Gourd?"

"Absolutely delightful, and no." She lowered her voice. "How was the prince? And don't lie; Blaise said he saw the two of you walking through the palace grounds last night, and he was far too drunk to keep it to himself."

Of course he did. I did nothing wrong except contradict myself, which I'd contend with later. Besides, I was full of contradictions; what was another?

Every minute since I left Farran's room, I couldn't think straight. There was a war in my heart between what I wanted and what I deserved—I deserved worse than nothing for what I'd done and for what was left to do.

I'd never be worthy of the way he looked at me, how he trusted me, and certainly not the way he made me come. The

Reina he saw, who he believed me to be, was someone who didn't exist.

I pinched the bridge of my nose and looked back at her. "Fine, I owe you, but it's a long story."

"I have time," Leena chimed as she sat on the bed, arms crossed with indignance.

"Can I propose something else?" I flashed a grin, the same one I wore when I had a bad idea but her face stayed the same. "I promise you'll like it."

"Already trying to get out of talking?"

"No. But these dresses are absolutely not going to work, and Avi hasn't scheduled any training," I said and gestured to the terrible green gowns hanging in the wardrobe. "We both deserve something better, and I can't believe I'm saying this, but if I ask Arden, we'll have something fit for the Crown in no time."

"A new dress?" Her face lit up. I wondered why the gods would gift one of their darkest powers to the brightest woman I knew. This kingdom would never be worthy of their *sunderone*.

I nodded. "I'll tell you everything on the walk."

She tried to rein in her smile by biting her lip. "You promise?"

I gave her a pointed look. "I would never joke about seeing Arden."

I meant it, and Leena knew. She was the only other person capable of seeing Arden in the same complicated way I did. In minutes, we were walking through the palace gates, towards the break in the wall leading to Lower Rowane.

The walk was close to an hour, and I told her about last night, about the queen, and about every one of my misgivings.

I didn't tell her Farran's secrets, about the glamour over my eyes, or what destiny expected of me; no one needed to know, *not yet*. I wasn't strong enough.

"That's everything," I finally said and nearly meant it.

Silence settled between us as we moved through the streets of Lower Rowane and dodged the few people who were up early. Leena's gold eyes watched the stones below. The lines on her brow were taut as she contemplated everything I'd said.

"You know he cares for you, right?" The way she said it was so matter-of-fact that it sank into my chest and became something else as we turned the corner. I said nothing.

Leena grabbed my arm and forced me to look at the rigid lines of honesty on her face. "You care for him, too. I can see it."

"Maybe, but it doesn't matter." *That was a lie. It did matter.* I cared for him, and I wanted him, but the higher the sun rose in the sky, the more I knew it couldn't end in anything but hurt.

I had too many secrets, too much of a past. Love was the only thing that could destroy me; it was a fate worse than death.

"Of course it matters." Leena scoffed.

I shook off her arm and kept walking. I wanted to tell her everything about myself, but I knew better. It would make her complicit, and Leena didn't deserve that. Or it would make her hate me, and I couldn't live with that either.

"Things like this don't last for me." I sighed and twisted to look at her. "What happens after the Armory? We're soldiers, *knights*, not ladies. Thera comes before everything."

"Maybe what you think is wrong. Once you rise, you're tied to him by the queen, and maybe it doesn't have to be so bad? We learned to trust each other. Why couldn't you learn to trust someone else? You don't have to be miserable."

Miserable was easier. "It's more complicated, Lee. Farran can't know about Arden. The closer to the Crown I get, the more danger I'm in. I told you about the boy I loved when I was nineteen, or did you forget?"

"No, I didn't forget," she said softly. "But haven't you punished yourself enough? It was an accident."

"No," I said sharply. I hadn't. "I don't even deserve your friendship."

Her hand gripped my arm and forced us to a stop. I looked at her. There was quiet rage in her eyes, and her jaw was tight. "Be upset about him if you want. *Fine.* Whatever you are is yours to ruin, but *us*?

"You picked me up from my fucking lowest, Rein; you know me inside and out just the same way I know you. I'm not your friend out of pity or circumstance. We earned each other, and there's no score to keep. If that's what you think, then I misjudged you in more ways than one."

I took a deep breath. "I'm not keeping score."

"Good, neither am I." Her face softened, and she let go of my arm.

I crossed the street towards Arden's estate while she followed close behind. It was never the seedy den nobles pretended it was.

The grand house stood in the middle of a street, lined on either side by row houses and street-level shop fronts with tattered awnings. The front of the house was shielded by a courtyard that could be mistaken for a city park . . . if the heavy iron gate wasn't padlocked during daylight hours.

The gardens within it were pristine: hedges clipped to perfect corners, tree branches hanging evenly overhead, and the groundskeeper raked and removed any leaf litter or disturbed mulch first thing every morning.

Leena peered through the bars of the locked gate. "I was expecting something a little grimier."

"Most people are very surprised to see he has taste." I smirked.

I pulled the string on the bell hanging from the garden gate. The sweet chime echoed through the courtyard, and a minute later, Declan walked towards us.

His face went through exactly six expressions before he reached the gate. "What are you doing here?" Every syllable sounded more worried than the last.

"Nice to see you, too. We're not deserters, if that's what you're thinking." I frowned. "We were invited by the Crown to the palace. Didn't Damien share that?"

"Yes, but I didn't know . . . who is she?" he stammered.

I glanced at Leena. "Leena Farrow, a friend of mine and perfectly trustworthy. Is he around? I have a favor."

"He'll be back shortly," Declan grumbled, his hand fiddling with the lock and a comically large key. "You're sure no one else followed you?"

"No," I said sardonically. "Led the entire Queensguard straight here."

Declan scowled. "Fine, come in. Quickly."

Arden designed the greenery specifically to change with the seasons. In the fall, there were several flowers that would bloom, and the trees were all a brilliant shade of red before their leaves dropped, giving way to rich, verdant evergreens. Leena ambled behind us to admire them.

The smell of the house was the first thing that transported me: a demure mixture of women's perfume, cigar smoke, and eternally burning incense.

We sat in the drawing room where the velvet settees had been rearranged and new art hung on the walls. Arden's current display seemed to be an homage to the naked human form: the last thing I wanted to think about, so I stared at Declan.

He wore an embroidered gold doublet, and his amber was neatly trimmed. It looked good, but he looked grown and every bit the nobles' son he was supposed to be.

"Leena used to dance with Moer," I said to break apart the tension. "I promise she can be trusted. She's not a noble."

"I'll take your word for it." Declan still looked skeptical as he poured the tea. There was an echo of my mother's judgment in his blue eyes. "Arden was hoping he'd run into you while you were here. Even had me clean your room the other day. You don't have to stay, but in case you wanted to."

My heart swelled a little, even if I'd never stay. "What else has he made you do?"

"Nothing, Reina. I've been mentoring with the library under a few Crown historians." *It worked.* If Declan never had to come back here after my rise, my oath was worth it—worth everything . . . He would be okay.

"That's great, you—"

"No," he spouted. "I did not ask Arden to do that. They were interested in me. It's probably because I was introduced as the brother of the *dreosen*. But, you know, Arden kept his promise? I would leave the moment he tried to turn me into you."

I winced and murmured, "I'm sorry."

"No," Declan muttered, and his eyes lifted to mine. "I'm sorry, but sometimes you still see me as a child. I'm fine. In fact, I'm more worried about you. That's why I rode out this summer; I needed to see *you* were fine."

The anger on my tongue dissolved.

"I told you I'd survive." My voice shrank as my chest constricted. "And maybe when I'm on the Queensguard, I'll get to stop in the library and bother you about dragons."

Amusement flickered across his face. "There's no world where you ask me about dragons."

"Did I tell you I saw one?" I retorted.

"You didn't ride it, did you?" His eyes widened as he leaned forward.

"No, of course not. I'm reckless, but I don't have a death wish."

Leena opened her mouth to add something, but the door opened behind us. We shot to our feet as Arden shuffled in, weighed down by several bags he promptly dropped.

"To what do I owe the pleasure?" Arden's sun-kissed face looked over both Leena and me. He took my hands in his and held them up to look at me over me like the glittering prize I was to him. "I'm delighted to see one rumor was true. Is it also true she's making a show to the nobles out of her demon wielder?"

"I'm promised it will be the talk of the night," I said solemnly. But I couldn't read the expression on Arden's face. It looked somewhere caught between scheming and wanting to pry more information.

"Have you thought more about our chat?" he asked, menace edging his tone as he dropped my hands. I didn't have an answer, and he quickly provided, "No need for you to worry, Reina.

You're well on your way to the Queensguard, and I do hope this beautiful lady will join you. Have we met?"

"Leena Farrow." She stuck her hand out. "Pleasure to meet you."

Arden took her hand and kissed it gingerly. I bit back the urge to roll my eyes. Leena was everything Arden loved in a woman, but never earned.

"Did you dance? I swear I've seen you," he remarked.

"I did." Leena looked at the ground and back up at his inquisitive brown eyes. "I danced for Moer."

He nodded. "Very good. I hope the Armory has been better to you than he was."

"Was?" Leena's eyes widened.

Arden's face shifted. "He passed about six months ago. Throat mysteriously cut in an alleyway. He had very few friends in Rowane."

Leena's expression was unreadable. Eventually, I'd ask Arden who did it, as I had no doubt he knew. Moer was on several lists and deserved his end. I hoped it fucking hurt.

Arden clapped his hands together, breaking the tense quiet. "I asked before, but I'll ask again: what brings you home, Reina? I know you're not here to say hello."

"You would be correct," I said, standing straighter. "I need a favor, and you're the first person I thought of."

"And that is?" he drawled, eyeing me curiously.

"Could I have money from my accounts to find a gown befitting Thera's *dreosen* and Emerald's *sunderone*?"

"Shadows, Miss Farrow?" Arden's gaze pivoted as he smiled. "Very impressive. A good gift, indeed. No need to pull from your account, Reina. It'd be my pleasure. I have open accounts at Aubra's and Fletching Lewis. The choice is yours. Either will have dresses in your measurements, my dears."

"That's gracious of you." I bowed my head slightly, knowing Arden liked it. A few times I'd asked Arden to stop having dresses made for me, but I'd long since given up. "Thank you."

"No, thank you, Reina," he crooned. "You'll want to hurry over, though. It might take time, but I trust you'll find something that will make them remember you. There's one in particular I'm thinking of."

I moved to the door. Arden tugged my arm and pulled me into him. His breath and the smell of tobacco curled around my neck as he whispered, "Should anything happen, run for the woods. You'll be safe."

I shook off his grip and glared. "I'll consider it. Thank you again."

Leena looked straight at me. Declan, too. I ignored them and hardened. "Let's go."

We left and the iron gates closed behind us. I walked briskly until we stood in front of Aubra's dress store.

I finally looked at Leena when we stopped. "Is this alright? Aubra is a wizard, I promise."

Leena smiled, but it didn't dissolve the uneasiness of Arden's warning, which clouded my thoughts. "This is one of those days where I remember who you used to be," she remarked. "I'm sure it will be perfect. "

"She's never let me down." I shrugged and pushed open the door.

Aubra, a squat old woman, came to the front and hugged me so tightly I might have mistaken it for a chokehold before backing away, hands lingering on my upper arms. "I thought I'd never see you again, Reina. And who is this?" She turned to Leena.

"This is a friend of mine and Lord Arden's. We require gowns to meet the queen."

Chapter 36

We returned to the palace shortly before midday to find Farran pacing the hallway while the other five third-years watched.

"Thank the fucking gods," Farran exclaimed.

His eyes surged like a storm as he barreled towards me. For a moment I thought he would reach out, but he quickly cemented his hands to his side.

"The crown prince was asking where you were, and we had to say we didn't know," he scolded. "It's not safe out there. We could have sent a guard with you."

"I had Leena," I retorted, but his face remained incredulous as he eyed the bags draped over my arm, as well as Leena's. I stepped back and stared at him. "I've never needed a guard in Lower Rowane, and I'm not starting now—just needed a dress."

"Told you," Vera said flippantly. "Sangrey shouldn't wear any old court dress. Not when she's being watched by the queen. She did what any self-respecting person would."

"I'm sure," Farran muttered. His eyes moved to Leena. "Farrow?"

"It's true," Leena said. "We weren't told anything about training, but we'll be out on the field in minutes, if it's an order."

"Right, it is an order," Farran said, and his gaze settled on mine. The storm lessened as he spoke, every word calmer than the last. "You and I need to figure a few things out before we wield demons in front of five hundred people. Prince Lorcan has extended his help."

"Five hundred?" I squeaked. It was undignified, but I didn't care. I was fucking terrified, and my heart clenched at the thought.

Waking up felt it all felt distant. Like something that happened a lifetime ago, not hours.

"If I could do more as your captain, I would," Avi said apologetically. "But the queen and Linden are the ones who set the order, Far. Your uncle also agreed."

"Thanks for the reminder," Farran grumbled, and I noticed his hair had yet to be combed or tied back; it looked wild. His arm reached to touch mine, but he withdrew it again, thinking better of it. "We should go, Sangrey. Bring the dress with you. You can change in the palace."

Leena hadn't left yet, and I caught her grinning. Damn her and her romanticism.

I draped my leathers over the dress bag and walked to the palace in silence.

My arms were already tired from the weight of the dress and leathers as we charged toward the front steps of the plaza. The great hall was overwhelmed by servants and nobility preparing for the masquerade.

Everything about the inside of the palace was grand, even in the wake of chaos with decorations and flower arrangements strewn everywhere. The ceiling stretched high above us, and marble-checkered floors ran into gray stone walls, colliding in a beautiful explosion of marble trim carved to look like the ivy vines climbing up the city walls.

Farran slowed and glanced back at me, as if he'd suddenly remembered I was supposed to be there. "Sorry if I was harsh. Cormac nearly had Linden call a search party."

Wordlessly, he took the dress from my arms and led us through a narrow corridor, away from the roving eyes of the palace and into a winding stairwell as gnawing guilt crept into my chest.

My life wasn't my own, and it never would be. It was becoming clear that working for Arden was the closest to freedom I'd ever have as more and more walls closed in.

"I'm sorry. I should have said something or told someone," I mumbled.

There was more I wanted to say, but I bit it back. The stairwell wasn't the place to talk.

We climbed in dizzying circles, one flight after another. He didn't have to say it. We were going to his room. After seven flights, we landed on his floor where I tried, covertly, to catch my breath.

Again, I waited for guilt to strike as I followed Farran pushed open his door. I thought being up here would remind me I did something wrong, but it never came.

I was so fucked. If this didn't end with both of us dead, it would end with one of us broken beyond repair. Everything about this, about him, felt like something clicking into place in the worst way. It scraped against my heart the same way fear scraped my chest: breathless and fucking terrified.

"Lorcan will be here in a minute." He hung the dress near the door as I laid my leathers and cape across a chair.

I tried not to remember how he'd kissed me, or how I looked in his mirror, standing beside him. Or what it would be like for him to fuck me on the desk.

Farran continued, "Cormac wanted to know if you would like one of the ladies to do your hair. I know you usually do it yourself . . ." His voice was soft and hardly jolted me from the reverie.

"Yes, please."

"Right, great. I'll send word." Farran looked awkward and unsure of what to say as he paced around the room.

At least he was wearing a tunic and trousers this time. *Could I ask him to kiss me again? No. Absolutely not.* A moment later, I had an answer as Lorcan opened the door and walked in with a stack of books in his arms.

Somehow, he was scrawny and six inches taller than Farran. Lorcan was svelte, where his brothers were muscular. He had long, dark blonde hair tied back and the same olive eyes as Cormac. For now, he wore a normal tunic and trousers with the same crooked smile as Farran.

Lorcan set the books down with a thud on a small chair near the entry. He didn't seem interested in going any further into his brother's room.

He turned to me. "Pleasure to meet you, Reina Sangrey. I've heard many things about you. Most importantly, you've got a curse like my brother, which has led our mother to believe you should help blow up an altar to prove your loyalty. I'm Lorcan, the second prince who can't shake the title."

Farran crossed his arms and glared, but a smile twitched at his lip. "You shouldn't say things like that in polite company, Lorcan."

"My apologies." The prince looked back at me, but he wasn't apologetic. "Farran said you're not thrilled about the situation, either. Understandable. There was a reason Cormac and I tried to talk her out of it, but we're just princes who don't understand what it is to rule. Never mind that Lord Riding and several priests agree with us."

Farran cocked an eyebrow. "She's letting you sit in during council meetings now?" he hedged.

Lorcan shrugged and reached down for a book at the top of his pile, which he held out towards Farran. "We can talk about what I'm allowed to do later. You wanted my help now, and the lady still needs to get ready. Our queen has high expectations," he reminded us.

Of course, the queen had high expectations. I was the demon wielder she was ready to sacrifice one of her sons for through a blood oath. I tried to ignore the way Lorcan's words twisted my stomach into knots.

"What do I need to do?" I asked, furrowing my brows.

"It's not all on you," Farran reminded me as he flipped through several of Lorcan's bookmarks. "Our mother is expecting us both to wield the demons and destroy the altar together."

I looked at Lorcan and asked, "Will they? It's an altar for Dreonna, their god. I'd be asking them to go against their nature."

Lorcan looked around the room and back at me. "As far as I've read, they should do anything you ask them to do. You wield them, and they kneel for you. I'd expect they do the same for Farran, but now you can pass the reins and he can hold them steady while you focus on destroying the altar. At least, that's what I'd recommend."

My eyes narrowed as I took in what Lorcan suggested. He had talked about this with Farran. "How would I use my magic?" I pressed.

"Farran told me you wielded a storm as described in a book I'd sent him." Lorcan grabbed another book from the pile and furiously flipped through it. "If you do that inside the stone of the altar, it will break apart, and you don't have to make the demons do anything." Lorcan paused and looked at me with a penetrating stare. "I don't care what the creature is; it's wrong for the queen to ask this of them."

"Do I have enough magic?" I whipped around to look at Farran, who glanced away from the page he was skimming.

"I'll be there," he answered, as if he had all the power in the world. Then he added, "I'll be drawing it out from the altar as much as I can. You will, too."

"It shouldn't be any different from the Armory, right?" I looked between the brothers.

"Only stronger," Farran shrugged as a smile tugged at the corner of his mouth, "but I think Thera's *dreosen* can handle it."

I glared, but directed my attention back to Prince Lorcan. "We'll waste magic if we practice, but are you sure this will work?"

Lorcan nodded. "I've never seen anyone destroy an altar with its own magic, but I checked with a few other scholars," he replied, looking at Farran as he flipped through the book in his hand to another paragraph. "The nobles won't know the difference. Mother might, but Cormac can handle that. It just needs to look like both of you wielded demons for the court."

"Thanks," Farran said with a somber nod. "Any other advice?"

"You're not gonna like it." Lorcan frowned. He glanced at me before looking back at his brother.

Worry creased around his eyes, and for the first time, I noticed Lorcan had a winding tattoo, like a delicate raised scar on his left hand and another of the Theranian crest on the right side of his neck.

Farran stared at his brother. "If you can say it to me, you can say it in front of her."

Part of me wanted to swoon at the conviction in his voice. Lorcan heard it too—one of his brows quirked up as he scanned the book again and he flipped to a page.

"Right, then. Far, you'll need more blood to be safe. Hers is a large gift; it's not like the ones Mother kept poisoning you and Father with. *Ontaros* were called leeches for a reason."

Farran winced but didn't break his concentration. "How much?" I didn't love the tone in his voice.

Lorcan shoved the book in his brother's hand and pointed to a paragraph I couldn't see.

"Gods," Farran exclaimed, and my eyes narrowed at his tone.

The room was silent for a minute before he shoved the book back at Prince Lorcan's chest. The cold calculation returned to his eyes, and Farran's gaze drifted to the floor.

He muttered, "I'll figure it out. Thank you." Lorcan opened his mouth to say something, but Farran gave a dismissive glare. "*Thank you.*"

I deserved to know. "How much?" I asked.

He didn't look at me. Instead, Farran stared at Lorcan, who picked up several of the books and returned to the door.

Farran's taut face softened for a second as he forced his lips into a small but sincere smile. "I truly do appreciate the help, brother. Warn me if anything comes up."

Lorcan nodded and backed out of the door.

I waited for the latch to click before I repeated my question, "How much?"

Farran's hand ran through his unbound hair, messing it up even more than it already was before he turned around. "Nearly three times what I took last night."

I blew out a haunted breath. "*Gods.*"

"You don't have to. We can figure—"

"No." I took a deep breath, and my gaze held his. "It's fine. If we do it now, I'll have time to recover. What time is it?"

He hesitated. "Three. We have until quarter after five."

Fuck. "Right, let's get it over with." I stopped beside his bed. "Wait, one request: can you have water put in the bath? I need—"

"Already done," he said so smoothly that the threads in my chest uncoiled and fluttered. "The palace prepares a bath before events. Something about being clean."

Either way, I held on to the same stubborn emotion as I walked to his bed and sat on it. My dagger still sat on the bedside table . . . I couldn't believe I'd left it there; I'd never left it anywhere.

Farran paused in the doorway and looked at me. His sapphire eyes held my own, though I had no interest in knowing what he was thinking, not right now.

I untied the green ribbon on my wrist, tucked it into a pocket, and held the dagger against my arm.

"I hate that it's happening like this," he finally said, voice barely above a whisper.

"How else would it have happened?"

He took a deep breath, and as he sat beside me, the knot of magic in my chest frayed.

"It wouldn't have happened at all."

His fingers laced between mine, and I didn't know who I was. I didn't know what this was or what it could be. I sat in the chambers of a Theranian prince, dagger in one hand and his in the other; it was the start of a very complicated joke.

I tried to push reassurance into my voice. "This is one of those times where we don't have a choice. Just like trial."

Farran nodded, and I pressed the cool blade to my arm. Beads of crimson gleamed against the steel as I drew back. Softly, he took the dagger and I leaned back, closing my eyes—letting the fire of his touch consume me.

He was gentle, even playful, but there was an urgency and a risk that hadn't been there before. Last night was a taste; today was the show.

As he took, our magic wove together, beautiful and inextricable from the other. He wasn't just borrowing . . . we were becoming. The power in me wanted to be shared.

It had waited so patiently for so long, but it wanted this in the same way I did. The knots strengthened, expanded, and morphed into a tapestry of power.

Then he pulled away.

"That's all I'm taking," Farran said decisively, as though I'd know how much it was.

My eyes stayed closed. I was floating, and every part of me was warm and calm. My arm tingled in his grip as he repaired the wound.

"How does it feel?" I asked, but my voice was far away.

The bed shifted. Farran laid next to me, and I knew it would only last a moment, but every part of me was desperate to hold on to it.

"Incredible," he murmured. "You're always incredible. Even when I was just supplementing your magic, I knew it was different. I caught glimpses—but this . . . this is nothing I imagined."

"And it seems to like you," I mused.

"Well, like magic calls to like," Farran said, as though it answered everything.

It didn't. It couldn't. Not all of this was magic. Most of it was complicated, dangerous, and terribly real. It was a choice even if it wouldn't last, not when Arden still occupied my thoughts.

If anything happens, run for the woods. Everything Damien Arden said to me still crashed against my chest when the room was too quiet.

Arden knew something, and I hated him for it. Maybe he was right about houses being brought to Rowane. And maybe he was right about my gift, but Damien Arden couldn't be right about everything.

For now, I hoped he was wrong about only one thing: I hoped he was wrong about the prince. I was exactly where I was never supposed to be, and I wasn't strong enough to end it.

Farran kissed my forehead, the bed shifted, and I was alone.

I was in no hurry to move. I stared at the ornate stonework above me. Pillars curved into archways, bonded together in stone and exploded into fits of leaves. The cavities in the ceiling boasted faded mosaics in a hundred colors that weren't silver or navy.

I admired it as the magic roared beneath my skin. The loss of blood left me light-headed, but reality came back heavier with every pulse. Maybe Farran had taken a part of my magic with him, or maybe it was the crushing weight of truth as it settled in his absence.

Whatever it was, it didn't stop what happened next. I plodded across the room to the massive tub sitting in the middle of the bathroom. Steam rose from the water, and my attention snagged on the array of oils, soaps, and a hundred other things piled on the table beside it.

I tugged my breeches off, piling my clothes on the floor as I approached the claw-foot tub. Blue and white painted ceramic decorated the walls, while solid dark blue shone beneath my feet.

In mere seconds, I drowned myself in the smell of peonies and the comfort of the warm water until there was a knock on the door. I hardly registered the sound, but I panicked, sinking into the water as it swung open.

My hands covered the important bits . . . Nothing would be more humiliating than one of Farran's brothers seeing Thera's demon wielder completely fucking naked.

"Lady Reina?" It was a voice unfamiliar to me, with an accent I didn't recognize. I froze and said nothing. "I'm here to help with your hair."

Oh, *right*. I breathed a heavy sigh of relief. "I'm in the bath!"

A woman who wore a pretty gold gown with simple embroidery strode into the bathroom with purpose.

"I'm Sera," she said, appearing petite and nearly my age. Her nose scrunched when she smiled. "It's a pleasure to meet you. Take as long as you need."

"Thank you, Sera. I'll be done in a moment."

Sera pulled a chair out from under a table and unfolded a pack of tools. I scrambled, and the water sloshed as I stood, wrapping a towel around myself and trying my best to dry off quickly.

When I was done, the maid guided me round to a chair. I sat in front of her, biting my lip as she dried and tamed my hair into something presentable with sparks of magic and tools I'd never seen.

Occasionally, I glanced at the mirror to see if my eye color changed—it hadn't. They remained brown and plain . . . just the way my father's were.

"There," Sera said with finality. She'd wrestled my hair into an elegantly taut bun resting high on my head, making my features look harsh and formidable. "When you change for the ball, you'll only need to pull out four pins. The rest will stay tied up and it will look nice with a dress, I promise. Do you like it?"

"I do." I smiled. "Thank you. What time is it?"

"Half past four," Sera replied as she packed her things and made to leave. "Happy Autane, and best of luck."

"Thank you."

The door closed, and I was alone again. I moved gingerly to avoid messing up my hair, and the awkward movements jolted me back to Arden's den.

For years, I'd make my hair, put on a pretty dress, and do what was required that night to keep his coin safe. Most often, he relied on me looking harmless, like one of his girls. And now I wondered just how many nobles would recognize me when I was paraded before them.

A formal silk tunic laid on top of my leathers, and it was much nicer than the cotton one I'd brought. It must have been Farran's because it smelled like him as I pulled it on and methodically dressed in the twelve layers it took to be a knight.

I clipped the emerald cape and attached my silver cord before I looked in the mirror.

I'd worn it all before, but the done-up hair made it feel infinitely real. Something in me sank with every fringe of silver and whorl of the emerald crest caught my eye.

It's what I always wanted; my place in the knighthood was carved into my skin regardless of what banners killed my mother, but it was strange to stand here.

The door opened without a knock, and I jumped. Farran gave me an apologetic look. "Sorry," he blurted from the doorway, but then he grinned as it closed. "Usually, someone else isn't in here."

He looked incredibly princely in his leathers, even if they were the same as mine. His dark hair had been slicked back into a knot, and for the first time, a thin, silver crown rested on his head.

Something warmed in me that was certainly not magic, but those threads stirred, too. I stared. I couldn't help it—*this was fucking real.*

"I know it looks ridiculous," Farran said and walked towards me, his gaze holding mine. I wondered if he felt the same. "If I didn't wear it, she would find a worse one."

"I forget you're a prince," I admitted.

"Me too," he said. "You look beautiful. Sera has a way with hair. She attends to several of the ladies in court."

I took a step closer, reached up, and pulled his lips to mine without hesitation. Heat danced on the edge of my tongue as he kissed me back, gentle and deliberate. His hands fell to my waist and pulled me into him. Power burned, and our threads tangled, entwining us like we were meant to stay locked together.

Farran broke the kiss but held me there. "I'm consumed by you." His sapphire eyes calmed and focused on mine. "All fucking day I've thought about how you taste, Reina."

His lips brushed mine again, and I wanted nothing more than to burn with him. If I could make a choice, I'd choose to stay here, in this. But we couldn't. Of course, we couldn't.

Farran kissed my forehead, my cheek, and my lips again. The buzz of heat followed everywhere he touched.

He groaned and took a step back. "Are you ready?"

"Thera's *dreosen* is always ready," I said tightly.

I know he didn't believe me, not truly. But I needed to say it. I needed to feel the words leave my throat because not a single part of me felt adequate as I followed the prince through the Theranian palace and into the queen's receiving hall.

CHAPTER 37

THE RECEIVING HALL WAS long and massive. At the far end was a dais decorated in silver with navy drapes. The silver throne of Thera sat atop and hanging behind it was a massive banner with the Crown crest. On either side, narrow windows scaled soapstone walls, and murals between each depicted a battle of the gods or any number of Thera's wars.

I hadn't paid enough attention to figure out which. Instead, I focused on my feet and the rhythm of my steps as I progressed down the empty hall toward the woman who punctuated my past and future.

I wondered if she felt it, too. The gravity of this moment.

Her Majesty wore a grand gown made of navy, embroidered with different depictions of the crest in silver. On her head sat a beautiful crown, gilded in silver with filigree detail in a run of thorns, vines, and lilies, as though it grew out of her raven-black hair.

Her face looked almost like it had in my Rite dream. Her olive eyes watched my every move as I stopped before the dais and dropped into a low bow.

Tonight couldn't be the night. She doesn't die in a gown.

"You may rise, Lady Reina Sangrey, and come forward," the queen beckoned, her tone commanding and short. *Good.* She was exactly who I wanted her to be.

I'd enjoy dragging my dagger through her once the oaths were fulfilled and no one else could die.

The queen's stare bore through my skin and into my very being. If she thought anything of me, she didn't reveal it.

I stepped forward, lifting my eyes. "It's an honor to serve, Your Majesty."

Cormac stood behind her. He looked past both of us toward the entrance of the hall, or perhaps one of the murals. He and the queen had the same eyes, but Cormac's held a glimmer of amusement, an emotion which was completely lost in the queen's; hers were assessing and sharp.

They raked over me.

"The honor is mine," the queen said after a pregnant pause. "You're the first *dreosen* to stand in this hall in nearly two centuries. And the first to stand for our Kingdom. Your arrival means more for the Crown of Thera than all of the Armory, and I hope you know that, Lady Reina."

"I look forward to honoring and defending Thera with the gift I've been granted," I replied.

All four Emerald makers stood to the right. Avernought did not look at me; he looked at the floor.

"I'm sure you do," the queen said. "I expect tonight will be the first of many."

"I'd be disappointed if it wasn't." My lip quirked up. The last thing I would do before the Queen of Thera was cower at her promises.

A brief, tight smile crossed her face. She didn't deserve my fear. She only needed to trust my loyalty—that was how I'd get close. Today was the first step of many.

Her gaze shifted to Farran, who now stood beside me. "Prince Farran, I expect you've kept your promise?"

Farran nodded and spoke formally, "I always keep my promises to the Crown, Your Majesty. Like Lady Reina, I too look forward to honoring Thera."

The queen's lips pursed. "For your sake, I do hope that's true. The nobles expect two demon wielders—as do *I*. This isn't a parlor trick, my son. This is how we honor Thera and the loyalty of those we serve."

She took a breath, and her eyes roved back. I shuddered instinctively at the power she held.

"You'll have nothing." No—I fought the memory. This wasn't the time.

"You're both to destroy the altar on the grounds with your demons, in the name of the Seven. The nobles arrive presently and gather in the garden," she drawled. "You will walk together. My guard will be behind you. I expect it won't take long."

I nodded. "It won't. I'm rather good at what I do."

"So, I've heard," the queen said with a cruel smile. "I appreciate your time and service. You are dismissed to the terrace. And, Your Highness?"

"Yes, Your Majesty?" he bit out, though Farran maintained his cool façade.

"Straighten your cape. You're my son, not a commoner."

I swear Farran growled as he fumbled with the clip on his left shoulder. With that, we bowed and left. Calmly, I walked away from my mother's murderer to do exactly as she asked.

My heart raced. Then it nearly stopped beating when we stepped through the palace doors.

The terrace buzzed with hundreds of nobles and Theranians. I needed to ignore them; I was here to follow an order.

Farran edged closer, his shoulder brushing mine. Heat and magic tangled between us and knotted together, even at the faint contact.

The urge to take his hand in mine clawed at my insides, but I fought it and kept my head forward, looking over the railing of the terrace. I reached for the magic in my chest. I needed to know it wouldn't fail me. *Not today.*

I gasped as I pushed the threads aside and found a cool, wet one—*waiting.* Usually, I needed to dig deeper, but they seemed to know they were needed tonight.

Farran elbowed me gently.

"Are you okay?" he leaned close. The threads all rearranged. My brows furrowed.

"Yes," I blurted. "I'm fine. How much longer?"

A horn blared and faded into the song of Thera.

"Now."

Of course. Of fucking course.

Behind us, several Queensguard knights lined up. Their dual silver cords were the most obvious marker of a castle guard along with the detailed, silver embroidery trimmed their sleeves and capes. We stood before them on the terrace steps. Then we processed down the sloping garden and towards the inevitable.

Five hundred faces stared at us. I kept my eyes straight ahead, trying to keep my expression steady and unreadable—a skill I'd been born with.

We passed our house; we passed Ruby, and I knew we passed several nobles who had seen me in Arden's den. None of it mattered, and I'd be damned if I'd let it.

I was Thera's fucking demon wielder.

A tapestry of magical threads stretched between Farran and I. They spun around us like a spider's silk only we could feel and see as they strengthened with every step towards the altar.

The procession didn't stop until we stood in the center of the row of roses along the forest's edge.

I wanted you to know what it was like.

Farran's voice reverberated through my thoughts from last night… It was a beautiful altar. More than that, it contained the blood of his father and centuries of blood from his ancestors.

Now we stood before the court of Thera, poised to dismantle it at the whim of a queen.

Rage boiled in my blood. She would pay for this.

The music stopped and horns blared, announcing the queen's arrival. She was accompanied by several of her guards while Lorcan and Cormac marched behind her.

I turned toward the altar. The sun set behind the trees in a brilliant display of orange and red which I was about to turn pitch black.

Nerves fluttered around my chest like a cage of mayflies as I breathed. I couldn't look anywhere but at the damn altar as I let my magic unfold.

The queen gave an address, but I didn't hear a word. The threads multiplied and reached across my skin until every part of me vibrated in the warmth of the old gods and their sacrifices.

I wondered if the altar knew we'd come to destroy it. I wondered if it would let me.

A breeze rippled through the trees, and the heat in my chest edged unbearably. I was keenly aware we were being watched but the eyes of the court fell away when Farran whispered, "*Now.*"

My right hand stretched out, and Farran did the same. I closed my eyes. My magic was alive and waiting. I pushed the threads aside and tugged.

With a screech and a roar, my eyes flew open. Two demons stood before me. They kneeled, their beady eyes meeting mine, and for the first time, I saw the true beauty of my gift in the black depths of their scales and talons. They could shred every noble who watched with jaws hung open. This wasn't a show; this was true power.

I forced myself to smile then commanded, "*Destroy.*"

That's the word that left my lips, that's the word the queen heard and everyone else within earshot. It's the word that rattled in my chest and anchored my feet to the ground like I'd been bound in iron.

But the demons didn't move. They didn't stand; they didn't turn. They only stared at me and the silence blared so much louder. The threads held, but they drained and I could hear everyone in the audience holding their breath.

I needed to do something—quickly. Farran's magic nudged against mine. I froze and hoped he couldn't see the panic in my eyes. I didn't have enough power to force the creatures to destroy the altar of their creator. It wasn't my choice to make.

Farran's nerves crept through the magic tethering us, but I wouldn't look at him. I needed him to hold the demons while I gave the queen a show.

Anger and refusal vibrated on the demon's threads: it was a warning that dragged across the base of my neck as the threads were taut, rigid.

Farran took them from me. The two demons remained kneeling, and I prayed to Dreonna they could read the thought I projected towards them: *we are being tested. I need you to trust me. Pretend this is your doing.*

I held my breath and didn't release it until they rose to their feet, swords in hand, and faced the altar of their creator as I asked for too much.

Impatience radiated from the crowd, and I knew it was taking too fucking long. My eyes flicked to Farran's. He looked steady, his jaw tensed, but he nodded. I lifted my left hand, faced my palm to the sky, and imagined the same seeping mist I'd conjured at the Armory.

Hot yarns of magic flared as it obeyed my command. Mist rolled in, white at first, but it darkened quickly into a shade of churning, bluish-black.

I tugged on another cold thread and wove it into the mist. The cloud concentrated and darkened to onyx as it became a pulsing storm. Wind picked up, and I forced the storm into the heart of the stone. It strained against me, but it would bend.

The threads became more alive. I dropped one hand, the other holding the storm aloft. A nudge rippled against my temple—I needed to be fast. I was getting close, and the demons felt it coming as they braced their wings. Or Farran called them back. Either way, they retreated, standing between us and the altar with their swords sheathed and wings hinged as they stood at full, terrifying height.

Then I pulled on the threads, hard, and forced every ounce of the energy and magic into the stone until the ground beneath me shook.

The altar exploded in a brilliant display of black mist and an inky black substance so similar to demon blood. Gold tendrils of burning old magic released from it like glitter, and stone flew in all directions.

I was sure it hit an onlooker; there were screams and shouts of chaos, but none of it touched me.

The debris should have pummeled us, but the demons had spread their wings to deflect it.

I stood still; my ears rang, and everything came back little by little. A demon was hurt, and the sear of phantom pain shot through my back as if it were my wing. I winced and finally dropped the threads to stare at the mess I'd made.

My demons kneeled, and there was a *whoosh* in my chest as Farran released them . . . They'd be dust in less than a minute. My heart twisted when I looked past them.

The altar was no more. The statue of Dreonna and the receiving stone below had blown apart and covered everything nearby in an oily sludge. Demon blood swamped the area and clung to the dying roses. I'm sure it splattered several of the nobles, but it was their fault for standing too close.

A roar of applause fully jolted me back to reality as red-cloaked healers closed in. *I did it.* We did it.

I turned to Farran. There was pride in his eyes as the demons turned to dust, but I could see the storm raging behind it.

We'd done exactly what the queen had wanted. I'd wrenched out a sliver of an old god's soul and destroyed it.

The queen clapped her hands together and spoke, but none of her words reached me. I wanted to run. I couldn't, so I waited to collapse.

My vision should have shivered, but something was wrong. With equal concern and curiosity, I reached for my magic. None of it had depleted, despite how much I'd spent. If anything, my threads were stronger, warmer, and hummed beneath my skin like a simmering flame.

The moment dismissal left the lips of the queen, we climbed the hill, and I ignored every eye trying to catch my attention.

My skin buzzed. My magic wasn't waning . . . it was a building storm, and it thrashed for release. If Farran touched me, I didn't feel it. All I felt was myself burning apart. This was worse than being empty.

Once my feet touched the stone of the terrace, I took off to Farran's quarters. I needed to get this cape off. I needed to feel less, and I needed silence. If I stopped, I would explode.

Farran raced to keep up and said nothing until he pointed out that I needed to turn left instead of right after I pushed myself up the several flights of stairs to his chambers and barreled through his door.

I ripped off the emerald cape, yanked off the Crown-embroidered leathers, and kept discarding clothes until I stood in the middle of Farran's sitting room, heaving in a silk tunic and trousers.

Magic burned in every vein like poison. I wanted to tear it all out with my bare hands, even my teeth, if that's what it took. I couldn't breathe fast enough.

The click of a lock sounded, and I whipped around. Farran stood with his hands up; *fuck*, I must have looked feral—I was feral.

"It's just me." He took a step closer. How was he calm about this? *Couldn't he feel it?* "You're safe; no one is coming in. Let me help you."

"I don't need help," I snapped.

His eyes held mine as though we were caught in a standoff. We weren't. I just needed to breathe, and I couldn't. Farran took another step. I tugged at the hem of the tunic, but my hands weren't my own.

"You were brilliant," he said gently. "But I think you did something else."

"What do you mean?" My eyes flashed.

He took one more step. His jaw ticked, but everything about him was soft and inviting. All at odds with the first officer who stood before me in leathers and designations. "To start, your eyes are usually quite beautiful, but they are glowing, which is very new."

"What?" I fractured and whirled to look in the mirror. My eyes glowed. Threads of gold and silver shimmered and moved in purple, not brown. The glamour had fallen. "What did I fucking do?" I spun back.

My frenzied stare held Farran's, and I needed him to look more panicked. His calmness infuriated me. It took every bit of crumbling control I had not to lash out.

Then, he took a step toward me. Reflexively, my hand snapped for the dagger.

"I suspect," he said and stopped in front of me, "The old magic in the altar found the next closest vessel. You don't feel drained?"

"I'm on fire," I rasped.

A smirk flitted across his face, but he quickly replaced it with concern. "It will level in a few hours. Cold water will help. Or *I* can."

I moved from the mirror to a chair. I gripped the back of it, knuckles turning white as everything in me raged and thrashed. "A few hours?" It was searing me from the inside out.

"I can help. Let me help."

Something in me broke apart; There must have been a crack in my chest. He stepped closer once more, and his fingertips touched my cheek. I almost buckled at the gentleness.

I leaned into his hand and pulled him closer until his lips brushed mine. It didn't feel like fire this time; it felt like being pulled into the calm of the forest. I kissed him deeper, and with every lash of tongue and cloying breath, the fire in my veins cooled.

But a kiss wasn't enough—I needed so much more of him. I wanted to suffocate in the rush as his gift drew the ancient, bottomless magic from me.

He pulled away, and I stood dazed. Floating on the edge of something I didn't have a word for. His blue eyes gazed at my lips, and he stared at me. The threads of our magic entangled as his forehead touched mine. Tears stuck to my lashes, but with every breath I returned to myself.

"Your eyes are normal again," he whispered. "How do you feel?"

"Much less on fire," I rasped.

Farran's arms wrapped around me. His breath was warm in my ear. "I was just going to hold your arm, but your idea was so much better."

"Thought it was." My head swam as his thumb stroked my cheek.

"Most people wouldn't survive that much magic, Reina. I can hardly hold it."

I pulled back to look; the same silver and gold threads glowed and moved in the depths of his eyes. My hand moved to his cheek. "Can you let it go?" I whispered.

"I don't want to waste their sacrifice," Farran said through gritted teeth. His arms dropped from my back, and I watched as he crossed the room in a frenzy to pry open a chest from underneath his bed. "I'm going to do something so you can still access it. I've only done it a few times before, but if it works, you can use it or return it to another altar."

"What are you—"

Farran said nothing as he frantically sifted through the trunk's contents, discarding things onto the floor until he pulled out a narrow, faded blue box and stalked towards me.

His eyes were wild. I imagine that's what I looked like a few minutes ago, and I couldn't deny the part of me that would love to put the magic to a different, selfish purpose. *Ancestors be damned.*

He cracked the box open: inside was a necklace made of a thick gold chain with inset black stones shimmering like the mirrored eyes of demons.

Softly, Farran said, "It's from my father's family. I took it when my mother no longer wanted it."

I said nothing—I only stared, mouth agape, as Farran placed the box on the floor, then took the necklace in both hands. Tendrils of silver and gold bound and wove themselves into the metal and stone.

The magic in his eyes dimmed and calmed until it flickered out and he finally looked at me. "May I?"

Words wouldn't come, but I nodded and turned, allowing him the freedom he needed to fasten the necklace. Delicately, he placed it on my chest and clasped it at the nape of my neck. His fingers lingered where they touched my spine.

The metal was warm, and it hummed. The magic twined and wove into my own the same way his did. I brushed my fingers across the stones. It responded with a quiver.

"It looks beautiful on you," he whispered into my ear.

As I turned around, the cool wash of the glamour slid back into place. Farran had already stepped away towards the door.

"It has almost all that magic," he said as he paced the room, looking for something else. "You'll know how to use it if you need it."

Farran opened the door and had a quick exchange with the guard outside before he closed it. I was at a loss and said nothing, just watched as he bolted into his bedroom and walked out a minute later dressed in formal wear.

He looked at me with a soft smile. "My mother is requesting me. Take all the time you need. I'll see you downstairs."

Chapter 38

I was grateful Farran left Creighton, his guard, with me. Summoning demons for the entirety of the Theranian court and destroying an altar to the gods left me shaky. I would not have made it down the seven flights of stairs in regular clothes—let alone a gown, slippers, and a mask—without him.

The dress was lovely, but it was heavy. An extravagant layer of embroidery was stitched into the thick silk in shades of green and silver, while the skirt billowed out behind me; a high slit on the right side gave me easy access to my dagger and the vial of *fharendought* from Arden. It could nullify any binding sigils, just in case.

Hefty pieces of silk draped over my arms that wanted to be sleeves, but they did nothing to hold up the weight of the gown; a steel-imbued corset supported the bulk of it. She'd even added clips to the bodice for my silver cord.

But it was the last piece of the dress that qualified it for Thera's *Dreosen*. Clipped to the points on the back, a bejeweled, emerald cape was the last piece of the dress. The glitter started sparsely towards the top and collected at the bottom in a pool of emerald, silver, and gold. She wanted me to glow and I was certain I did.

My feet hit the bottom of the stairs, and the din of excited conversation and the drawl of a violin echoed through the stone corridor. I'd performed, and now I could enjoy the evening as if I were just a normal person in the court—like everyone else.

I thanked Creighton for his help and strode towards the ballroom. This part I could do alone. It wasn't hard to find the party, even in a palace.

The necklace around my neck thrummed like a second heartbeat as I walked; the ancient magic felt part of me. I could do this. I wasn't the girl who snuck in here in the dead of night to pierce the heart of a page. I was a woman and a soldier here at the invitation of the queen; I'd earned my place.

Even more, the power folded beneath my skin was worth more to her than her son. Farran. Should I ignore him? He'd hate that, but he is my first officer. Even the *dreosen* shouldn't act too familiar with the prince. Not in front of the court. Or were the rules different for us? I'll let him take the lead.

Tightening the black mask on my face, I took a deep breath and joined the throngs of well-dressed nobles as they filed into the ballroom. It was a party for the ages and the air of excitement was contagious.

I stood near the wall, searching for anyone I recognized. There were hundreds of beautiful gowns in every color, and so many faces behind intricate masks.

"Impressive show, *dreosen*, and a beautiful gown," a familiar, deep voice complimented as they approached from behind—Avernought.

Apparently, I wasn't hard to find even with a mask.

His eyes were evaluating through the plain black mask covering only half his face. He wore a deep green doublet with fine, gold embroidery.

"Glad you got the chance to see, my lord," I said tightly. "No regrets about pledging me to the queen?"

"None." He cleared his throat. "Only that she forced you to do something so egregious. I do apologize for my recent absences. Her Majesty kept several of us in Rowane for meetings. I'm afraid that's why I've missed the last several Atrium appearances, but Arden promised to keep you abreast of any information."

Avernought lowered his voice and leaned closer.

"I also see the prince remains close to you," he added. "I take it your past has remained an unbreeched topic? Arden worries you might be distracted."

I glared. "The prince has nothing to do with this. The queen won't win her wars without demons. She has no choice but to keep me close."

"You think she didn't see them kneel for you?"

"What?" Confusion creased my forehead. They'd always kneeled. It wasn't news.

"Nothing." He glowered back at me. "Nothing at all. My interests are tied to you, and I only hope I wasn't wrong."

"What else has Arden told you?" I demanded.

"Damien isn't the only one who knows you, Reina. Now that the entire court has seen, you need to watch yourself. I expect a return on my investment."

"Appreciate the advice."

"Plenty where that came from. Be alert." Avernought nodded at me and walked away; surely, he caught my dour expression.

As Avernought left, Arden's words traipsed around my head while I moved through the crowd: *run for the woods—you'll be safe*.

The ballroom we stood in was staggering. Marble floors met stone walls in bursts of colored tile. Pillars stretched to ceilings that must have been three or four stories high, and chandeliers hung between a thousand banners of strung leaves all suspended by magic.

I grabbed a glass of sparkling wine from a passing tray and took slow sips as I looked through the crowd. I recognized several faces; some from my time with Arden and some as Armory makers. Tonight was a generous display of the queen's court, but I wanted to find my friends.

"Reina Sangrey, a pleasure." General Linden appeared in front of me. He was squat and severe-looking, even in his formal attire, weighed down by his own designations.

"An honor, General Linden," I replied with a bow. "I'm here to serve. My gift is Thera's."

"Indeed, it is." He smiled at my well-practiced words, but a narrow gaze scrutinized me.

I shivered. The man wasn't entirely unpleasant, but every part of him seemed more sinister up close. He stood only a foot away from me, and now I could see he was haunted. The shadows on his face reminded me of Arden; they were both men who traded in flesh.

"You look quite beautiful following an awe-inspiring performance. I know it was difficult, but it means everything to the Crown that you did well. I'm pleased to have run into you so early in the night," he remarked.

"Oh? And why is that?"

"I need to speak with Lord Avernought, but there might be reason to shorten your time in the Armory. It's uncommon of course, but we'll have further conversations with your maker about your importance to the Crown."

"Whatever the Crown deems appropriate."

He nodded. "Indeed, Lady Reina. Enjoy your evening. I'm sure we'll speak more about this. Her Majesty has many ideas for you."

"I look forward to them. Enjoy your evening, General Linden."

I gave a curt bow, and he disappeared. Shorten my time in the Armory? That would free me of two oaths, and there was nothing I wanted more.

A few minutes later, my eyes finally found the person I'd been looking for. Leena was across the room in her beautiful satin dress shimmering on her frame in a dark shade of green. Her unbound curls were tamed to one side and trailed down her back in blonde rivulets.

She'd tied a gold filigree mask to her face and looked like a goddess as she stood with the rest of our house in their varying shades of green.

"Leena! You're radiant," I exclaimed as I approached, and she hugged me.

"By the Seven," she said when she finally let go of me. "Holy gods, you did it, and now you look like this? You look like a queen in that dress. Aubra was right to make you keep the cape. And the necklace? Where did you get it? Actually, don't tell me yet. I have a few guesses."

"I'm sorry I wasn't there to get ready with you. I did promise—"

"Never apologize for breaking a promise because you were requested by the Crown," she said. "That's why we're all here, remember?"

"It's a relief to see you," I admitted.

"A lot's happened, that's for sure." Leena lowered her voice and gave me a wicked grin. "A week ago, you hadn't fucked a prince of Thera."

I ignored the jab but smiled despite. "What did I miss?"

She bit her lip and looked around. "Nothing much. Jaxon ran us through some drills earlier. We dueled some of the Queensguard knights in the arena. Have you seen it? I couldn't imagine dueling there. It fits at least a thousand people."

"Here's hoping we don't find out," I muttered.

Aixen and Varyn joined us as the music picked up and the wine flowed. I retold the story of destroying the altar at least four times and heard several versions of what it looked like from Aixen, Vera, and anyone else who felt the need to weigh in.

It wasn't until Tomas started to tell his version as the music came to a sudden stop and horns blared. Thera's song filled the ballroom, and the Queensguard Knighthood filed in wearing their Crown leathers and navy capes as they formed an aisle for their queen.

The three princes entered first. Farran and Lorcan wore thin-banded crowns and walked behind Cormac, whose crown was a smaller version of their mother's. They all donned the same silver masks, but there would be no mistaking who they were.

Even through the mask, Cormac's face was the most severe I'd seen it, while Lorcan and Farran's appeared blank. Something had happened, judging by the shifting of the crowd.

The queen strode in behind her sons without a mask. She wore a well-fitted navy gown cut from the same fabric as her sons' doublets. When she reached the dais, the music stopped and she pivoted to face her court.

The queen's fingers pressed to her neck, and tendrils of yellow sprouted from them as her voice filled the room.

"I wanted to thank everyone for being here tonight at the close of Autane. Again, I was reminded how successful our harvests have been this growing season, and though the days grow shorter, darker, and colder, we have all the means to face winter. The Seven are pleased, and we are blessed. Today proved it.

"So long we have waited for the demon wielder who would triumph over the old gods once and for all. We've all seen today that the impending darkness will be of no consequence to Thera. We are stronger not only by our dragons but by our Queensguard Knights and the demons we thought were lost. There is only the future and the generous Seven gods of Thera. All else is lost."

Applause rippled through the ballroom as the Queen flashed a lukewarm smile, but she wasn't done. Not yet. She raised her arms and continued.

"Many have requested a display of Armory talent, and tonight we will provide it. Our demon wielder was only the beginning; the Emerald and Ruby captains have promised a round of duels in exactly one hour to give the court a taste of what gifts protect us all.

"Finally," she said, unclasping her hands and gesticulating. "Before the night gets away from us, I have only one more announcement. It gives me the utmost pleasure to announce to the court the engagement of my sons."

Sons. All the blood left my face. Whispers filled the room like smoke.

"His Royal Highness the Crown Prince of Thera, Prince Cormac MacLaine, is formally betrothed to Lady Rosalind Verdura." A pause. A breath, and an eternity as I clutched my glass. "Prince Farran MacLaine is formally betrothed to Thera's beloved *dreosen* and the first of her name, Lady Reina Sangrey. We wish them all happiness and a fruitful marriage as the gods see fit."

My breath caught in my throat. The room stopped. Maybe the world itself. Everyone swiveled to look at me, and my legs threatened to give out.

Did Farran look terrified, too? It didn't matter. I was too far away to see, and part of me didn't want to know. I grabbed my skirt to run, but Leena gripped my arm, holding me in place. She was right; I knew she was right.

I was suddenly and irrevocably exposed. There wasn't a face in the room who could forget me. After my name, I heard nothing else the queen said.

Rage simmered against my skin, nearly frothing as uproarious applause filled the ballroom as the ringing in my ears drowned it out.

Leena tugged my arm and whispered, "Go up there, Reina. You have to dance with him."

Him. The Prince of Thera. Farran. Betrothed. The word stuck in my brain.

Leena pushed me.

Sometimes, we don't get choices.

This was just another one. I wanted to scream; I wanted to drag my mist of thrashing demons over the dais, but every eye of Thera watched me—again. So I put one foot in front of the other and approached the royals with a tight smile . . . my oldest magic trick.

I buried my biting words and bowed as I approached. Lady Rosalind Verdura did the same beside me, and neither of us stood until the queen invited us to rise.

My eyes locked onto Farran's. Even through the mask, he looked pale.

The princes stepped forward and took our hands. The ice in Farran's gaze felt impossible and at odds with the warmth of magic between us, but he led me to the floor.

Our bodies moved apart and back together with precision, knowing exactly the steps we needed to perform. It wasn't until the tempo shifted and more couples joined us as Farran led me into a dip and pulled me into him for a moment too long just to whisper in my ear, "Never like this."

When the song ended, he pulled me in again. I wanted it to feel the same; I wanted to enjoy it, but all I felt was dread wrapping its hand around my spine. "I need some air."

Farran nodded, and I walked to the terrace. Alone.

In my absence, several people swept in to congratulate their prince. This was far from the evening I had in mind. I stood on the terrace; my hands gripped the balcony as I peered into the garden below. I wanted to run, to scream, to do something other than suffocate in the open air.

A hand touched my shoulder, and I spun to see Leena standing there, looking at me, her face pinched in concern. "Did he know?" She asked, stopping beside me. Her delicate but deadly hands braced the railing as she looked out, mirroring me.

"I-I don't think so," I stammered. "No."

"Are you going to get out of it?"

"I don't know, Leena. I don't know about any of this."

"I'm sorry, Rein." Leena squeezed my hand. "We'll figure this out. I'll do whatever you ask."

I closed my eyes and ran my hand over the necklace; the warmth of the threads within it vibrated under my touch. Hatred for the queen coursed through my veins for every ounce of magic it contained. "Go back in and have fun, Leen. I'm fine—I'll be fine. I just need a moment."

"Of course," she said. Her hand squeezed mine again, but I didn't look up. "If you run, I'll understand."

"I won't miss the duels," I promised.

Leena let go of my hand and kissed my cheek. "No matter what," she whispered.

I sighed and said it back, twisting the ribbon tied around my wrist. "No matter what."

She returned to the ballroom, and I listened as the rap of her shoes faded. More people left the ballroom for the cool air on the terrace, but I ignored them. I didn't just need the cool air. I needed the breeze to remind me I was still alive. Still whole. Still, somehow, Reina Sangrey.

I was Arden's viper once, and now I'd be Thera's fucking princess. All of it was wrong, impossible, and irrevocable—I was going to throw up.

The memory of my Rite swelled back. The blood on my hands, the queen's last gasping breath and exactly what she'd said. I always wondered about it, but it was suddenly so much clearer.

The kingdom you rule will be devoid of life.

Princess was far too close to queen, and I wouldn't consider the possibility. Not when Farran was the third prince. I was a lot of things, but I wasn't that cruel.

The cold bit at my bones, but I wasn't ready.

I can do this. I repeated again and again as I tried to hold on. Everything shifted underneath my stupid, slippered feet. *I can do this. I'm Reina Sangrey.* I turned to go back inside, but my eyes immediately caught Farran's.

I froze. *I couldn't fucking do this.* There was too much, and now it lived in the swirling depths of those damn blue eyes.

"Walk with me?" Farran looked so much like a damned prince. From the emerald doublet perfectly fitted to his broad shoulders, to the hair without a piece out of place, and to the damn crown tangled in his fucking hair.

A crown I knew he hated with even more ferocity than I did at this moment.

"I suppose I don't have much of a choice?" I mumbled.

He frowned and extended his arm. The threads in my chest relaxed and warmed in his proximity, and I cursed them; I didn't want the reminder. Yesterday was years ago.

I didn't take it. Instead, I stalked away from the terrace, knowing he'd follow. I ambled down the stairs into the same garden from the night before. The moon was bright and cast shadows as we walked.

A thousand emotions sat heavy on my shoulders, because all I needed was more time. More time to tell him who I was in Lower Rowane, and *why*—any truth now would be a betrayal, and all of it turned sour on my lips: *I was trapped.*

"She told Cormac and I moments before we walked in," Farran finally said as we rounded another row of hedges, away from everyone else. "I'll speak with her tomorrow and try to find a way out. I'll tell her you're of more use to Thera as a knight than a princess. Cormac will agree with me."

"It won't work," my voice croaked. "She decided."

"You don't want *this*, Reina," he pleaded like it would make a difference.

I stopped and glared at him, his expression strained. "You don't know what I want." I regretted the words as soon as they left my lips. Hurt flashed across his face, and I sighed. "I don't know what I want. I just want a choice, just *one* fucking choice, and this was never one I thought I'd have."

My head snapped up to make sure no one had heard.

"It's fine," Farran said lowly. "This is a dead end. Creighton is guarding the entrance. No one can hear us."

A small relief. I looked up and saw a pergola with a bench at the end of the hedgerow. I kept walking and didn't look at him until I sat down. My feet were killing me, and this dress was far too much. Farran remained standing and stared at me. He stared as though my face could tell him what we were—like I had any idea.

I gestured to the space next to me. "You can sit."

He did, and I leaned into the warmth like it was second nature. Then I jerked back, unsure if he noticed, as he pushed some of my skirt aside.

"I wanted a choice, too," he finally said. "My mother did this. I'm sure she thinks she's clever."

I said nothing. I couldn't. Part of me agreed; the Queens-guard was only a knighthood. If she wanted her weapon close, she'd keep it where no one would dare to touch it—where *I* couldn't betray it without ruining myself, and where no other kingdom could reach.

"I should have suspected it," I whispered.

Farran's hand squeezed mine. "No. You cannot blame yourself. What's done is done. Tomorrow, we'll fix it. No, fuck that. I'll fix it. It never should have happened, not like this."

Not like this.

A breeze drifted through, and I shivered. His arm wrapped around my waist as I untied my mask and watched him do the same.

He whispered, "For what it's worth, I would have chosen you. Demon wielder or no, I've meant everything I've said to you, Reina. This is the only day with you I wish I could take back. You deserve better, more than this."

The emotions swelled back: the guilt and hurt. Tears welled in my eyes. Deserve was the wrong word to use, and the emotions curdled in my chest.

"Farran," I said his name gently. My magic curled around the word. His gaze steadied on mine as I forced out measured honesty. "I do want you. Crown or not. But—" My voice cracked as my hand reached for his cheek. "I've never been a choice for you either, and you know that. Your life was sworn to me before we met. You don't know me."

"I know enough." His hand grabbed mine, and his eyes were fierce. "The day I met you in the Armory felt like I was meeting the rest of my life, so don't ever think I didn't have a choice, Reina. Every moment we were together, you were a choice I made. I chose you that night on the beach. I chose you those nights in the woods, and I'd choose you every day after this—blood oath or not. I hate that I swore it. I hated the oath until the night I found out the *dreosen* was you."

Farran stopped talking. His arm stiffened on my back, and his eyes looked at the ground; he never meant to say what he did. Something in my chest shivered, and gods be damned was I undeserving of this moment.

"I lied to myself every time I said it was a mistake," I breathed, and a sliver of truth spilled out. "The first time you kissed me, I never wanted anything else."

His voice hardened. "You don't want the crown, Reina."

"I want you," I murmured, and it was the truest thing I could say.

He took both my hands in his. "You are strong and beautiful, Reina Sangrey. You want to be a Queensguard Knight. That's all you've ever wanted. If we go through with this, you need to understand we don't go back to the Armory, not the same way—"

I looked at him, and it struck me. I froze. Not returning would be a death sentence. I had to go back to the Armory. There was no other way. A twinge in my back dripped with grief, and the words came out of me as a whisper, "The Queensguard doesn't marry."

His expression pained. "Rules can be broken. I'll be the Prince Commander, but you . . . you'd be a princess. You'll have your demons; you'll be expected to use them when it's needed, but you become infinitely more important than just a knight."

"Why?" My eyes flashed. "Don't tell me a princess can't hold a sword when our goddesses led wars. Besides, your oath requires it. I have to rise to the Queensguard."

His voice was low and sobering. "If anything happens to Cormac before he has an heir, the Crown falls to *us*. Our duty to the Crown changes with a marriage vow. Even after your rise."

I was silent. My head spun . . . My heart wanted so much of this, but I couldn't. What was I supposed to say?

"We'll find a way," Farran said, his voice hardly above a whisper. "If you're sure about this, let me try to get it right."

"Get it right?" I repeated, my brows furrowing as I pondered his words.

Farran kept my hands in his as he moved from the bench to the ground in front of me, his gaze steady, as every nerve in my body stiffened. He looked at me with the same gaze I'd fallen into before.

"I've spent these last months choosing you because you leave me in awe of your kindness, your strength, and your grace in facing the impossible. I never want to know another day without that feeling, without that awe. If you choose, I pledge my life, my future, and my sword to you, Reina Sangrey."

Farran's hands squeezed mine; tears brimmed my eyes as I pressed my forehead to his and said the only words I could gather, "My heart is yours."

All of this was self-indulgent and tenuous, but none of it was a lie. I meant every word, even as the truth crawled closer. I meant every word, and it would kill me later. I was sure it would.

His thumb brushed away a tear before he kissed me. Slow and deep, like we had all the time in the world when we had anything but.

Too soon, Farran pulled away. "I'd love a second chance to dance with my betrothed."

Betrothed.

It was real. I was fucked, and so was he . . . whether or not he knew. My heart hammered in my chest. So much was said, and so much left unsaid.

This wasn't the plan. This was everything I was warned against, and I was falling. The hand of fate closed in around my neck, and all I could do was choke out *thank you.*

"I would love nothing more," I said with a fretful smile.

We tied our masks back on and walked through the garden to the palace. Tomorrow would be for worrying. I knew exactly the venom running through my veins. Sooner or later, whatever we had would shrivel into a grief-laden memory just like everyone I'd loved before.

Music and laughter rolled out of the jovial room and onto the terrace as we approached. Aixen danced in circles with one of Cormac's guards, while Leena spun on the floor with a woman who wore a beautiful cherry gown.

Farran and I as the prince and the *dreosen*, the demon wielder of Thera—*betrothed*.

It was indulgent to stand in the middle of the ballroom, with the fire of his hand in mine and his other on the small of my back as our bodies followed the tempo of the music. He spun me and reeled me back to his chest.

His breath was hot on my neck. "I know I told you I loved the dress, but it wasn't the whole truth."

I turned as the tempo slowed; my chest against his as we swayed.

"You're sleeping in my room tonight, *Princess*." The tug of desire dragged across my skin and he growled, "And I expect to end this night buried inside you with that dress on my floor, doing *everything* that would make the Seven blush."

I shuddered in his arms and spun around, pressing my lips to his ear. "Only if you spread your wings."

"Anything for you." He bit the lobe of my ear while I flushed.

This was the other side of the precipice and everything I wanted to hear. Shock still locked my limbs and screamed at me, insisting this was a dream, until Farran leaned forward and his lips touched mine.

The world fell away, and I kissed him back. I wanted too much more, but I quickly remembered we were in a room filled with all of Thera.

"Ignore them," he whispered. "I'm the prince, and you just agreed to be their princess. We'll figure this out. I promise."

Farran kissed me again before I protested. *Gods*, did I want more than a kiss. His lips were so soft and controlled, but I shivered at the memory of how they felt last night. When the song ended, Farran didn't let go of my hand.

I opened my mouth to say something, but he had spun around when a guard tapped his shoulder and whispered hurriedly.

It wasn't Creighton, nor a Queensguard Knight; it was someone else from the palace. "I'll be back," Farran said and kissed my cheek. "I need to speak with my brothers."

He disappeared through the crowd, and I noticed several women stared at me, whispering. I supposed that was something I'd need to get used to because there was no more hiding: I would be their princess.

It wasn't my choice, but I'd play the game, so long as Farran was at my side.

And so long as it brought me closer to the queen.

For no reason, Arden's words haunted me again. *Just in time to watch the war begin.*

I shivered and took a sip of wine as my other hand moved to the necklace hanging weightlessly over my chest. It pulsed with the old magic of the altar.

The Queen of Thera could pretend all she wanted that the old gods were gone, but I felt them, and they waited. She needed their power because the truth was the new gods had nothing.

CHAPTER 39

Once I regained my confidence and composure, I strode through the crowd to find Leena leaning against a pillar near the entrance of the ballroom. Her gold eyes surveilled, watching with an intensity that concerned me.

"You look much better dancing with Farran when you have color in your face."

I glared, but my face softened. "Who were you dancing with?"

"A Ruby soldier from a province in the South. She was trying to teach me how they dance there. It's quite exciting, actually. I'll show you when we're not in these gowns." Leena lowered her voice and leaned towards me. "Does something seem . . . off to you?"

"Outside of my engagement announcement and the queen expecting duels any minute?"

Leena nodded, though her face returned none of the playfulness. "We're all wearing masks. Several of the guards just moved, and the queen's dragon riders left about twenty minutes ago."

My eyes narrowed as I turned to watch the room. "How do you know?"

"I watched. They all have the same signet on their collars. Jaxon always wears it, and they all left together. Seems a bit suspicious, is all. Where's your prince?"

I winced. "Speaking with his brothers. Maybe they're running a drill on the border in the morning."

"Perhaps. But there are several men I don't recognize who aren't dancing." Leena looked at me with steeled eyes and asked, "Did Arden warn you about something this morning?"

I froze. Of course, Leena caught it.

"He told me to run for the woods."

"Perhaps we should get closer to the doors." Her gaze flicked to the other side of the ballroom where we caught Aixen spinning across the floor with a different nobleman in a silver doublet.

I swallowed. "Arden is wrong more often than he's right."

"You're heard what they say about blind roosters," Leena muttered.

I didn't, but I wouldn't panic. The beating heart of magic hanging from my neck and the cool weight of the dagger on my thigh were my anchors. If anything came, I was ready to fight. I was always ready to fight, especially with the way rage simmered in my blood.

The music stopped. All eyes in the room swiveled to the dais where General Linden stood beside the queen, fingers pressed to his neck and flanked by several Queensguard knights.

Their stoic faces scanned the crowd while Avi and the Ruby Captain stood at attention, one positioned on either side of the general.

Linden's voice filled the room, booming, and grating in equal measure. "We've heard your concerns about the cost of maintaining the Armory, and tonight we hope to show you what it's capable of." He paused as murmurs rippled through the audience. "Each of my Armory captains have chosen three soldiers for a duel so that you might glimpse the power protecting us and our Crown. Soldiers, join me at the dais."

Leena's shoulders slumped, but she drew them back and walked towards the dais without a parting word. What was there to say? Of course, Avi picked her. Shadows were nearly as rare as demons. The crowd parted for her, and Leena stopped beside Avi with her hands clasped.

She looked radiant, like she belonged on the dais in the dress, power searing through her. Soon, the court would see her for who she was, and maybe they'd forget about me.

Vera and Aixen stepped up next. My eyes roved over the three Ruby soldiers opposite. I knew their names and a few other stories, but we never talked about gifts on our trek to Rowane. All I remembered was the captain wielded light, and he wasn't dueling.

Fuck, I needed to be better at assessing threats. They drilled it into us the first two weeks at the Armory and assumed we'd learn in practice. I should have known what they could wield, but I wasn't dueling.

The Queensguard fanned out, clearing the center of the ballroom. I shuddered as Leena's words drifted over me again. Where were the dragon riders? My head swiveled towards the other doors leading in from the great hall. Farran and his brothers walked back into the room, their faces unreadable.

Should I go up there? No one told me the rules, but I had no interest in crossing the crowd, so I remained against the pillar, leaning as I stood on my tiptoes to see better just in time for General Linden to announce the first duel.

"Aixen Reid of the Emerald House and Tara Steitz of the Ruby House—to your positions. The duel begins on your mark."

Linden's hand fell away from his neck, and he took his place beside the queen who sat in her silver throne. Aixen strode to the center of the ballroom and faced Tara. She didn't wear a gown, rather a long, ruby and gold-trimmed jacket brushing her ankles. Aixen looked sharp in his own tailored emerald doublet and coiffed flaxen hair.

The ballroom was silent, barring the scuffle of feet as they circled one another and waited; Aixen never struck first.

Two lines of tension formed between Aixen's eyes as he circled. Silver dripped from his right hand like beads of water. Then it formed into a scabbard extending as a part of his arm that couldn't be knocked loose.

Tara hardly registered the magic. Instead, she stopped in her tracks and closed her eyes. Briefly, Aixen looked like he might charge, until a snap rang through the room with the deep crack of a bone cleaved in two.

There were several shocked gasps as two Taras stared at Aixen. Each held a long, narrow sword and smirked, daring Aixen to strike. He sprang forward, towards one of Tara's forms, but his sword swung at empty air and he cried out as it struck the marble ground. He pivoted as her second form reappeared, rearing her saber at him.

Liquid silver splayed out in a jagged shield. Tara struck the shield and metal sang on contact. Aixen twisted his hand, sending silver to swallow more and more of the sword until it consumed her hand. It weighed down her shoulder, forcing her to her knee.

He didn't have time to register how panicked she looked as he let go and scrambled to his feet, forging another sword out of thin air to parry back the other Tara who closed in on him with vengeance in her eyes.

Swords screamed as he blocked every sweeping hit and pushed her back. Then, with a flick of Aixen's wrist, a root of silver careened towards her, knocking her off balance. She faltered, but Aixen didn't.

The point of his sword pressed into her throat, and shock filled her eyes. He had a choice, and his silver drew back as Tara's double dissolved into mist at the end of his blade.

Her true form, paces away, was freed from the silver hold. Shards of it clinked as she shook loose and drew a long knife from her waist. Then she ran at Aixen with animalistic ferocity.

Before he shifted his silver into a shield, she'd ducked under his arm, grabbed his waist, and pressed her knife to his throat.

His silver vanished entirely . . . It was Tara's choice now. Applause rang through the room, but Tara didn't drop the knife. My heart hammered. I was ready to knock her to the floor until two knights separated them. I sighed in relief, and the center cleared.

Next, Vera strode forward in her own green gown and kicked off her slippers. Across from her, a scrawny man from Ruby analyzed every move with stark yellow eyes as he entered the ring. He was all limbs, gangly and imposing.

Vera stood in the center with a smile, both arms stretched out as she tethered herself. She had no weapons, while a too-large broadsword hung from his hip. There was no way a man like him could hold it steady long enough to win a duel. He underestimated Vera.

Linden's voice rang. "The duel begins on your mark."

Vera didn't wait; thick, thorned vines sprang out of the marble and threw the Ruby man backward. Her lips curled into a smile as our *balen* stepped forward—she looked like the earthen goddess, Balris, as vines trailed behind and power surged green and wild beneath her skin.

The room gasped. I craned to look, rebalancing on the tips of my toes. The Ruby man dragged himself to his feet, but he wasn't the same.

No, he'd transformed into something *other*. His clothes had torn apart, his face lengthened, and every muscle tripled in size. He towered over Vera and everything else in the room as he lumbered towards her.

He roared, and the sound reverberated, scraping against my chest like the talons of a griffon while Vera's eyes went wide.

She drew back and dragged on her magic. Her eyes flashed a vibrant green, and the Ruby soldier charged, claws outstretched. Luckily, the transformed soldier was clumsy where Vera was lithe. She met every swipe with a whipping vine. Frustration twisted his face as he fought them off.

Then a thick magicked root sprang out and trapped his leg; he cried out, and the tenor of it shook my ribs as his broadsword flew across the makeshift arena. He was too strong and tore out of the grip like it was an old, fraying rope and not a root the size of my thigh.

Vera needed to be faster. She screamed. More vines lurched for him and transformed the center of the ballroom into a forest until the right tendril grabbed his neck and dragged him to the ground, clawing at his throat. Vera hadn't won yet.

Power still surged in undulating green as she waited with bated breath. She wasn't letting go until he surrendered.

The soldier transformed back into his human form. Vera gasped but urged the thorned vines and roots even as the soldier tried to crawl out. They coiled around him in a mess like roiling constrictors, protesting his efforts.

He yelled and struggled, every movement tearing more and more of his skin. He had no weapon. She had trapped him, and it was over as several knights blustered between them.

Vera retracted her vines, leaving the Ruby soldier standing naked in the ballroom, surrounded by debris and riddled with cuts. He smiled coyly and bowed towards Vera before being escorted out by a fellow Ruby soldier.

Applause was delayed, but it was raucous when Vera walked back to the dais with a grin. She'd earned the win almost too easily. Beside her, Leena gulped. It was her turn now.

Farran stood behind them, and I caught him whispering something that turned up the corner of her lip just before she stepped into the ring. Blood from the Ruby soldier speckled the marble, and several of Vera's vines still laid limp between cracks in the floor.

Any assurance Farran gave Leena drained the moment she stopped in the center and realized every eye in the room was on her.

I knew Leena inside and out. This was a performance for the court, which was everything she tried to escape, but here she was, again: in a pretty gown, parading around for coin she'd never see.

The violence was different, but the implications were the same.

Leena's hands fisted at her sides, and her jaw tightened as the last Ruby soldier walked out. Something slithered down my spine; a keen and cold sense of dread I couldn't shake.

It was the same woman Leena had danced with earlier. The Ruby soldier wore a full cherry-red ball gown with matching gloves, and a maker's cord stretched across her chest. She stared down the bridge of her nose at Leena, who tipped up her chin to meet it.

I didn't catch the woman's name, but it was mesmerizing to watch the two square up and circle each other as they drew their gifts.

Shadows gathered in Leena's hands like a concentrated storm while the woman watched Leena with razor-sharp eyes—no indication, yet, of what power lay behind them.

Black seeped from Leena's feet and raced towards the woman in wild, coordinated streaks. They collided with her in a cloud of smoke and tipped her off balance. But she easily regained her footing, extended her arm, and something clear hurtled towards Leena. Leena's eyes widened, and I gasped.

Leena gripped her shadows to block the ice, meeting in a spectacular shatter. People screamed as I realized it wasn't ice—it was glass, fucking glass.

Another shadow erupted from Leena instantaneously as the Ruby soldier pelted her with glass daggers in a hailstorm of crystal. I could barely see through the storm of black and the glitter of broken glass.

Leena shrouded them in her shadows as the two gifts collided, punctuated by explosions of glass. Until the howl and shriek of a fucking shadow hound cut through. My blood turned to ice.

That was a death sentence if the soldier didn't back off. I cursed and kicked off the pillar, needing to get closer. I needed to see Leena. She wouldn't use a shadow hound in a duel unless something went wrong.

I pushed through a few people. Everyone in the crowd squinted and craned, trying to see through the wall of shadows closing them in. Glass kept shattering within it, muffled as rain on the Atrium ceiling. Another step. I was almost there, but then a hand grabbed my arm and jerked me back.

I whipped around and glared. Aixen stood there, his doublet torn and a shadow of concern across his face as he stared into the same storm of black in the center of the ballroom.

"Don't even think about it," he muttered. "Leena will be fine."

"This is taking too long!" I protested.

His jaw was tight and limned with concern. I could see the twitch even as he tried to reassure me. "They're evenly matched," he said.

A ball of fire screeched overhead and barreled through the wall of shadows like they were nothing. It crashed and exploded only a few feet above the dais, colliding with a tapestry and setting it alight. Screaming and confusion erupted.

Aixen looked around, shaking the silver from his hand, shaping it back into a sword as he pressed closer to me, his other hand still tight on my arm.

Where the fuck was Leena? I didn't hear the hound. Then I glanced over my shoulder and the shadows had vanished as more fire flew over us, followed by a blast that sent glass shards flying in a thousand directions. We ducked to shield our faces.

The sound of steel rang as Queensguard knights drew their swords at once and sprinted for the dais. There were shouts of, "*Get the queen!*" and "*Dreites!*"

Dreites. My blood ran cold. The palace was under attack.

People screamed, and several scattered from the area around the dais, but nothing else happened, not yet. I reached for my dagger and eyed the exit, but I didn't grab it, not yet. *Run for the woods.*

I didn't trust Arden, but I didn't trust this either. I pulled Aixen through the crowd toward the terrace. He walked in step with me, like a fucking guard, but I didn't have a sword, just one dagger, surging magic and a few demons if they'd still listen to me.

I scanned the room as we hurried and accidentally made eye contact with a man I didn't know. Something shadowed over his face and turned sour in my stomach. He snarled and sprinted for us. Aixen dragged me by the arm, but we couldn't move fast enough.

The man was on me until Aixen spun and caught his chest with his sword, silver surging forward through the man in a spray of crimson.

Blood splattered us as the man fell. There wasn't time to breathe—or notice how wet my dress was—we had to keep moving.

Step by step, we made it through the thrashing, screaming, shouting as everyone clawed for escape. I reached in my gown, grabbed the vial, and downed the bitter roots from Arden. A sigil wouldn't stop me tonight.

Fire hurtled overhead, more shards of glass crashed like cursed rain, and the sound of steel drowned out everything except for the sudden intrusion of a voice I wouldn't acknowledge that I'd heard before.

It itched against my scalp like a long-forgotten night terror.

"*We've only come for the* dreosen."

My face blanched, but my feet didn't stop. The fuck they didn't.

The woods—I needed to get out. The terrace was so close, and Queensguard knights closed in, but I didn't trust them either. Not right now. I sprinted and barely heard Aixen curse as he shoved people out of the way.

Avi and Blaise also had to be around somewhere. I hadn't seen Leena since her duel began, and I hadn't seen Farran.

For a split second, I hoped it would stay that way. No one goes down with me . . . not tonight.

My feet pounded on the terrace, and cold night air struck my face. I flinched. The massacre behind us echoed and writhed as the dreites tore the ballroom apart.

Another hand grabbed my arm. I whipped around to see Avi, her sword bloodied and eyes wide.

"Don't move," she commanded. "They're not taking you."

Avi, Aixen, and Blaise closed around me like we faced a pack of fucking wolves and not several dreites with magic beyond comprehension. Tomas ran for us. Flames spread out behind him in the impressive shape of wings as I unsheathed my dagger.

It was all I had as more shouting punctuated the air and people fanned out from the terrace, away from where we stood. Queensguard knights ran towards us. I reached for the necklace with my other hand and tugged on the magic, hoping it would turn into something useful.

I needed to run and I needed no one else to follow. I was ready to stab anyone who tried.

Run for the woods.

I backed up. More faces closed in, and Tomas threw a blast of fire at the crowd: a single warning . . . but it didn't work. A stream of propulsion collided with it and sent us all flying backwards, knocking the dagger out of my hand. I tumbled down the terrace stairs and saw red as my head hit a step. Pain rippled through my skull.

I groaned and desperately yanked a thread. A demon appeared at the top of the stairs, but it simply stood as the taste of blood filled my mouth.

The thoughts and commands wouldn't come. Something was wrong.

Get up, get the fuck up. I cursed at myself and tried to scramble onto my feet, but hands dipped under my armpits and dragged me onto my legs before I mounted them myself.

Shadows filled the terrace. Leena was alive as I swayed as the grip tightened around me. I lifted my knee and brought my foot down as hard as I could on whoever held me. I needed to get to the woods. I was out of options.

Nothing, not even a grunt of pain. I wriggled, kicking haphazardly and twisting to bite—

"Not so fast, *valdronna*," the captor's voice whispered into my ear, and a chill clamped around my spine as my magic locked.

I felt sick all over again as the sharp edge of a dagger pressed against my throat. My vision wavered; I squinted through the starry patterns and saw my demon standing before me, but it didn't move; it did nothing but watch. My head throbbed. There was more indistinct yelling.

Whoever held me waited for something or someone. No doubt a dreite. "Fuck," he muttered. Good.

The dagger fell. Abruptly, he started to drag me to the forest line. I struggled in his grip, attempting to kick and bite, and scream, but I wasn't strong enough. Every muscle in my body was too heavy.

I clawed at my magic, but it fell through my fingers like dry sand until another vicious wall of propulsion struck. It sent us both flying.

I landed hard on my elbow, and the pain crackled through all of my body as the world turned over. This time I vomited and tried to roll to my feet, but my body wouldn't obey. The pain was blinding. I couldn't give up.

"Let her go!" someone shouted as I tried to get to my feet, while my other arm dangled and seared. I stood, swaying like a tall, thin pine in the wind, but I was breaking.

Stiff arms caught me again and crushed my arm, sending a jolt of pain so sharp I cried out. A dagger weighed on my throat again, cold and hungry for blood. I forced my eyes open. Through tears, the palace appeared to be on fire.

"Do it," I choked. My voice was coated in vomit and blood. My words sounded like they'd been scraped over stone and left for dead .

The dagger bit my neck as the dreite took another step back.

The bones in my elbow ground. and I screamed. On the fucking Seven.

"Don't come any closer," he shouted at whoever walked towards us.

I forced my too-heavy eyes open. The garden didn't come into focus, but I made out the bits and pieces swimming around my failing vision.

Several people stood in front of me. Fire leaped, and the pure blue of light magic spilled from someone's hands. Any other details faded away.

"Let her go," Farran's familiar voice threatened, cutting through my pain. The silver of his wings and their outline against the inferno made him look like a god through my unfocused eyes.

The princes were on either side of him, each with several guards and knights—every single sword drawn and ready, magic in hand.

The man holding me jerked. Again the dagger bit, and I yelped. The pain was unbearable, and I was sure tears streamed down my face unbidden.

"I'm fine," I spat, trying to mask the pain. No one needed to know I couldn't fucking stand. "Take me, but no one else."

"*No!*" Cormac bellowed, and I wished he hadn't. I wanted this to be over. "The Crown will meet any price. If any harm comes to her, it will be considered an act of war. She is Theranian."

Theranian. The word swirled around my brain like thick smoke, and my head lolled. It was all too heavy. I was going to die—maybe not here, but certainly later—and all the men could do was talk.

"I have no intention of harming her, Prince. Perhaps your mother never told you, but your *dreosen* belongs to us, and we're taking her back. There is no price to pay. There is no price we will accept."

I blinked. Several large Queensguard knights, steeped in magic, stepped closer.

My elbow throbbed, and I squeezed my eyes and tried to focus and drag out some of the pain, but my magic didn't bend, it didn't shiver.

Everything I had kept slipping away, just like in Beven. My eyes swiveled and caught Farran's somehow. There was a beautiful storm in them. It raged as he realized it, too. I was cold and hot all at once, and maybe this is how death felt.

Farran rushed forward. "Remove the sigil by order of the Crown. It will *kill* her." His voice was soothing, even when it commanded. Sigil? How? My knees buckled. They all saw it, and they all lurched, but the dreite tightened his grip and pulled me closer. I screamed as my elbow ground and the blade went deeper.

"It will not," the dreite barked. "You know nothing of what she's capable of." Anger and panic laced his voice as it vibrated against my back. He was cornered, but this wasn't over.

The dreite was wrong; it would. The thrum of magic had disappeared, and the flicker of my own heart faded as my consciousness waned. If he let go, I'd fall to the ground in a heap of limbs and gown. . . I was nothing now.

My demons had abandoned me, and the Crown had no teeth in the wake of the dreites. The Queen miscalculated and now neither side could let me die, even if I begged for it.

"Fine—If you take her, you take me too."

No. My eyes rolled open for a brief second, just enough to catch Farran holding his palm up to silence his brothers and their guards.

The dagger loosened against my throat . . . the demon wielder, and a prince of Thera . . . How could they say no?

Some force of magic blasted from behind Farran, forcing him to his knees, and I screamed. That was the last thing I remembered before it all went black.

Just in time to watch the war begin.

CHAPTER 40

SUNLIGHT STREAMED THROUGH A window, and soft bedding ruffled beneath my aching body as I woke. Everything felt deeply unfamiliar: it was much too quiet, much too still, and the sheets in the palace certainly weren't this soft.

My head swam, heavy with the memories of what had come before. Farran's voice . . . my friends' faces . . . a blade to my throat. I swallowed as fear coalesced, and my magic was nowhere to be found. I shivered in its absence and tried to move, but even my arms felt too heavy.

I closed my eyes. Breathing as memories continued to flood, slowly at first, then swift—Arden's warning, destroying an altar dedicated to the old gods, a celebration . . . and then the betrothal.

My betrothal . . . to Farran. *Farran.*

"Take me, too."

I sat straight up, remembering how I screamed. He had to be here . . . wherever here was. Throwing back the sheet, I winced at the pain in my elbow. Someone had mended it so the bones didn't grind, but it was still tender. Standing on wobbly legs, I was at least thankful someone had dressed me in a tunic and trousers.

I needed to find him—*now.* I needed to know he was safe. Sparing a quick glance out the window, the landscape was foreign to me. It wasn't the palace, and I was nearly sure we couldn't be in Thera. We were hostages.

The door opened, and I spun around, instinctively reaching for my thigh but neither a sheath nor dagger was there. Nor was there a knife in sight.

A woman stood in the doorframe, dressed in plain clothes with wide eyes. "You're awake. Let me—"

"Where is Farran? The Theranian Prince? Tell me now," I barked.

"Oh," she said, face paling. "Down the hall. Let me bring him to you, Your Majesty."

Majesty? I was betrothed, that's what I remembered. Nothing else changed. What else happened? How long was I out? A few minutes later, footsteps shuffled again. The woman guided Farran into my room. He stared at me warily.

His blue eyes raged as they held my gaze. My heart cratered. Something was terribly wrong.

Farran cleared his throat, his voice cold in a way I'd never heard before. "When were you going to tell me you were the Queen of Noterra?"

"*What?*" I gaped.

There was no air in the room. The words sucked it all out. What he said was wrong, a lie.

"No. No, that's not true. It can't be." I looked around the room, anywhere but his eyes. It couldn't have been true. Arden's viper, traitor to the Crown, and destined to murder the Queen of Thera, but never that.

"Do not lie to me," he ground out, eyes cutting straight through my confusion as my heart rattled in my chest.

"I'm not," I whispered, but the rage in his face only burned brighter.

"You have been unconscious for two days," he said. "We're one day south of the Noterran capital, because they didn't want to travel any further with you in that condition, and I don't want to go any further with a woman I don't recognize. I'll be returning to Thera and telling my mother it was all a fucking mistake," He spat the one word I never thought he'd use and took a step closer. "You know, I was *terrified* when he held the knife to your throat, Reina. Is that even your fucking name?"

"Yes." I steeled against the accusation in his voice. Tears brimmed in my eyes, but I refused to let them fall. Instead, I clung to the bit of anger knotted in my chest. "Please, *please* let me explain."

"I'm leaving for Rowane tonight. I don't care what you do as long as it doesn't kill me." *The oath.* Fuck. My heart pounded in my ears as I clawed through my brain, looking for something to say.

Taking a shaky breath as I stared at the floor, I straightened and spoke as clearly as I could. "I am Reina Sangrey. My mother was a noble from Noterra. She died with my father in Lower Rowane, at the hands of the Crown by order of treason. That's the truth. I swear to it on every god and star, above and below."

"She died according to the Theranian law. Being a noble from the Darklands is treason."

"So is worshiping the old gods, even if your father is the prince consort," I snapped.

Farran glared back. "Your father was the fucking king."

I shook my head. "A noble maybe, but never the king. The king had no heir. He died in the streets of their city when Thera attacked with dragons. That's the history—it was in your books and mine." I looked up at him. "Truly, if that's what they're telling you, I didn't know."

Farran remained skeptical. "What happened after your mother died?"

"I worked for a friend of Avernought's," I said, watching the way his face measured my words. "I promised to serve the Queensguard in exchange for my brother's safety."

"Who?" he demanded.

My jaw tightened, and I stared ahead. "It doesn't matter."

"It matters to me. I will find out, even if you choose not to tell me." A threat underlined his words like a promise.

I wanted to lie. I wanted to scream, but we were past that, and the words came out as a whisper of admission. "Damien Arden."

"The traitor? The one who's shown up to court and told everyone he'll have a hand in the end of Thera? Tell me, did you work in his dens? Were you sent to Armory to fucking lure me away? Or maybe you're supposed to find a way to the crown prince instead? Gods fucking know—"

"*No.*" The words I wanted to say died on my tongue.

I didn't know the lie; I didn't know myself. My eyes burned with tears, and I wouldn't hold them back much longer.

"I never worked in his dens. Arden trapped me in a blood oath when I was ten—"

"Prove it."

"Farran—"

"Show. Me."

I bit my lip and hesitated. Not like this, never like this, but there was no way out, no other shred of proof. I turned my back to him and lifted the tunic so he could see the shame carved into my back . . . the same way his was carved into his chest.

We were both owned, body and soul, and there was silence as his eyes burned into it, tracing the mark.

I knew what he saw. I cried the first time I saw it: a snake slithered along my spine cloaking a dagger. This far away from the Armory, I knew the oath was fragile—his would be too.

Today, the snake laid in wait for something finite. For anything that could change my fate. The moment it happened, it would strike and choke the breath from my lungs and his.

"Say something," I pleaded as the tunic slipped out of my fingers.

Farran breathed, and I wished I hadn't. "You're Arden's viper."

And there was nothing I could say but, "Yes."

"And Noterra's Queen."

Slowly, I turned to face him as my heart fractured. "I didn't fucking know."

"Arden is a traitor, and I let you into the palace. The *viper* of Rowane slept in my fucking bed."

"Arden saved my life and my brother's when your mother would have killed us."

Farran jerked his head back and looked at the ceiling. He was exasperated. "That's what happens when someone betrays the Crown, or do you think you're above it, because Arden found a way to make it fucking impossible?" He looked straight at me, his eyes too calm and voice too even. "The Queensguard has an order to kill on sight when they find his viper. Did you know that?"

I swallowed. "No." But I suspected.

He looked past me, out the window, and whispered, "You nearly killed Cormac."

Anger flashed. I'd never touch a prince even if Arden had begged me, and he knew better. "That's a lie."

"Is it?" Farran pressed.

I look at the wall behind his shoulder. It was plain gray stone. "I've never had an order on a prince; Arden's guild doesn't play with royalty." I kept my tone even, but everything in me shook. "If I had received an order, I would've finished the fucking job."

It was the wrong thing to say, but it was true.

His jaw ticked. "How many did you kill for him?"

"He held my oath over my head. If I fought back, he would . . . he was creative about punishment."

Farran's eyes flared and seethed. "Why didn't you leave?"

"I couldn't." I glared. "My debt to him could only be repaid by my rise to the Queensguard. That's the condition of the oath. That's how I saved my brother. I tried everything in my damn power to get out of it."

Silence drifted. There was nothing I wanted to say.

"I meant what I said," Farran said in a whimper, his tortured gaze lifting to mine. Tears lined his voice as I tried to hold back my own. "You tricked me. I fell for Reina Sangrey, the self-assured *dreosen*. Not Arden's fucking viper and enemy to my family."

I deserved this. I hung my head; this wasn't the worst of it.

"I'm still Reina," I mumbled.

"For your sake, I hope that's true." He paused, eyes sharpening on mine as I dared to look. "You know marrying me to the *dreosen* was my mother trying to consolidate her power. I'm not playing two sides of a war when she finds out who you are. That you do alone, Your *Majesty*."

I bristled, even as my heart splintered. "I'm not a queen."

"Every soul in this fucking castle believes differently. It's only a matter of time before you see the same."

"I don't want it." I choked.

"You think it's a choice?" His voice was empty and tired. So was I.

"No."

He nodded and left the room without a parting word.

Betrothed in front of the entire court of Thera, with no escape in sight. It was a joke; I knew better than to let myself get close to him, and here I was. Funny how immediate retribution could be when it was deserved.

I curled back up on the bed and drifted into a fitful, pained sleep that was nothing but a string of unbidden memories that didn't end until a serving girl dressed me for dinner.

The castle wasn't extravagant. Stone floors, stone walls, with a few crooked paintings hung between hallway doors. Wherever we were, it was damp and cold, save for the few paces around one of the nearly ten roaring fireplaces we passed.

I'd seen more mantels now than people as I followed the serving girl through the maze of stone into a dining room where a long table had been set for dinner.

Two more fireplaces flickered on either side of the room. I was the first to arrive, and she sat me at one end of the table. I didn't deserve this seat. Not in a thousand years.

Footsteps echoed in the hall and I rose, exhausted and completely out of my depth. Several dreites I didn't recognize came into the room, bowed, and sat intermixed with a few faces I did know. It didn't matter. I hated them all the same.

My sleeping magic shifted uncomfortably in my chest like it had in Beven, in the woods. This time, rage simmered beneath it.

Farran sat to my right and pretended he couldn't see me. I felt sick again, out of place, time, and out of everything else.

To my left sat a woman who was neither dreite nor human; the tips of her fingers were black, and her nails were long like talons. She regarded me curiously, head cocked to the side. Her face was smooth and haunting but beautiful, while her eyes were a bottomless void.

I knew I withheld so much truth from Farran, but I needed him to believe that this—all of this—was unknown to me. I lied about plenty, but not this. Everything would have been different if I knew about this.

"Your Majesty, if I may." A man stood up.

I recognized him as the priest with silver eyes who held the dagger to my throat. He was the same dreite from Beven who slaughtered the nobles in Valois's library. I stiffened.

"Reina," I said with a glare. "That's my name. I have no title, and I would not like one."

Farran's gaze drilled through me. I couldn't change his mind, but I had hope. I wasn't ready to lose him . . . not like this.

The dreite cleared his throat. "Reina. It is good to see you awake. I'm Cassius, former hand to King Garek and current Crown Regent of Noterra. We apologize for how this situation was handled. We didn't believe the rumors at first and sought to see for ourselves.

"The seers promised us that our heir hadn't been lost in the purges, but we had to wait until specific gifts showed themselves before we knew for sure . . . It wasn't until your display in Beven—"

"My home is Thera. I've never known the Darkland." My gaze narrowed. "And why should I believe you after everything you've done? Held me at knifepoint? Dampened my power? Took my demons—"

"You misunderstand," Cassius snapped.

"Explain."

Cassius looked around the table with pursed lips before he looked at me. "We only meant to amplify your power, but miscalculated what you're prepared for. Your reaction in Beven and at the palace was proof of your claim, leaving us with no choice."

"Proof?" I scoffed. "I nearly died."

"No," he said too quickly. "That was power. It was your magic, realizing its full potential. You have to trust us. You are safer here where we can train you. There's reason to believe the Theranian Queen knows exactly who you are."

"That's impossible," Farran interjected. "If she—"

Cassius interrupted the prince with a wave of his hand. "The man you took from our southern keep along the strait would have revealed it."

My eyes narrowed, and Farran tensed to my right.

"What do you mean?" I demanded.

"His name was Victor. He served the Noterran capital until he crossed the border to share the truth we suspected with the Theranian Queen. We caught him just before he crossed, but your Armory house delivered him anyway, straight to the walls of Rowane, believing he was a priest.

"Because of that, we had to devise a much more aggressive plan so we could protect our heir. Though, perhaps, the queen has already beaten us." Cassius's eyes swiveled from mine to Farran's.

"This is ridiculous," Farran said with disbelief, but ice lined his tone. "The Darklands fell; they are an ungoverned wasteland. You cannot pluck a girl from Thera and stick a crown on her head because she has a power like your dead king. There is no proof of her parentage."

"The power is proof of her parentage." Cassius glared. "You are smarter than this, Your Highness. Similar magic from your father also pulses through your blood. And, if I'm not mistaken, you were also prepared to put a crown on her head? You recognized her eyes belong to Dreonna well before you knew who she was."

Silence swept through the room in a storm, and something in Farran relented.

A woman looked directly at Cassius as she spoke without an introduction. "We toe the line of war now that we have taken what is falsely assumed to belong to Thera." She had long, dark hair and robes holding golden traces of the moon and its cycles. "The Theranian Queen must have known a union between her son and our queen would strengthen Thera's claim to Noterra. She's been preparing for war since the possibility of the *valdronna* was brought to her attention. Or do you still prefer *dreosen*?"

"I prefer nothing," I said harshly. "I have no interest in Noterra."

"I believe you'll find yourself quite taken with our land," another dreite said. His words went unacknowledged, and Farran cleared his throat.

My gaze swiveled to him. He'd straightened his shoulders as he surveyed the room, both hands splayed on the table as his gaze settled on Cassius. He looked every bit like a fucking prince.

"How would Noterra wage a war?" Farran asked. "Thera has dragons, nearly fifty keeps along our borders, and front lines thousands deep before we even broach our Queensguard. What do you have?"

"The answer," Cassius said with a spreading grin, "is very much protected from the Theranian Crown. However, you saw a sliver of what we can manage in Beven. Every one of our generals is a long-lived priest or priestess, where yours are children. We've also had centuries to learn how to live without dragons."

"And we've had centuries to learn how to use them," Farran replied, anger seeping through the seams barely holding him together. "Is there somewhere I can have a private discussion with my betrothed?"

The word was a rock in my chest. There was no warmth in his voice; any memory of Autane and the words spoken in the garden were a distant dream I couldn't hold on to.

Cassius nodded and looked towards the ethereal woman to my left. She promptly stood, motioning for us to follow with her long fingernails. We walked in silence down a different hall, into a small, dusty library where books scaled the walls, and yet another fire crackled.

With not a single word, the heavy door closed and we were alone. Farran twisted the iron lock and looked back at me with his damn blue eyes. I leaned against the desk. Every part of me was weak, from my willpower to my muscles. Being alone with him did nothing to help.

He took a few steps closer, the coldness between us expanding. "I don't trust you, but I believe some of that was true."

I could accept that for now.

"What do we do?" I asked sincerely.

"If we don't get back to Thera, there will be war. Thera isn't ready for it. I've seen what the dreites can do, and our forces are too spread out—"

"Your mother knows who I am." It was the only thought I had. My eyes rose to his as my hand ran along the dusty, rough-hewn edge of the desk. "She wants the Noterran Crown."

"She's always wanted it," Farran sighed.

"I need a few more days."

"Then you do so without me. I'm leaving tonight. The oaths we've made will get us killed if we stay." I had to return—*no matter what*. I knew that, and I didn't need reminding; The Queensguard was always a promise, never a choice.

But I had no interest in leaving before I had an answer.

"There have been five acts of war in the last three days," I said, watching his jaw tighten. "And we were taken by dreite priests after destroying an altar to their gods. I have no doubt your brothers are looking for you. We were taken like hostages, and the Crown will negotiate our release and buy time to avoid war."

"We aren't hostages, and you have no experience negotiating."

I searched for his gaze and held it. "If we leave in the dead of night, we don't get answers. They'll keep coming for me, and I'm not leaving until I have my guarantee that I will rise to the Queensguard. No one will die. I can control this."

"You have no power unless you're planning to take a crown you know nothing of, in a kingdom which has taken you by force," he said with a rising temper I hadn't seen before.

"We'll see about that." I pursed my lips and brushed past him to the door.

Our magic reached for the other, and the sudden rush gave me pause. It was a twitch of warmth from deep in my chest I never wanted to feel again. I needed the cold, hollow space. The warmth between us was a weakness.

I didn't look back as I returned through the halls to the dining room where I stood, gripping the back of my chair instead of sitting.

"Cassius?" I asked. "Can I count on the strength of Noterra in a negotiation if I should request it?"

"Of course," Cassius said confidently. "They are *your* forces."

"Reina." It was a warning. Farran's blue eyes swirled as they met mine. "You cannot negotiate with her. She will not. She's destroyed Noterra before, and she'll do it again."

His gaze was hard and unwavering, just like mine. "I didn't say we were taking an army, just that I'm protected." I turned to the rest of the table. "We will stay until the Theranian Crown comes for us. Until that happens, we negotiate the terms of my crown."

"No," Farran snarled. "I'm not waiting. I'm going home."

"Please don't do this," I said. My voice tightened. "You know I need you, Farran. I can't do this without you."

"Then maybe you should come back with me, and we can figure it out. With people we *both* trust. Here, you operate on the word of strangers."

"I don't trust the Crown either." I bit my lip and stiffened as I clipped my words. "I need you for this to work."

"Reina, please."

Tears welled against every will I clung to. I turned and stared at the fire. I wasn't going back to Rowane—not yet. If I let Farran, I wasn't sure he'd come back, and panic barreled into me.

"Seize him." I breathed, but I didn't turn around.

He cried out and begged as my heart shattered the second time . . . but I didn't flinch, because I was already the monster in his story. Chairs moved, and magic flashed as they bound him.

I didn't look, and I didn't dare move as they carried him out, screaming my name.

Fuck.

PREVIEW

Once, when I was eleven, I found a snake in the branches of a hedge as I pruned it. He was beautiful with obsidian scales that reflected the green leaves and the sky above, intermixed with stripes the deep rust color of wet Theranian clay.

The snake slithered towards my outstretched hand as though he somehow knew we were the same. Without hesitation, he wound himself around my arm to my shoulder.

His split black tongue tasted the air for danger while his beady, void-black eyes took in the world from his new perch. Perhaps he liked the warmth of my skin. Perhaps he wanted something else.

I couldn't leave him in the garden. Something about him didn't belong there. He was far too trusting, too special, too *something*.

I couldn't bear the thought of losing him, so I put on my best perfume, batted my eyelashes, and begged Arden to find me an enclosure where I could keep him safe.

Arden's finger reached out and twirled a lock of my hair before letting it fall.

"Of course, my dear," he sighed with resignation.

The enclosure arrived a few hours later, the same size as Declan's desk. Eagerly, I filled it with hedge cuttings, logs, a bowl of water, and anything else I thought a snake might like.

The snake seemed happy at first. His head perked up whenever I came into the room, waiting on the highest branch. In the evenings, I'd carry him around Arden's estate just to scare the ladies and even some clients I wasn't supposed to talk to.

During the quietest hours of the day, I'd tell the snake all about myself and he stilled on his branch as though he listened. For those weeks, he was a friend when I had none.

"He sees something in you," Arden said as he watched the snake unfold its grip on my neck, to slither down my arm and sniff the cold cucumber soup we had for lunch.

When the third week came, something changed. The snake ignored me. He wound into a tight ball in the corner. Even my coaxing with a mouse couldn't rouse him to move.

On the fourth week, he lunged for me. It felt like a betrayal, and I slammed the door. Tears burned in my eyes, and on the fifth week, I woke to him thrashing against the walls.

He hated it; he wanted to be free. He *trusted* me, but I broke it the minute I put him in a cage.

The very next day I released him into the garden, crying so hard I hiccuped. I soured the one thing on earth that understood me, and I never saw him again.

That very same wracking guilt swelled back and crushed my chest like an iron vise.

Instead of Arden's estate, I stood in an empty room of a Noterran castle. And instead of a trusting snake, I had trapped the prince of Thera in a dead kingdom because I couldn't bear the thought of losing him completely.

The kingdom you rule will be devoid of life.

Was this how it started?

I always wondered what the Queen meant in my Rite vision. Her words meant nothing to me until these last few days. Now I saw them with distressing clarity.

There wasn't a single choice waiting for me. I was always a weapon, undeserving of the way Farran had looked at me when he thought I was someone else. Inherently, I knew it, but I was selfish.

I hadn't seen the prince since the guards dragged him away two days ago.

Cassius assured me he was fine, but I wasn't. I was splintering apart. The fire in his sapphire eyes consumed every waking thought and raked through my chest, shredding it apart like an overcooked roast.

I ordered his arrest because everything I knew about myself was a carefully constructed lie. Leaving in the middle of the night wasn't a possibility, not with all the raging questions threatening to push me over the edge.

But I warned him. I told him the truth; I deserved nothing. He ignored my warning, but now he wouldn't make the same mistake again. Now he knew I wasn't worthy of anyone.

I'd release him today. I had no choice when Theranian forces were now two days out. Once they retrieved us, we'd return to the Armory and survive another year, pretending the past was nothing but an inconvenience. Or he'd expedite my rise just to execute me the moment the oath faded to nothing.

Had Arden known all along who and what I was? He never cared for me, not truly, but if he or Avernought knew I was royalty and *still* tied me to the Armory—I would kill them both.

I'd given up so much of myself to be exactly what they wanted me to be, and for what? It didn't matter what title I held. I was only good for death—pretending I could be anything else was a delusion.

THANK YOU!

THANK YOU FOR READING The Emerald Dawn. I hope you enjoyed your time in the Kingdom of Thera. Reina's story continues in Sapphire Noon.

As an indie author, reviews mean the world. They make the countless hours of moving commas around and tearing out my hair worth it. If you enjoyed the story, please take a moment to rate and review on <u>Amazon</u> or <u>Goodreads</u> so more readers can scream with you.

Acknowledgements

THE CRAZY THING ABOUT writing a book is actually writing it and then rewriting it like one hundred more times until it finally looks like the thing you saw in your head the first time.

Nothing about Reina's story would have been possible without the constant encouragement of my family, friends, and the patience of my husband who somehow managed to enjoy the first draft (of twenty?) after a month-long writing delirium that vomited up the bare bones of the Demon Wielder series.

Emerald Dawn wasn't the book I thought I'd publish first but now that I'm sitting here I can't imagine starting this journey any differently. It's been a learning curve, it's been intense. I've made mistakes I won't make again, but I can't wait to share more of Reina and Farran's story with the world.

I've thanked my family but now I want to thank everyone who put in the work. To Cassie, Patrick, Kathleen, and Rae who not only had to read the book at various stages of editing, but who also have had to deal with my unhinged snapchats and rants while I make myself cry at wine-bars: this will not be stopping.

I also want to thank Sarah, Ashley, Stacey, Mihai, and Wren for making Emerald Dawn the best it could be and supporting me at the various stages it took to get here. I hope you're all ready for the whirlwind that's waiting in Book II.

Lastly, thanks to *you*—the reader. It's a great honor to share my little stories with the world, and a greater honor for someone to take the time to read them. I hope you enjoyed Reina Sangrey as much as I've enjoyed writing her. Thank you for reading.

Allison Trebacz is an author who belongs in a forest and lives in a desert. She writes about romance in nearly godless worlds and dreams of being able to wield a sword. For as long as she could remember, she was obsessed with stories about imaginary people in fictional words—clearly, she never grew out of it and has no intention to.

Her natural habitat is a coffeeshop where she can be found hunched over a latte, poking at her computer or in her home, daydreaming of trees and annoying her two cats, dogs, or husband.

Stay up to date on her latest:

Instagram: @allisontrebacz_author
TikTok: @allisonimagining
www.allisonimagining.com

www.ingramcontent.com/pod-product-compliance
Lightning Source LLC
Chambersburg PA
CBHW021411010826
48972CB00014B/1090